DOCTOR WHO

THE TARGET STORYBOOK

DOCTOR WHO

THE TARGET STORYBOOK

Based on the BBC television *Doctor Who*
adventures from 1963–2019.

BOOKS

1 3 5 7 9 10 8 6 4 2

BBC Books, an imprint of Ebury Publishing
20 Vauxhall Bridge Road,
London SW1V 2SA

BBC Books is part of the Penguin Random House group of companies whose
addresses can be found at global.penguinrandomhouse.com

Penguin
Random House
UK

First published by BBC Books in 2019

www.penguin.co.uk

A CIP catalogue record for this book is available from the British Library

ISBN 9781785944741

Publishing Director: Albert DePetrillo
Project Editor: Steve Cole
Cover design: Two Associates
Cover illustration: Anthony Dry
Interior illustrations: Mike Collins
Production: Sian Pratley

Typeset in 11.75/18 pt Georgia Pro
by Integra Software Services Pvt. Ltd, Pondicherry

Printed and bound in Great Britain by Clays Ltd., Elcograf S.p.A.

Contents

In memory of Tommy Donbavand

1967–2019

Gatecrashers
Joy Wilkinson

Work 116791

It was exactly like a pizza parlour in Sheffield, except that there were no doors or windows, it wasn't in Sheffield, and there was a dead, grey, alien girl lying on the tiled floor. There seemed to be no way in or out, except for the TARDIS, whose systems had picked up a six-digit code that piqued the Doctor's interest as they shot away from 17th century Lancashire. Her initial analysis suggested it was a discount takeaway offer so she'd tracked its origins in hopes of collecting a Mega Family Meal Deal.

As it turned out, the code was something else entirely.

'Teleporting!' said the Doctor, sonicking a large oven emblazoned with the brand Pizza-Porter, followed by another string of six numbers. She opened the door and peered inside. 'You put the pizza in here, set the customer's coordinates, and *Ping!* off it ports, piping hot. Brilliant! No need for mopeds, or legs, or any interaction at all. Hmm, maybe that's not so brilliant.'

'There's been an interaction here,' said Yaz, interested in the physics of deep-pan transportation, but also aware that the Doctor was trying to ease the distress of the real discovery. Sorrow swelled in Yaz's chest as she took in the dead girl's face, young but waxen grey. The whole body was drained of colour, at odds with her bright sparkly dress – and with the bright silvery blood congealed where her head had struck the tiles. Yaz homed in on darker grey patches on her arms: bruises, in a pattern she recognised from too many domestic violence cases back home. 'Looks like there was some kind of a struggle, someone grabbed her and she fell. A robbery gone wrong?'

'Doesn't make sense. What's there to rob here?' Ryan looked around the kitchen, shook a can and sprayed globules of yellow fat into the air. Even with his appetite for fast food, this was a step too far. 'Spray cheese! No one would die defending that. And there's no money here. It's all credits, like ordering through an app.'

'Maybe it was personal?' Yaz ran with it. 'She looks like she'd finished her shift and was going on a date. Maybe they came to pick her up and one thing led to another?'

'Her name was Iz,' the Doctor was clicking on a red band around the girl's wrist, like a high-tech step-counter, revealing its data and a logo: FreedomCo. 'We need to find out who Iz was, then we'll find out what happened to her.'

'Maybe she went mad.' Graham stared at the wall. He'd traced it all the way around the room, looking for hidden exits, listening for sounds from beyond, finding nothing. 'It'd drive me mad not being able to go outside. Not even being able to see out.'

'There could be something out there you don't want to see.' Ryan shuddered.

'Result!' The Doctor showed them a series of six-digit numbers on Iz's wristband. 'Coordinates for the places she has access to. Work. Home. Mall ... Um, that's all.'

'Sounds about right for most of my mates in Sheffield,' said Yaz.

Ryan nodded. 'Plus a trip to Ibiza once a year if you're lucky.'

'Yeah, but that code would get wiped,' said Graham. 'Limited use, one-week-only.'

The Doctor was sonicking the wristband. 'Perfect − unlocked the Plus-One function, so you two −' she snapped the band around Yaz's wrist − 'can use this to check out her home while me and Graham take a trip to the mall in the TARDIS. You've memorised all the coordinates, right, Graham? Only kidding. It's all in here.' She tapped her head with the sonic. 'In the sonic, I mean. I'm not Derren Brown!'

She grinned and headed to the TARDIS. Graham followed and crashed into her as she stopped, turned back, suddenly serious.

'I'm being daft because this scares me. Graham's right, this place is dangerous. This isn't a locked room mystery − it's a locked world, where girls can die and no one will know or care who did it because whoever's in charge must want it that way. They want control. So they won't like us. *Be careful.*'

Home 114592

Yaz and Ryan let go of each other's hands as soon as the teleporting process was over. They were cool with grabbing each other to escape from rampaging monsters, but somehow it felt awkward holding hands without the threat of imminent death.

'You all in one piece?' Ryan checked his particles were in order, while Yaz took in the room.

It was a small, sad cell of a bedroom, without even the luxury of a barred window.

Yaz sniffed the air, frowned, and then listened to the floor, as Ryan watched her, bemused. 'Careful, Yaz, you're getting like the Doctor!'

Flattered, Yaz shared her findings. 'Listen to the floor. You can hear the hum of the freezers, and smell the pepperoni. Bet you this place is above the pizza parlour, so ...'

'Iz's home and work are in practically the same place and she doesn't even get to have the fun of a staircase. This planet really sucks.'

Ryan opened the wardrobe. It confirmed his analysis. The clothes were all the same – pizza parlour uniforms. 'She really didn't get out much. Tonight must've been a big deal, until it went wrong.' He shut the wardrobe; it was bringing him down. Making him angry. His life hadn't been much better than Iz's, until the Doctor showed up. 'We've gotta solve this, Yaz. Or what was her life for?'

Yaz looked under the single bed and found a pile of pizza napkins. She gasped. Ryan came to look as she leafed through them, reverent. Iz had drawn on them, but these were no doodles. There were alien faces, landscapes, and flowers, lots of flowers, twining around the rest of the pictures, intricately rendered in blue ink. 'Beautiful!'

'Wonder where she saw all that if she'd never been outdoors?' Ryan marvelled.

'She must've dreamt it.' Yaz felt tears threatening to sting her eyes, but she didn't want to dampen the artworks, so she placed them carefully back beneath the bed. 'She might have been trapped, but what an imagination!'

'Bad guys don't like imagination, do they? Dictators lock artists up, or get rid of them. They're dangerous. Iz could've been a rebel, planning a revolution?'

'In that dress? I dunno …' Yaz looked around, one last time and noticed – even the wallpaper was hand-drawn. Tiny biro blue flowers, painstakingly marked onto the paint. 'Let's go and tell the Doctor what we know. See what she's found out.'

Mall 382601

White clouds drifted across a stunning golden sky, stretching away over rolling hills in the distance.

'All simulated, just pretty pictures!' The Doctor brought Graham back down to Earth, or whatever planet they were on, ending his reverie at the mall ceiling.

'I knew that,' he fibbed. 'It's very realistic though, best I've seen yet. And I've seen more than my fair share of simulated realities by now.'

The walls of the mall showed a mix of TV channels. Shoppers who weren't staring in store windows stared at chat shows, news and adverts. On the news, Graham spotted 'Ronan Sumners, Mayor of New Port City'. The Doctor followed his glance to a grey-haired, grey-skinned man beaming benevolently as he was interviewed. She had an innate distrust of benevolently beaming leaders, and mentally filed him away for future investigation.

'So this is New Port? Give me the one in Wales any day!' Graham watched the alien shoppers, going about their business in the mall – old folk dozing in the food court, toddlers rampaging through a soft play, bored teens hanging around. All grey like Iz, but otherwise eerily like the shoppers back in Sheffield, or any mall in the universe for that matter. But something – apart from the fact that it was essentially a giant prison – was troubling Graham as they made a circuit of the mall.

'Not being funny, I love a bargain, but none of these shops sell dresses like Iz was wearing. That was proper fancy boutique get-up. And there ain't none of that here.'

'I never had you down as a fashion guru, Graham.'

'Charming!'

'But I'm liking it! Go on?'

'Well, malls normally have levels – lifts, escalators – but this one doesn't.' Graham looked up at the clouds again. 'What if there was a whole other world above that ceiling?'

'Fashion guru and town planning genius. Come on!' Inspired, the Doctor bounded up to a bored grey sales assistant at the counter of a clothes shop. 'If I wanted to get a really posh frock – not saying your shop's frocks aren't fancy, they're very nice, if you like frocks – but I mean even fancier, where would I go?'

The sales assistant frowned, mildly diverted. 'The Black Zone. If you could go there. But you can't or you wouldn't be asking.'

'We might be able to,' Graham chipped in. 'A girl we know worked in a pizza parlour and she went there.'

'She's lying. No one gets to go unless they're born there or they win the lottery.' The girl peered closer at the Doctor's coat, intrigued. 'What zone are you two from?'

'No zone. All zones. To be honest, I find the concept of zones is usually unhealthy.' The Doctor leaned in, matching her curiosity and raising it. 'I'll tell you how to make a coat like mine, if you tell me everything about this "lottery".'

Work 116791

Ryan paced in circles and Yaz sat on the counter, looking down at poor Iz, imagining her life trapped here, as they waited for the Doctor and Graham to come back.

'Want to play tiddlywinks with the frozen pepperoni?' said Ryan. 'I guarantee you'll beat me.'

'Tempting, but no, thanks.'

'Well, I can't stay here. It's doing my head in. Let's go and find them.'

Yaz suspected it was a bad idea, but the inertia was getting to her too. She could feel her limbs stiffening like Iz's must be. This place was like a living death.

'OK, we'll just go and look, stretch our legs, then come straight back.' Yaz clicked through the codes on the wristband, searching for the 'Mall' – but she must have pressed the wrong switch, gone the wrong way, because suddenly the wristband vibrated slightly, as if she'd hit her 10,000 step target, and another code flashed up.

'Ryan?'

He peered over her shoulder. Read the new six-digit code and the word: 'Party.'

He looked at Yaz, eyes widening. She knew what he was thinking, and spoke first: 'We'll go to the mall, find the Doctor and Graham, then we can all go to this code.'

That wasn't what Ryan was thinking. 'What if it's gone by then? One of those codes for a limited time only, and if we wait, we'll miss the party.'

'Iz went to that party,' said Yaz, 'or she was going to. Whatever happened to her is what led to this.'

Ryan grabbed a napkin and pen. 'We can write down the code and leave a note for them, but we've got to go now. We might be too late already.'

TARDIS

'We should go get Ryan and Yaz.' Graham had no clue how the TARDIS worked, but he had a very strong intuition that the code the Doctor was inputting was not the one for Iz's work.

'We will. Very soon. But it's not like they're going anywhere.' She focused on her calculations of the last two digits. 'And we need to get to the Black Zone, fast, before any evidence of what happened to Iz is cleaned up.'

'Are you trying to figure out the winning lottery number so we can get access too?'

'Sort of, but that's not quite how it works. She said everyone's Home code goes into the lottery draw and one is selected at random. That person is then sent another special six-digit code that entitles them and their lucky Plus-One to access the prize.'

'A fabulous showbiz party and a whole new life in the Black Zone. I got that bit. I just tuned out at the numbers.' Graham blushed, and moved swiftly on. 'So, if we can't get that special code, how are you going to get us there?'

'That girl reckoned we were right, about the Black Zone Mall being directly above the Grey Zone Mall. So if the codes are based on the physical coordinates of each location – and it's safe to assume they are, based on the proximity of Iz's Home code to her Work code, which indicate she lives right on top of her Work – then it's really not that hard to figure out what the code must be to move us up to the floor above.'

Graham took a moment to compute – a moment longer than it took the Doctor to finish inputting the code – and the TARDIS set off. Briefly.

'You've taken us upstairs, right?' Graham caught up. 'Basement to ground floor.'

'Ground floor to penthouse,' she grinned, rather pleased with herself. 'Come on.'

Outside 393602

Her grin froze as they stepped out of the TARDIS into a broken cityscape. It looked like Sheffield might if it had been bombed and abandoned for a century. Empty streets. Cars smashed up, rusting. Lawns overgrown. But this city wasn't abandoned. Some of the old buildings weren't crumbling and the windows and doors were bricked up to make them fit-for-purpose in the new regime. Newer buildings were dotted around the landscape, custom-built with sheer blank walls. Impenetrable fortresses. There was a huge one right next to where they'd landed, the size of several aircraft hangars.

'Ah, *that* must be the mall,' the Doctor kicked herself. 'We went sideways not up. That's annoying!'

'What's that?' Graham stepped forward to point out a strange building on the horizon, a hybrid of old industrial and gleaming high tech, as if Apple had refurbed a steelworks.

'Don't!' The Doctor pulled him back. She pointed to the roofs of the bricked-up buildings, where inverted black satellite dishes stood mushroom-like on their stems. 'Force-field generators, protecting them.'

'From what?'

'From the teleporting system. Can't you sense it?'

Graham tried, but got nowhere, so she tried to describe what was setting her nerves jangling. 'It's like when a space shuttle – or a car – just misses you by an inch, a nanometre. All around us right now, there are invisible superhighways whooshing bodies from this code to that code. Constantly moving. A skyful of Spaghetti Junctions! That's what's smashed up those cars and buildings. Anything without a force field could get hit at any moment. It's a mad system, never seen anything like it before. Normally teleporting only exists in cultures that have become very advanced, but here it's like the teleporting came first and the rest of the world has been made to adapt around it. It's even more dangerous than I thought.'

'So we should get back in the TARDIS?' Graham edged towards the door.

'We should – but you're right. That building *is* interesting.' She eyed the horizon. 'Looks like some kind of power plant, maybe for the teleporting system.' She was tempted to calculate a code for it, but Graham put his foot down.

'You couldn't get us upstairs in a mall, there's no way you can get us over there safe, and we need to get back to the others. Anything could've happened to them.'

Party 993366

The first room, where Yaz and Ryan ported in, was small. It was around the size of a large changing cubicle in one of Graham's fancy boutiques. It had a full-length mirror and coat hooks. On one of them was a crumpled pizza parlour uniform. On the floor was a cheap pair of trainers, worn down, kicked off. Iz had been here not long ago, changing from her old self, getting dressed up to party. Yaz couldn't imagine what would make her go back.

'Maybe she was gonna turn back into a pumpkin at midnight and—' Ryan broke off, noticing something unusual, for this world at least. 'Hang on – is that – a door?'

The mirror was exactly the size of a door and around its edges was a very slight gap.

Yaz's reflection grinned at Ryan's reflection as she realised he was right. Her hand reached out and pushed. The door opened into—

The second room, which was bigger, more like the corridor that leads into a cinema screen or theatre. Dark walls and plush red carpet. A roped section to one side.

'For the press, I bet.' Yaz flashed back over all the hours she'd wasted watching broadcasts live from the red carpet – or maybe not wasted now it had helped her figure this out. 'She got all glammed up, then posed for her photo here.'

'Why would they take her photo? She was just a girl from a pizza parlour.'

'She used to be, but now she was special. She must have won a prize – for her art maybe? A talent contest? That opened doors for her. Literally. Got her this invite, and they took her photo to show the world – dreams can come true!'

'I guess the party was down there.' Ryan peered down the dark corridor. It was silent. Unsettling. They had definitely missed the party, but he knew that they still had to look. There could be a clue, or cleaners they could grill. They had to know the truth.

Ryan and Yaz went cautiously along the red carpet, towards a door that had no intention of hiding. It was big and grand and framed with ornate gold. They held their breaths, went in.

It was tiny, like an elevator, with barely enough room for both of them. The door closed behind them. There were no doors in front. It was totally sealed and lightless like a coffin.

Suddenly the coffin dropped.

Ryan yelled out, panicked. 'Port us out of here! Port us out!'

'I'm trying!' Yaz stabbed at the wristband. No codes flashed up. 'It's not working!'

She grabbed his hand. They gripped each other tight, as they plummeted down.

Work 116791

Pizza orders were racking up when the Doctor and Graham returned to the parlour. The Doctor scrolled through the staff protocol on the till, where customer demands flashed red. 'It'll trigger an alert to HQ and someone will come out to see what's up.'

'That's a good thing,' said Graham, crouching by Iz, to take his mind off worrying. 'They could tell us what might've gone on.'

'More likely they'd clean up, stick her in the freezer and carry on,' the Doctor mused. 'That's what this world is. Everyone in little boxes, minding their own business.'

'Says the woman who lives in a box!'

'That's the opposite of this place. That's about going anywhere, everywhere. Getting to know people. Helping them. This place – it's all about keeping you in your place. Speaking of which, what's keeping Yaz and Ryan? Surely Iz's home can't that big!'

Graham spotted something under the counter. The pizza napkin note, blown under when Ryan and Yaz teleported out. He retrieved it, recognised Ryan's scrawl.

'They're not at her home. They're here.'

TARDIS

'It's not working.' The Doctor tried the code a third time.

'You sure you've got the numbers right? His handwriting's shocking.'

'It's not that. The place exists, but it's been blocked. It's as if the teleporting doorway to that location has been locked.' Her brow furrowed at the data the code was throwing back at her. She raced around the console. Graham's worry rocketed.

'Doctor, wherever Iz went to, it wasn't any party. We can't let Ryan and Yaz—'

'I know. I'm trying – we can't port there because they've blocked it. But if I can use all the codes we've already got – Iz's and the outside and all the customers' codes – maybe I can figure out exactly where it is and we can find another way to get there.'

'A way that's not the TARDIS?'

She nodded, her fingers racing across the console, so much slower than her brain. Hands were irritatingly inefficient in many ways, but they still had their uses. So did feet. Hers stopped dead as the map zeroed in on the Party coordinates and beamed out a holographic image of the location. Graham recognised its hulking mass.

'The power plant. That's where the party is?'

'And the nexus of the energy given off by the superhighways. The teleporting core.'

Now Graham's mind was racing to all kinds of dark places, while in reality he knew they were stuck. 'How the hell are we going to get there?'

The Doctor was a step or ten ahead. 'I believe your local term is "Shanks's pony"!'

Outside 393602

The Doctor stuffed her backpack with supplies from the pizza parlour and the TARDIS. Graham got his head around the full insanity of her plan.

'You want us to *walk*, all the way there, through the spaghetti junction of invisible, deadly superhighways that you just told me under no circumstances to go near?'

'Yep! Precisely. Unless—'

'We can use a force-field generator?' Graham asked hopefully.

'Climbing onto these death traps to get one would be more dangerous than walking. Nah, I was going to say – unless you can get that moped working?'

Graham was so dumbfounded by her suggestion that he suddenly found himself picking the moped up from where it had been left many years ago, right by where the TARDIS stood now. It wasn't like a moped from Sheffield, but Graham could find his way around operating most modes of transport, apart from the TARDIS. He flicked a few switches. The engine grumbled, annoyed at being stirred from its long slumber, but with a few more flicks and a couple of kicks, it was humming.

The Doctor was thrilled, even though he warned her: 'We're still going to get killed. Just a bit faster, that's all.'

'Not with this!' She pulled something from her pocket. Graham hoped it was some kind of mini force-field generator, but it was a backscratcher. The telescopic kind that pulls out, to scratch those hard-to-reach itches. The Doctor extended it fully and taped it to the front of the bike, horizontally, like a very weedy lance with a little hand at the end.

'That'll give us a bit of warning if we're about to hit something. And this'll help too.' She pulled a canister from her backpack. Spray-cheese.

She sprayed a blast in front of them and watched the globules settle. Most dripped to the ground like thick buttery rain, but the distant drops sizzled as they hit a highway.

'There you go. I've got your back. Well, front. What I'm saying is: we'll make it.'

'You want me to drive this thing while you sit behind me spraying cheese?'

'Exactly! But I'm happy to swap if you'd rather be on cheese duties?'

There was no time to argue. Graham got on the moped, revved it up and set off, weaving his way across the wasteland as the Doctor perched pillion, letting out a constant plume ahead, from can after can. The horizon was further than it seemed. Much further than the cans and the backscratcher would last – its metal fingertips were already bitten down by the sizzle of the superhighways. Graham gripped the handlebars, thought of Ryan and Yaz, and kept going.

The Core 300875

Ryan and Yaz couldn't hold hands any more. They were locked in separate boxes now, even more coffin-like, despite the cushioning beneath them and the clear lids. With every code, their lives seemed to have got more restricted, leading to this moment.

The grey man returned. He had stunned them as soon as their elevator hell-ride stopped, locked them up in their boxes in this stark white room, and taken a fluid sample from the base of their skulls. He used a bio-tech device, half-syringe, half-insect, its proboscis rigid and sharper than any needle. Even though they were stunned, they felt the sting as it punctured. Yaz wanted to scream as it probed deep. Ryan wanted to be sick. But neither dared move a muscle as its drinking-straw tongue foraged through their brain tissue, seeking out its nectar. Just a sip to begin with. So the grey man could scan the contents and see how much they could supply. Now he had the results.

'What exactly are you?' He gazed at them, fascinated, impressed. They'd clearly passed his test with flying colours. 'You both have higher levels than any Gornt. You could keep the system running for weeks. I could actually take some time off at last!'

'Higher levels of what?' Yaz demanded through the glass – then figured he might respond better to gentle bribery. 'Tell us what you're doing and we'll tell you what we are – and where you can find more of us.'

The grey man considered, clearly tempted.

Ryan pushed, 'Go on, I bet you're dying to tell someone how clever you've been, dreaming all this up on your own. It's all a secret, isn't it? That's why there's the party, the photos, so that no one knows?'

'And that's why you're alone.' Yaz added the final shot, that really got to him.

'Being alone is good,' the grey man snapped. 'I'd be alone all the time if I could. It boosts my levels.'

'Are you sure?' asked Yaz, realising provocation worked best of all. 'Because you said our levels were high and I hardly ever get a moment to myself!'

'Impossible!' he dismissed her, but their plan had worked and he couldn't help opening up. 'Sperantium is the chemical that fuels our imaginations. It peaks in our youth, the precious years when we are still physically constrained, but our minds are ranging at their widest, when the impossible seems real, as though you can break boundaries and go anywhere in your head.' He spoke as if giving a well-rehearsed lecture – he must have imagined this moment often. 'I found a way to harvest sperantium and use it in the world. So we can move through space as fast as you can in your imagination.' His grey eyes lit up with wonder and pride, showing them a warmer side – a glimpse of how he might have started out, before the coldness and cruelty kicked in. 'The fuel reserves taper off in later years, but isolation can help to restore it. That's a happy side effect of my system. That it creates more fuel to keep it running.'

'Your system sucks!' Ryan punctured the happy moment. 'You lock people up, use them as fuel and for what? Just so's you get to play with your stupid toys?'

The grey man sighed, shook his head. 'One would think that, with your levels, you wouldn't have such a limited perspective. My system keeps them safe. When people could go wherever they liked, there was chaos – hate, pollution, terrorism. Our world was too big. We got lost. Now our world is smaller, simpler, safer. Only a few have to die so that the rest can live in peace. And even fewer after today, thanks to you two.'

'Three. What about Iz?' Ryan asked. 'The girl you killed – from the pizza parlour?'

Finally a flicker of recognition. 'I didn't think she knew anyone – she didn't bring a Plus-One, unfortunately. But I didn't kill her. She had some kind of panic attack at the photoshoot and ported back. I thought perhaps she had an inkling of what was to come, but I don't see how. I tried to retrieve her, but – she fell.'

'So you just left her there to rot?' Yaz cut in, disgusted.

'She's no use to me dead. The sperantium instantly dissipates. Her company would deal with the body and report back to me and then she'd be replaced and no one would care. Most people will think she's living happily ever after in the Black Zone.'

'What's the Black Zone? Death?'

The look on his face answered her. 'That's enough questions. You'll find out soon enough. It's time to top up the system.' He took out a brace of the insect syringes.

'Wait! We haven't told you yet – where to get more of us.' Yaz flashed a panicked look at Ryan, seeing they were both heading straight for the Black Zone.

'You don't imagine I believed that you'd tell me the truth, did you?' the grey man chuckled. 'I can get my answers from your autopsies.'

The bugs' spindly legs tapped, eager to feed. Yaz and Ryan kicked against their prisons, but there was no way out. The syringes plunged into the access tubes behind their skulls. They felt the sting—

Suddenly everything went black. Loud and black and then very light, as the wall fell away, revealing the Doctor and Graham, in a huge swirling cloud of smoke and dust. They'd blown the room wide open.

Ryan and Yaz were safe in their boxes, protected from the explosion, but the man was thrown back hard onto the ground, unconscious. The Doctor recognised him straightaway, even without the benevolent smile.

'Ronan Sumners, Mayor of New Port City.' She pointed a finger at him. 'I just knew it!'

Graham eased out the wriggling syringes and stamped on them, just to be certain. 'Normally I'd never harm a fly.' He shuddered. 'But these are seriously grim.'

'Tools, that's all. Non-sentient.' The Doctor sonicked the locks, letting Ryan and Yaz out of their boxes with only an itchy bite mark. They filled her in on Iz, sperantium, the whole messed-up system, so that by the time Ronan came to, he blinked up to see the Doctor standing over him, filled with righteous fury.

'You want people with imaginations?' she glowered down. 'You have to set them free. Let them see things, go places, meet each other and understand how it all works so they can make it better than you managed to. That might mean risking some chaos, danger. But it's worth the risk. And it's not like your way has paid off. That blood leaking from your skull will kill you, unless you give this up and let me help.'

Ronan raised a hand to his skull and felt the sticky wetness – silver liquid leaking out where his head hit the white marble floor. He looked up at the Doctor, with disdain, and breathed one word: 'Terrorist.'

Quick as a flash, his hand reached for his wristband – quicker than a flash, the Doctor got there with her sonic. It pulsed, as Ronan ported out. Not to his chosen destination, but to one of the codes the sonic had stored. Iz's Home, Work, Mall, or—

'Uh oh, that's really bad.' The Doctor had recognised the code. 'I forgot that was in there.'

Graham didn't recognise it. None of them did, so she had to reveal his destination.

'The Pizza-Porter. Hopefully it won't automatically switch on.' She pulled a face, implying it probably did. A horrible image, Ronan heating up like a deep pan. *Ping!*

'You offered to help him, which was more than he deserved,' said Yaz.

The Doctor nodded, grateful for the reassurance.

Even so, Yaz could sort of see why Ronan would call her a 'terrorist'. The Doctor was everything he'd built this world to insulate against – a free-thinker who wouldn't be boxed in, and who happened to have an old stash of Nitro-9 cans in her backpack. She got busy on Ronan's computer, pulling up his maps of the city. 'We need to find his TV studio and send out a warning so that no one else gets hurt. Then we're going to do some demolition!'

Everywhere

The last blast shattered the great wall of the mall and hundreds of Gornt emerged, blinking into the open. It was safe outside now. The Doctor and gang had blown the core and the superhighways were all gone. The only danger now was the people, and they didn't look so dangerous. They looked—

'Beautiful!' Yaz gasped.

As the alien sunlight touched the Gornt, their skin blossomed, changing colour from grey into blue – a shimmering, intricate pattern, like a full-body tattoo of flowers.

'Iz knew – she dreamt this!' Ryan marvelled once more, at the girl he never knew. Maybe she'd imagined him and the others too, strangers from way across the universe who'd come here to be the friends she never had, fighting for her death to mean something. He put his arms around Yaz and Graham.

'Her sperantium levels must have been off the scale!' Graham smiled, moved. 'Imagine how much more she could've done and dreamed of, given the chance.'

The Doctor nodded, watching the Gornt bloom. Now they could smash down the rest of the walls and go as far as their imaginations would take them. She had no idea what her own levels were, at her age and after all she'd seen, but it gave her hope.

She closed her eyes and imagined where they could go next.

Journey Out of Terror
Simon Guerrier

We had left Vicki behind!

In all the time I travelled with the Doctor, this was the worst moment. Oh, our lives were constantly in danger but this was our mistake. Losing a child is a schoolteacher's nightmare. And I simply hadn't checked. I'd fled into the TARDIS, desperate to escape that awful, haunted house – and the Daleks.

I remember the desperate sense of relief, just to be back inside the ship. My head and heart pounding, I was in no state to talk to the others so I went to get us all cups of water from the TARDIS food machine. My hands shook at the controls but I composed myself, and breezed back into the main control room to hand out the water. The Doctor and Ian were busy with some contraption the Doctor was building, all wires and complex circuits.

'Where's Vicki?' I asked, glancing round. That's when the awful truth hit.

'But I thought she was with you!' the Doctor snapped at me.

'We left her in that madhouse,' said Ian, stunned.

'You have to take us back,' I told the Doctor.

Ian took my hand. 'Barbara,' he told me, his voice breaking, 'the Daleks were right behind us. They must have killed her.'

The poor girl, in that dreadful place alone. What she must have felt, realising we had abandoned her. And then—

'No!' said the Doctor. His face was stern, his eyes glimmering. 'I won't accept it!'

I wanted to believe him, I so wanted to believe. 'Ian is right, though, isn't he?' I said. 'You can't take us back. The time mechanism of the TARDIS is broken.'

The Doctor didn't answer but brushed us out of the way of the table top of controls. His fingers danced nimbly over the handles and levers. The round column of glass in the centre began to turn. Lights flickered, and from the depths of the ship underneath us there came a rumble like an oncoming storm.

'Whatever you're doing, the ship really doesn't like it,' Ian protested.

But I understood. 'You can bypass the time mechanism.'

'That really would be impossible,' said the Doctor as he worked. 'But did I not observe that our last destination was *not* within time and space?'

Had he? I turned to Ian, who only shook his head. 'You said you thought the house was some kind of dream.'

'Very much more than that,' said the Doctor, fussing over the controls. 'It was solid, tangible. Indeed, those creatures were even a match for the Daleks!'

'I saw Count Dracula,' I said. 'And Frankenstein's monster. Characters from stories.'

The lights around us dimmed, and the growl of the TARDIS engines became ever more strained. I held on to the control panel for support, and the Doctor put a hand on top of mine. He smiled at me so kindly. 'Yet you still believed, didn't you, my dear? You entertain the most extraordinary ideas in the dark corners of your mind. I mean, not just you – the whole of your species. Monsters, demons, creatures of the id. Occasionally, in times of stress, these dreams can surface and have formidable power. The remarkable thing is what happens when enough of you believe in the *same* extraordinary things!'

The room was getting dark now and eerie, the Doctor's bony face lit only by the panel of controls. I shivered with sudden cold. 'You mean if we share stories, we combine those forces.'

'Exactly! You nurture it and it grows. When enough people all believe the same thing, it can achieve existence.'

In the fading light, with the thrum of the engines, it seemed almost possible. But I'd always been the more credulous one on our adventures.

'You're talking about a realm of make-believe,' Ian scoffed.

'A land of fiction,' the Doctor nodded. 'I have heard tell of such domains, but to actually venture into such a place ...'

'Where the normal rules don't apply,' I said. 'So we wouldn't need the time mechanism to go there. Then how do we move through it?'

'Cross our fingers and wish,' said Ian, with a smile.

I scowled at him. 'Ian, this is a chance to save Vicki!'

'Sorry.'

'Chesterton is right,' said the Doctor. 'In his own cynical way. We make ourselves receptive to these cumulative forces. I have programmed the conceptual geometry. The telepathic circuits are aligning. Now we add that wish. Concentrate, both of you, on what it is we most desire.'

He placed his hands over two discs inset into the panel before him and solemnly closed his eyes. I did the same, and wished.

Nothing happened. I glanced at Ian, who shrugged. The Doctor's lips were moving, speaking silent words. Still nothing happened. Ian was going to say something but I shot him a glance. He raised his hands in surrender, turned and walked away. And, in the gloom, he immediately tripped over.

So much for dignity! I felt like such a fool as I lay there in the semi-darkness. But that's why I tripped over the book.

I'd forgotten the battered old hardback, found in one of my voyages into the TARDIS interior. Now, seeing it again on the floor, I felt the hair on the back of my neck stand on end. The dust jacket showed three peculiar robots, single-eyed hemispheres with spindly arms and legs, moving through the cosmos. Above them, the garish title: *Monsters from Outer Space!*

It wasn't the book that made my blood run cold, but the thought of when I'd last seen it. Time was difficult to judge in the TARDIS, but I'd been looking through that book perhaps that very morning, or the previous day. The memory made me utterly ashamed.

As Barbara helped me to my feet, I showed her the book.

'I was reading it earlier,' I said. 'Vicki came over and asked what I thought. I couldn't tell her that I barely understood a word.'

'Is it badly written?'

'It's the knowledge it assumes on the part of the reader. Scientific concepts well beyond our time.'

Barbara nodded. 'But Vicki grasps them with ease. She's a child from the future.'

'I was ashamed of my ignorance. So I fobbed her off, shifted round so she couldn't read over my shoulder. Made it clear I didn't want her hovering around.'

Barbara started to tell me not to torture myself, that she'd been cross with Vicki for some minor mishap, too. I was no longer listening. Idly flicking through the pages of the book, I'd found a comic strip. And in the scratchy-looking pictures—

An awful shiver ran through me, what my mother used to say was someone walking over your grave.

'Barbara, look – it's us!'

There we were, on the printed page. Barbara, the Doctor and I – and Vicki, too. A story, with the four of us its heroes!

The panels showed us being discovered by a family of astronauts – mum, dad and awkward teenage daughter – who accused us of being stowaways and endangering their mission to save Earth!

That was just the first page and I wanted to read on but Barbara – the real Barbara – took the book from my hands.

'We're wearing the same clothes,' she said. 'Your polo neck, my jumper.' What was more, Vicki looked just as we'd last seen her – a cowl-necked top like Barbara's, and her hair in bunches. Barbara shook her head in wonder. 'It's exactly what I wished for.'

'What can it mean?' I said. 'We've never met these people.'

'Oh, I should say it's perfectly obvious,' mused the Doctor, his eyes open and alert. 'These things haven't happened *yet*.' He lifted his hands from the control panel and came over to join us, donning his spectacles to examine the book.

'Now this is most interesting, most interesting indeed. The likenesses here are very striking, the composition realistic. As if it's sketched from the life.'

I found myself glancing round. 'You mean we're being watched.'

'They must have one of those machines,' said Barbara, gesturing to the huge, round computer bank by the interior doors. The Doctor's Time and Space Visualiser was like a giant television set for viewing any moment in history. Barbara shuddered. 'Someone watches us, then copies it down in a book.'

'Perhaps they do,' said the Doctor. 'But this could be something else.'

'You mean, we've arrived in your land of dreams?' I asked. 'We've become fiction ourselves?'

'I rather think we have,' said the Doctor with glee. 'This is a most encouraging sign. If the scenes depicted in this book really took place, but we are yet to experience them, then it tells us something vital.' He tapped the pictures with one bony finger. 'We will be reunited with Vicki.'

Of course, Barbara was thrilled but I was determined to remain cautious. 'It doesn't tell us how we're reunited.'

'It can't tell us everything,' said the Doctor. 'That would interfere with future events. But we may proceed in confidence. Sometimes, that's all that's needed.'

I tried to turn the page to see what happened next – but the Doctor snapped the book shut.

'I wanted to see if the Daleks turned up,' I protested. 'We could be putting that family in danger. There's a girl, a child, on board.'

The Doctor considered, then flicked the pages quickly, locating the comic strip. He allowed himself the briefest sight of the pages that followed, then snapped the book shut again. 'No Daleks,' he said. 'I can assure you of that.'

'Why not?' said Barbara. 'They were right behind us.'

'Something must happen,' I said. 'And in the near future, because we're wearing these same clothes in the story.'

'So,' said Barbara, 'sometime soon we're reunited with Vicki. We escape the Daleks for good. Then we encounter this family.'

'Your box of tricks,' I said to the Doctor, indicating the half-finished device on the plinth. 'It must work against the Daleks.'

'Of course it will work,' said the Doctor. 'I said it would, didn't I? Really, you could both do with showing more faith.'

For emphasis, he patted the control panel beside him. The TARDIS suddenly lurched, the engines protesting with an almighty groan. Barbara grabbed me and I clung on to the controls for dear life. The central column rose and fell, as it did when in flight.

And then it settled. The terrible thrum of the engines faded. The lights came on around us.

'What happened?' said Barbara. 'What was that?'

The Doctor inspected the controls. 'We've landed. Breathable atmosphere. No sign of radiation or toxins.'

I'd learned enough of the controls to spot something in the readouts. 'We've landed but we're still moving.'

The Doctor beamed. 'Just like on Captain Maitland's spacecraft, when we encountered the Sensorites.'

'Then we're on another ship,' said Barbara.

'We could be on the Daleks' version of the TARDIS,' I said. 'They've caught us up at last. Is your device ready?'

The Doctor shook his head. 'Another hour. Maybe two.'

'We don't have any more time,' I said. 'Not when there's a chance to save Vicki now.'

The Doctor looked ready to argue. But he worked the control for the TARDIS doors, and they hummed slowly open.

Darkness waited beyond. Mist curled gently round the doors towards us. I would have said it didn't seem very inviting, but the Doctor and Barbara were already heading out.

I followed the Doctor into dark, oppressive heat. The steam felt clammy against the exposed skin of my face and neck and hands. I could barely see anything and the Doctor had to stop me from walking right into a girder. Slowly my eyes adjusted to the murk.

We had landed in a space the size of a classroom, but without any edges or corners. The wall curved smoothly round us, crudely cast from metal. It hissed and ticked in the heat. A walkway fixed to the wall spiralled upwards through the steam to a hatch in the ceiling, high overhead. I thought the ceiling was dizzyingly distant then realised the false perspective: the room narrowed the higher it got. We were inside a section of a cone!

Around us, boxes were stacked containing technical supplies – circuit boards and machinery I didn't recognise. I turned to the Doctor, sure he would explain. But his attention was on the dimensions of the walkway, a nervous look on his face. I quickly made the same connection that he had.

'That ramp could have been made for a Dalek,' I said.

He took my hands in his. 'My dear, you had better wait in the TARDIS.'

I shook him off and started up the ramp. 'If Vicki is here, we have to find her.'

'Careful,' called Ian. 'There isn't a rail and it goes up pretty high.'

'It's much too dangerous!' agreed the Doctor.

'Then,' I told them, 'you'd both better stay by the ship.'

After a disconcerting, steep climb, the ramp ended about four feet below the hatch in the ceiling. By the time I got there, Ian had caught me up. He didn't say anything – he didn't dare. We examined the hatch workings together until the Doctor joined us.

'Why haven't you opened it?' he said, breathlessly. 'That's what the wheel is for.'

'We don't know what's on the other side,' I said.

'We discover that by opening it,' chided the Doctor.

'It could be an army of Daleks,' said Ian.

'No, I don't think it could be,' said the Doctor, his eyes narrowing. 'That wheel suits humanoid hands.'

'But the ramp,' I said.

'It's suggestive, yes. But the hatch suggests otherwise. I recommend you open it.'

Ian gripped the wheel with both hands. 'And if you're wrong?'

'Then you'll be entitled to say so, young man.'

Ian tried the wheel. It didn't budge. He put his back into it. I reached around him to grip more of the spokes. We heaved – and it still didn't shift. I thought Ian might do himself an injury. And then, gradually, it began to move. With a scrape of metal on metal that set my teeth on edge, the wheel slowly turned. It picked up pace, caught by its own momentum, and soon got away from us! We couldn't stop it, until—

Clang!

Ian and I both fell back in a tangle of limbs. We lay like that, horrified, as the noise reverberated round us, filling the conical chamber. It was like being inside a great bell.

The Doctor glowered until the sound died away. 'Well,' he sighed. 'I suppose it's cordial to announce our presence to whomever might be here.'

We got up and Ian pressed his shoulder against the hatch. I helped, pressing my palms against the door. The muscles in my arms and shoulders ached from turning the wheel, but the door started to lift. Again, once it was moving it became easier. As soon as it was upright, it fell backwards – with another echoing clang. We didn't wait this time but hauled ourselves into the next room, Ian reaching back to help the Doctor scramble up after us.

We were in a higher, narrower part of the cone, tapering to a single point above our heads. But whereas the room below had been bare except for boxes, this room looked furnished and comfortable. We climbed out onto a thick rug, on which sat a coffee table and sofa. There were bunks built into the walls, with cosy-looking beds. One bunk was obscured by a pair of curtains. The curtains wavered, where someone inside held them shut.

'Hello?' I said, taking a step forward. 'We don't mean you any harm.'

From behind the curtain, something growled. The curtain twitched – but did not open.

'Can you understand us?' I said, taking another step. The growl grew louder.

Ian tried to stop me. 'That doesn't sound human,' he said.

'We're trespassers here,' I told him. 'No wonder they're frightened.'

'We must find out where we are,' said the Doctor, striding to the bunk and yanking back the curtain.

Immediately, something huge and hairy sprang out at him, and they both tumbled back on to the floor. We ran to help but the thing was all over the Doctor, snarling and snapping. That didn't stop Ian, who threw himself at the thing and tried to wrestle it away. It did no good, so I took the other side and tried to shove it back with brute force.

It had all been so fast, all I saw was noise and size and hair. But as we struggled to prize the snarling thing from the Doctor, Ian laughed.

'It's a dog! I think it's a deerhound.'

Why hadn't I seen it before? *Of course* it was a dog. 'A pet,' I added, seeing the collar round its neck. Something bobbed from the collar, a heart-shaped pendant. As I fought to keep the dog back so the Doctor could wriggle free, I leant round to read the word engraved there.

'Bunny?' I said. The dog tensed in response to its name but continued to worry at the Doctor's shoe. 'Bunny,' I said in a kinder, mumsier toner. 'Who's a good dog?' The dog continued on the shoe but stopped snarling. I reached a hand round to nuzzle Bunny's head, in the spot between his ears. 'Oh Bunny, who's a good dog?'

That did it. Bunny flopped heavily into my lap and let me dote on him.

Ian watched in astonishment. The Doctor sat up with all the nobility he could muster, his bow tie loose and his waistcoat hanging open. The sight of me and the dog made him smile.

'Well,' he said. 'Whatever next?'

'Please,' said a terrified voice up in the bunk. 'Please, don't hurt my dog.'

The girl lay at the back of the bunk, brandishing a wrench. She couldn't have been more than fifteen, her hair in a sleek, Louise Brooks bob, and her wide, expressive eyes adding to that Silent Movie feel. Her boiler suit was at least a size too big for her, and apparently moulded from plastic.

Barbara had the deerhound to keep on friendly terms so I talked to the girl. I didn't get up from the floor or make any move that might frighten her further. But I addressed her in a companionable tone.

'I'm Ian, this is Barbara and the Doctor. What's your name?'

The girl only prodded the wrench in my direction.

'Oh dear,' I said. 'Don't you have a name?'

That offended her, as I hoped it might. 'I'm Julia Jett!' she said.

'Yes, well, it's very nice to meet you, Miss Jett,' said the Doctor. 'You and your exuberant hound. I should say he thought to protect you from us. But as Barbara said, we really mean you no harm.'

'Look,' said Barbara. 'Bunny and I are already the best of friends.'

41

She had a knack with animals, and with children. Julia watched Barbara with the dog, then shifted slowly forward. The three of us – and Bunny – remained exactly where we were, presenting no challenge as Julia slipped down from the bunk. She wore thick socks, in stripes of two bright shades of blue, which made her seem all the more girlish.

'How did you get here?' she demanded, the wrench still clasped in her hand. 'What do you want?'

'We got here by accident,' said the Doctor. 'And we want nothing but to be reunited with a dear friend of ours.'

'I know what you are,' Julia told us. 'You're stowaways! And now you're endangering my vital mission to save Earth!'

'I can assure you we're nothing of the sort,' exclaimed the Doctor, starting to get to his feet.

'No, wait a moment,' I told him. 'I know those words! Stowaways, a vital mission. They were said by the man in the comic strip.' I turned on the girl. 'They were said by your father.'

Julia blinked. 'My parents are asleep. I stole Mum's rocket so I could fix the satellite that's broadcasting the signal.'

'We're in a space rocket!' I said. The table and sofa gave a cosy, domestic feeling but now I looked for them I could see the control panels and display screens for controlling flight, and even a porthole with its own little curtain. The sight of it unsettled me. 'Hey,' I said, pointing it out to my friends. 'I've seen that before.'

The Doctor blanched. 'The story in that infernal book!'

'But it's different,' I said. 'In the book, the girl is with her parents.'

Barbara put her hand up to her mouth in horror. 'And we're with Vicki. But now it's different.'

The Doctor looked agonised. 'I'm afraid Barbara's right,' he said. 'The story has changed. And Vicki is no longer part of it.'

I wanted to argue, to shout and scream. But not in front of Julia, the wide-eyed child who'd been terrified enough just emerging from her bunk. I took a breath and tried to focus on something, anything, practical we could do.

'You said your parents are sleeping,' I said to Julia.

'That was in the story as well,' said Ian. 'Everyone on Earth is sleeping.'

Julia looked surprised we didn't already know. 'Not everyone,' she said. 'But most people. Because of the satellite.'

'Which satellite?' asked the Doctor.

Now Julia laughed. 'Seriously?' We explained we really didn't know anything. 'Colsat is dead old,' Julia told us. 'It was launched in the late 1970s for broadcasting ordinary colour TV. And it worked OK. Then last year there was interference in the signal. People complained but they could still watch their programmes and they didn't want to pay for a launch to get Colsat repaired. So they left it. The signal got steadily worse but people insisted that they could make out what was on the screen, and that anyway the poor sound and picture made things better because you had to concentrate more.'

'But what about this sleeping condition?' asked the Doctor.

'It's what happened next,' Julia told him. 'People started getting sleepy. It didn't matter when you'd been watching – the effect could hit you hours or days later. People fell asleep in the street or at work.'

'And not just in front of their television sets,' nodded the Doctor. 'So you didn't realise the cause.'

'Plenty had ideas. But that only made it worse. There was panic. Eventually, the Prime Minister addressed the whole nation – on TV.'

'Oh dear,' said Ian. 'I've heard a few political speeches like that.'

I laughed, as did Julia, but the Doctor wagged a finger. 'This is all very serious. A whole country asleep, perhaps a whole world! And how do you plan to wake them?'

Julia's smile faltered. 'No one's managed to.'

Now the Doctor smiled. 'You worked out the cause of the problem. And then you stole up here in a rocket ship to try and put it right.'

Julia blushed. 'Someone had to. It could have been anyone.'

'I don't think so,' said the Doctor. 'Your family will be proud.'

'I don't know,' she told him. 'I was being rude to Mum and got sent to my room. That's why I missed the Prime Minister.'

'Then there's the little matter of stealing a space rocket,' I said.

'That required ingenuity and not a small amount of pluck,' said the Doctor.

'Well, of course *you* approve,' I said.

'Why ever not? Julia is going to save everyone. With our assistance, of course.'

I turned to Ian for support. 'What do you expect us to do?' he asked the Doctor.

'This ingenious girl had almost done it entirely herself. She got the rocket into space and was all set to fix the satellite. But then why hasn't she? Well, I'll tell you. Think of the effort you both expended on that bulkhead door.'

'I couldn't move it,' said Julia. 'I couldn't get to the equipment. But now I can.'

It proved a little more complicated than that.

Barbara and I lugged up box after box of heavy equipment from the room below, where the TARDIS had landed. Meanwhile, Julia showed the Doctor over the control systems in the crew room. The Doctor would have made a wonderful schoolteacher – the sort the pupils all loved but who drove the governors mad. As I hefted another box up into the crew room, I saw how he encouraged the girl, how he hung off her every word, as if she were the teacher. No doubt, this kind of spacecraft was child's play to him, but he listened in rapt attention and I could see how it made Julia grow in confidence.

I caught Barbara's eye at one point, and she looked horribly torn. We'd seen the Doctor bond with Vicki soon after the loss of his beloved Susan. Could he really be replacing Vicki in his affections so quickly? I wanted to say something. Barbara stopped me. It wouldn't be fair, she said, not in front of Julia. We would bide our time. But we wouldn't let the old man abandon poor Vicki.

By the time we were carrying up the last, extra-large box between us, the Doctor and Julia had unpacked most of the previous cargo and assembled the machinery. They'd built a kind of robot spider, only with dozens of legs, many wielding technical instruments. Bunny scampered round the thing, huffing and sniffing, hoping it would be a new playmate.

'Then the robot fixes the satellite,' I said. 'Can it be as simple as that?'

Julia and the Doctor exchanged glances. 'I thought it would be,' said the girl.

The Doctor nodded. 'If everything had gone to plan. I'm afraid, my boy, that Julia not being able to open the bulkhead door has led to some delay. The delay has used up precious fuel.'

'We don't have the fuel to get to the satellite?' asked Barbara.

'We might just, but there's no room for anything else to go wrong.'

'Then don't get anything wrong.'

The Doctor smiled at her but still looked concerned.

'That's not all, is it?' I asked.

The Doctor came over to join us, away from Julia working on the robot so she wouldn't hear. 'If we use up the fuel on getting to the satellite,' he said, 'there's no way she can get home.'

'Surely they can send another rocket,' said Barbara.

'If anyone's awake,' I countered.

'It's not so simple as that,' said the Doctor. 'They might be able and willing, but they still couldn't get here in time. There is limited oxygen on board this vessel. It might have been enough for Julia and the dog, had the three of us not taken our share.'

'We've oxygen in the TARDIS,' I said. 'We could siphon some off. Or just open the doors.'

But the Doctor had that inscrutable look on his face. He'd already made his own plan.

'You want her to join us in the TARDIS,' said Barbara levelly. 'You'd take her from her whole world, from her family, to assuage your guilt about losing Vicki.'

'If we don't take Julia with us,' said the Doctor, 'she dies.' Now he turned to Barbara, and we were both shocked by his expression, the awful look in his eyes. 'My feelings for Vicki have not wavered. But we are where we are, and this girl needs our assistance.'

He and Barbara stared furiously at one another. Then Barbara relented. 'All right,' she said. 'We help her. And then we go back for Vicki.'

She didn't let him answer, but turned sharply on her heel and went over to join Julia. 'We've been thinking,' she said breezily to the girl. 'About what happens afterwards ...'

*

Julia was delighted, and that made it worse. 'You won't miss your family?' I asked. She explained that her parents would never forgive her for turning down the chance to travel in the TARDIS. They were explorers, pioneers – a generation of the space age.

I found that profoundly sad. 'Don't you enjoy travelling in time and space?' she said.

'Of course,' I said – a little quickly. 'It's not always fun. Sometimes it's very dangerous. And I miss my home.'

She considered. 'The Doctor really can't take you back to where you came from?'

'I don't think he ever can,' I told her. I don't think I'd admitted it before, not even to myself, and saying those words it was as if a terrible weight lifted from my shoulders. Or the last vestiges of hope.

Then a light flashed on one of the panels. 'We're coming up on the satellite,' Ian told me.

The Doctor and Julia now ignored us, all attention on the controls. They peered through the porthole, the glass etched with a vertical straight line marked just like a ruler. It didn't seem the most sophisticated – or reassuring – way to measure our approach. We watched, tensely. Bunny nuzzled at my hip, but even he knew not to make a sound.

'Up by four,' said the Doctor.

'Up by four,' confirmed Julia, working a lever.

'Counter-clockwise two, no three.'

'Counter-clockwise three.'

'That's good. I should say that's excellent. Yes—'

And we hit something, hard. The whole room shook and there was the most awful scraping, tearing noise from outside.

Then we rumbled to a stop. Ian helped me to my feet, and we found the floor tilted at a sharp angle. The Doctor, hanging from the control panel he'd been operating, smiled sheepishly back at us.

'A perfect rendezvous,' he said. 'More or less.'

He helped Julia untangle herself from the controls and together they clambered over to the airlock. Julia wanted to do one more check of the spider-legged robot, but the Doctor tutted that they'd already been over it so many times, and shooed her away.

'The air is already getting thin,' Ian said quietly, so that only I would hear.

Julia operated a switch. The door closed on the robot, a warning light flashed and the chamber depressurised with a noisy hiss. Then a clunk, the room around us trembled – and the robot had been released to the vacuum.

The Doctor and Julia returned to the main controls. Ian and I joined them – not easy given the sharp tilt of the room. I pinioned myself against the back of the sofa and helped Ian scramble up after me. The Doctor and Julia took up most of the porthole window, but I could just about see.

Out in the dark, the robot fell gracefully, eerily, silently towards a huge metal latticework, on which were harnessed all kinds of radar dishes and antennae. The structure was enormous – the robot kept falling, smaller and smaller and smaller, until I could barely see it any more. But no – it finally hit the huge latticework. I saw its legs suddenly flex and catch on. Then it nimbly skittered away, lost in the shadow of one of the radar dishes.

The Doctor drummed his fingers on the controls in front of him. He'd never been one to wait patiently. 'It will work,' Julia told him, and he smiled.

It was an agonising wait. Ian had been right, too – the air had definitely thinned. I was conscious of the sound of my own ragged breathing, and the panic rising inside.

And then there were voices. A babble of them, all at once, as if a hundred different radio sets had all just been switched on. 'Well, good morning!' chuckled a plummy announcer – I think they still had the BBC in the future. 'Bonjour,' said another. 'Buenos días.' 'Buongiorno.'

Julia beamed. The Doctor patted her hand. 'Yes, that's most satisfactory. But what a lot of noise.' He turned a dial and stilled the voices.

'Doctor,' said Ian, breathlessly. 'We can't stay up here much longer.'

'No,' said the Doctor, his eyes fixed on Julia. 'My dear, are you ready to join us?'

The girl nodded, enthusiastic. 'I can bring Bunny, can't I?'

The Doctor didn't looked thrilled. 'Of course,' I said. 'We couldn't do without him.'

So we made our way back down the sloping room to the hatch in what had been the floor. The storeroom below also tilted sharply, the spiralling walkway now a corkscrew.

'We'll never get down it,' I gaped. 'Not all of it points down!'

Ian had picked up the dog and now surveyed the prospect below. 'Look, there are handholds – and ropes.'

I couldn't think how I'd not seen them before. But yes, all along the wall were a series of crescent-shaped holes, just the right size for our hands and feet. It wasn't exactly easy, but we began our descent.

Ian had to climb one-handed, his other arm tight round the dog. Julia and I helped the Doctor – though he insisted he didn't need it. In fact, I let Julia do most of the helping. It was important that these two bonded. I saw it in both their faces: the excitement, the sense of fun at the start of this new adventure.

It wasn't how I felt at all.

Giddy from the lack of air, hollow inside from the sense of betrayal I felt about Vicki, I had to concentrate on every step and handhold. But at last we reached the upended floor, on which stood the TARDIS at a precarious angle. The Doctor fussed with the key, and the door creaked open.

That was when Bunny launched himself from Ian's arms and straight at the Doctor.

The Doctor fell back with a yell. Julia tried to grab the dog, but it turned on her – and bit her! Snarling, barking, it barred the open doors of the TARDIS. I got the Doctor to his feet, but there was no way we could get past.

'Bunny, please!' wailed Julia, her cheeks now streaked with tears. 'We have to go.'

'It's scared of the TARDIS,' I said. 'It can sense it's something strange.'

'There's nothing strange about my ship,' said the Doctor. 'But there's something strange about this dog.'

The dog snarled at him, but the Doctor stared defiantly back, hands gripping the lapels of his coat. 'I'm right,' the Doctor continued. 'Aren't I, Miss Jett?'

Ian and I whirled round to Julia. She only had eyes for the dog. 'Please,' she told Bunny. 'If we stay, we die here.'

The dog stopped snarling and gazed up at her, such a forlorn look in its eyes. Then it bowed its head, twisted round and walked into the TARDIS.

Or it should have done. Instead, crossing the threshold, Bunny seemed to unravel, like a thread pulled from a carpet. Once moment there was a huge dog, then only dust in the air.

'Bunny!' called Julia in horror.

Ian grabbed her arm to stop her following the dog. 'What happened?' he asked.

'You're not surprised,' I told the Doctor.

'No,' said the Doctor, sadly. 'I don't think Julia is, either.'

Julia stood transfixed by the space where her dog had been lost. Then she shook her head.

'We're in the realm of dreams,' said the Doctor. He indicated the skew-whiff room around us. 'All this is merely a story.'

'And the dog,' I said. 'And Julia?'

She turned to me. 'I feel real,' she said. 'The more time I spend with you, the more you believe in me.'

'I should have realised,' said the Doctor. 'We made ourselves receptive. And I wanted so desperately to rescue Vicki. The forces here couldn't oblige, but they lured us here with the thought that we might be reunited with her – offering us hope.'

'But it would make no sense to find Vicki here,' said Ian. 'So they tried to give us ...' He looked at Julia. 'The next best thing.'

'To keep us here in this dreamland?' I said. 'So we become characters in a story ourselves?'

'I dare say, my dear, yes.' The Doctor nodded to himself. 'We'd have climbed into a make-believe TARDIS and had make-believe adventures that always ended well – fixing the time mechanism, foiling the Daleks, rescuing Vicki ... Fortunately for us, it seems my ship is too strong to be subsumed into this realm.' He raised his voice, addressing the shadows above us. 'You'd have to get rid of the TARDIS first, wouldn't you, hmm? And that would be quite inconceivable!'

I felt angry. 'You tricked us,' I told Julia.

'I'm what you made me,' she said. 'All of you.'

'We wanted to save you,' nodded Ian. 'To feel less bad about leaving Vicki behind.'

I wanted to argue but he was right. I'd been furious at the Doctor for bonding with this girl, when I'd really been furious at myself.

'We can't take her with us,' I said. 'Can we?'

The Doctor sighed. 'I'm afraid it seems not.' He took the girl's hands in his. 'I am sorry.'

'Without you,' she told him, 'I'll return to the darkness. The empty void.'

'Oh, not at all,' he chided. 'We might have been the spark of your existence, but you're your own person now. An individual with a universe to explore. To the people waking from the reign of that satellite, you'll even be a hero.'

The girl smiled. 'None of them are real.'

'They are if you want them to be,' said the Doctor.

'But what about the air?' Ian asked him.

'What about it?' he snapped back. 'Do you really think I would leave this poor child without air? Absurd! No, I admit I wanted her to come with us. But when we were upstairs I also fixed the secondary supply system. She will be quite content until the inevitable rescue.'

He winked at me – so quickly I might have imagined it. The old goat was making it up! And yet he said it with such conviction that I believed him. So did Ian. And that was all it took.

Around us, valves started to hiss as the secondary supply came on, flooding the compartment with cool, refreshing air. Ian laughed, realising what the Doctor had done.

'Could we really wish for anything?' he said.

'It's not the wishing,' said the Doctor. 'It's the making it credible.'

So I concentrated on something very simple, something I could easily picture in my mind. A form, with texture and weight, emerging from the TARDIS.

'Bunny!' exclaimed Julia as the dog bounded towards her.

We left the girl and her dog after that. Oh, it was cordial – she hugged the Doctor and I shook her hand. But we all felt awful leaving. Would she really survive? And if she did, how would she fare in a cosmos she knew to be fabricated?

The Doctor set the TARDIS controls, piloting us out of this realm composed of thought and back into time and space. 'There,' he said at last. 'There.'

'How would we know if we were still in a story?' I asked him, teasing.

'Oh Ian,' said Barbara, horrified. 'Don't. I feel so ghastly for that girl. And so guilty.'

The Doctor clasped Barbara's hands and tried to soothe her. I turned away, and spotted the book discarded on the floor. *Monsters from Outer Space!* I went over, picked it up and flicked through the pages. There was no trace of the comic strip we'd seen before. It had been a projection, an illusion.

'I blame myself,' Barbara was saying. 'Not just for Julia, for Vicki. I should have made sure she was with us!'

'It's my fault,' the Doctor insisted. 'My own stupid fault. I shouldn't have moved the TARDIS.'

I told him not to blame himself, that we were all responsible, together. That's what Julia had told us, wasn't it? Our combined guilt and need had created her.

And that gave me a thought. Together we had power. Maybe *together* we could fix the time mechanism of the TARDIS and find our way back to Vicki. In fact, I had a better idea. What if, I suggested to the Doctor and Barbara, we stole the Daleks' working time ship from them and used *that* to get back to Vicki?

The Doctor looked utterly horrified. And then he looked delighted. 'I say yes! Yes, yes!'

And so began the next chapter.

It's been quiet since the TARDIS left. There's the clunk and tick of the rocket itself, the hum of the computer. I haven't the heart to turn on the radio and listen to all the voices. They'll only say whatever I want to hear. It's the same with the rescue mission from Earth. They'll arrive when I want them to, they'll be whoever I want.

Instead, I snuggle with Bunny and listen to his breathing, so grateful that he's here. There's just him and me.

And you.

You sustain me, as you read these words. Imagine me sitting here, snuggled up with my dog on a rocket in orbit round Earth. I'm easy to imagine, aren't I? You can easily picture me. Perhaps I remind you of someone you know.

That's it. You make that connection and I become that little more real. It's unsettling, isn't it? That feeling, that emotional response, it can feed me, too.

I'm real now. I'm here, a child adrift in space with only her dog for company. At least, while you keep reading.

Please don't turn the page.

Save Yourself
Terrance Dicks

The Doctor sat in a luxurious anteroom deep in the heart of the Capitol, the governing building of the Time Lords. He was waiting to hear if he would live or die. He had been condemned to death for Time Interference by the High Council according to the strict provisions of Time Lord law. Then a visitor from the mysterious Celestial Intervention Agency had told him of a possible way out. The Council apparently were still undecided.

The Doctor felt tired, as if he'd been waiting here a lifetime.

A guard appeared at the door. 'Come, Doctor, they are ready for you.'

The Doctor was marched along a corridor and into a larger room. He stood gazing curiously around him. He was in a small audience hall with a circle of benches surrounding the Lord High Chancellor's chair. Elaborately robed Time Lords occupied the seats.

'Well, Doctor,' said the Lord High Chancellor, 'which is it to be, exile or death?'

'Exile would suit you best,' said the Doctor. 'If I was executed there would be a terrible scandal. Disappearance into exile would give a better chance of hushing the whole thing up.'

'It would also have the advantage of preserving your life,' said the Lord High Chancellor.

'A formidable argument,' agreed the Doctor. 'What do you want me to do?'

'It's a matter of a mission,' said the Lord High Chancellor. 'Several missions in fact. It has come to our notice, Doctor, that while your interference has sometimes run contrary to our interests, on other occasions it has assisted them. We have a number of missions in which, under our guidance and control, you can work for us.'

Oh, do you! thought the Doctor. But he said nothing.

They made an incongruous pair. The High Chancellor stood tall and stately in his flowing robes. The Doctor's check trousers were more than a little baggy. His well-worn black coat had seen better days, and his shirt was definitely wilting. His gently comical face was crowned by a mop of black hair.

'Now to the first,' said the Lord High Chancellor. 'There is an unprepossessing planet called Karn in which we take some interest.'

'In which you take considerable interest,' said the Doctor. 'Karn is the home of the Sacred Flame, which creates the Elixir of Life. Many Time Lords would have died without its restorative effect.'

'Something we prefer to keep quiet about,' said the Lord High Chancellor. 'Now we have received word that Karn has been occupied by a hostile force.'

'How did you receive word?' said the Doctor.

The Lord High Chancellor paused. 'You know, I am sure, that Karn is the home of the Sisterhood, a semi-supernatural cult. Personally, I believe its proceedings are little more than mystic mumbo-jumbo. However, it appears to have occasional erratic glimpses into the future. Recently, one of our telepaths received a message with the news I have given you, insisting that it was of vital importance to the Time Lord race. Whether this is true or not we simply do not know.'

'And you want me to go and find out,' said the Doctor.

'We can furnish you with your TARDIS and any help you need.'

'Why don't you send a force of your own?' asked the Doctor.

'Scandal, publicity, galaxy-wide interest,' said the Lord High Chancellor. 'Go and find the truth for us, Doctor, and we shall know how best to act.'

'I have some conditions of my own,' said the Doctor.

'You are in no position to bargain.'

'I think I am. You want me to do this mission very much. Something tells me you are unable to find anyone else prepared to do it.'

'Well,' said the Lord High Chancellor, 'what are your conditions?'

'The death sentence is to be annulled. Double Jeopardy.' (This meant that the sentence could never be re-imposed.)

'The number of missions is to be strictly limited – the precise number arrived at by pre-agreement.'

'Of course, Doctor. Strictly limited.' The High Chancellor seemed amused as if by some private joke. 'What next? You must have more demands.'

'I'll try to think of some when I have time.'

The High Chancellor turned to a guard. 'Take him to his TARDIS.'

The Doctor was marched along endless corridors to a small blank room which held the familiar blue box of the TARDIS. The guard ushered him inside. The Doctor felt a rush of welcome as he gazed around the control room. And yet, something felt different. The console looked a little more battered, as if it had been through a good deal since he'd left it to go on trial.

'There have been some modifications,' said the guard.

The Doctor peered at a bank of instruments. 'You've added a Stattenheim remote control unit, I see. Giving you dual control?'

'Your TARDIS will take you to Karn and, in due course, bring you back here, but that is all.' He saluted and left the control room.

The Doctor stood for a moment, his hands resting gently on the central console. 'Got you in chains, have they, old girl? Never mind, we shall be free again one day.'

His hands moved over the controls and the central column began its rise and fall.

*

The journey was not long. The central column slowed down, and the Doctor heard the familiar landing noise of the TARDIS. He switched on the scanner.

He was gazing down into a steep valley at the end of which there stood a castle. There were many such castles on Karn. Like most of them, it was half-ruined. The Karnians, once a high-tech civilisation, had destroyed themselves in internal wars many years ago.

'Well, I suppose I must see what the Sisterhood were trying to warn us about.'

The Doctor left the TARDIS and stood shivering a little in the bleak winds. He stood on a desolate, rocky plain wrapped in Karn's prevailing gloom. Suddenly, he remembered his fur coat. He was about to go back inside and fetch it when a deep voice boomed out:

'Halt! Do not move or you will be shot down.'

The Doctor looked up and saw a small group of black-clad guards with levelled space rifles.

'All right,' he sighed. 'I shall stand quite still.'

The guards clattered down the path towards him. Soon he was surrounded.

One of the guards stepped forward. He was a large thuggish-looking man with a square jaw, evidently the Guard Captain. He glared at the Doctor. 'What are you doing here?'

'My craft – the blue box you see behind me – crashed down here.' He clasped his hands together and looked up guilelessly. 'I was going to ask whoever lives in that castle for their help with repairs.'

The guards conferred for a moment. 'Shoot him?' suggested one of them.

The Guard Captain said, 'No. *He* said that anyone arriving here was to be questioned.'

The Doctor noticed that 'He' was pronounced with awe and reverence. 'Who is this *He*?' he asked the Guard Captain.

'He is our Leader. He is going to bring us to glory and conquest. No more questions. Come.'

They set off on a long and gruelling march across the rocky terrain. The pace was ruthless. At last the jagged black shape of the castle loomed over them.

They marched to the main gate. The Guard Captain exchanged a quick word with the sentries, and they were admitted into a high-ceilinged stone passageway.

The Doctor looked round curiously. He noticed two things about the castle. Firstly, that someone had worked very hard to destroy it. There were broken columns and great chunks of masonry fallen from walls and ceilings. Since then, someone – presumably someone *else* – had worked very hard to restore it. Smooth surfaces had been dusted and polished, and rubble neatly stacked in corners.

The corridor ended in an elaborately carved stone archway. Beyond the archway lay a throne room. Like the rest of the castle, it was battered but restored. A throne stood at the head of a flight of steps. Guards were posted about the room.

The Doctor turned to the Guard Captain. 'What now?'

'We wait until He is ready for us.'

The Doctor looked round the throne room. The waiting guards, like the Guard Captain and his men, all looked somehow similar. Tall men with swarthy skins, thin noses, bushy beards and moustaches. 'You're Trastevarians, aren't you?'

'Yes,' said the Guard Captain proudly. 'A race of warriors.'

'A singularly militant and destructive race,' said the Doctor. 'I thought you'd been all but wiped out – driven to the remote fringes of the galaxy.'

'So we were. But now He has come to lead us, we shall return. He has promised us fresh planets to conquer.'

There was a sudden fanfare, and all eyes turned to the door behind the throne.

It opened and a man appeared, not particularly tall, but lean and wiry. He wore a black velvet doublet studded with jewels. 'Bring him!' he bellowed.

Guards seized the Doctor and dragged him to the foot of the throne. He looked up at the gorgeously black-robed figure, at the eyes behind the round pebble glasses.

'You,' the Doctor breathed.

It was the War Lord.

'Welcome Doctor,' he said. 'I knew the Time Lords would send an agent to investigate in time. I hoped so very much that it would be you. Now, kneel!'

'To you?' said the Doctor. 'Never!'

The War Lord turned to the guards. 'Make him kneel!'

The guards seized the Doctor by the shoulders and tried to force him to his knees.

They didn't succeed.

The Doctor squared his shoulders and set his muscles, and his whole body became like a rock. Panting and red-faced, the guards gave up their efforts.

'Stronger than he looks, sir,' gasped one of them.

'Mind over matter,' said the Doctor. 'Or, more accurately, I have a mind and you don't matter.'

'Let him stand, then,' said the War Lord, his fury showing only in his eyes. 'How can you do that?'

'Venusian meditation grants the enlightened soul the most precise muscular control.' The Doctor straightened up. 'A far more interesting question is how and why you're here. I thought I'd witnessed you being executed. Temporal dissolution no less!'

'The most elevated of my race, Doctor, have stolen technology from all the higher powers of the universe. They have kept pace with Time Lord technology and, in some instances, surpassed it. When my atoms were dissolved into space, my superiors recaptured them and reassembled me- as you see, as good as new.'

'So much for the "How",' said the Doctor. 'Now for the "Why".'

'Several purposes, Doctor. First to kill you for ruining my splendid scheme.'

'It was a hair-brained, half-cocked scheme. It was already collapsing under its own weight.' The Doctor smiled disarmingly. 'I just added a little pressure.'

'I shall revive the scheme, on a smaller scale at first. My reserve guard of Trastevarians will attack a number of wealthy planets and recruit further armies. Once we have sufficient forces, we shall destroy that Earth of which you are so fond. Its populations will be cannon fodder in the great conquests to come, and those who do not fight will slave for us maintaining a galactic supply depot for our wars across the cosmos.'

'I see,' said the Doctor angrily. 'What you sought to do by stealth you now intend to do quite blatantly. But the Time Lords stopped you once; you can't be so foolish as to believe they won't stop you again.'

'Indeed I am not,' said the War Lord, seating himself upon the great throne. 'Which is why I shall destroy the Time Lords. You know what is on this planet, Doctor. The sacred fire that creates the Fountain of Life upon which the Time Lords depend for their multi-lived immortality.'

'Depend? Nonsense!' the Doctor retorted. 'It helps in rare cases, that is all.'

'My own War Chief's life was saved by it,' said the War Lord. 'When I first encountered him in a Trastevarian jail, he was so close to death that he regenerated. He said the elixir was vital to the regeneration process.'

'Perhaps he said that so you wouldn't consider him weak!' the Doctor shot back.

'Why should I believe you?' The War Lord produced a glistening black sphere from the pocket of his robe. 'This is my people's most powerful explosive. It will destroy the Fountain and with that gone, the Time Lords will die out.'

'You're deranged!' cried the Doctor. The elixir might not be vital, but it had still saved countless lives both on Gallifrey and beyond. No wonder the telepathic cry had gone up as the Sisterhood sensed the danger they were in! He couldn't let the War Lord destroy something so precious.

'Deranged, you think?' You can scarcely stop me,' the War Lord said, signalling to his guards to seize the Doctor. 'If you will not kneel to me, then my men will remove your legs. You will regenerate perhaps – but there will be no elixir to help you ...'

He was interrupted by a strange wheezing, groaning sound. A blue box materialised from nowhere beside the Doctor.

The War Lord jumped to his feet. 'Time Lords!' he shrieked. 'So you have sent for your Time Lord armies? Too late, Doctor.' Leaping away from the throne, the War Lord ran to a curtained alcove and ripped away the curtain. In the alcove stood a smooth black column with a domed top. He disappeared inside. The black column vanished with a screeching, grinding sound.

The Doctor too was on his feet. He ran to his TARDIS and opened the door with his key. The door swung open to reveal an empty control room. He turned to face the Guard Captain.

'No Time Lord army,' said the Doctor. 'Just me. I'm rather glad now that the Time Lords gave me a remote control unit! Your War Lord is gone. He has abandoned you. Now I am in charge. You will obey my orders.'

The Guard Captain stared at him uneasily.

'Do you hear me?' rasped the Doctor. 'Soon the Time Lords will be here. Obey them and you will come to no harm.'

The Guard Captain came to attention and saluted. 'Sir!' He turned to the other guards. 'There are new orders. They are to be strictly obeyed.'

In an authoritarian society, thought the Doctor, *people obey the voice of authority.* He went inside the TARDIS. The door closed behind him, and the box vanished with the same wheezing, groaning sound with which it had arrived.

Inside the TARDIS, the Doctor patted the control console.

'Well done, old girl! Hurry now. No time ... just a short trip through space.' He raised his eyes upward. 'I'm sure the Time Lords can steer you where you need to go?'

Already the central column was slowing in its rise and fall.

As the TARDIS landed, the Doctor checked the scanner but all was gloomy. He opened the doors and went outside. He was in a low cavern in the heart of the mountains. The smoky air crackled with heat. In the centre of the cavern, a low wall surrounded a fiery pit.

Beside it stood the War Lord, the black sphere in his hand. He was haranguing a small group of black-clad and hooded women, the Inner Council of the Sisterhood. 'Here is the end of your precious Elixir of Life. This device will blow the central fire to fragments. The minerals will not melt into water, and even the Fountain itself will flow no more.'

'You think so?' The Doctor stepped forward. 'Well, we shall soon see, shan't we!'

At the sight of the Doctor the War Lord retreated. 'Stay back,' he warned.

'Leave,' the Doctor told the Sisters of the Inner Council. 'Go, now. Fetch help!'

'Help, Doctor?' The War Lord laughed, his eyes wide. He seemed almost unhinged. 'Nothing can help you now.'

'Then let me help you,' said the Doctor. 'To be destroyed atom by atom and then reassembled ... that would send anyone quite mad.'

'If I am mad, you would be well advised to surrender.' He raised the black sphere. 'You know that I intend to use this.'

'Set off that device here and you'll destroy yourself as well as me,' the Doctor replied calmly, continuing his slow advance.

Suddenly, he darted forward and lunged for the black sphere. The War Lord tried to dodge, stumbled over a rock. The black sphere slipped from his hand.

'Oh, my word!' The Doctor dived under the sphere and just barely caught it, clutching it to his chest.

With a snarl, the War Lord was back on his feet. The Doctor put down the sphere and closed with him. They grappled furiously.

The War Lord, like the Doctor, was much stronger than he looked. But neither was used to hand-to-hand combat. The Doctor locked his muscles together once more, allowing the War Lord to waste valuable energy trying to shift him. But it was a mistake. The War Lord turned from him, ran and grabbed the black sphere from the ground. Then he sprang up onto the low wall encircling the pit.

'No! You mustn't!' The Doctor bounded across the room and scrambled up onto the wall close beside the War Lord. They confronted each other and then grappled again.

It was a brief and furious tussle.

The Doctor's foot slipped, and he fell backwards away from the fire. As he did so, he knocked the War Lord's legs from under him. With a scream, the War Lord toppled and then plunged into the fiery pit, still clutching, the Doctor realised despairingly, the black sphere.

Warriors of the Sisterhood, armed with spears, hurried into the smoky cave.

'Get down!' the Doctor shouted, rolling away from the pit. 'Down, I say!'

There was a sudden thunderous roar from behind and the cave filled with black smoke.

The roar gradually faded, and the smoke thinned. Cautiously the Doctor turned to look behind him. Black smoke was still jetting from the pit. He held out his hand and it was soon covered with fine black dust. He brushed it away.

'Well. I don't think "the most elevated of his race" will reconstitute *that* into another War Lord!' he said with satisfaction.

One of the Sisterhood called upwards in a high-carrying voice: 'How fares the Fountain?'

The Doctor waited tensely. The smoke in the air was somehow parted by a telekinetic force. The supernatural wind whistled down into the pit. The sound of a magnified *drip, drip, drip* filled the cavern like a watery heartbeat. Then the noise faded and the wind died away.

A voice called back: 'The Fountain flows.'

All was well, thought the Doctor. The Fire of Life had absorbed both the War Lord and his device.

He addressed the shaken Sisters. 'Stay here and wait. Time Lords will come and help you. Guard the Flame.'

Then he hurried back to the TARDIS.

In the Council Chamber, the High Chancellor sat worriedly upon his chair. What was it that Earth poet had said? 'Uneasy lies the head that wears the crown.' He knew the Doctor was an unreliable agent, and yet that very unpredictability was often the source of his success. For how long could he hope to harness it?

The wheezing, groaning sound of the Doctor's TARDIS interrupted him. The Doctor emerged and threw himself onto a bench. He and the High Chancellor studied each other for a moment.

'Déjà vu,' said the Doctor suddenly. 'I have the most curious feeling I've been here before ...'

'I briefed you here, Doctor,' said the High Chancellor.

'That's not what I mean.' The Doctor was looking about mistrustfully.

'I presume you were successful?'

The Doctor gave a brief account of his adventure. 'The Sacred Flame and the Fountain of Life are safe, and the War Lord is gone for good.'

'Let us hope so.' The High Chancellor sighed and sat back in his chair. 'The War Lord's superiors are at large still. The thought that their technology may outmatch ours troubles me deeply.'

'Well, that's your concern. Mine is for the happy ending I've just earned for myself.' The Doctor smiled broadly. 'Where you shower me with thanks and rewards and give me my TARDIS and my freedom.' He paused, then said quietly, 'But you're not going to do that, are you?'

The High Chancellor smiled. 'Not quite yet, Doctor. Now as to your next mission ...'

The Doctor jumped up. 'We agreed there would be only a limited number!'

'Indeed we did, Doctor. We've agreed that many times.' The High Chancellor's smile was almost regretful. 'And each time you sit in the waiting area, your memory is wiped of all the missions you have carried out for us already.'

The Doctor's face had grown grave. '*All* the missions?'

'Each, for you, is the first,' said the High Chancellor. 'So that each time you act for us with the full force, hope and vigour of a man fighting for his life and freedom. Believing that success will bring the repeal of his sentence.'

'You mean you're using me over and over and I don't even know?' The Doctor was red-faced with anger, hopping from foot to foot. 'Saving your bacons, time after time?'

'We are Lords of Time, Doctor,' the High Chancellor said. He pulled a device from his cloak and pressed a button.

The Doctor sat in a luxurious anteroom deep in the heart of the Capitol, the governing building of the Time Lords. He was waiting to hear if he would live or die. He had been condemned to death for Time Interference by the High Council according to the strict provisions of Time Lord law. Then a visitor from the mysterious Celestial Intervention Agency had told him of a possible way out. The Council apparently were still undecided.

The Doctor felt tired, as if he'd been waiting here a lifetime.

A guard appeared at the door. 'Come, Doctor,' he said. 'They are ready for you.'

The Clean Air Act
Matthew Sweet

It is time to tell the truth to our children. The battle to feed the nation has already been lost. By the middle of the 1990s, British supermarkets will no longer be stocked with fruit from the Commonwealth or meat from South America. Those territories, like ours, will be managing their own domestic famines. They, like us, will be obliged to put their own populations first. But this task will be barely possible. In these islands, the soil will be exhausted, the rivers lifeless, the coastal seas depleted of life. The air will be bitter with the chemical by-products of the synthetic food industry. Only one strategy will allow us to pull back from the complete collapse of the ecosystem. We must ask the coming generation to take on the most heroic task humanity has yet attempted. To refrain from creating unsustainable new lives. To build a new world, clean, breathable, uncrowded.

A child brought me to this realisation. Her name was Sally Hesketh. Two years ago she appeared at my constituency surgery, a seventeen-year-old with straight brown hair and a serious manner. I noticed she was holding a copy of *New Ecologist* magazine, and assumed I was in for a lecture about the Sleaford bypass. Sally, however, had a much stranger story to tell. It concerned the death of her parents at Oak Green.

That name once carried no strong or particular association, beyond, I suppose, the bucolic sturdiness adored by modern property developers. Now, of course, it has become synonymous with one of the most shocking tragedies of peacetime – an event that has cast its shadow over every subsequent perfect summer afternoon.

When Sally Hesketh came to see me, the Rowlands report was only a few weeks old. She had read it, but was not persuaded by its findings. I asked her why. She opened her satchel and produced a bundle of exercise books, their pages black with notes. For more than an hour, she spoke to me of luminous paint and military aircraft. She quoted the Radioactive Substances Act (1960). She drew a graph describing the half-life of radium-226. And she said that none of these explained why her mother and father were dead, and why so many of their neighbours lost their lives that summer.

I was sympathetic but unconvinced. I asked her to recall the grave atmosphere at the public inquiry; Lord Rowlands' dogged questioning of the military witnesses; the moving and dignified apology delivered by a senior military officer attached to the United Nations.

Sally prickled at the mention of this officer. She was, she said, grateful for the compensation. The monthly cheque was funding her campaigning life. She had used the first instalment to buy a bolt-cutter. But, she argued, the Ministry of Defence had no case to answer. It had never used the site to dispose of instrument dials from wartime bombers. There was nothing toxic buried beneath her parents' house.

On that hot Sunday afternoon, she said, death had come from the air. From the air above Oak Green.

From Charles Grover, *Last Chance for Man: A Penguin Special*

Jo Grant felt it happen. At first she thought it was some vibration in Bessie's engine. The Doctor, excited by axle grease and petrol fumes in the way that some men are stirred by patchouli oil, was always adding components beneath the hood. Not all of them agreed to live in harmony. Later, in her statement for the UNIT files, Jo tried to describe the sound, but the words eluded her. *A low whistle. A rushing noise. A disturbance of the air*. She crossed each one out, then wrote them back in again.

For the Doctor, it began with one of those *Jumping Jehoshaphat* moments; he'd spent the morning at a scientific conference at Tarminster University, where he'd ended up annoying everyone as usual, firstly by snorting during the keynote and then by eating all the sandwiches. (Jo had admonished him with more tact than he deserved.) Then, not long into the journey, a glance in the rear-view mirror revealed a shocking sight. A man, lying in the lane, about fifty yards behind.

The Doctor yanked Bessie into reverse. As the car screeched backwards, he noticed, half-hidden by the hedgerow, the edge of a modern housing development. The man must have run from one of the gardens. Now he was on his back, twitching on the tarmac. The Doctor leapt from the car to examine him. The man was dressed in a football shirt, and in his left hand he clutched a pair of barbecue tongs, the ends of which appeared to be stuck together.

'There's been an accident,' gasped the man. His eyes were wild. The Doctor murmured some soothing words, and asked Jo to ring for an ambulance. But Jo was already belting down the path that ran behind the backs of the houses.

When she turned the corner, Jo assumed that she was looking at the aftermath of an explosion, though there was no sign of a blast. The residents of the estate had been scattered across their own back lawns. A young father struggled, dazed, in the web of his own rotary washing line. His three children formed a hyperventilating heap at the bottom of a rocket-shaped climbing frame. Every garden contained a similar scene of disarray. An old couple floundering beneath their parasol. A boy felled in the act of fixing a punctured bicycle tyre. Only one garden seemed untouched. Here, a girl of around fifteen was sitting on a metal-framed sun-lounger, a magic painting book balanced on her knees. There was a jam jar beside her on the grass. The girl was dipping a brush in the water, and using it to reveal the picture. Jo thought she seemed a bit old for that kind of thing.

'Do you have a phone?' asked Jo. 'I need to ring for help.'

'Help,' repeated the girl, blankly.

*

UNIT arrived at dawn. Jeeps settled on driveways. A mobile HQ, draped in camouflage, blocked access to the communal garages. Captain Yates supervised the evacuation, packing off residents to friends and relations in Tarminster. After that, the only sounds came from the birds in the trees, the traffic on the bypass, and the squad of soldiers led by Sergeant Benton, who collected test samples from lawns, living rooms, drains and dustbins, and laid them, like tributes, before the door of a scuffed-looking police box, perched on the back of a flatbed military truck.

In the late afternoon, the Doctor emerged, frowning and disappointed.

'Do you know those newspaper headlines that say: *Scotland Yard baffled*?' he asked. 'Well, I know how Scotland Yard feels.'

Captain Yates tried to be encouraging, but found he'd simply cued an aria on the frustratingly non-toxic nature of the samples collected at Oak Green.

'It's not in the air. It's not in the water. It's not in their food. It's not in their bodies, either, according to the hospital. But something nearly choked these people to death. And I have absolutely no idea what.'

'Fancy a bit of a patrol?' asked Yates. The Doctor concurred.

As they toured the estate, he peered suspiciously at hedges, collected some coins dropped on the pavement, even lifted a discarded lolly stick and gave it an experimental lick. Something caught his companion's eye, too.

'She's come back,' Yates sighed. 'And with her little Midwich Cuckoo, I'll bet.' Yates moved purposefully to the nearest house, pushed at the letterbox and began talking through it. The occupant, clearly conceding that a frosted glass panel did not confer invisibility, opened her front door.

'Everyone else has left, love,' said Yates. 'You should think of that daughter of yours.'

'But nothing happened to us,' protested Mrs Hesketh, a human barricade in an A-line floral dress. 'The ambulance crew said we were fine. I don't want to spend a week sleeping in a sports centre.'

'It's only for a couple of nights,' pressed Yates. 'I'm sure it won't take us long to work out what happened here. Will it, Doctor?'

The Doctor, down on his hands and knees, was using a drinking glass to listen to Mrs Hesketh's lawn. He flapped a hand in the air, indicating that he did not welcome any interruption.

'If the UN is sending in the worm-charmers,' said Mrs Hesketh, 'I don't think we can be in that much danger, do you?'

Yates showed his impatience. 'Is your husband in, Mrs Hesketh?'

The Doctor leapt to his feet, and began checking his jacket for grass stains. 'Mrs Hesketh is within her rights, Mike,' he beamed. 'She isn't in the Army, you know. You'd need to apply to the courts to remove her. As for the rest of her family – I think they're keeping Jo entertained.'

From somewhere inside the house came a clattering noise. The unmistakable voice of Jo Grant exclaimed, 'Buckaroo!'

Mike Yates rolled his eyes in an unmilitary manner, and left them to it.

'Drink?' asked Mrs Hesketh. The Doctor didn't mind if he did.

In the kitchen, he found Sally Hesketh prising apart a custard cream. She seemed uninterested in the game that was being played for her benefit. Jo, with implacable jolliness, was gathering up handfuls of small plastic objects. She flashed the Doctor a conspiratorial look.

'Here's his saddle,' said a voice from beneath the breakfast bar.

Mr Hesketh, not a tall man, rose to meet the velvet high-rise in his kitchen. 'Are you with the military?' he demanded. 'We're not in Chile, you know. Not yet.'

'This is the Doctor,' said Jo. 'You can trust him. He's fighting the system from within. Aren't you, Doctor?'

'Well,' said the Doctor, rubbing the back of his neck. 'I'm a civilian, if that's what you mean.'

'The Heskeths called 999 when we arrived,' explained Jo. 'The gas didn't seem to affect them.'

'If it was gas,' said the Doctor. 'Any theories in this house?'

'There are all kinds of chemical pollutants blowing around in the atmosphere,' said Mr Hesketh. 'We're breathing them in all the time.'

'And you didn't see anything usual?' pressed the Doctor. 'A strange smell? A light in the sky? Any of your neighbours behaving strangely?'

Mr Hesketh shook his head. Mrs Hesketh opened a bottle of homemade wine. The Doctor pronounced it absolutely marvellous, and then began looking for somewhere to pour it. His eye was drawn to the goldfish bowl on the kitchen table.

'His name is Cousteau,' said Sally. She split another biscuit and licked out the filling.

The Doctor bowed in the direction of the bowl. 'Jacques Cousteau thinks the human race will grow gills and live under the sea,' he said. '*Homo aquaticus*. Fancy it, Mr Hesketh?'

'Not really,' said Mr Hesketh.

'But you're worried, aren't you? You and Mrs Hesketh and Sally. About the fate of the world. About – what's the phrase? – the population bomb?'

'Isn't everybody?'

'No,' said the Doctor. 'They're not. Most Earth people are pretty complacent. But you've thought this through. I can tell that from your bookshelves.'

Mr Hesketh declined to take the bait.

'Try me,' said the Doctor. 'You may find I agree with you.'

'We thought we could start it here. One of those small, stable communities they were always going on about in the books. It seemed modern at Oak Green. The architect was Swedish. It already looked like the future.'

'What sort of future do you desire?' asked the Doctor.

'Oh, the usual,' said Mr Hesketh, a forlorn note in his voice. 'The cities reborn. All those urban rivers liberated. The streets reclaimed from the cars. Everything free and breathable. Crops growing at the Oval. Trout swimming in the Thames.' Tears pooled in Mr Hesketh's eyes. 'Pretty stupid, eh? Nothing's going to change. We've lost already.'

In the aftermath of the Oak Green incident, Tom and Jenny Hesketh were profiled in the press with the rest of the victims. They were, the public learned, botanists who met in the field. Tom was working for a large multinational agribusiness. Jenny was a backpacker with a knapsack full of specimens. You may recall the photograph of their unconventional wedding ceremony on a hillside in Papua New Guinea. The newspapers insinuated they were cranks; reproduced the last school photograph of Sally, taken before the Heskeths decided to educate her at home. The photograph was unfortunate. Sally positively glared into the lens. I think it was the reason why some people speculated that she bore some responsibility for what happened. She once showed me her collection of poison pen letters. Most took witchcraft as their theme. One depicted her communing with the occupants of a flying saucer.

In the years between, she has turned over every detail of her final week of family life. I soon discovered that too many questions made her irritable. 'The best way to describe it,' she told me, 'would be a kind of house arrest.' Her strong impression was that her parents were attempting to shield her from events that had occurred, and some that were yet to come. They kept the windows shut. Sometimes, her father would slide open the patio door, allowing the whisper of a breeze to disturb the curtains. Despite this, a strange holiday atmosphere prevailed. She was allowed to eat anything she pleased and stay up as late as she wanted. She was even permitted to watch ITV.

She knows that trauma has robbed her of some of the details and added others to which she, on reflection, can give no credit. Of one thing, however, she is very sure. She recalls that there were two kinds of people at Oak Green that week. The uniformed ones her parents declined to let inside the house, and others, dressed as if they were on their way to a rock festival, who seemed to be part of a protest group. I was happy to tell her that I could put a name to it. The organisation was one I helped to found. One that, after reading this book, I hope you will be persuaded to join.

Last Chance for Man, pp.23–4

On the third day, the Save Planet Earthers pitched up. Three tents appeared on the roundabout at the entrance to Oak Green, containing earnest young people in sensible shoes and sour-smelling denim. When they saw a UNIT jeep approach, they quickly organised themselves into a picket line.

Brigadier Lethbridge-Stewart pulled off his mirrored shades and wished them a cheerful good morning.

'We know what's going on in there,' said their leader, a tall young woman in a yellow T-shirt. 'We know.' She was waving a sheaf of photocopied papers on which the Ministry of Defence letterhead was visible.

'Radioluminescent paint,' said a man who, the Brigadier thought, had clearly cut his own hair. 'From the dials in your aircraft. The toxic legacy of imperialist wars of aggression.'

The Brigadier's eyes followed the arc of the documents. 'I don't suppose,' said the Brigadier, 'that you'd consider sharing your theory with the military-industrial complex?'

'Move over, General,' said the woman in the yellow T-shirt, leaping into the jeep and snaking an arm around the Brigadier. 'Anoushka Masterson. You may remember me from last summer's nude sit-in under Nelson's Column. We made the front page of the *Daily Chronicle*.'

It was clear that the Brigadier did remember. 'Drive on, Sergeant,' he snapped.

The jeep moved forward. Anoushka waved to her comrades like a GI bride off to a new life in Baton Rouge.

'Don't do anything I wouldn't do!' yelled the man with the haircut.

The Brigadier blushed deeply. So deeply that he was almost grateful for the irregular spectacle that greeted him as the jeep rumbled into the estate. Mr Hesketh was tearing across the front lawn of his house towards Sergeant Benton. Seconds later, Benton was flying backwards under the influence of a punch to the face.

The Heskeths' garden was soon a crowded place. Mrs Hesketh arrived with a wet flannel for Sergeant Benton's black eye. Mr Hesketh babbled his apologies: he'd seen Benton collecting a sample from garden compost, and was worried about damage to its delicate microbial culture. Yates and the Brigadier pondered whether the assault came under UN jurisdiction, or was a matter for the local police. Anoushka went round introducing herself to everyone, and started an enthusiastic conversation with Jo about a demo she was planning at Stonehenge.

Benton and Yates exchanged glances.

'What did she say her name was?' asked Benton.

'Masterrsson,' said Yates.

'You don't think ...?'

They peered carefully at Anoushka in her combat pants, yellow T-shirt and close-cropped hair.

'He's good,' said Yates. 'But he's not that good.'

Nobody was more surprised than Anoushka by the treatment she received from UNIT. She'd almost been looking forward to a fight. Instead, the Brigadier made her a cup of tea and listened carefully to her thoughts on the meaning of her MoD documents. He respected her disinclination to name her sources and agreed that she had discovered evidence that suggested Oak Green had been used to dispose of hazardous wartime waste. She watched as he instructed a quiet little corporal to send telexes to Geneva and to Whitehall, briefing them on the situation and requesting a specialist team trained in the extraction of dangerous materials.

The following day, they arrived. Capable-looking scientists in asbestos trousers, who studied the photocopied documents, walked round Oak Green with theodolites and Geiger counters, and set a small excavator to work on a patch of ground at the very edge of the estate. By the evening they had pulled a stack of Army crates from the earth. The Brigadier watched them being prised open. Each was densely packed with small metal containers, discoloured by decay. A scientist lifted one up with a pair of crucible tongs. The Brigadier could just make out the lettering on the side. SPAM.

The men from UNIT were disappointed when the order came to leave Oak Green. It had been a pleasant assignment. No ancient evil had risen from the earth. No extraterrestrial being had parked its tank on their lawn. The Brigadier had even acquired a light tan.

Yates and Benton made one last tour of the estate to tidy up the damage caused by their occupation. They scrubbed boot prints from linoleum, gave emergency relief to ailing plants, returned household objects removed for testing. Then they roared off in the mobile HQ, taking a slice out of the grass verge.

The Brigadier followed in his jeep. As he left the estate he saw that the Save Planet Earthers were ending their occupation of the roundabout. Jo was helping Anoushka gather up poles and tent pegs. The Brigadier stopped the car.

'Have you seen the Doctor, Miss Grant?'

'He's gone to the radio telescope at Beacon Hill,' said Jo. 'He said they had some printouts for him.'

'May I offer either of you ladies a lift to London?'

'I'm so sorry, Brigadier,' replied Jo, letting him down gently. 'We're going to Stonehenge.'

'You'll still need transport.'

'We'll follow the ley lines,' said Anoushka.

'And what will you do when you get there?' asked the Brigadier.

'Keep your eye on the *Daily Chronicle*,' said Anoushka.

The Brigadier saluted and roared up the lane. Moments later, a new convoy arrived. The residents returning to reclaim their homes. And the Heskeths waiting to welcome them, proffering glasses of homemade peapod wine.

On the day of the Oak Green incident, the barbecues burned bright. The air was hot and lazy.

And then, suddenly, the air wasn't there.

Jo and Anoushka were heading for the Heskeths'. They wanted to say goodbye and to return Mrs Hesketh's copy of *The Silent Spring*. As they neared the garden gate, the shockwave hit them; the force of some profound and violent and change in the environment, raging over the gardens of Oak Green. But not over the Heskeths'. It was as if the world was being drowned, and their little part of it was kept safe beneath an upturned goldfish bowl. Jo and Anoushka were on the wrong side of the glass. It was impossible to take a breath.

Jo looked up and saw Mr Hesketh standing at an upstairs window, gazing over the hedges of the estate. Later, she realised what he was looking at: the hand of death scattering his neighbours to the ground. Families expiring together, as if some new Pompeii had sent its cloud upon them. Men dying with their aprons on.

Anoushka and Jo hurled themselves towards the garden. Jo had the sense of passing through the skin of a giant soap bubble. They fell, gasping, onto the front lawn.

Mr Hesketh was already on his doorstep. He looked nervous, as usual.

'You can come in,' he said. 'On one condition. That you say nothing to Sally about what you've seen. We could save you. I'm not promising anything. You seem like good people. But you mustn't upset Sally.'

'All your neighbours are dead, Mr Hesketh,' said Jo. 'We need to call UNIT. Get the Doctor back here.'

'No,' said Mr Hesketh. 'It's too late for that now. I'm afraid I have to insist. One word to Sally, and that's that.'

'I could beat you in a fight,' said Anoushka. 'No problem.'

'We mustn't fight,' said Mr Hesketh, looking nervously up at the sky. 'We must have lunch. And after lunch, everything will be fine. This is about Sally. It's all about Sally.'

Jo and Anoushka made a silent agreement to bide their time until opportunity arose. Mr Hesketh opened the door. Mrs Hesketh was preparing a rice salad and some baked peppers.

'Will it stretch to five?' asked Mr Hesketh.

'I think so,' she said. 'Shall we eat in the back garden? We can enjoy the good weather. And we're not overlooked. It's private there.'

Mr Hesketh rolled open the patio door and moved the dining table outside. Jo thought of the scene in *Carry On Up the Khyber* in which the British pretend that the Indian Mutiny isn't happening. She checked Mrs Hesketh's face for signs of madness. Their hostess handed her the cutlery and a dish of sliced tomatoes to Anoushka. Sally brought her drawing things to the table, and barely looked up. Mr Hesketh poured orange juice.

'Only the packet stuff, I'm afraid,' said Mrs Hesketh.

The adults ate lunch in silence. Sally appeared not to register their awkwardness. Jo noticed a bee fussing in the air above the hedge, as if it were trapped behind a window. As trapped as they were.

Pudding appeared.

'It's going to be OK,' said Mr Hesketh, quietly, and more to himself than anyone else.

'Will all this pass?' asked Jo. 'Like last time?'

'I think you're asking the wrong person,' said Anoushka, with a touch of aggression. She was looking at Sally.

Sally held up her pad. She had sketched the main avenue of Oak Green. In place of the tarmac, there was a river, alive with a fanciful number of fish.

'Where are the people?' asked Anoushka. 'Where are all your neighbours?'

'I'm afraid they've breathed their last,' said a voice from the kitchen. Standing at the patio door was a towering figure sheathed in shiny black rubber. The Doctor removed his breathing apparatus and peeled off the hood of his wetsuit. He drew down the zip, releasing his bow tie from captivity, then extracted his entire body.

'Tarminster Diving Supplies,' he explained. 'They hire, but I'm afraid I had to use all my powers of persuasion to get them to waive the deposit. All I had was these, you see.' He reached into his trouser pocket and produced a number of copper coins.

'I picked them up on the first day. I was looking for a toxin. A contaminant. But really something was taken away from Oak Green, not added.' He dropped the coins onto the table. They were fused together. 'Cold welding,' he said. 'Only happens in a vacuum.'

'Go to your room, Sally,' said Mrs Hesketh.

Sally flashed an angry look at her mother, but did as she was told.

'What's happening here, Mr Hesketh?' asked the Doctor. 'Mrs Hesketh?' He picked a slice of tomato from the salad bowl. 'For the second time in ten days, the air has vanished from your little patch of England. But you are untouched. How do you explain that?'

'It's her,' hissed Anoushka. 'It's that girl.'

'Do you think so?' said the Doctor. 'I'm more inclined to blame the parents.' He looked pointedly at Mrs Hesketh, who poured the Doctor a glass of peapod wine.

Mr Hesketh was less circumspect. 'We're just ordinary people, Doctor. People who want what's best for the planet. What's best for the children, like Sally. Soon the air will be clean again. They're going to lift it all up and give it back to us fresh.'

'Who's they?' asked the Doctor. 'Anybody on Earth?'

'We can't speak about that,' said Mrs Hesketh, firmly.

'Tom,' said Jo. 'If this is about aliens, then the Doctor and I, we know about this kind of thing. You wouldn't be the first person to make a bad deal with an extraterrestrial.'

Anoushka stared. Mr Hesketh frowned, as if irritated by the idea that Jo considered his experience commonplace.

'Look,' he snapped. 'We know there's a risk. We saw that last week, when all the ambulances came. And soon it's going to happen again, everywhere. The air will be snatched for just a few moments, then blown back new. And humanity will breathe again. We'll have saved the world, and we won't even want any credit for it.'

'What about today, Mr Hesketh?' asked the Doctor. 'Would you like credit for what I saw on the way from the main road? Oak Green is the site of an atrocity.'

'Those people didn't die in vain,' said Mr Hesketh. 'The system had to be tested first – a tiny sample to prove they can take it all. We ... we can build a memorial for them.'

Jo thought that she had never seen the Doctor look sadder.

'You listen to me, Mr Hesketh,' he said. 'I went on a little drive this morning to the Beacon Hill Research

Establishment. I asked them to collate some satellite data for me. They couldn't make head or tail of it, but I saw what it meant. You could call it a great hand reaching out across the universe. And it didn't look very friendly. Nobody is going to launder the Earth's atmosphere for you. It looked to me rather as if they were going to steal it.' He took a sip of the wine, and wondered why he was bothering to be so polite. 'Do you know,' he said, 'this wine is absolutely revolting.' And he tipped the contents of his glass into the compost bin.

This small action produced extraordinary results. Tom Hesketh leapt up as if he had been scalded, and loosed a great primal scream. Anoushka reeled backwards. Jo picked up a dining chair and held it up like a lion tamer. Mrs Hesketh sat, statue-like, at the head of the table, staring straight ahead. Her eyes were black and dilated. Jo thought she could see something moving inside them, like the fronds of an anemone pulsing in a rock pool. Her attention, however, was distracted by a new and alarming sound. An insistent thudding coming from inside the compost bin.

Jo backed away instinctively. The Doctor, however, did the opposite. He rolled up a sleeve and thrust his hand among the eggshells and broccoli stalks in the compost bin. Something snaked around his wrist. Something that threshed and gathered in the organic mulch. When he pulled his arm from the bin, it was caught in a thick tuberous vegetal mass, quiveringly alive, and as unexpectedly huge as a lug of human hair teased from the bath.

With baffling speed, the creature sprouted fresh tendrils, drove them into the earth, and brought them up to ensnare the Doctor's legs. It was, Jo realised, trying to knit him into the lawn. She picked up a knife from the table, but the implement was whipped from her hand. She looked round to see that Mrs Hesketh was responsible – or, rather, one of the long, wet roots that was burgeoning from her body. Mr Hesketh had seen it too. He stared at his wife and gave a low wail of despair.

'Listen to me, Jo,' said the Doctor, spitting out a root that was trying to slither into his mouth. 'Take the breathing apparatus. You and Anoushka will need it to get Sally through the vacuum.'

Jo began to protest, but stopped when the atmosphere above their heads gave a sudden convulsion. The bubble of safety around the house was collapsing. The sky was falling in.

'Save that girl, Jo,' said the Doctor. 'And don't let her look back.'

Jo knew this was blackmail. 'I'll be back for you,' she whispered. With tears in her eyes she handed the Doctor's oxygen cylinder to Anoushka, and they hurried through the patio doors.

Mrs Hesketh was now almost unrecognisable. She had become something between a tree root and a nest of centipedes.

'They said Jenny would be OK,' moaned Mr Hesketh. 'She ate the root. I found it and dug it up. But she tasted it.

And the taste never went away.' Tears were streaming down his face. 'They said she'd be all right!'

'Of course they said it,' gasped the Doctor. 'They're liars. Just like your bosses. They cultivated you, Mr Hesketh. They cultivated you.'

Tom Hesketh looked like an animal stunned on its way through the abattoir. He didn't know whether to run, or fight, or scream. Circumstances made the choice for him, by robbing the oxygen from his body. He fell to the grass, insensible.

The Doctor's lungs ached with the effort of breathing. Tubers rattled and snapped around him. They made a sound like laughter. A thin tendril slithered down his ear canal. The shape that had once been Mrs Hesketh joined in the scrum, pushing a bunch of fibrous fingers into his mouth. The Doctor bit down hard on them. His mouth ran with sweet acidic sap. The taste was surprisingly pleasant.

It was at this moment that he stopped fighting. Or discovered that he had joined a different kind of struggle.

He imagined himself standing beneath a chemical orange sky. He saw the exhausted surface of a world many light years away; let his gaze follow its salt flats and dead pastures to the horizon. He felt connected to the mind of something infinitely old and cynical; something that had reached out across space to the small blue shape of the Earth. He saw Tom Hesketh, younger, faster, optimistic, trekking through the forests of Papua New Guinea. He saw him digging at the root of a jungle plant. He saw Jenny. She was herself, but also part of the root; dry and twisted, like an illustration of a mandrake in a medieval book. The Doctor felt he knew the Heskeths intimately; that he could have answered any question about their histories and habits; their life in England, Mr Hesketh's worries about the morals of his employers. He knew all about Sally, too. He could even recall his being present at her birth.

Then his vision took him skywards. He saw the Earth's atmosphere streaming through space, roaring up from Oak Green and forming a great funnel through the stars. And he realised that this was not some mirage produced by oxygen desaturation, but the sight of something real; that the alien body in which he was entangled had formed a link between the English soil and a burnt-out planet circling a distant star; that the breath of one world was being used to replenish another.

Tubers curled around his head and over his eyes. He imagined uprooting them, dragging them from the soil as they twitched and shrieked and chittered. And with this effort of will, he found strength in his body, twisting his arms and legs to snap some of the ropes of root-flesh that pinned him to the grass. His right hand made contact with something cold and metallic. He tore an arm free to pull the object towards him. It was Sally Hesketh's sun lounger. Blindly and desperately, he used the dregs of his energy to slide the folding frame of the lounger into the mesh of tendrils, and slammed both sides together like a pair of jaws.

Sap bubbled over his fingers. He heard a sound like someone stamping on a head of celery. But as the air escaped upwards, silence muffled everything, as if the Heskeths' garden had been plunged underwater. The Doctor drove the jaws of the sun lounger together again. And again. And again. But a fifth time proved impossible. Metal touched metal, cold-welded together in the chaos of Oak Green. An airless chaos, in which even the death-scream of a monster would not have been heard.

Exhausted, the Doctor allowed himself to sink into a pleasant dream. He seemed to be lying on a bed of fabric – canvas, perhaps? He had the sensation of being dragged on his back over the grass and through a hedge. Then came the noise. Nature demonstrating its abhorrence of a vacuum. The air crashing back down from space like a sky-borne tidal wave. The voice of Jo Grant, imploring him to wake up. And, finally, a low howl, dwindling over the gardens.

Nothing stirred on the Heskeths' back lawn. The compost bin was silent. The remains of a tomato salad were scattered on the patio, not far from those of a suburban English couple, and Earth's latest alien invader, guillotined in their floral-patterned sun lounger.

Jo cradled the Doctor in her arms. 'I thought you'd gone!' she cried.

'Thank you for coming back to me,' whispered the Doctor.

Oak Green is now a restricted site. Those who attempt to visit face the discouragement of sentries and barbed wire. Five feet below the crates unearthed by UNIT, several barrels of toxic paint were discovered. The men who buried them in August 1945 were doubtless dreaming of their demob and the girls back home, and recorded the wrong figure on the paperwork. One surviving serviceman told the inquiry that he thought someone had been drinking on duty that day. Much was made of this in Lord Rowlands' report — a document that, I fear, fully justifies the suspicions raised against it in the radical press.

I share the anxieties of this generation. I also see the smoke rising from the factories. The soot that gathers on the trees and in the brickwork gets into my lungs, too. I am convinced that mankind's present path leads to a world of ash, slag and clinker. But I remain hopeful that the planet's most imaginative inhabitants will find a way to sidestep this future, using technologies that will cause us to look back on the era of coal and oil and gas as a kind of dark age.

And this is why I must decline your kind offer to write the foreword for your book. I am in sympathy with many of your views, but I am also of the opinion that man has not yet had his last chance. Not quite.

When that moment comes, the choice will be clear. It will be a choice between a new way of life, or going the way of the dinosaurs.
Yours faithfully,

Dr John Smith

Punting
Susie Day

'Oh, I do love the autumn,' Romana declared, from her transport on the river. 'All the leaves ... the colours ...'

'At least with something as simple as a punt nothing can go wrong,' said the Doctor as he slid the pole into the dark waters of the Cam. 'Just the water ... a strong pair of hands ... and a pole.'

'Punting is surprisingly fast,' observed Romana.

'Is it?'

'Yes. You promised me sedate. In fact, I think the word you used was "stately". And this is really not—' Romana gripped the edge of the punt, as her back was pressed into the cushions by a sudden burst of speed. 'Doctor, you don't have to show off.'

'I'm not trying to.' The Doctor kept his balance, barely, as he planted the pole into the riverbed and pushed off again. 'I really do have a strong pair of hands ...'

'Look!' Romana flung out her arm, pointing at the sky behind them.

He turned to see it: a black obelisk obscuring the idyllic view. It was hurtling towards them, and sending the river's peaceful flow into a frenzy, moving them far faster than a punt pole ever could.

The Doctor stowed the pole crosswise and leaped into the belly of the punt.

'Whatever are you doing?'

'Evasive manoeuvres.'

He knelt before the gramophone resting by Romana's feet. With a twist, off came the horn. With a press and a satisfying click, the record turntable lifted off like a lid. Beneath was a reassuring tangle of circuitry and wires.

'Ah,' said Romana. 'What do you think? Amplification? High-frequency oscillation?'

'Bit of both, hmm?' said the Doctor, one eye on the obelisk.

He hooked out a series of yellow and blue wires, allowing Romana's smaller fingers to reach a dial beneath. She twisted it till it would twist no more, then deftly reattached the wires, directing the power back to the gramophone's primitive speaker.

'I'm not sure this'll work, you know,' she said, frowning as she replaced the disc.

'It's that or pre-emptive sinking,' said the Doctor. He twisted the horn back into place. 'Ready?'

Romana nodded.

The Doctor gripped the pole, and rose unsteadily to his feet. 'Then let's dance.'

With the end of the punt pole, he knocked the gramophone's arm onto the disc, and set it spinning.

No music filled the air – but the pulse of the ultra-high-frequency soundwave was enough to set the rushing river's surface thrumming in little splashes.

The obelisk rippled, its sharp edges buckling. It grew silvery, transparent, spinning slowly like a silky frock.

'It's working!' said Romana, delighted.

The pull of the artificial current slackened. The punt returned to a smooth glide through the water.

The Doctor retook his post at the stern, and dropped the pole in deep and out to starboard. If he just could steer around the inconvenient interruption, they could stick to his plans. There was going to be a picnic. There would be scones, and jam. Possibly a little light drama; a minor catastrophe. But nothing too taxing.

The gramophone made a dramatic bang.

A light waft of smoke drifted from its interior.

'You didn't really want sedate, did you?' asked the Doctor hopefully, as the swirling obelisk hurtled towards them. The punt accelerated suddenly, knocking him backwards – but before the inevitable splosh, it swept them up into its embrace.

Typical.

Just typical.

There he was, with a lovely, straightforward yet charmingly whimsical plan to become immortal. Every component part was neatly being laid out upon the board before him. He'd even made little people to go on it. In outfits. They weren't strictly necessary; he just liked to be thorough and, since Rassilon had left him a nice chessboard with a croupier's stick to play with, that was what he'd decided to do.

The rest of the plan – to clear his path to the Tower, getting all those Death Zone nasties out of the way – that was his own. There was a hint of cruelty in it, perhaps. Some might call it sadism. But it was all quite practical, really. He'd constructed the whole thing with consummate care for the glorious predictability of the most irritating Time Lord ever to pass through the Academy.

And what was the most predictable thing of all, he reflected miserably? That the Doctor would mess it up.

The only surprise was that it was only one of him.

'On reflection,' said Romana, 'I preferred the river.'

The obelisk had swept them, punt and all plus a small square of Cambridge, into the time vortex – and got stuck. There it held them in a warping time field: a semi-transparent silvery pod, with unstable walls like a bubble. The punt was steady beneath Romana's feet but when she reached her arm out to its edge, her fingers elongated eerily. If she tried to press against the flimsy-looking wall of their contained space, her hand contracted. It was a funhouse mirror of a ship; a one-room TARDIS with its dimensional control on the blink.

'You broke it,' she said accusingly, watching her hair shrink as she peered too closely into the fast-moving silver swirl of the vortex beyond.

'I did not! I temporarily disabled it. If I'd broken it, we wouldn't be here. And strictly speaking, *we* broke it. Team effort.'

'Where exactly is here, anyway? Not counting ...' She gestured unhappily at the lapping water that had travelled with them; a portion of riverbank, a murky sky, and a large slice of limestone bridge had come too.

'Here is nowhere, technically.' The Doctor ruffled his curly hair, frowning. 'That's the time vortex. And we're—'

'Stuck in it.'

This was literally the case. The distorted edge of the obelisk had fused with the swirling maelstrom of the time vortex. And the vortex's powerful pull was tugging at the obelisk's unstable borders.

'Will it hold, do you think?' asked Romana.

'It wasn't built to,' said the Doctor, his fingers growing long as he felt around the edges of the space. 'And that's not my fault! But let's not take chances, shall we? I don't much fancy sitting around waiting to find out.'

Romana had already crawled across the punt to rifle through his coat pockets.

'Do you mind? I might keep something personal in there, you know.'

She laid out her findings: an inventory of sorts. A yoyo. A crumpled paper bag of jelly babies. Several feet of string, tied in a knot. K-9's old whistle. A stub of pencil, and three coins, all of different currencies.

'See? There. That coin, the blue one with the hole. Cleopatra gave me that to say thank you for – oh, something. It bears deep associations. A litany of feelings. Why, if I ever lost it I'd—'

Romana picked up the coin, balanced it on her thumbnail, and flipped it at the shimmering wall of the obelisk.

It hung in the air for an instant, warping from a clean circle to a flattened oval. Then it was sucked out into the vortex. Gone.

Romana looked up at him, pointedly.

'All right, all right, no time to waste, I agree. We need to detach ourselves. Any ideas?'

'What about all this?' She gestured at the bridge.

'Oh, no need to worry about that. It's Cambridge. They've got lots of bridges. Besides, it'll give them something to discuss for a century or so. They do like to talk in Cambridge.'

Romana shook her head. 'Not a problem for them. A gateway for us. If we can resonate the stone to the right frequency, we can restore the obelisk's stability. Perhaps even follow it back to where we started.'

'Go back? I don't want to go back! If someone's going to be so rude as to scoop me out of my time and place, I'd like to meet them.'

Romana sat back on her heels. 'Scoop,' she said.

'Besides, it might be important. I have been known to be summoned in an emergency, you know. I'm quite handy.'

'Scoop,' said Romana again, more firmly this time.

'Scoop?' The Doctor looked blank – then the penny dropped. 'Time scoop?'

Romana looked around, nodding slowly to herself. 'I knew I recognised it from a history book: just took me a while to place it. But it has to be one. I wonder who made it.'

'You know perfectly well who made it,' said the Doctor, rubbing his chest unhappily. 'Only Time Lords would be so silly.'

'It can't be. The High Council banned using them on Gallifrey centuries ago.'

'That doesn't mean some fool won't have changed their minds. Or gone rogue. Dug it out of the records and decided to give it a whirl. Why scoop up me, I wonder?'

'Or me,' said Romana quietly. Then she frowned. 'Are you all right?'

The Doctor was still rubbing his chest, his face growing pale and peaky. 'I don't seem to be all right at all,' he said weakly, sinking to his knees with a grimace. 'I have a nasty feeling that when they scooped me up, they might have tried to scoop the rest of me up too.'

'Your other regenerations? That's incredibly dangerous.'

'Even more so when it doesn't work.' The Doctor held a hand in front of his face, glaring at it as it grew pale and indistinct.

'Do you think they're trapped like us, here in the time vortex?' Romana stood, peering out at the silvery glow beyond.

'I hope not. But if they've made it to Gallifrey, me being here won't be doing them any good at all. Pulling us out of our time streams is hazardous enough. If we stay here, I might drag them in too.'

'Doctor, I don't want to worry you further ... but look.' Romana reached out and grabbed his hand, which returned to being reassuringly stable and solid, and hauled him to his feet to see.

Outside the obelisk something was moving.

Several somethings.

Large dark shapes, approaching in an odd dipping motion, and screaming: a savage shriek that tore through the silence.

'That doesn't sound like a rescue party,' murmured Romana.

'Living in the vortex?' said the Doctor. 'I think not.'

The shapes drew closer, and more distinct, their dipping motion suddenly explained.

Wings.

They were flying. Six of them, vast skeletal pterosaur-like creatures. Their bones were covered with a thick dark blue membrane, stretching tightly across sinew. A light dusting of brighter blue ran down the spine. Their beaks were long, and cruel. Their wings were tipped with sharp claws, their bony feet the same. Their gliding flight held grace, and ease. But there was no denying what they were – or at least, what they were some close relation to.

Harbingers of death.

The grim reapers of the vortex.

As they swooped close to the shimmery edge of the obelisk, the Doctor felt one beady eye fix upon his own, and he swallowed.

*

This was all so very unreasonable.

Weren't Presidents meant to be in charge? Wasn't it meant to make his life simple?

Yet here were the upstart Castellan and dreary old Flavia, insisting on throwing another spanner into his already somewhat spanner-strewn plans.

The Master.

To 'help'.

Of course, the ghastly fellow could take the place of the missing Doctor. Mop up a Cyberman or two; take out a Dalek. He'd only put them there to up the stakes. Keep the Time Lord on his toes. It didn't matter, in the great scheme of things.

He just didn't like being overruled.

No wonder Rassilon invented that silly coronet.

'Stay still,' hissed Romana, through tightly pressed lips, as she nervously lowered herself down into the punt.

'You first,' the Doctor hissed back.

The creatures circled, their wingbeats loud. He'd read the texts. Mederi: the cleaners of the time vortex. Vast, eternal, and single-minded.

They were beautiful, the Doctor marvelled. In their own distinct way, of course; not to all tastes. That powerful motion of the wings. The unexpected kingfisher-bright blue dappling their backs: feathers, were they? That eye that had caught his: so curious, so knowing.

Still, if one was about to be ripped into oblivion, it hardly helped that the messenger was pretty.

He blinked, looking again at the nearest Mederi. That brightness running across the spine; that iridescent glow, like—

Music blared from the gramophone, a shockingly loud and sudden noise that startled the Doctor – and sent the creatures flapping in alarm away into the murk.

'I had a feeling they wouldn't like Brahms,' said Romana, beaming with pride.

'Do you know, I live for Brahms.' The Doctor sat down beside her, breathing rather heavily. 'I don't suppose you found a hyperlight drive while you were down there? Dimensional charts? Steering wheel? I feel a powerful urge to be somewhere else.'

'Not quite. But I've been thinking. That history book: the page on time scoops. It's primitive, but there's a navigation system of sorts in here. Simplified, of course: a one-way ticket. I don't think this ship is stable enough to travel – certainly not to detach from the vortex. But I think we might be able to open a connection to the destination point. May I?'

She held out a hand, looking sterner when it wasn't filled.

'Very well,' bristled the Doctor, sliding his sonic screwdriver from his pocket and placing it into her palm.

It didn't take her long to locate what passed for a time scoop's navigational drive: it was simply a string of dimensional coordinates, hardwired into the virtual circuitry of the obelisk's internal space. Once identified, it was then a matter of reconfiguring the input of the gramophone circuitry to connect the two – then translating the output to something more useful than music.

With a burst of static, and some atonal grinding, the horn of the gramophone once again came to life. A conversation, indistinct but comprehensible. Familiar accents: voices he knew, but hadn't heard for some years. And some distinctly troubling content.

'Did he just say the Doctor no longer exists?'

'Shh!' said Romana, tucking her hair behind her ear to listen.

'Removed from history! Me?'

'Doctor, really!'

'And they brought the Master in to help. Help! Him!'

'If you keep quiet, we might actually be able to work out who's behind this whole affair.'

Bristling at the sound of the Master – of all people – being given the Seal of the High Council, the Doctor managed to hold his tongue as the Council's plan was set in motion.

'And now, we wait,' said a voice.

'I would prefer to wait alone,' said another.

'Would you now?' the Doctor murmured. 'I think we've found our culprit. It would have to be someone with full access to all Rassilon's old bits and pieces. Stands to reason it would be the top man.'

'Borusa? We should warn the Council.'

'Never mind the Council. I'm more worried about so much of me being scooped – and deposited in the Death Zone, no less.' The Doctor mulled. 'We can't leave me to sort this out. I'm hopeless when you get me together: nothing but squabbling.' The Doctor took back the sonic screwdriver. 'I say, do you think we could beef up the power on this thing?' He nudged the gramophone with his boot, sending a burst of static rippling up the walls.

Romana pushed his boot away and squinted, thinking. 'We are stuck in the time vortex – the greatest power source imaginable. We'd need to find a way to harness it without damaging the stability of the obelisk's dimensional bubble, though. It's risky.'

'Risky is one of my several middle names!'

'If you get sucked through the wall like that blue coin, what happens to your other selves?'

'Oh, they'll be all right. A little cosmic heartburn, maybe. Nothing they can't—'

He sat down with a graceless thump, his legs giving way without warning. His indistinct fingers drifted in front of a face he could no longer feel. It was an odd sensation: as if he were a completed jigsaw puzzle someone was trying to lift whole, and chunks were starting to drop off around his edges.

When he came back, two small hands were resting on his chest.

'Don't go fainting on me again,' said Romana firmly, though her eyes were soft.

'Noted,' he said, sitting up. 'So: need to travel, without the walls falling apart and killing all of me. We need a dimensional stabiliser. Happen to have one under that hat?'

'No. But I know where we might borrow one, sort of. At least, I hope so.'

Before long the punt was a mess of circuitry and string, as Romana worked, and the Doctor largely did as he was told, while trying terribly hard not to be violently ill over the side of the punt.

'There,' she said at last.

She set a slow pulse running from circuit to circuit. The walls of the obelisk glowed with it: randomly at first, and then in a rhythm; silently at first, and then with a familiar rising and falling sound that lifted all four of their hearts.

This was rapidly becoming a disaster.

Of course the techie had been unable to rescue the Doctor's lost regeneration from the vortex. Borusa could hardly explain the whole business to the annoying little chap – nor impress upon him quite what a problem this was.

So the Doctors might get sucked into the vortex: he could live with that. But his funny little friends with their frilly collars and their ankle-twisting weren't going to clear the path in his place, were they?

There was nothing for it. He'd have to change the plan. Cast suspicion elsewhere, and quickly, before coming up with another way into the tomb. He hunted through the chests and drawers in the secret chamber. He found a fetching pair of skis and a very ugly set of teacups before laying his hand on just the thing: a nicely ominous box of black scrolls.

*

'The TARDIS!' said the Doctor, clapping his hands with delight.

The obelisk echoed with the comforting sound of the ship in flight.

'I can't make a full connection,' Romana said quickly. 'I thought it might materialise around us, but it's held in some sort of force field.'

The glowing walls of the obelisk began to swirl as they had when it had scooped them up, showing lights and colours, patterns and movement – until it landed in a corner of the TARDIS console room. It didn't vanish away. They viewed the room as if through a gauzy curtain, all aswish.

The Doctor beamed, peering through the veil to the brightly lit room beyond. The people in the console room seemed blurred, distorted.

The Doctor began to wave his arms. 'Hello! It's me! I got trapped in the vortex! You're in the Death Zone!'

'They can't hear you.'

'It's Borusa! He's behind it all!'

'We're out of phase, Doctor. Different time streams.'

Her words made little difference. He was still shouting 'Cocktails? Pineapple? This is no time for a drinks reception!' when she twisted the dial of the gramophone, and sent the obelisk swirling back through the vortex.

This time it materialised in total darkness.

'Where are we?'

Romana cleared her throat. 'It'll make sense in a moment, I'm sure. That TARDIS had a new console readout:

a monitor, tracking your other selves.' She had thought it rather tacky, the little screen, but it was useful enough. 'I should be tuned directly into it now. If we can just warn one of them ...'

And, she reasoned privately, if proximity to his other selves stabilised his status as well, no harm done.

Out of the darkness came a dim, flickering light.

A flaming torch.

'Look! We're underground.' Romana stared up at the rocky cave ceiling above them, again through the thin gauze of the obelisk, as the orange flames lit the way. 'Gallifreyan catacombs, I suppose.'

'I never wore that coat!' grumbled the Doctor, as a small man approached, silhouetted by the torch. 'Oh! Brigadier! How are you?'

The younger Doctor and the older Brigadier disappeared into the next tunnel, arguing and quite oblivious to their presence.

Unfortunately, something else was not.

There was a distant shuffling sound, like footsteps on the cave floor. The Doctor caught the merest glimpse of fur and fangs, eyes and claws before the air split with an unholy roar.

'Yeti!' he cried, jolting back as the beast's great furry arm connected with the dimensionally compromised wall of the obelisk – and began to pass through it.

Static burst from the breach, the charge sending the Yeti into a greater rage. It was even more determined to get in now. With another ear-splitting howl, it lunged again—

And its arm was sliced in two, as Romana sent the obelisk spinning away to safety.

A heavy, hairy claw landed in the punt with a thud.

'Not quite the souvenir I'd have chosen,' said the Doctor, wrinkling his nose as he kicked it under a cushion. 'Where next?'

'Above ground,' Romana reported. 'See if we have any more luck warning the other you that's here ...'

Here, apparently, was a blasted rocky hillside, dotted with slate.

And Cybermen.

'Oh dear,' said Romana.

'Sarah!' said the Doctor brightly. 'How lovely to – oh.'

Sarah Jane Smith was in the process of lifting a large rock, and hefting it down the hill directly towards them. It somehow missed both the obelisk, and the troop of Cybermen marching up the slope.

'This isn't working,' said Romana.

'Yes, I know.' The Doctor frowned. 'She was always much cleverer than that, you know.'

'I mean this!' said Romana, kneeling beside the gramophone and wrestling with the dial. '*This* isn't working!'

The hillside faded from view as the obelisk lurched into flight again. This time, there was no quick trip to land and stare into another spot of the Death Zone. Instead, the obelisk appeared to be being dragged against its will.

The walls warped. The sound of the TARDIS supporting its flight grew stretched and distorted. The moment they ceased, the connection that was keeping the dimensional bubble of the obelisk in place was lost. The very space it occupied began to stretch in one dimension, contract in another, pulling at the Doctor and Romana's bodies in an agonising assault.

Then, without warning, it stopped.

'What did you do?' asked Romana, gasping for breath.

'No idea,' said the Doctor, panting too. 'I thought it was you. It worked, after all.'

The obelisk had returned to its previous stable state. The punt was intact, the bridge and the rippling water too. They were back in the time vortex.

'It's as if we never left,' said the Doctor. 'Well, apart from ...' He nudged the Yeti arm with his toe.

But Romana was shaking her head. 'No, it's not. It's not at all. Look.' She raised a shaky hand and pointed.

The silvery swirl beyond was as impossibly bright and rapid as ever. But now, there was a tear in its fabric. A wound in time itself.

Romana's voice was heavy with guilt. 'The power source. I used vortex energy to build enough power to connect to the TARDIS's dimensional stabilisers. I programmed this ship to draw on that power, enough to pull us away from where we'd fused to the wall. I thought it would repair itself. I never imagined—'

'Now, now,' said the Doctor, flapping a casual hand. 'Tearing a hole in the fabric of time: we've all done it. Or something like. We'll just pilot ourselves back into the hole. Plug it up. Work out how to get back out again later, hmm?'

'It's too late. Look.'

The edges of the tear were glowing eerily. Something viscous and yellow was growing there: an infection in time.

Even as they watched, it was taking hold. First the edge of the tear was overtaken. Then the swirling silver energy vortex began to be encroached. As it spread, the infection left behind decay: crumpled blackened matter like the ashes of a paper fire.

'The infection. It's eating time,' whispered Romana.

'That's not all it's eating,' the Doctor whispered back.

He took a small step closer to her, revealing a foul yellow glow at the base of the obelisk. It had infected that too.

'We'll just have to reconnect to the TARDIS,' said the Doctor. 'Fly away.'

Romana shook her head, accepting his hand in hers as he urged her back along the punt, away from the slow but determined spread of the infection. 'If we do, we'll spread the infection with us. Take it to Gallifrey. Infect the whole planet. Destroy it all.'

'Tempting as that sounds, I suppose it wouldn't do. So: no flying away. No staying here.' The Doctor pouted. 'It's quite the conundrum.'

Romana stumbled a little as they edged away down the punt, tripping on the Doctor's coat.

There was a bright tinkling sound.

Something had fallen from the pocket inventory: something small, and silver.

The Doctor grinned. 'Perhaps we won't need them after all.'

He reached down, and snatched up K-9's whistle. Pressing it to his lips, he blew hard: seven times, for an emergency.

'Doctor. I don't think K-9 can travel in the vortex. Or deal with infections.'

'No, he can't. But *they* can.'

She heard them even before he nodded to the swirl beyond: the wingbeats of the Mederi.

'No, Doctor! They'll be infected too! This'll spread the decay all through the time vortex!'

The Doctor smiled. 'Not the Mederi themselves. They're just the mode of transport. That bright blue, do you see it? I thought they were feathers. Couldn't understand why they were so very iridescent – not Mederi physiology at all. Until I remembered. Carpasial parasites.'

Romana frowned. 'Aren't they extinct?'

'In our time and space, certainly. But they seem to thrive rather well in the vortex, don't they? Lots of tasty infected time to chew up, like maggots in a flesh wound. Clears the infection right up.'

A stream of iridescent bluish speckles were now busily removing all traces of the foul yellowish substance from the edges of the obelisk. The decayed areas were being knitted together again, not neatly but well enough for safety.

The Mederi, meanwhile, swooped lazily around them, as if admiring of the plan.

The Doctor reached down, and grabbed the severed Yeti claw. 'Here you go! Good girl,' he said, hurling it at the obelisk wall.

It lingered in the air as the coin had, before elongating and being sucked out into the void.

The nearest Mederi swooped on the claw with a caw, snatching it up in its beak in one bite, and flapping away satisfied.

'Bye bye!' The Doctor waved. 'Now if I can only do something to free us fully ...'

Romana shook her head miserably. 'There's nothing more we can try.'

'I don't mean *I*, I.' He grinned. 'I mean, I, I, I and I ...'

There was much excitement on Rassilon's bier in the heart of the Dark Tower. Those infamous Time Lords who'd hoped for a taste of immortality found themselves transmuted back from stone to flesh for the first time in aeons. It was a chance to twitch and blink and peer about – and to notice a new arrival between them.

'Lads. *Lads*. Check out the new one,' said Left.

'Hello!' said Far Left.

'Shhh,' said Right.

'Get this. He only used the time scoop,' said Left.

'He never,' said Far Left.

'And tried to use the Doctor. The Doctor!' said Left.

Far Left made a whistling sound through his stone teeth. 'Impressed you made it here at all, mate. Doctor sorted you out, did he?'

'Well, stands to reason,' Left said sagely.

'Shhh!' said Right again, more urgently this time.

A deep rumbling laugh boomed out above them.

'I warned you,' hissed Right.

'Welcome, welcome,' boomed the voice of Rassilon. 'A new immortal has joined the pantheon: Lord President Borusa has played my game and lost. For his benefit, I shall recommence my reading of the great history of Gallifrey: *The Memoirs of Rassilon*. Chapter One: the Birth of the Great-Great-Grandfather of Rassilon.'

Right groaned softly.

'Don't worry, mate,' Left told the new arrival. 'There's a good bit in about 96 years.'

'You did it!' Romana beamed.

'Yes, didn't they,' said the Doctor obtusely.

'Weren't we just walking into the TARDIS a moment ago? Oh look! You've got your pole back.'

'Full service, those Mederi.' The Doctor grinned broadly. 'If I had control of the time vortex, I'd probably want to tidy up a thing or two ... Look, they've given Cambridge its bridge back too.'

'But borrowed some leaves, apparently,' said Romana, staring at the bare trees on the riverbank. 'Have they messed about with the weather? I don't remember it being this cold. Or the sky ...'

A light snow began falling upon the punt. Romana turned her face up to it as it frosted her hat.

'Oh, I do love the winter ...' she said.

The Dark River
Matthew Waterhouse

Nyssa looked across from the bed she sat on to the humanoid machine lying shattered on the TARDIS floor. Ever since she'd met the Doctor and Adric she'd been caught up in endless carnage, and the dead android (was 'dead' the right word?) was just another piece of wreckage.

'It was such a magnificent machine ...'

The boy sitting next to her was flabbergasted. 'That machine tried to kill you!'

'It was a slave, Adric ...' She sighed. 'It was only doing what it was told.'

The best medicine for melancholy is activity. She sprang from the bed and went into the control room.

'Tegan will still be at the house,' said Adric, following. 'Now you've destroyed the android, it's perfectly safe to go there ...'

He touched buttons and pulled levers and scratched his head and thumped the console. Finally the central column began to rise and fall.

'We've dematerialised,' he said gleefully. 'We're moving!'

With a thud, they weren't moving any more.

Nyssa switched on the scanner.

'We haven't gone anywhere!' said Adric flatly. 'We're still in the woods.'

'Try again. Wait.' She touched his arm. 'These aren't the same woods. They're denser.'

'We must have moved a few feet.'

'Look at how bright the sun is. We've moved more than a few feet!' She glanced at the information display. 'We've moved thousands of miles!'

'You're kidding.'

'I wish I was.'

Adric ran a hand through his hair. 'Not time too?'

'Time too!'

'We mustn't panic,' said Adric. 'Are we still on Earth?'

'Mmmm.'

'*That's* a relief.' He smiled as if to say this made everything OK.

'I'm glad it's a relief for somebody,' said Nyssa.

'I pressed the wrong button, that's all. If I try this one ...'

Nyssa looked at the screen and let out a small gasp. 'I think I ... Did *you* see movement?'

'Nothing.'

'In the trees. The thick trunk on the left.'

Even as Nyssa spoke, a man hurried into the clearing. He was tall, in his middle twenties, with skin the shade of milky cocoa. His face was a picture of abject terror and utter exhaustion. He wore tatty rags and broken shoes. He looked right across at the TARDIS, ran towards it, then, baffled, veered away into a clump of thickly leaved trees on the right.

Seconds later, three long-bodied, dribbling hounds pounced into the scanner's vision, followed by a man on horseback, clutching a rifle. This man's skin was red as uncooked beef. He pulled up his horse and fired into the trees.

Adric pulled the door lever. 'They're chasing him, Nyssa.'

'You can't just run out there. You'll be killed!'

Adric had reacted without thinking. He ran into a harsh, oppressive heat. Baked, cracked earth, but the greenery dense, overgrown. From somewhere out of sight there were sounds: violent barking, the call of an aggressive voice. The muffled sound of running water. Adric entered the trees. Branches and leaves slapped his face.

The knotty growth had given the boy a sense of running into thick, dark woods, but he found himself beyond the trees in twenty seconds. The rushing water which had seemed so far away was right there, a massive, wide river. The man in rags was trapped on the bank, the ravening dogs in an arc in front, three but one, like Cerberus broken apart.

Then all was confusion. From behind the boy, the crack of a gun. He spun to find its source, then snapped back as the man in rags folded, rolled down the bank and splashed into the water. The boy made to move towards the body, then spun again. He raised his hands instinctively. Too late. Another crack. Terrible pain in Adric's left side. All this in a second.

A shuffling movement. Unconsciousness.

*

The man with the gun, on foot now, looked out at the body in the water, then down at the boy. He used his boot heel to lever the boy onto his back, so he could see the young dead face. The boy's top was stained with blood and ripped right through where the bullet had pierced him.

The man's boot manoeuvred the boy to the edge of the bank as if he was a dead bird, then with a kick pushed him down into the water.

'Dumb kid. Curse you, James. Cost me a goddamn fortune.'

The tide moved the bodies downriver. The killer whistled to his dogs who came to him.

In the clearing he patted his horse's nose. He vaguely noticed the blue box, but was too worn out to care about it. He mounted his horse, laid his rifle across his lap and trotted off, back bowed, dogs following.

On the scanner Nyssa watched the man and his vicious hounds trot away. She had expected to see mere brutality in his face. In fact he looked so drained and prematurely aged she felt a tinge of pity for him.

'We've got to get back to the Doctor and Tegan,' she said to the time rotor. 'Which means finding that boy! Let's hope he hasn't got himself into trouble.'

Nyssa hurried from the ship, in the direction Adric had taken. Beyond the deceptive trees, she found herself looking down into a deep wet morgue. There were two bodies face down in the water, the man's head and left arm entangled in weeds, the boy tenderly bobbing back and forth against him as the tide tugged. A long thin lace of blood drifted into the river.

'Adric!' Nyssa started to scrabble down the bank, but an agitation in the weeds made her stop. The man's head broke the water. He apparently did not notice her, seemed to be focused only on dry land which was air and survival, as opposed to the river which was a drowning death. Adric's body brushed him. He grabbed it roughly by the shoulder and dragged it shoreward, a fresh swirl of blood following after. He threw the boy's body onto dry land and pulled himself after it.

He raised his head. His eyes met hers.

Nyssa detected in him a commingling of terror and strength and a kind of battered nobility. But what he saw in her she could not imagine.

What he saw was not a person but a type. He noticed her hair, multitudinous ringlets like he'd seen many times before. Wealth and whiteness were what he saw.

He knew what was to come. She'd scream. They always screamed, his mother had told him they always screamed. Her face would distort. Their faces always distorted, became ugly. A dead blood-drenched white boy? A big black man? 'Murder! Murder!' she'd cry, finger pointing, raising a mob. Always there was a mob, easily summoned, as if in a state of perpetual waiting for just such an opportunity. They'd lynch him. He wondered for a second if he even cared. He couldn't have killed the boy, didn't have a gun, but what difference would that make?

And yet, what was supposed to happen, what he had been brought up to believe always happened, did not happen. This young woman did not scream or accuse. He read in her eyes a willingness to trust and decided he would trust too, in truth the only alternative being to await the mob.

And they ceased trying to interpret each other and turned simultaneously to the dying boy.

There was an oval of sticky blood on the boy's left side, which was already beginning to dry in the searing heat. The man tore a ragged circle of bloodstained cloth away from the wound. There was a horrible ripping sound, as if even the material was crying in pain.

Nyssa raised the boy's wrist, felt for a pulse. 'He's gone.' Her eyelids batted together as if to stop tears coming.

The man put his thumb and first finger on Adric's wrist.

'There's somethin'. Faint, but somethin'. Look, still breathin'. Don't got long to live, though.'

'There may be hope.'

'That accent. Not from these parts?'

'Not by any means. Are *you* all right?'

'Only a graze. Wet 'n' tired is all.'

'I need to get him back to our, uh, blue shed. Will you help me carry him?'

'You can't move him. Not without a stretcher. He's just gotta lie here.'

'Will you stay with him? I can get some medical supplies from the shed.'

Nyssa made her way back to the TARDIS where she found some ointments and bandages and cotton wool. She collected a fresh set of Adric's clothes. (An automaton called K-9 had programmed the TARDIS's mechanical tailor to manufacture several.) In a wardrobe she found another duplicate outfit, this consisting of a long coat, a shirt with question marks on the lapel, striped red and white trousers, cricket shoes, a straw hat.

'I don't suppose he'll mind.' Nyssa smiled, thinking of the Doctor. 'We will get back to you and Tegan ...' Resolute, she put both sets of clothes over her arm and went back outside.

She found the man leaning over Adric, whose eyelids were beating in semi-consciousness. Then they closed again. The man held in his fingers, sticky with blood, a reddened bullet.

'Pretty much came right through the other side. Don't look it, but this is one tough kid. Should be on his way to the afterlife.'

They wiped the wound clean and bandaged it. Then they made the boy comfortable and wiped his sweating brow. Throughout the scorching morning and early noon they waited. Mostly the boy's groans and the river's rush were the only sounds, but every so often a passing steamboat disturbed them. When this happened, the man ducked into the bushes until it had passed.

'You gonna take me back there, I suppose? To the farm?'

'I'm not taking you anywhere you don't want to go. Might I ask your name? I'm Nyssa. Nyssa of Traken.'

'Nyssa of Traken? You sound like some kinda princess from an old story. Carry yourself like a princess too, come to think on it. I'm James Harviss.'

'Hello, James Harviss.'

'The boy?'

'This is Adric.'

'Adric what?'

'Just Adric.'

James put his hand gently on the boy's face. 'Just Adric, eh? Well then, I'm just James. James is the name my mother called me. Harviss ain't my right name. The name of the family owned my grandmother. So I'm just James.'

Nyssa handed him the pristine clothes. For James, new clothes were an unimaginable luxury. He turned his back and pulled off his ragged shirt, exposing four deep, disfiguring welts like long gnarled twigs. A minute later he was dressed in his new clothes.

'You wear them well,' said Nyssa.

Something even stranger happened. Nyssa changed the bandage and Adric's wound was already knitting together. What ought to have taken days or weeks was occurring over a period of a few hours.

'That's impossible,' said James.

'Adric's rather special. Whatever you do, don't tell him that.'

As the afternoon sun glistened on the water, the boy's eyes suddenly opened, fully alert, as if he'd been finger-snapped from hypnosis. He focused on a collar, on question marks.

'Doctor ...?'

'You a sorcerer or somethin'?'

Adric's capacity for swift healing, standard on Alzarius, always impressed elsewhere in the two universes. This gifted boy with his hot-house upbringing had begun to see this power as another example of his personal excellence rather than mere biological good luck. He was about to agree that he was a sort of sorcerer, but Nyssa interrupted.

'How do you feel, Adric?'

'Some pain in my side but tired more than anything. Doctor ... Have you regenerated again?'

'This isn't the Doctor, Adric. This is James. He's a new friend. He saved your life.'

Nyssa asked James what his plans were. He shrugged.

'Get away from here.'

'Why did that man want to kill you?'

'Didn't. Wanted to wound me. I'm too valuable to kill. But I played dead like you saw.'

The time travellers looked puzzled.

'You two are the strangest kids I ever saw. You don't know nothin' at all, do you?'

'So tell us.'

'I'm a *slave*, Miss Nyssa. Know what that is?' He spoke with quiet, aching intensity. 'That man, he *owns* me. I've been *owned*, all my life. When I was fourteen my first owner put me in chains and sold me at the slave market upriver at the big port. They washed me down first to make my skin look glowin' and healthy and Phillips felt my arms and legs and was satisfied, so he went and bid for me and then I belonged to the Phillips Plantation. Warn't nobody tellin' him any different.'

'We had slavery where I come from,' said Nyssa, 'but we outgrew it millennia ago.'

'Ma'am, here it's the *law*. The *churches*, they tell the pious white folk it is all fair and moral and good to whip me and beat me and there ain't nothing I can do to change it, except *get the hell away*. Y'know, they sold my wife down the river and they treated her so bad she died. I won't be seeing her no more, not in this life. I got this big sad feeling inside me and I couldn't stand it no more. I'm gonna get to a free state or die trying. Me, I ain't got nothin' to lose.'

'I want to help,' said Adric.

'Adric,' said Nyssa, 'that's kind of you but we have, well, other responsibilities. The Doctor and Tegan ...'

Adric rubbed his hands over his eyes in a show of exhaustion. 'James saved my life.'

'We can't abandon the Doctor ...'

'If you kids gotta go, you gotta go,' said James.

Adric signalled to Nyssa to follow him a few feet. Out of James's hearing, he hissed, furious.

'*I'm not abandoning anyone!* James saved my life, Nyssa. Plus, the TARDIS is a *time* machine, remember? We can go back now or in three months and no time need have passed for the Doctor and Tegan!'

Nyssa remained frosty. 'You think you can control the TARDIS with such precision?'

142

'Look about you. This is Earth in the future, so we know the Terileptils didn't succeed.'

'Do we?'

'We can visit a hundred places and go back to the Doctor and Tegan when we're seventy-five if we want and it won't make a shade of difference to them!' Adric threw his hands in the air. 'If you want to go, go. I'm staying. Goodbye. Send them my best wishes!'

'Adric, Adric.' Her tone had softened. 'You're being awkward.'

'I'm at the awkward age, I'm *supposed* to be awkward. I bet you were awkward when you were a teenager!'

She smiled. 'I've never been awkward.'

'Of course. Little Miss Nyssa the Perfect Princess has never been awkward. I wish I was with Tegan. She's infuriating but at least she doesn't act like she's perfect.'

'I can't believe you're talking like this.'

Adric reached down and scratched his knee absently. He replied more calmly. 'You know I don't mean it. I'm tired and worried and my side hurts.'

He looked desperately sad. Nyssa held his hand for a moment. She went back to James.

'We'll help you.'

'You crazy? Helping me is a *crime.*'

'I'd be dead without you,' said Adric.

'My plan is, there's a loggin' company a few miles downriver and, get ahold of a raft there. Head south on the Mississippi all the way to the Ohio river, then I can maybe go north. Travel by night, rest by day. We got all the fish we need out here –' he thumbed towards the rolling water – 'and when we come to townships we can maybe find bread, fruit, some meat even.'

'I'm good at stealing,' said Adric usefully.

'He's a boy of many talents,' said Nyssa. 'No doubt the blue shed will be safe for a few days.'

'No one ever comes here,' said James. 'Which is why I used this path tryin' to escape.'

They made their way along the bank to the Jefferson Logging Company. Here there were several pretty sturdy rafts, floating on the water, roped to trees. Hooked over the low thin branch of a bush someone had abandoned an old brown jacket and in its pocket, to James's great pleasure, there was a corn cob pipe, some tobacco and matches.

The final rays of sunset faded. In the star-strewn night they pushed out.

'Welcome to our railroad, children, the great Mississippi ...'

'The Missippi River,' said Adric, feeling the strange word on his tongue.

'Mississippi, he said.'

'Missippi ...'

'Miss-iss-ip-pi,' said James.

'Missippi.'

'You keep missing an "iss",' said Nyssa.

'Mississississippi!'

'That's one "iss" too many.'

And they embarked on their journey.

The current moved the raft along swiftly. James put on his hat and lit the pipe. Adric and Nyssa lay back, hands under heads. The sky was vast, the lamps of starlight numerous, laid out before them on a velvet cloth.

'It's like looking at a whole galaxy,' said Nyssa.

James offered Adric the pipe. He took a pull and spluttered. James held it out to Nyssa, who wrinkled her nose in her most princessy fashion.

They were all quite silent and, whatever the future might hold, they shared in those journeying hours the sense of helping James get to somewhere better. Early on, many of the buildings dotted along the banks were warmly lit. As night wore on, house lights were extinguished, but those of the places of pleasure grew brighter. Here and there, church spires were outlined against the sky.

There was for much of the night no sound but the running of the water, cicadas in the reeds. Once a distant accordion was heard. Once a fiddle. There was laughter. There were shouts and fights. Sometimes there was a paddle steamer's plash, water whirling about the great big wheels, maybe bound south like them, briefly alongside before passing, maybe northbound upriver against the tide.

Dawn came, slaves were already at work in the cornfields.

They poled the raft towards a thicket and bathed. Adric's wound was nearly healed but James's scars were forever.

They took turns to wrap themselves in a blanket and wash their clothes. Adric removed his badge and pinned it to the blanket while his clothes dried.

'You a sheriff?' asked James.

'A what?'

'A lawman?'

'Do I look like one?'

'Then what's the badge about?'

'It's to say I'm clever,' said Adric. 'A mathematical genius, to put it modestly.'

'When did you ever put anything modestly?' asked Nyssa.

'If some guy comes around makin' difficulties,' said James, 'you might wanna tell 'em you're a lawman.'

James fished. On the second day Adric sneaked into Hibbertstown and came back carrying a big loaf of bread and some peaches, and cradling a large fruit, its skin many shades of green.

'Riverfruit!' Adric ate greedily, thinking without nostalgia of his home planet. James and Nyssa guzzled juicy peaches.

On the fourth morning, far from any township, they perhaps relaxed too much. They swam and fished and lit a fire.

There was a rustle in the bushes. A bird? A cat?

'Damn,' breathed James.

'What you doing here?' It was a very old man, with a tatty white beard and little round glasses propped on the tip of his nose. He had a rifle slung on his back which, with a single deft movement, he swung into his arm. Old as he was, he could handle a gun. He looked right at Adric.

'What you doing here?' The voice was not less threatening for being thin, withered.

'Hello, sir,' said Adric. He pushed out his chest in a preening fashion, which made the sun glint on the gold edge of his badge. The old man squinted.

'You a sheriff, boy?'

Adric glanced at James. 'Sure am.'

'You look mighty young to be a sheriff. Hey, what town you from, boy?'

'Alzariusville.'

'That Alabama way?'

'Pretty near, yeah.'

'Uh-huh? And this purtty girl, she your wife?'

'I am not!' said Nyssa, hands on hips.

'Yet,' said Adric.

'No,' she said with a flash of invention, 'I'm known as Mississippi Nyssa!'

'Truly?' said the man. A salacious smile skimmed his features. 'You know Nebraska Nancy by any chance? She was a hot one!'

Nyssa fell quiet, little spots on her cheeks.

'So you ain't from round here, kid. Whatcha doin' here?'

'I'm an intern at the local Sheriff's department.' He pointed to James. 'Escaped, see. Takin' him back to his owner ...'

'Escaped? What's he doin' in them swanky clothes? Stole 'em, I'd wager.' The old man expelled a big gob of spit which landed between James's feet. 'Dunno why they can't learn to be grateful fuh what we done for 'em.'

'We?'

'White folks.' The old man rubbed his nose. 'Sheriffs just keep gettin' younger and younger. Seems mighty rum to me. You're lucky I didn't blow your two young heads off. This is my land, thought maybe you were gonna steal my horses or somethin'.'

He wandered back through the trees, grumbling about kids being sheriffs.

'I could really take to being a sheriff. It's cool.'

'I don't understand. Just what is "white folks"?' asked Nyssa.

'You a fool, girl? White is *skin*, girl. Like yours.'

Nyssa looked at her hand. 'But we're not white. Look, my skin is pink.'

'You wanna know what white is to me? I tell you, people who'll put a rope around my neck and leave me hangin' from a tree. That's white. And they'll be hanging you two as well, for helpin' me. 'Cos if there's one thing they can't stand it's white folks who help black folks.'

'This planet,' said Adric, 'is a madhouse.'

At night the sense of escape and the cool of the river and the sheer beauty of the landscape made danger seem distant, but in the broiling day they were more cautious than before. Even as they ate and sometimes laughed, the constant hum of fear was now their companion.

*

On the fifth night it was James's turn to keep lookout while the others slept. The days of travel and the oppressive heat were taking their toll, and Adric and Nyssa fell quickly into deep sleep. Adric was dreaming of numbers when he was shaken awake. It took several seconds for him to gather his senses: the question marks, the hat, doctornonotthedoctor (one blur of semi-thought), the running of the water. He could not tell whether he had slept half an hour or eight hours until he saw that the river was still dappled by the last traces of dusk.

'Uh?'

James was alert, pointing.

A few hundred yards across the river, a steamboat was puffing south, in the deeper water mid-river. It came from behind and then for a few moments ran pretty much parallel. Its name was arced above the paddle wheel, *Washington Irving*. A couple of figures were visible in the pilot house. Some large crates were stashed at the back of the lower deck. And one blue packing case. No, larger than a packing case, more like a shed ...

'Nyssa! The TARDIS!'

'The TARDIS?' She followed his finger. 'The TARDIS!'

'We left it safely in the woods!'

'It's not in the woods now!'

The *Washington Irving* passed ahead of them and soon rounded the bend ahead. Wild panic gave way to a moment of hurried but sober planning.

'Next port, one of you needs to find out the destination of that boat,' James said. 'Probably Orleans.'

'Where are we now?' Nyssa asked.

'Left Missouri, I believe. Into Arkansas.'

The raft now rounded the bend, and the river ran straight as far as the eye could see. The *Washington Irving* was some distance ahead of them.

'It seems to be in a terrible hurry,' said Nyssa.

At that moment the steamboat began to shift uneasily from left to right to left again, then rightward. Then it lurched sharply, almost touching the bank, before semi-circling back near mid-river with a massive spray of water. It rocked.

'It's lost control,' said James urgently.

It shivered like a wet child. Passengers and crew emerged onto the decks. Frightened voices called out. The chimneys emitted shrieks like nightmare apparitions. Great flags of boiling steam spurted upward. The *Irving* spiralled northwards, threatening to bear down on the raft, but then rotated to face south again.

'What's happening?' shouted Nyssa.

'All that steam! The boiler's overheatin'. Which is a disaster. We've gotta get this raft as near shore as possible.' James began poling like crazy. There was only one pole, so Adric and Nyssa were helpless to assist.

The *Washington Irving* spun again and again, creating its own whirlpool, thrusting great waves in its wake in all directions. A huge wave rolled towards the raft.

'Take my hands, fast!' roared James.

Adric took one and Nyssa the other and, as the raft titled ninety degrees, they leapt, as if playing some childish game, hitting the water's edge and pulling themselves through mud. Several pieces snapped off the raft and the bulk of it rolled away, mossy underside upward.

The boat, whirling madly, caromed from the bank a few dozen feet downriver right into the water where the raft had been mere moments before. The crates on deck were thrown off, so forcefully that several hit dry land, shattering, projecting clothes and books and trinkets outward and upward. A calico gown entwined in a willow hung like a ghost.

'The TARDIS!' cried Nyssa despairingly.

The heavy blue box toppled over the rail, rolled in the air and, with a fountain's billow, was swallowed by the river, maybe a dozen yards from shore, a hundred downriver from where the trio lay, soaked and muddy and bruised.

The boat now sprang a half mile downriver. The chimney released more great howling sheets of steam. There was a deafening explosion, followed by a ghastly space of nothingness.

'The passengers? The crew!'

'Explosion like that, Nyssa, there ain't gonna be no survivors. Happens a lot.'

James's hat – the Doctor's hat – drifted by.

There were no lights visible on their side of the river.

'We're stuck in nowhere,' said James.

'Those poor people ...' said Nyssa, looking at the motionless riverboat.

Adric put his hands over his face. 'What a mess. And it's my fault, isn't it, Nyssa?' he said. 'If we'd gone when you said we should, we'd be back in London. Now we've lost the TARDIS.'

'You couldn't have known ...'

'What's to become of us? What's to become of the Doctor and Tegan and Mace?'

'At least we know where the TARDIS *is*.'

'Deep inside a horrible muddy river where only the fishes can get at it. Maybe the door broke off. Maybe it's been flooded I can't imagine water'll do the dematerialisation circuits much good ...'

'We'll need to find help,' said James. 'But there ain't nothing we can do until daylight.'

Unable to fight tiredness, they fell into fitful simulacra of sleep, but it was still the heart of night when Adric and Nyssa awoke and leant against a tree bole, looking at the dark river. James was already wide awake, sitting in front of them, knees up, his head resting on a fist, looking out.

Adric was thinking a bit more clearly now. 'I've just remembered. The Doctor once planned to immerse the TARDIS in that London river to flush out the Master, so I know it's waterproof. We just have to work out how to get it out of there. Oh! Look!'

On the surface of the water the unlit light showed like a buoy. Low tide was coming to the Mississippi.

Too tired for more than muted jubilance, the minds of the bone-tired travellers floated like driftwood again into states of half-sleep. Then a grey dawn came. The whole TARDIS roof could be seen now and the POLICE BOX sign below. A crane settled on the light for a second, then flew away.

James gasped. 'What in the name of all that's holy are *they* doing round here?'

A dozen young men, some black, some white, some Hispanic, and a somewhat older Chinese man, were walking with an eerie purposefulness along the bank. They carried coiled ropes. A horse and cart plodded behind them, one of the men holding the reins. None so much as glanced at the ruined steamboat. The Chinese man pointed at the blue box.

'Curiouser and curiouser,' said Nyssa.

James signalled that they should slide behind a bush.

The young men, near now, dived into the river. They trod water in a circle around the TARDIS. The Chinese man stood on shore, calling instructions. Some of the men disappeared under water for several seconds at a time.

The ropes were gathered around the box at different levels. It took a long hour's tugging to manoeuvre the spattered TARDIS inch by inch towards the bank until, with a squelch, it was released from the river's muddy grip.

The horse and cart was brought forward.

'Hello,' said Nyssa, coming out of hiding. 'It's kind of you to rescue our shed!'

Apparently no one heard her. The group placed the TARDIS on the cart.

'We'll take charge of it,' said Adric, showing himself. 'Thanks awfully.' He put his hand onto the nearest man's arm but the man did not register the touch. 'It's like they're hypnotised or something. Under someone else's control.'

Nyssa looked anxious. 'Like the villagers controlled by the Terileptils?'

'Zombies,' said James, who had come out too. 'Heard tell of them in the old religion.'

'I thought zombies were supposed to be dead,' said Adric. 'These people are warm to the touch.'

The Chinese man tilted his head as if listening to something far away. Then he pointed to Adric. One of the Hispanic men approached the boy, clutching wet muddy rope.

'You're not going to tie me up, are you?' As his hands were pulled behind him it was clear this was the intention.

'Leave the kid alone!' shouted James. The man softly pushed him away. In moments all three travellers were bound, and yet without the slightest show of violence. They were very gently placed on the cart. They sat down, backs against the TARDIS door.

'Don't seem to wanna harm us,' said James.

The Chinese man climbed on the wooden seat and whipped the horse, which laboriously pulled its heavy load up the bank to a flat dry path.

They were heading south again. In breaks in the trees they saw glimpses of the mangled remains of the *Washington Irving*, each time more distant. Then the path curved and the steamboat was lost to sight.

'Funny,' said Adric. 'Even if we're in danger the Doctor always seems able to explain what's happening. I haven't a clue.'

'Me neither,' said Nyssa, puffing out her cheeks like a trumpeter and blowing out air. 'I think the Doctor's guessing half the time anyway.'

'Especially since he regenerated.'

The road was stony. They were rattled about for several hours. There were occasional settlements along the way. They passed people on horseback who threw them very odd looks. The sun rose in the sky. It became unpleasantly hot. At what they supposed was approximately lunchtime, they stopped outside a small grubby-looking tavern, into which their horseman disappeared for a good half-hour. He came out with three unappetising bowls of catfish. He spoon-fed them in turn, answering no questions. They set off again.

James was fascinated by the box.

'It's a sort of boat,' said Nyssa, 'for travelling long distances.'

'By magic?'

'By means the people in your time and place cannot understand.' She sighed. 'Not that I understand the TARDIS well myself,' she added.

Dusk came. They stopped in a small town. The horse was changed and they rode on. All through the night they journeyed. The trio managed to sleep a bit, even as they were shaken about.

Then suddenly they stopped, alongside a rickety three-storey clapboard house rather oddly placed a few hundred feet inland up a slight hill, looking down to a steamboat landing and the river. Three wide steps led up to the porch, where several chairs and a swing and a rocking chair and a few low tables lent an air of friendly invitation.

A massive man leant against a wooden pillar at the porch's edge. He was six feet two inches tall and pretty much as wide. He wore a pristine white summer suit and a white hat, which looked like they'd just been delivered from an upscale New York store. He had skin of extremely rich darkness and darting, alert, intellectual eyes. A big cigar between his teeth emanated bluish fumes.

The horse whinnied and stamped its hooves. There were the first reddish hints of dawn. The three friends had travelled for the best part of twenty-four hours. All bones ached. The Chinese man lifted them off the cart one by one and untied them.

The large gentleman beheld the TARDIS with a look akin to enchantment. He took in a last big puff of his dying stogie, threw it to the ground, dipped into his pocket and pulled out a fresh one, which he lit. He stepped nonchalantly off the porch and reached up to the TARDIS on the cart. He patted it like he owned it. Then he spoke to the Chinese man.

'Thanks a lot, Li Cho. I've got you a room down at the Riverview Hotel. Imaginative name, ain't it? You can head back tomorrow.'

Li Cho separated the horse from the cart and cantered down towards a little cluster of buildings near the landing. The man in white turned to the travellers.

'Girl, that purple outfit of yours kinda puts me in mind of Traken. Am I right or am I right? You, Mister,' he pointed to James, 'you're in the wrong goddamn country for cricket.

And you, kid,' he added, looking closely at Adric, 'well, I ain't got no *notion* where *those* clothes come from, but it sure as hell ain't Arkansas.'

'We would appreciate some explanations,' said Adric.

The large man smiled, as if to say that there would be explanations only when and if he felt like giving them. 'Sit yourselves down and relax, y'all. You're gonna be here some time so might as well learn to like it.'

Adric and Nyssa took the swing. They rocked back and forth. James took a chair next to them.

'Truly terrible, that steamboat explosion,' said the stranger, with a melancholy shake of the head. 'Terrible, terrible.' He looked at the flame on his cigar. 'Damn inconvenient for me too. Took a whole extra day to get that blue box here.'

'Who are you?' asked Nyssa.

He puffed out smoke in a full, generous cloud. 'You can call me Doc Ashberry. You?'

Nyssa did introductions.

'Hi, y'all. So you friends of the Doctor? Just like me.'

'I suppose we should be surprised to meet a friend of the Doctor,' said Nyssa, 'but after the last day I'm beyond being surprised by anything. How do you know him?'

'There ain't no harm in my tellin' you. We go back a long, long way. Back to the Time Lord Academy. Amazing to think he's right here in these United States in 1847.'

'Actually ...' began Adric, but Doc wasn't listening.

He removed his hat to bat away a wasp, stepped off the porch and reached up to the TARDIS on its cart, patting it fondly. 'Battered but beautiful. Been a long time waitin' for somethin' like this to happen.' He hopped back onto the porch. Despite his size, he moved with lightness and grace. He dropped into a rocking chair. 'Didn't think it'd be the Doctor ...! Knew him when he was real young, then as a little guy with an umbrella, for a while he had a dumb-ass scarf, then he took up the recorder ... Hey, what face you know him by?'

'Never mind that. How did you *find* our TARDIS?' asked Nyssa. 'We left it I don't know how many miles away.'

'It ain't your place to ask questions, honey. it's your place to accept the situation. But dammitall, you all three seem like nice people. Look, it's gettin' a little bakin'. Wanna come in to the cool?'

Doc opened the door into the house. They crossed the threshold.

'My Lord,' said James. The simplicity of this remark belied his obvious bewilderment. 'Ain't never seen nothin' like this. Seems like I stepped into a dream.'

If what James saw was unimaginably alien and incomprehensible to him, it was hardly less surprising to Adric and Nyssa. It had echoes of their familiar TARDIS, its light green walls indented with discs like theirs. However, it was a wholly different space. In one corner there were armchairs and tables and a cabinet which contained several bottles of whiskey. There was a big case of cigars. There were rows of books in what looked like expensive bindings, leather, gold edging. In another corner, there was a small kitchen. Doors led to a number of back rooms. Right in the middle of the main area standing a full two storeys high was a gigantic circular tube, inside which were countless unlit lights. There was a single long console desk on which could be seen a quantity of dials and buttons, some of them familiar to Adric and Nyssa.

'See, I fled Gallifrey real young. Got my hands on this TARDIS Type 29. It was a pretty beat-up old thing even then. "Rescued" it from the Museum of Classic Space Transportation.'

'It's bigger on the outside than the inside,' observed Nyssa.

'Yeah, the damn "relative dimensions" component went kaput three hundred years back. Dammit, shoulda waited for a newer model. Impatience, see, that's my flaw. This old 29 was just fine for a long while, even after the relative dimensions blew, but the time rotor ran outta juice and I've been trapped right here fifty long years.' He patted the console. 'Her "search" function's been waitin' for another TARDIS to happen along ever since. A TARDIS lands inside of a hundred thou miles even for a second, I hear about it. The moment yours turns up, knew exactly where it was in them Missouri woods. Own half the gamblin' joints hereabouts, so instructed my head guy out there to get a hold of that TARDIS and ship it on out to me. That journey along the river, followed its every movement. Knew when it'd fallen into the water. What TARDIS type is the Doctor's? Type 39 I'd hazard, 40, 41 maybe?'

'Type 40,' said Adric. 'He says it's not his forté.'

'Goddamm it, that's just the sort of thing he *would* say. Course, Type 40s are overdue for the junk heap but it'll be OK.'

'How do you communicate with your men ...?' mused Nyssa.

Doc thumped his console, not without humour. 'You love pepperin' me with damnfool questions, don't you? See, my guys, they got chips in their skulls!'

'Talkin' about those zombies?' asked James.

'I guess all sufficiently advanced science looks like voodoo if you don't know better. See, I can activate my boys at the gamblin' houses. They won't remember. Even Li Cho, once he gets back home, won't know he ever left, just go right back to managin' a little gamblin' house. Good guy, Li Cho, very fond of him. And I can *hear* everythin' they hear, so when you kids start pipin' up about that box I knew you were, uh, persons of interest ... You all look like you could eat a horse. Let me you cook up a little breakfast.'

They followed him to the kitchen, where he began to fry steaks, eggs, green tomatoes and hominy grits.

'Did you know a Time Lord called the Master?' asked Nyssa.

Doc looked up sharply from his pan. 'Is *he* around here?'

'No. He killed my father.'

'Gee, truly sorry to hear that. He was always a bad apple, that guy, even at the Academy. The only guy I ever met that was smarter than me. Pity he's such a jerk, bless his hearts!'

'*Bless* him? Surely not.'

'Local lingo, honey. The more you hate a guy, the more you give him your blessin'!'

They all took huge plates of food back to the lounge.

'This is really nice,' said Adric, taking the half of Nyssa's steak which she didn't want.

'My mamma taught me the world was full of strange stuff but I didn't ever imagine this,' said James, looking at the big glass tube.

'You ain't seen nothin' yet,' said Doc.

Once they'd eaten, they sat in contented silence for a bit.

'That was a great breakfast if I do say so myself.' Doc looked at the trio of friends apologetically. 'Well y'all, no more hesitatin, folks. We best get down to business. We're gonna make a little exchange. Your TARDIS for mine.'

'You can't have the Doctor's TARDIS!' Adric blurted out.

'Hey, look at it from my point of view. I've been trapped here a good long time. Fair exchange ain't no robbery. You kids are gonna give me the key to your TARDIS and you can settle down comfortable here, with the Doctor when he shows up – where the hell *is* that guy? You, Adric, in a couple years you'll be ready to enjoy a shot of whiskey and a good cigar. And maybe the two of you'll get together ... Might not be a very long wait till the next TARDIS moseys along ...'

Nyssa had spent much of her childhood observing the political machinations of her home planet and perhaps this was why she demonstrated, at least on the surface, remarkable calm as she said, in a sort of negotiating voice,

'We don't have the right to give the Doctor's TARDIS away. You've been very kind to us but we have a responsibility to him.'

'Dammit, you're gonna disappoint me, ain't you?'

He reached into one of the deep, deep pockets of his cool summer jacket and pulled out a small black metal object.

'Didn't wanna have to do this. James, will you stand over there, please? Don't want you to get hurt, brother. Now, kids, if you'd both put your hands up I'd appreciate it. Great. It's terrific that you kids are around 'cos it coulda taken me months to figure out how to break into that blue box. I hate to do this 'cos I like you both. You may think, I bet that ain't what it looks like, a Colt pistol from 1844, I bet it fires stun rays or somethin' like that. You'd be wrong. It's a pistol. But this barrel here contain six little bullets. Now I don't wanna use 'em but I've been waitin' a good long time and I'm just about done with this place. Give me the key to the Doctor's TARDIS.'

'They ain't givin' you nothing!' shouted James. He leapt towards Doc Ashberry and landed a sharp sidelong chop with one hand on the back of Doc's neck, while with the other he snatched the gun. He couldn't know it, but he'd inadvertently performed a move which would have been recognised by martial arts experts as from the extra-planetary discipline of Venusian Karate. But the gun slipped from his fingers and flew into the air. Nyssa caught it. She pointed it at Doc, who had fallen to the floor and was rubbing the back of his neck.

'Gun's too light,' said James. 'Ain't no bullets in it.'

Nyssa opened the barrel. It was empty.

'Dammit, James, of *course* there ain't no bullets in it,' Doc grunted. 'Never killed no one and ain't startin' now.'

'Calm down, everybody,' cried Adric, flapping his hands for attention. 'Doc, you say your time rotor is "out of juice"? You mean your battery's flat?'

'Ain't that simple, kid, but basically, yeah.'

'Then can't we use *our* time rotor to charge *your* time rotor ...?'

Doc had a cable in one of his storerooms, which they trailed from a plug at the bottom of his time rotor, out onto the porch and along to the cart and into the blue box, to a similar outlet on the underside of the control console. The Type 40 time rotor, in non-dematerialisation mode, rose and fell.

It was a molasses-slow job. Doc's machine had been inert for so long it showed scarcely any response for hours, only a single flickering dial suggesting anything was happening at all. Until, as night came round yet again, a low animal groan was heard. A light began to flash, just one at first, slowly, then another, then more, one up here, one down there, until finally the Type 29 rotor became a spectacular dance, a whirling dervish of spinning, multi-coloured lights.

The giant rotor launched upward and very nearly touched the ceiling, before plummeting down again and repeating the action.

*

'It's been nice to meet you, kids,' said Doc, puffing on his cigar. 'You too, James.'

'We'll send your regards to the Doctor,' said Nyssa.

Doc's eyes widened in mock horror. '*Au contraire*, my dear! I would like it if you didn't mention me, OK?'

'What's the problem between you and the Doctor?' asked Adric.

'Some questions are best left unanswered, kid. Jus' keep our meeting to yourselves, comprende, amigos?'

James let them chatter on, barely hearing a word. He was standing on the porch, looking out to the river. It was beautiful now. A frigate bird swooped overhead. Cicadas buzzed.

But he remembered the broken raft.

He remembered the Phillips Farm.

He could feel the welts on his back.

He remembered his wife.

He went through the door. 'So this is some kind of magic ship?'

'Remember what I told you about science and voodoo? It ain't voodoo.'

'But it can take me away from here?'

'Oh, it can take you a mighty long ways from here.'

'Where you goin', Doc?'

'Don't rightly know, James. Somewhere pretty, I hope.'

'Can I come?'

Doc drew in fresh smoke, blew it out through his nose, looked thoughtful. 'The moth that wants to go to the stars, eh? Well … Well, I guess I might find myself havin' a few adventures 'long the way. Guess I could use an assistant.'

'Companion,' said Adric.

'Guess it might be useful to have a guy around who knows Venusian Karate. If you think what you've seen is wild, that's only the beginning. It's gonna be pretty mind-blowing.'

'You'll travel in space,' said Nyssa.

'And time,' said Adric.

'But you'll get used to it,' said Nyssa.

A big, warm laugh came from Doc. 'Whenever we Time Lords take on helpers from other planets, it's damn incredible how quick they go from disbelief to takin' it all for granted! Dammit, hop on board, James. Hop on board. Come in and sit right down. By the way, where you get that cricketing gear?'

The final farewells were brisk.

'I'm antsy to get away,' said Doc. 'Maybe see you kids again some place, some time.'

'Hope so,' said Adric.

The old three-storey clapboard house faded and was soon gone. Doc and James had lit out for the vast territory of space and time.

'Dammit all to hell!'

'You can drop the accent, Adric.'

'Tarnation! Let's quit this damn planet!'

'*Adric!*'

'Sorry!'

Through an open door Nyssa saw the dead android. 'Just another slave ...'

'We do what we can, Nyssa. We can't work wonders. But you and I just did a lot for two remarkable people. It's something. More than something.'

'I suppose you're right.'

'Of course I'm right, Nyssa,' he said with his sweetest smile. He was, she realised, the gentlest boy she'd known. 'I'm always right. Ninety-nine times out of a hundred.'

'You may not know this but when the Doctor's away you have a habit of talking like him. Which is fairly trying.'

'He's right ninety-eight per cent of the time so I have the edge,' he said. Then, peering right into the coloured lights at the heart of the time rotor so he did not have to catch her eye, he added, 'Nyssa. I'm not ... I mean I don't ... I mean I'm not ... but I think you are a very amazing girl.'

'I don't imagine I will ever meet a more marvellous, astounding boy than you, Adric.' She became suddenly business-like. 'We must get back to the Terileptil base. The Doctor and Tegan are depending on us.'

'Yes. And when we've rescued them we really must get Tegan to her airport as soon as possible ...' He applied his Doctor-ish 'thinking' face. 'The fast return switch has had time to recharge. If we press this button I think it will take us where we were aiming for ...'

'Why not try thumping the console again?' asked Nyssa, smiling. 'It's far more likely to work.'

Interstitial Insecurity
Colin Baker

Anyone who had encountered the Doctor in his current persona, in their past or his, would have struggled to recognise the Time Lord who stepped uncertainly out of the dock in the space station courtroom.

To say that he was shaken would be an understatement. He had been unceremoniously plucked out of time and space and placed on trial when in the middle of a cataclysmic series of events on Thoros Beta, culminating in the death of his travelling companion, Peri. Having just been forced to watch the horror of that event, via the Matrix, as part of the evidence against him, he was left shattered, dejected and confused.

The Matrix, the supposed interference-proof repository of the minutiae of every Time Lord's actions, was at odds with the Doctor's own memory. But he knew with sickening certainty that his mind had been attacked and scrambled by Crozier's mindwarp machine, and he was still struggling to reassemble his memories and relate them somehow to what he had just witnessed. Had he really attacked his friend and companion so savagely when she was so unbearably vulnerable? Had he stood by, colluding with the reptilian Sil and his fellow mentors, while her young human body became a container for the consciousness of the vile Lord Kiv? Had he so callously betrayed her? It made no sense. If only his own memory were functioning properly. If only he could disperse the fog in his head and find the truth. If only Peri were not dead. If only ...

The Doctor started to shake.

'Are you ready, Doctor?' The Inquisitor stood nearby. She was elegantly dressed in flowing white ceremonial robes, with a red scarf draped across her shoulders, her stern features framed by the high double axe-head of white silk that signified her office. She was customarily measured and controlled, but the occasional lapses of protocol displayed by both the Valeyard and the Doctor had combined to unsettle her composure. 'If you are to offer evidence that can enable us to view in a different light what we have seen already, then this is your only opportunity. The secrets of the Matrix are as available to you to prepare your defence as they were to your prosecutor, the Valeyard, in preparing his case. If you are ready, the bailiff will escort you.'

The Doctor merely nodded. The bravado he had been showing in the courtroom had been blunted by the impact of what he had just witnessed. No childish pun came readily to his lips, provoked by hearing the name of his hated adversary. Unusually, he was at a loss for words.

The court bailiff led him to the Matrix entrance door, which was flanked by two impassive guards. The Keeper stood outside and with a fussy flourish opened the door.

'The Seventh Door, Doctor. I believe previous versions of yourself have visited the Matrix, but please don't expect on this occasion, given the section you will be visiting, to see or experience anything familiar. The Matrix will find its own way to interact with you. Take all the time you need, Doctor. There is absolutely no rush. However much time you may think you have spent inside, we will nonetheless see you in a few minutes. You will be undertaking your research in between the layers of time, as it were.' All this delivered with that particular air of superiority possessed by all guardians of secrets.

The Doctor was already aware of the many temporal peculiarities of the Matrix, so merely nodded again and entered. A thought struck him.

'How will I know how to—'

The Keeper interrupted, speaking over his shoulder as he departed. 'All the help you need will be available when you need it.'

The door closed, and the Doctor's eyes, ears and other senses adjusted to the environment that they suddenly found themselves having to process.

A corridor. Another corridor. A series of corridors. A wry smile crossed his face as he remembered. He and Peri had vied with each other on so many occasions to be the first to articulate the interchangeable nature of the countless corridors they had fled down during their time together. Would they really never share a moment like that again? The smile died away. 'But these corridors are actually different,

Peri,' he said aloud. 'Similar admittedly. But not exactly the same! Small mercies, eh?'

He paused and looked around. An unexpected voice jolted him. The tone was pleasant, even reassuring, which made its suddenness no less startling.

'That's because these are corridors created by you, Doctor. You must need them to be here and different, so they are.'

The voice was calm and youthful. But there was no one to be seen. The sound wasn't in his head; it had a normal, open acoustic, but the wide corridor remained frustratingly empty in every direction.

'I see. In that case, if I have a *need* to see you ...'

'Then you will. Do you? Have a need?'

'Yes.'

As if she had always been there, a child, a young girl in a plain pale blue dress trimmed with white lace, was sitting in an old-fashioned wheelchair, right in front of him, with the long thin fingers of her alabaster-white hands entwined on her lap. She smiled disarmingly. It occurred to the Doctor that she was the embodiment of the stereotype known in every sentient society throughout the universe that offered varieties of gender – the girl next door. In different circumstances, he would have warmed to her immediately.

'Hello, Doctor.'

He knew better than to demonstrate any doubt that the girl in front of him might not be up to the task, whatever that task might be. In the Matrix, nothing is ever as it seems and, although his memory of the time spent here by several of his previous incarnations was sufficient to make him grateful that his current interlocutor seemed friendly and open, he was nonetheless cautious.

'Hello. Are you my promised helper?'

'My name is Anosia, Doctor, and I hope that I will be able to help you,' she replied. 'I am the custodian, if you like, of the Recorded Pantemporal Data in this closed sector of the Amplified Panotropic Complex of the Matrix. Quite a mouthful, eh? I like "Helper" better, I think. When the Time Lords are threatened and the truth is required to counteract or minimise the threat, then it is my job to enable and assist the search for that truth. It is unusual, I confess, to be consulted in a merely judicial enterprise. However ... My services are at your disposal ...' She paused and looked at him in a way that he couldn't quite interpret yet then added, '... apparently.'

The Doctor returned her gaze. He knew he was possibly being manipulated by the Matrix in presenting him with a guide that he would be likely to respond to spontaneously with ease, but saw no reason to doubt that this was the only game in town. He decided he would, at least for now, take her on face value.

'I am on trial, Anosia, and I need to extract evidence from the Matrix that will demonstrate my innocence ...'

'I know, Doctor. You want to see your own future timeline. I am fully briefed on all the events of the trial and am therefore able to assist you to prepare your defence. Follow me, please.'

With seemingly minimal effort, she propelled her chair forward at a speed that the Doctor managed to match only by breaking into a rather undignified brisk trot behind her. His senses battled with each other to integrate and make sense of his differing perceptions of the surroundings. Then he noticed that neither her hands nor her wheels were moving. Glancing down, he added his own legs to the list of immobile appendages.

Noticing his confusion, Anosia smiled and stopped. 'Ah, Doctor, you haven't visited this area of the Matrix before, of course. It lacks the comparative stability of the other more frequently visited areas, dealing as they do with the relatively fixed nature of the past and rolling present. Nothing is quite as it seems here, nothing at all. The Matrix is being kind to your senses in less controversial matters – like travel – by offering you what you expect to see rather than confusing you with the dimensional oddities of the present future.'

'The present future?'

The Doctor was getting irritated, despite his best endeavours given the evident benevolence of his guide, as she began to explain the peculiarities of their environment.

'You will be aware, of course, Doctor, that our privileged experience of the four dimensions can confuse. It is our practice in this sector to refer to the future of a visiting Time Lord in this way because, while here, he or she is viewing an event from a subjective three-dimensional point within *my* four dimensions. The future you request sight of is – as it is shown in the present – the present future for you. Should unusual circumstances prevail that resulted in an alteration – however slight – to that future, then it would become a past future and be replaced by a *new* present future at the moment of change. The variable fluidity of the passage of time, Doctor, is why Time Lords have such strict rules and codes of conduct. I know you are aware of this, despite what others may sometimes suggest.'

Before the Doctor could engage with this classic example of what seemed to him typical Gallifreyan sophistry, Anosia smiled sympathetically, waved her hand as if to dismiss any implied criticism of him and continued.

'I shall offer you some future events in which your judgement and the safety of others were at risk, Doctor. Examples that demonstrate your absolute adherence to our cardinal tenets and rules. Is that acceptable?'

He nodded.

'Good. How would you like to experience your present future history, Doctor? Sitting, standing, recumbent ...'

To his immediate regret, he interrupted. 'Sitting on a park bench, for all I care. Please just get on with it.'

He should have known, in this environment, that that was a stupid thing to say.

As he sat on the park bench, waiting to watch his present futures, the Doctor struggled to accommodate the conflicting emotions that were now assailing him. He had been out of control of his own destiny since the moment the Time Lords had plucked him from Thoros Beta. He had failed to protect Peri. His memory was fragmented and the little he *could* remember was frightening. He was struggling to hang on to any certainty that his actions had matched his desire to do ... what? The right thing? Can the right thing always benefit everyone? Who is the ultimate judge of what is right, anyway? Surely not the Time Lords ... and yet ... he himself was a Time Lord ...

His turmoil was interrupted by Anosia's quiet clearing of her throat. 'Are you ready, Doctor?'

Once again he nodded and immediately found himself embedded, as an unseen observer, in a series of perilous situations in which, to his admittedly biased eye, he had behaved – would behave? – properly and caused no harm as a result of his own actions, whilst in most cases improving the lot of those he encountered.

The Doctor anxiously scrutinised the detail of each scenario with particular attention to the ability of the Valeyard to twist the narrative to suit his vindictive agenda against him. He soon learned that his uncanny ability to turn up anywhere in the universe at a time of chaos, war, confusion or cruelty would continue undiminished and was relieved to discover that he never took the easy way out, but always did what he could to help. He had just witnessed himself successfully persuade the Grand Cosmophage of Mihr that uninhabited moons were considerably tastier than inhabited planets, especially when accompanied by the music of pangalactic megaptera, when he momentarily slumped.

'Anosia,' he suddenly said. 'Do you think I could clear my brain for a moment? This is all a bit overpowering and my mind is not operating with its customary forensic clarity. I hate to admit it, but I need a break and the Keeper was at pains to explain that time in here passes at a different rate to that within the courtroom, so whatever I do will not inconvenience the Inquisitor or the Court.'

'Indeed, Doctor.' Anosia smiled reassuringly. 'In fact the only restriction as to when you return to the Court is that you cannot do so *before* you left. Your point of return is currently set as being after a reasonable break for the court officials and the prosecutor. Is there anything I can do to help revive you?'

Never was the Doctor known in this particular incarnation to miss an opportunity for a cup of tea. 'I don't suppose you could conjure a cup of Earl Grey tea and a biscuit or two, could you?'

'They're already on the table next to you Doctor, I think you will find.'

They were.

'Only one cup?' The Doctor wanted to find out more about Anosia and a tea break could help achieve that. 'You won't join me?'

The wheelchair glided over to him from the vantage point where she had been observing his immersion in his 'present future'. 'Thank you, no. But it was very kind of you to suggest it.'

For the first time in this rarefied environment, the Doctor looked carefully at her. Had he been in error in thinking her a child? She was slight of build and it was not easy to estimate her standing height, so perhaps it was the simplicity and friendly openness of her demeanour that had led him to so characterise her? She was certainly unusual. An unsettling combination of passivity and strength, gentleness yet latent power and an openness that could perhaps be concealing a myriad of deceptions.

'Anosia,' he ventured. 'How do you come to be here? I can't imagine there are many times when the High Council authorises access to a Time Lord's present future. You cannot surely spend all your time here, alone and inactive, waiting for the odd occasion when a Time Lord is reluctantly granted access to these records in order to try to frustrate the best attempts of his fellow Gallifreyans to terminate his ability to regenerate.'

A smile flickered across her face and she looked thoughtful. After a pause she looked up sharply with an expression he had not seen before. Her eyes radiated something that combined deep sadness with anger.

'Your fellow Time Lords do not like visitors to Gallifrey seeing evidence of imperfection. My personal mobility is even more limited outside the Matrix on our home planet and I make our lords and masters feel uncomfortable. Gallifrey is vain and self-serving, despite all its protestations of altruism and benevolence. I am useful in here and an embarrassment out there. The loneliness does not perturb me, after aeons of averted eyes and excuses; in fact, it is a relief.'

She smiled and all the depth of feeling she had just shown was replaced by her customary amiable candour.

The Doctor had long ago become aware of the arrogance and self-serving nature of his race, but was still saddened to hear how Anosia had been so shabbily used.

'Anosia, I will, I promise, do everything within my power when I leave here to ensure that you—'

'Doctor,' she interrupted, 'I have seen enough of your lives in preparing for this process to know that you are both naturally and by circumstance different from all but a few other Time Lords. But that is a promise you cannot keep. As I have told you, you will remember nothing of your time with me – nor indeed that I even exist – when you leave here.' Her tone became briefly forlorn. 'That of course is why I can be so candid with you. It also means, I am glad to say, that when I have less amenable visitors than yourself – and I have had many of them I assure you – I can be as forthright as I like with them, as they too remember nothing when they leave.'

The Doctor looked dejected at this reminder of the subtlety of his current position and couldn't immediately find any words to express his heartfelt regret that he couldn't help this ill-used young woman.

'Don't look so glum, Doctor. Your desire to help me reinforces my inclination to be more open with you than I have been instructed, but more of that later. In the meantime,

I have found a possible extract from your future time stream that might suit your purposes very well.'

He waited expectantly.

'It concerns events on an Intergalactic Liner that harbours a massive threat to all on board and which would, if allowed to continue, bring about the deaths of everyone on the planet Earth, which I know has a particular place in your hearts, Doctor.'

'Earth? Or Ravalox, Anosia?'

'Before the Sleeper debacle, Doctor. Earth Year 2986.'

'Right, thank you.'

'More tea, Doctor? I might join you this time.'

Sipping their Earl Grey, Anosia and the Doctor immersed themselves in the mysterious events in and around the hydroponics centre on the *Hyperion III*. And while the Doctor gave every appearance of concentrating on the unfolding drama, he also began to notice small tells that made him think that Anosia seemed more interested in his reactions to the unfolding events than she had been during the exposition of previous narratives, interposing brief confirmatory comments to support his increasing belief that this story would serve very well as evidence of his probity.

As the holo-show ended, the Doctor abruptly, but in a manner that suggested mild interest rather than any stronger emotion, said, 'Forgive me, Anosia, for asking you this, but I have the impression that you'll recommend this particular timeline extract as one I should produce in the farrago of a trial that currently embroils me. I am therefore wondering why that is the case. I am usually very good at reading people – indeed I pride myself on it most of the time – and as far as I can recall, in my present iteration, I have only been perplexed, but sufficiently intrigued to take a risk nonetheless, once before. Her name was Charlotte Pollard and in many ways you remind me of her.'

He stopped and stared at her, waiting for a response. Her deep brown eyes met and held his gaze. Then she swept a lock of auburn hair from her forehead and gazed down at her pale hands for a moment.

When she looked up, it was, for a second, as if her personality had completely changed. She sounded and looked no different than she had seconds earlier, but it was if one of several veils had been removed and she had evolved from the innocence of youth to the self-control of young womanhood in the brief time that she had glanced away from him.

She seemed to sit higher and with less vulnerability in her wheelchair, as she said, 'I implied earlier that I was told how to guide you through the evidential extracts available to you. Any of your choices would, in fact, have been acceptable to your prosecutors, although the story of the Vervoids and their implacable purpose was their first choice.'

'Was it?' the Doctor asked cautiously. 'In which case I'll go for the one with the young Queens in England, I think – and the older companion. I liked the cut of her jib!' he added.

'I think that would be a mistake Doctor – and this is what I am instructed to withhold from you at all cost ...'

'Yes?' the Doctor prompted.

'Doctor, I have been their creature for too long. All their promises of freedom and a better life on Gallifrey have proved to be worthless so ...' She took a deep breath. 'The testimony you have seen with me has already been suitably and subtly edited for viewing in the Inquisitor's Courtroom with a view to destroying you. You have been seeing the true course of events; what the court will be shown however has already been adjusted to demonstrate your guilt in many different ways, and you will not remember.'

'Editing? But I thought that was impossible ...?'

'Of course you did. That is what they want everyone to believe. But I cannot connive at your destruction, when you are literally the only compassionate or caring Time Lord I have ever met.'

'Go on, Anosia,' he said gently.

'As always, Doctor, the truth is banal and shabby. The Vervoid evidence was the preferred option because it required the least editing. Quite simply that. The final scene that you saw, where you revealed that you had set up an herbarium containing Vervoid seeds genetically modified to remove their aggressive genocidal tendencies, assured the benign future of that previously savage species. That scene left you free of any possible charge of committing genocide yourself. The excision of that scene, however, would guarantee your conviction of that most heinous of offences. You would have chosen a story that exposes you to a charge of genocide. You would have no knowledge of the true events as, once you've left here, your memories of what you witnessed with me will be completely erased.'

'Anosia! This doesn't help me. I'm going to forget all this, so how is your exposure of this farce going to assist in any way? I won't remember!'

'But I will, Doctor.' Anosia moved her wheelchair until her face was an inch from his. 'I don't forget, and all I have to do is reinstate that excised scene prior to the transfer to the trial room, make a couple of other minor restorative tweaks to the story and you will be exonerated. The other evidential offerings available to you are too difficult and fragmented to restore without drawing attention in advance to my part in their restitution.'

The Doctor gazed intently at the disarming young figure. Everything she had said made sense. Given the memory/reality switch when he exited, he could say or do nothing that had the benefit of what he had learned in the Matrix, so he had to make a decision now. If he didn't trust her, what other way was there? And how extensive was the conspiracy against him?

'When I was given my instructions, Doctor, I realised that this time I was not merely being used to airbrush Time Lord history for the purposes of Public Relations. My mission this time seems personal and vindictive, without any greater good that is usually argued in these situations.'

'Thank you, Anosia. Truly, thank you,' the Doctor said slowly. 'This is quite hard to assimilate. I can tell it has been quite a risk for you to share all this with me. Can I ask you who "they" are? Who is pressuring you to do this – is it the Keeper? The Inquisitor? The Matrix itself? Who is my enemy, Anosia?'

'I don't know, Doctor.' As he went to voice his frustration, she continued: 'I see the Keeper occasionally but he is invariably business-like and pedantic, with no signs of a hidden agenda. The only other Time Lord I have seen recently is unlike any I have encountered. When he visits he has the key of Rassilon and seems able to come and go at will; he appears to have a greater knowledge and understanding of the Matrix than anyone I have ever met and knows how to manipulate the data so that the external layers show no sign of disruption. He has shared some of his knowledge with me so that I may navigate parts of the shadow Matrix with similar ease. He has an arrogance that exceeds even the excesses of the worst High Gallifreyans and seems immune to the effect of the Matrix's mind wipe on exiting here. He says that is because he is the High Council's chosen prosecutor.'

'The Valeyard.'

By the time the Doctor spoke the name, he was beyond surprise or anger. Who else could it have been? But why? What had the Doctor done or what might he do in the future to produce this level of murderous hatred from a man he had never met before?

'He has never used that name with me, but is very fond of saying that he is Schrödinger and you are his pet cat, whatever that means. It appears to amuse him to repeat it.'

A silence laden with frantic reassessment on one side and anxiety on the other charged the atmosphere in this non-place, drifting in its non-temporal state.

'Why are you telling me all this, Anosia, knowing that I won't remember?'

She became suddenly more intense and driven. 'Because, Doctor even during the short time between this moment and your return to your trial, I want us both for a moment to know the truth of what has happened here in this festering, putrid backwater of the Matrix. And unlike you, I will remember ... If I could find a way to help you remember, believe me I would.'

'The Valeyard will punish you. Hurt you ...'

She seemed to repress a smile and reassured him, 'In here I am completely safe, Doctor. Now I must go and restore the evidential narrative and ensure at least that you will receive the justice you have every right to expect. The door is behind you.'

Before he could frame the words he wanted to say to her, she had gone in such a complete way that it was as if she had never been there and everything that had happened had taken place in his mind.

He turned and wandered slowly towards the door, which opened and revealed the Keeper waiting on the other side.

'Before you exit, Doctor, have you selected your evidential strand and are you ready to leave in the knowledge that you will now forget everything you have seen?'

Desperately trying to file every bit of information in some hidden corners of his mind, the Doctor testily responded, 'Do I have any choice, Keeper?'

'No. Put your seal on this if you will, Doctor.'

The Keeper handed him the document and seal. The Doctor obliged, still willing his mind to retain what he'd learned and stepped through the open portal.

'Here you are, Doctor.'

The Keeper handed him his copy of the document.

'What's this?'

'Just a copy of your acknowledgement that at the point when you forgot the detail of your visit to the Matrix Data Bank, you were entirely content with the discharge of our obligation to you. It was prepared by Matrix Protection Operative, Anosia.'

'Never heard of her,' said the Doctor as, slightly dazed, and with a strange sense of emptiness, he headed back to the Trial Room.

Had he still been on the other side of the Door, he would have heard the Valeyard's familiar tones.

'My child, you have performed extremely well, although I must confess I began to doubt your allegiance, so good was your performance. Your apparent desire to help that smug, meddling fool was beautifully enacted. Now … I know I promised you an end to your confinement here, but you will have to wait just a little longer, I'm afraid, until all my plans are complete. I'm sure you understand. And though I trust you absolutely, my dear Anosia, I have already made the appropriate copy of the Vervoid saga, to save you from being tempted to make choices you might live to regret. So for a while longer you must enjoy the limitless facilities of this spectacularly dull but, oh, so useful, place.' He began to laugh.

Anosia sat in her wheelchair, with tears easing onto her cheeks, listening to the sound of the Valeyard's laughter echoing around the Matrix and making the empty teacups rattle.

The Slyther of Shoreditch
Mike Tucker

Private Matt Doe stared into the thick November fog that wreathed the streets of Shoreditch and felt a shiver ripple along his spine. It wasn't the fog itself that caused his unease, but what the fog might conceal ...

Doe had only been transferred to the Intrusion Counter-Measures Group a few weeks ago, and in truth he'd considered it to be a cushy posting. Sure, he had had heard the rumours about why the unit had been created – a rapid-response team to react against unknown and unusual threats – but he hadn't believed a word of that. He had been convinced that the ICMG was nothing more than a propaganda tool, a reaction against intelligence that hinted at Russian experimentation with parapsychology – ESP, spoon bending, all that rubbish ...

This morning had changed that view.

This morning he had been confronted by a robot monster from another planet; a robot monster armed with a death ray. And now Matthews and MacBrewster lay in an East End morgue.

He could still see the expressions of agony and surprise etched onto their lifeless faces. They had been good soldiers, good comrades, and their lives had been snuffed out by something so incomprehensible, so alien, that Doe still felt the whole thing was some terrible nightmare. If it hadn't been for that little scientist ...

He shivered again and checked the magazine on his L1A1 Self Loading Rifle. Bullets hadn't meant much to the thing in the junkyard, but the rifle was all that he had, and at least now he knew that the robot things *could* be destroyed.

A sudden noise from a side alley made him start, and he spun on his heel, swinging the muzzle of his rifle towards the sound.

'Who goes there?'

He peered into the fog, listening intently for the tell-tale whirring sounds that the thing in Totter's Lane had made. What was the instruction that they had been given? Aim for the eyepiece ...

Finger hovering over the trigger of his rifle, he edged forwards into the alleyway, wincing at every crunch that his combat boots made on the cobblestones. The strange noise came again and Doe frowned. This wasn't a mechanical sound; it was more organic – wet, slithering ...

His boot suddenly skidded on something slick, and his leg shot from under him. As he struggled to retain his balance, his rifle slipped from his fingers, clattering onto the cobbles.

Cursing, he reached down to retrieve his weapon. To his disgust, the stock and barrel were covered in some kind of thick, evil-smelling slime, presumably the same stuff that he had slipped on. Grimacing, he looked around for something to wipe his hands on, but as he did so he realised that something huge and terrible and alien was emerging from the fog in front of him.

Not far away, the Doctor looked up as distant gunshots shattered the quiet of the still night air. One, two, three ... then a muffled scream and the bubbling roar of something that had no place on this planet.

The Doctor closed his eyes in despair. Things were spiralling out of his control in ways that he had never anticipated, and at such speed that it was proving near impossible to react in time to prevent casualties.

Certain that the distant scream marked the end of another innocent life, the Doctor was about to make his way in the direction of the sound to investigate when movement in the window of a nearby pub caught his eye.

A man was waving at him.

A man whose face he recognised.

A man he'd last seen on the surface of Skaro, lifetimes ago.

All thoughts of investigating the gunshots forgotten, the Doctor crossed the road and pushed open the heavy wooden door of the pub. At the far end of the virtually deserted bar sat a man in long grey robes, a half pint of beer on the small round table in front of him. He beckoned for the Doctor to come and join him. The Doctor approached him warily. *Any* Time Lord showing up at this particular space-time event would be unwelcome. But for it to be *this* one ...

The Time Lord smiled genially at him as he approached, raising his glass in greeting. 'Ah, Doctor, how nice to see you again after all this time.'

The Doctor sat down, eyeing him suspiciously. 'Making ourselves at home, are we?'

'I did some research on local delicacies before I arrived,' said the Time Lord in the supercilious tone that the Doctor always found so infuriating. 'Bitter shandy seemed appropriate.' He took a sip of his beer. 'I can't say that I'm overly impressed.'

'What are you doing here?' snapped the Doctor. 'If you are looking for my earlier incarnation and Susan ...'

'I'm not interested in whatever criminal activities you or your granddaughter might have been involved with,' the Time Lord interrupted. 'Not my department. My duties have a more specific focus these days.'

'And what might those duties be?

The Time Lord took another sip of his beer, peering along the long hook of his nose with a mischievous gleam in his eye. 'Can't you guess?'

The Doctor nodded grimly. 'Daleks.'

The Time Lord placed his glass down on the table and leaned forward conspiratorially. 'The actions that we took on Skaro to subvert the development of the Daleks all those years ago appear to have had unforeseen consequences.'

'We?' The Doctor raised an eyebrow. 'I seem to remember that I was the one who had to do most of the dirty work.'

The Time Lord ignored him. 'Even though you failed, the Daleks long ago learned of our attempt. They have always considered it a pre-emptive act of aggression and plan to retaliate.'

The Doctor said nothing.

'The Daleks' recent acquisition of time corridor technology has raised the possibility that they might be able to successfully counter-strike,' the Time Lord went on. 'They intend waging a war with us that will take place in four dimensions and they have given this campaign a name – *Pa Jass-Vortan*.'

The Doctor translated the Dalek phrase: 'The Time War.'

The Time Lord nodded. 'Fortunately, their temporal technology is primitive, but they are fast learners and formidable engineers. The High Council is concerned that it is only a matter of time before they successfully breach the Transduction Barriers, and then war will truly have broken out ...' He gave the Doctor a pointed look. 'I don't suppose you have any thoughts as to what the Daleks might be looking for here in this time zone, do you?'

The Doctor said nothing. He knew all too well what the Daleks were looking for, and he wanted them to find it, but trying to explain to a member of the Time Lord elite that he was about to hand over one of the most powerful temporal devices ever created to their mortal enemies was unlikely to go well.

Realising that the Doctor wasn't going to say any more, the Time Lord gave a deep sigh and shook his head. 'Very well, Doctor. Keep your secrets. But be warned, the game you are playing is a dangerous one, and there are worse things than Daleks to contend with.'

As if on cue, the unearthly roar that the Doctor had heard earlier echoed out through the fog again. A few of the other patrons looked up at the noise, but swiftly returned to their pints.

'You recognise that sound, I assume?' said the Time Lord.

The Doctor nodded. 'A Slyther.'

'And no ordinary Slyther. Scientists from the Imperial Dalek faction appear to have augmented it with mechanical prostheses in the same way that they have augmented themselves. It is now functioning as a highly sophisticated biomechanical tracker.' He took another sip of his beer. 'I was hoping to discover what it is tracking.'

The Doctor rose from his seat and hurried out into the street, peering into the swirling mist. He had already miscalculated once by not realising that his plan would attract the attention of more than one Dalek faction. The fact that the renegade Daleks had already recruited human allies to assist them was bad enough, but for the Imperial Daleks to have brought a Slyther was catastrophic. It had already killed. He needed to deal with the creature, and quickly ...

As the eerie, undulating cry rang out again, the Time Lord appeared at the Doctor's shoulder, smoothing out his long, grey robes ... 'Of course, if we knew what the creature was after it would be easier to track it and return it to its proper space and time.'

'You would do that?' The Doctor glared at him suspiciously.

The Time Lord smiled benignly at him. 'Think of it as a favour for services rendered.'

'Right.' The Doctor set off into the fog. 'Well, come on, then.'

'What? Wait ...' The Time Lord hitched up his robes and hurried after him. 'You mean you know where the creature might be?'

'Oh yes,' said the Doctor. 'I've got a pretty good idea.'

'An undertakers?' The tall, gaunt Time Lord stared up at the sign on the stern, stone building in disbelief. 'What in Rassilon's name are we doing here?'

'You wanted to know where the Slyther would be heading,' snapped the Doctor. 'Well this is it ...'

'But surely it's your TARDIS ...'

'The Slyther isn't hunting me,' explained the Doctor. 'It's hunting something I brought with me, and this is where the trail will lead it.'

He crossed the road, searching for any sign that the creature had been here. To his relief the building seemed secure; perhaps the Time Lord had overestimated the Slyther's enhanced abilities.

He was about to say as much when something caught his eye: a drain cover had been pushed aside, and the pavement around it was wet with pools of thick, faintly luminous slime. It had been here, and it had not found what it was looking for.

The Doctor's mind was racing.

The Daleks had obviously brought the Slyther to Earth to sniff out the Hand of Omega – presumably by homing in on its chrono-spore. But they – and he, for that matter – had fundamentally misjudged the nature of Omega's Temporal Manipulator. It was a smart device – literally. Once it realised that it was being hunted, it had been smart enough to cloak its unique energy signature so that it would evade just such detection. The people who had come into contact with it, however, were a different matter ... They would be marked, tainted, easy prey for the Slyther.

There was a huge black hearse parked on the street outside the shop.

Grabbing the Time Lord by the arm, the Doctor ushered him towards it. 'You and I are going for a little ride ...'

The hearse sped through the silent London streets. The Doctor knew that only three people had physically interacted with the Hand of Omega – his previous self, his granddaughter and Mr Donlevy, the owner of the undertakers. Donlevy was the only possible target. The Slyther had traced him from Totter's Lane to the undertakers, and now it must be tracking him to his home address, using the sewers to move through the streets of London undetected.

Desperately hoping that he could remember where Donlevy lived, the Doctor sent the hearse hurtling around another tight corner oblivious to the cries of distress his passenger was making.

Finally they arrived in a street that he recognised, and the Doctor brought the big car to a juddering halt. A terrace of imposing Victorian houses loomed over them, their façades bleached almost to monochrome by the fog. The Doctor clambered from the driver's seat and nodded in satisfaction. His memory hadn't let him down.

He leaned back in through the open door of the hearse. 'You stay here and keep watch.'

'Me?' The Time Lord looked alarmed. 'On my own? But the Slyther could be here at any moment!'

'That's what you're watching for.' The Doctor pointed at the horn on the centre of the steering wheel with the tip of his umbrella. 'If it turns up, press that.'

Not waiting to hear any further protests, the Doctor turned and hurried across the road to Donlevy's house, checking that the drain covers in the wet road were undisturbed as he went. Pushing open a small iron gate, he made his way up the short path to the front door. Unsurprisingly, given the hour, the house was dark, the sash windows swathed with nets and heavy velvet curtains.

Pulling a safety pin from his hatband, the Doctor inserted it into the lock and moments later there was a soft 'click' as the door swung silently open. He slipped inside and closed the door behind him.

The Doctor stood for a moment in the darkened hallway. For him it had been so long since he'd last set foot here; taking tea with Mr Donlevy and his wife in their front room as they had discussed the arrangements for the interment of his casket. Arrangements that might, tonight, get them killed.

From upstairs the Doctor could hear the sound of stentorian snoring. That at least was confirmation that the Slyther hadn't yet found is target. Cautiously, he started to make his way up the stairs, painfully conscious of every creak that the wooden steps made beneath his feet.

There were four doors leading off the landing. From the snoring it was fairly simple to deduce which one was the master bedroom. Quietly, the Doctor opened each of the other doors in turn. The first door led to a small, very floral bathroom, the second to a well-presented guest bedroom but behind the third door he found what he was after.

The long, black coat of an undertaker lay neatly folded on a single bed, a top hat resting on top of it, and a sombre-looking suit was draped over a chair alongside. But it was the tall wicker basket on the far side of the room that caught the Doctor's attention. A basket stuffed with overalls and aprons waiting to be washed.

The Doctor hurried over to the basket and started rummaging through the laundry. He needed something that had absorbed enough of the Hand's chronon fallout to confuse the tracking instincts of the Slyther; something that Donlevy had worn close to the skin.

With a cry of triumph, the Doctor pulled out a pair of long johns from the basket. As he did so a strange, undulating cry echoed from the street outside, followed moments later by the urgent beeping of a car horn.

Realising that he might only have moments to spare before the Slyther tried to gain entry to the house, the Doctor turned to leave, only to discover Mrs Donlevy in the doorway, clad in a pink dressing gown and matching pink slippers, staring at him and the long johns in astonishment.

'Um ... good evening.' The Doctor thrust the underwear towards her. 'Are you happy with your wash?'

'I'm sorry?' Mrs Donlevy stammered, backing away.

'I'm in the area testing a new washing powder – washes whiter than white – and am offering you a free trial.' The Doctor edged towards the door as more frantic beeping sounded from outside. 'Ah! My laundry van is ready to go. Excuse me!'

With that he turned and fled down the stairs, wincing as Mrs Donlevy let out a scream that could probably be heard the length of the street.

'Brian! Wake up! There's a pervert in the house! He's stolen your long johns ...'

The Doctor burst out of the front door and into the garden, skidding to a halt at the sight that confronted him. The Slyther was emerging from the drain in the street like toothpaste being squeezed from a tube, its huge, undulating body slick with slime, tentacles thrashing wildly as it pulled itself onto the tarmac.

The Doctor could see the Time Lord inside the hearse, gesticulating wildly as the monstrous creature came closer and closer.

All along the street, lights were coming on in windows, curtains twitching. Spurred into action by the bellow of anger and sound of heavy footfalls coming from inside the house, the Doctor dashed towards the hearse and threw open the rear doors, waving the long johns frantically at the Slyther as he did so.

'Here boy!' He whistled loudly. 'Is this what you're after?'

Three of the creature's sensory organs swung in his direction and the Doctor saw its body stiffen as its biomechanical detectors locked in on the unique chronon signature of the Hand of Omega. The Slyther gave out a hiss of triumph, heaved itself from the drain and gathered itself to strike.

The Doctor scrambled into the back of the hearse. 'Drive!' he yelled.

'What?' blustered the Time Lord, sliding over into the driver's seat. 'I'm not sure that I can operate this ... thing.'

'Of course you can!' cried the Doctor frantically as a probing tentacle curled into the back of the hearse, grasping at his foot. 'I thought that Time Lords transcended such simple mechanical devices when the universe was less than half its present size!' He batted at the tentacle with his umbrella. 'Now drive!'

The engine spluttered into life and, with a grinding of gears, the hearse lurched forward, wrenching the Doctor's foot free of the grasping proboscis. He hung on for dear life as they accelerated down the street, tyres squealing on the wet cobblestones. The Slyther surged after them, screeching in anger at its prey having eluded it.

They took the corner at the end of the road sharply, with a screech of tyres, the Doctor sliding around wildly on the polished teak in the back of the hearse. Through the rear window he watched as the Slyther tore a drain cover from the roadway and vanished back down into the sewers, obviously happier tracking them from underground.

'Slow down!' bellowed the Doctor. 'We don't want to lose it!'

'We don't want it to catch us either,' said the Time Lord, bringing the hearse jerkily to a crawl. 'I'm assuming that you have some destination in mind? Or do you intend to let that abomination chase us around the streets all night?'

The Doctor did have a destination in mind – it had been there the moment the Time Lord had revealed to him the augmented nature of the Imperial Daleks' Slyther.

He carefully explained the route that he wanted them to take. As he revealed the ultimate destination, the Time Lord's eyebrows raised in amused approval.

'Interesting . . .'

Before the Doctor could elaborate further on his plan, the hearse started to vibrate alarmingly. Moments later, the manhole cover that they had just driven over was sent spiralling into the air as easily as someone might flip a coin and, with an unearthly roar, the Slyther burst from the sewers.

This time the Time Lord didn't need to be told anything. Throwing the hearse into gear he stamped down hard on the accelerator, but it was too late. Seemingly anticipating what its prey might do, the Slyther lunged forward – thick, fleshy tentacles shooting out from its undulating body, snatching hold of the car's bumper and bringing it to an abrupt halt.

Clouds of acrid smoke rose from the spinning tyres as the Time Lord stamped down hard on the accelerator, trying to break the Slyther's grasp, but as tentacle after tentacle took hold the vile creature's grip became ever more secure.

With a hiss of pleasure, the Slyther hauled itself on top of the hearse, eager to get at the passengers within. As it did so, the weight that that had been holding the vehicle back was suddenly released. The hearse shot forward, careering wildly down the narrow street.

In the back, the Doctor was now surrounded on all sides by the quivering bulk of the creature; slick, oily flesh pressing against the glass as it searched for a way of getting inside. It was, thought the Doctor, an uncomfortable premonition of what it might be like inside the belly of the beast.

'Doctor …' The Time Lord was struggling to keep his icy composure. 'What do you want me to do?'

'Keep going, of course!' shouted the Doctor. 'At least we're taking it in the direction that we want.'

The Time Lord muttered something incomprehensible under his breath. The Doctor doubted that it was anything complimentary.

The hearse rounded another corner, its suspension groaning with the extra weight that it was now carrying. The Doctor could hear the Slyther's claws on the roof as it scrabbled to keep a hold on the speeding vehicle.

'Doctor,' cried the Time Lord, almost on cue. 'Is this the place?'

Craning his neck, the Doctor strained to see out through the windscreen. To his relief the electricity substation was right ahead of them; squat brick buildings no more than ghostly shapes looming from the fog behind a tall wire fence at the far end of the street.

Perhaps alerted by the voice of the Time Lord in the front of the vehicle, the Slyther stared to move on the roof, sliding itself forward, thin tentacles starting to probe at the handles driver and passenger doors, the wet folds of its body undulating down across the windscreen.

'I can't see!' screamed the Time Lord. 'My vision is—'

'Just keep the wheel straight!' shouted the Doctor. 'We're almost there.'

Seconds later, the air was filled with the sound of rending metal as the heavy hearse smashed through the wire fence of the substation. The Doctor wrapped the long johns around his head for protection as he was spun around the rear of the hearse like laundry in a tumble dryer. The ground was wildly uneven; for one horrible moment it seemed that the hearse would roll onto its roof, but miraculously it stayed on all four wheels. Moments later, the hearse rocked to an abrupt halt.

Suddenly aware that the thick, slimy flesh of the Slyther was no longer obscuring the view through the glass, the Doctor kicked open the rear doors and scrambled out of the car, looking around frantically for any signs of the creature.

Scattered about him, severed tentacles thrashed and quivered on the gravel forecourt, and for a brief moment the Doctor thought that the crash through the fence might have disposed of the monster without the need for him to put his plan into effect. An angry hiss put paid to those thoughts as the Slyther emerged from the shadows. The severed tentacles began to squirm their way across the gravel towards the body of the creature, which reabsorbed them one by one.

Aware that a new attack would surely follow, the Doctor checked on his unlikely companion. The Time Lord was sitting dazed in the driver's seat, a livid gash on his forehead showing stark and red against the corpse-like pallor of his skin. Grabbing hold of his arm, the Doctor dragged him out of the hearse.

'Here,' he said bundling the long johns into his arms. 'Hold these for a moment.'

With a wary eye keeping watch for any sign of movement from the Slyther, the Doctor started to pull at the twisted web of wire and fence posts that had entangled itself around the hearse's bonnet and bumper. A length of wire had wound itself around the axle – if they needed to get away in a hurry, the car wasn't going to be much use to them.

'Doctor …' A scrape of gravel made the Time Lord point. The Slyther was starting to edge towards them. 'That creature is getting rather close …'

'Almost got it … ah, ha!' With a cry of triumph the Doctor pulled free a long length of wire with the twisted stump of a steel fence post still attached to one end. 'This should do the trick.'

Trying to ignore the angry hissing of the approaching Slyther, the Doctor quickly tied one of the legs of the long johns onto the trailing end of the wire. 'Now, do exactly as I say. When I tell you to run, run as fast as you can.'

'Run?' The Time Lord stared at him. 'I've *never* run.'

'Then it's time you started.'

The Doctor turned to face the approaching Slyther. The creature had finished reabsorbing its severed tentacles, and soulless black eyes glared at them with malevolence.

The Doctor jumped away from the Time Lord. Momentarily distracted by the movement, the Slyther's eyestalks swung in his direction, before swivelling back towards the Time Lord and the source of chronon contamination that he was carrying.

It gathered itself to strike.

'Run!' yelled the Doctor. Hoisting up his robes, the Time Lord turned and fled, the length of wire that the Doctor had tied to the long johns trailing behind him.

With a bubbling roar, the Slyther gave chase, terrifyingly fast. The Doctor realised that he had only moments. He dashed towards the substation transformers, desperately hoping that he had correctly judged the length of wire that he needed.

There was a sudden cry of alarm and the Doctor tuned in time to see the Time Lord catch his foot in the hem of his robes and go sprawling in the gravel.

The Slyther reared up over him.

'Throw it!' yelled the Doctor. 'Throw it away from you!'

The Time Lord chucked the bundle of long johns, with its trailing wire, as hard as he could, and the Slyther surged after it, a sinuous tentacle snatching it out of the air. At the same instant, the Doctor heaved the fence post, still attached to the other end of the wire, into the substation's tangle of transformers, switchgear and distribution cables.

Immediately, the sky above the East End lit up as showers of white sparks exploded hundreds of feet into the air. A deafening crack, louder than thunder, echoed through the fog and, louder still, a high, keening screech pierced the night as the power of the national grid surged down the length of wire and into the Slyther's body.

In seconds it was all over.

The Doctor shook his head, his ears ringing. The air was filled with the acrid smell of burnt flesh and fried electronics. He gazed sadly at the charred lump that had one been the Slyther. It had been the Dalek implants that had been its undoing. The Doctor had no real idea of whether the surge of electricity would have had any effect without those additions; Slythers were notoriously difficult to kill, but since this one had so much Dalekanium threaded through its body ...

'Well, Doctor ...' The Time Lord had clambered to his feet and was brushing the dirt from his robes, trying to regain some of his earlier dignity. 'Your plan, it would seem, was successful.'

'Yes,' said the Doctor without enthusiasm. 'So it seems.'

'I can only hope that whatever you have planned for the Daleks themselves can be achieved in a somewhat less explosive manner?'

'Oh, I sincerely doubt it ...'

'Then you will forgive me if I take my leave of you. Your pace of life is a little too ... frenetic for my tastes.'

The Doctor nodded to the smoking remains of the Slyther. 'You will dispose of that?'

'Of course. The creature was no less a victim of the Daleks than any other life form. Even in death it deserves to be treated with some, dignity, don't you think?'

The Doctor nodded gratefully. 'Thank you.'

The Time Lord reached for the Time Ring at his wrist that would whisk him back to Gallifrey, then hesitated. 'Before I go, it's only fair that I make you aware of the oncoming storm ...'

The Doctor frowned 'Storm?'

'It doesn't end here. Whatever you have planned, it's a skirmish, nothing more. The war – the *Pa Jass-Vortan* – is spreading its tendrils through the space-time continuum in ways that even we don't fully understand yet. The outcome is far from certain, and far from promising.'

The Time Lord pressed his hand onto the Time Ring, and both he and the shrivelled remains of the Slyther started to fade into insubstantiality. 'Our paths are destined to cross again, Doctor, and sooner than you might wish ...'

Before the Doctor could ask anything further, the Time Lord was gone, a ghost fading into the mist.

The Doctor stood for a moment in the still, cold quiet of the November night, aware that it might be the last moment of calm for quite some time. He realised that he had become complacent. It was time to move the Hand of Omega to its final resting place ...

As the sound of distant sirens started to intrude upon the silence, the Doctor turned on his heel and started to walk back towards the road.

The Hand of Omega could wait until the morning. Right now he needed a cup of tea.

We Can't Stop What's Coming
Steve Cole

'The whole planet is riddled with time distortion!' The Doctor said so with a thrill of a grin, as if this were the highest praise. 'No wonder the TARDIS was drawn here.'

I sighed. 'So we have to go out and investigate, do we?'

'Ah, Fitz. Course we do!' He looked at me, and as usual I found myself thinking how stony-cold his eyes were, despite the twinkle and the air of the poet. 'I mean, really, leave this place, without knowing what was going on? How could I live with myself?'

'How do any of us manage to live with yourself?' Trix teased, feet up in an armchair across the control room. 'Hint. We pretend you're just our cab driver. You'll stop talking if we give you nothing to go on.'

The Doctor beamed at her. 'Are you coming out, then?'

'Nope,' Trix said.

'I'll come,' I said. 'Just so you can do your thing, yeah?'

'Readings. Samples. Quick trans-temporal biopsy.' The Doctor smiled, smoothed out the tails of his dark green coat and dusted down his waistcoat. 'We'll be back before Trix even realises we're gone.' He threw the lever that opened the TARDIS doors. 'After me, Fitz?'

'Obviously,' I said.

The Doctor led the way outside onto your basic blasted heath. Sort of a Clapham-Common-after-solar-flares type vibe. I closed the doors to our magic police box.

'Yes! Yes, yes, yes.' The Doctor was waving some weird instrument around the rocks and the stunted trees. 'This environment is definitely at odds with the rest of the planetoid.'

'You mean the rest of the planetoid isn't rubbish,' I suggested.

'This environment around us, it's from a different geological period. Everything's different.' He licked a finger and held it up to a breeze I couldn't feel. 'It's been picked up from somewhere else and just dumped here.'

'Like me.'

The Doctor blew me a kiss and looked back at his gadget. 'Yeah, I'd say that a limited area, maybe two miles square, was scooped out of one planet maybe 10,000 years ago and transplanted here in the relative present.'

I walked over to join him. 'Someone's got a big old bucket and spade.'

'Time-scooped, I'd say. Thing is, there's a ban on that kind of technology.' The Doctor sighed. 'Or there used to be, anyway—'

Next second this big hairy Neanderthal jumped down from nowhere (or possibly a ledge) and started screaming and hooting in our faces. Grey skin, wild hair, big dark eyes and bigger bright fangs.

I swore and pegged it back to the TARDIS. 'Come on, Doctor!'

Another one jumped out from behind the police box with a shriek and showed me the wooden club it was holding. I got a really good look.

WHACK! Right between the eyes.

'Shut up, Marcett.'

'What?' he protested. 'Jakarta, I never said anything! I was—'

'Even before you do. Shut up.' I held up my hand, tried to summon some strength. My boots were already caked in mud, it looked like rain and we had no teleport option until all targets were cleared. Why did Head Office insist on these stupid team-building exercises? 'I know that none of us want to be here any longer than we have to, but if you've heard the same rumours I have about "slimming down" the department, you'll know it's worth trying our best.'

'But—'

'But nothing, Marcett. Listen.'

I surveyed my so-called hunting party. Marcett, big and biting his lip, just one overenthusiastic breath away from bursting out of his too-tight khaki uniform. Thredmeyer, green eyes grown bigger through her glasses, her pith helmet run aground on the black cascades of her perm. And Bacchari, six gangling feet of sweaty apology whose fatigues hung off him like they wanted to be anywhere else. I couldn't blame them. My team of three barely functioned as accountants, let alone as hunters ready to take on unknown prey in this godforsaken wilderness.

'Do we really need all this firepower?' Bacchari was peering down the wrong end of his laser rifle. 'The gun, the grenades, the head-melter ...'

'Don't moan,' said Thredmeyer, counting the laser-bullets in her several belts. 'We don't know what's coming for us.'

'No, we don't,' I said. 'So, like I said, quiet for a minute. I'll go over the rules—'

'I'm not killing anything,' said Marcett firmly.

'I'm sure they'll be simulated life forms.'

'So? They're still alive!' Marcett shuddered, which set his whole uniform quivering. 'I can maybe catch something, Jakarta, but I can't kill it.'

'Well, we can't get off this rock until all targets are removed,' I said. 'None of us are going to enjoy it, but if we start by going over the—'

'I might enjoy it.' Thredmeyer practised drawing her disruption gun. 'I used to like hunting speelsnapes back on my mother's farm, with an old taser pistol. But weapons like these ...!'

Bacchari pulled nervously at his shirt collar. 'I'm sorry to interrupt, but don't you think it's weird Head Office want to use an accounts team to field test these weapons?'

'Maybe they want to check they're idiot proof,' I suggested.

Bacchari was immune to sarcasm. 'Are you aware how much cash the Company's spent on developing these weapons?'

'Of course I am,' I said, gritting my teeth. 'I'm Team Leader, Munitions Accounts.'

'And you've had me writing off the research overspends for years.' Thredmeyer aimed the disruption gun at Marcett and pretended to fire. 'Finally I get to have some fun with the things. Pew!'

Marcett jumped nervously in the air. 'Don't!'

'Sorry,' said Bacchari, like this was somehow his fault.

'The rules!' I snapped. 'Now there's no way off this rock until we've done the exercise, so if I could just explain—'

'No need, Jakarta. We can't lose!' Thredmeyer was caressing one of the many phosphor bombs in her custom shoulder holster. 'I mean, the prey's not even armed, right? How tough can it be to kill?'

A howling cry rose up from behind the chalky rim ahead of us.

We all swore together. Now there's team building.

I woke up and the Doctor was crouched over me. His face was lined with concern. His hair was a mess. His grin soon sparked to life, though. 'Welcome back, Fitz. How was your nap?'

'Rubbish.' I sat up and felt a whirl of nausea, tasted the thick iron tang of blood in the back of my mouth. 'Is my nose broken?' Then I smelled ripe hairy armpits and the stink of latrines and I groaned. 'No, it's working. Ugh, god, is it working.'

We were in a cave the size of a church hall. Twelve fires blazed around the perimeter. There looked to be one way in and out, a cave mouth blocked by one of the Neanderthals. It sat there, hunched and huge and hairy, baring its horrible teeth. My instinct was to get up and run. That's when I found my ankles were tied together, and so were my wrists. The Doctor was similarly hogtied.

The Doctor stared back, enraptured, like he was presenting a wildlife documentary. 'Our hosts are fascinating,' he murmured.

'Hosts?' I spluttered. 'They're hairy maniacs! They've got us!'

'Our hairy maniacs who have us are fascinating,' he tried again. 'I've counted just four of them on my little gadget.' I saw the doohickey was still clamped in his hand. 'Small for a tribe, don't you think? They tied us up and dragged us to this cave. From the butchered animals hanging from the roof, I imagine it's a larder.'

'I hate your imagination.' I looked around. Sure enough there were sides of raw meat hanging from spikes in the walls. 'Well, that's fab. Are they going to eat us?'

'I imagine it's on their to-do list. Still, they've got plenty to eat here before they start on us. We're several days from the butcher's block, I'd say.' The Doctor nodded to their guard. 'Would you say these are advanced technological creatures?'

'Armed with big sticks instead of lasers? I'm guessing no.'

'I thought that! But look, Fitz.' The Doctor nodded to the grey hairy monster crouched in the mouth of the cave. 'See that red thing on her neck?'

I saw it, lit by the flames. 'What is that? Metal or plastic?'

'Both. As far as I can tell – my view was blocked a bit by her armpit – I think it's a DNA marker. The others have one too. *Someone* wants to be able to tell them apart from a larger herd. Part of a study of some sort.' The Doctor looked thoughtful. 'I wonder. Sometimes conservationists tag endangered animals to keep track of them.'

'Yeah, well.' I sniffed and almost choked on dried blood. 'That thing's endangered if I get my hands on it.' The Neanderthal growled at me and I woofed back sarcastically – in my head, at least. 'Come on then, Doctor. How do we get out of here?'

The Doctor smiled. 'Perhaps the conservationists who tagged these creatures will come to check up on them and rush to our rescue!'

'That's your plan?'

'It's my dearest wish, Fitz.'

'I see.' I nodded. 'We're stuffed.'

'Don't say that.' The Doctor looked at me, his eyes pale in the firelight. 'There's always Trix.'

It wasn't me who led the way up the ridge. I nominated Marcett, told him it would look good on his annual appraisal.

'Please, Jakarta.' His uniform was showing ever-larger sweat stains. At least I hoped it was sweat. 'Don't make me do this.'

'Sooner we're done here,' I told him, 'sooner we teleport back to Head Office and get our bonus.'

'There's a bonus?' Thredmeyer's pith helmet nearly shot up in the air.

Bacchari was suddenly in my face. 'Sorry, how much are we talking?'

Mmm, now *you want to hear the rules,* I thought. 'There's one thousand credits per kill on offer. And an extra thousand for whoever kills the most.'

'Just for shooting sims? What are you losers waiting for!' Thredmeyer was already marching up to the top of the rim. Bacchari scrambled after her while Marcett puffed and panted to catch up.

I couldn't blame them, I suppose; each of them barely pulled in a thousand credits in a year. Soon, all three of them were letting rip with their rifles, sniping at their target – and at each other: 'You missed!' '*You* missed. I got its arm.' 'Sorry, but I'm the one who's taking that thing down ...'

I heard a primal shriek rise over the gunfire, a sound I'll never forget. As I reached the rim I saw a hairy, distorted figure with an elongated head, like no life-sim I'd ever seen in the company brochures. It was wounded, bloodied, screaming with rage as it swung round to face us. And its eyes. Oh, god, its eyes. They were windows to its pain and fear.

Thredmeyer broke those windows with her disruption gun. The gun made a fierce hissing noise and the creature began to shake and smoke. It never stood a chance – just jerked into silence and fell face down in the dirt.

'Kill is mine!' Thredmeyer whooped. 'One thousand credits!'

But as the smoke cleared I saw something else. A woman, with pink skin and blonde hair, on her knees, clutching her neck. 'Stop firing!' I snapped.

Thredmeyer grinned at me. 'Why, Jakarta? To give you a chance to get the kill?'

'Whoops.' Bacchari fired off another laser round. The ground in front of the pink girl exploded and threw her backwards with an indignant shout. 'Sorry!' he called after her. 'Went off by accident.'

'She's only a sim,' said Marcett. 'You don't have to apologise.'

Bacchari shrugged. 'Sorry.'

'Everyone just stop a minute,' I insisted.

'We're meant to be hunters,' said Thredmeyer sulkily. 'You said it, yourself, Jakarta: sooner we clear the targets, sooner we can teleport back to the Company.'

'I'm not a target,' said the pink girl, getting up and brushing herself off. She held up her hands and walked up the hill towards us. Even from here I could see the red welts on her throat from where the hairy thing had grabbed her. 'No need for alarm. I'm here to make your job easier.'

'Who are you?' I said. 'You're no sim. The company has nothing like you on its books.'

'That's because I'm wildly experimental.' The pink girl smiled. 'Look, before you ask, we're here because you are.'

'Who's *we*?'

'Me and my two ... component sims. We're kind of an organic weapon. Load us into that big blue box there and watch us go off.' She turned to Marcett, who was sweating more than ever now, his healthy grey pallor drained almost to white, and gave a sympathetic cluck. 'You've no stomach for killing things, have you? So use us! Powerful enough to clear all your targets in one hit – so you take all the credit and none of the risk.'

'Sorry to stare.' Bacchari was looking the pink girl up and down. 'You look so real. You sound so real.'

'Clever, isn't it? Just wait till you see the other two. So lifelike.' She led the way over to a cave and gestured. 'They were taken in here by your targets. Remember, the sooner you clear those targets, the sooner you teleport back to the company ...'

Bacchari shrugged. 'I suppose we *are* here to test new weapons.'

I looked down at the still smoking corpse of the thing my team had killed so sloppily. All targets dealt with in one hit? That had an appeal.

'All right, we'll go in,' I decided. 'Marcett, you stay out here and keep watch. If anything follows us in there, you shoot it in the back.'

Marcett nodded. He looked terrible.

'You OK?' I said.

He let me know by closing his eyes and pitching forward onto his face.

Me and the Doctor, we heard the screams from our cosy little hellhole. The sound was distorted from echoing down god-knew-how many tunnels. We looked at each other as our hairy sentry roared in response and lumbered away. Quick as a flash, the Doctor held up his hands to me.

'Untied!' I breathed.

'Another one I owe you, Harry,' the Doctor murmured, setting to work on my own bonds. He'd just freed my ankles when we heard the sound of distant gunfire.

'Cavalry?' I suggested.

'Possibly, Fitz.' The Doctor stared into the darkness of the cave mouth as a bloodcurdling howl went up. 'Or else a whole new fire underneath our frying pan.'

As he spoke, the sentry came hobbling back inside, grunting and groaning. She was limping badly. Another hairy monster, bigger and shaggier, ran into the cave and gripped her arm, helped her to walk. He saw me and the Doctor up on our feet and his eyes narrowed, jaws opened.

'Run for it!' I yelled, and started away. But the Doctor didn't follow. He couldn't. I saw that his legs were still tied. He'd wanted to free me first. Of course he had.

The huge hairy creature left the wounded sentry and charged at the Doctor. The Doctor launched into a forward roll that carried him clear. 'Let me help her!' he commanded. 'I'm the Doctor.'

The monster ignored him and grabbed for me instead. I wasn't fast enough. It took hold of both my arms and lifted me up like a living crucifix ready to ward off evil – or two grey-skinned women in weird army gear, at least, as they came edging into the room.

'Let rip, Thredmeyer!' one shouted.

'No!' the Doctor bellowed. 'I'll deal with this.'

He didn't. Our sentry, wounded as she was, staggered towards the two women – who both opened fire. Red energy beams tore into the shaggy form. Then bursts of bright green light started exploding all about her, hurling her body this way and that. It was horrible. She fell beside one of the fires and still they went on firing. The Doctor was bawling at them to stop but the gunfire was so loud.

Then I was thrown aside, hit the ground hard. Winded, I saw the anguish on the face of the monster still standing. He took an angry stride towards the army girls but the Doctor hopped up behind him and brought down a rock on the red tag on its neck. There was a brief shock of blue and the thing went down clean and fast.

At last the gunfire died and I heard Trix's voice from beyond the cave mouth. 'Stop firing, for god's sake! You could hurt Fitz and the Doctor.'

'What the hell . . . ?' I breathed.

'Hell is other people,' said the Doctor, and bounced right on up to meet them.

My heart was hammering and my thoughts were scattered but I guessed the pink girl had lied to us as soon as the man came hopping over, all wild-haired and eyes flashing. Weapons are tools, their character is dispassionate – rarely excitable.

'Lasers, phosphor bombs *and* a disruption gun?' He broke the ties at his ankles and gestured to the corpse of the monster we'd just gunned down. 'All that against teeth, claws and a wooden club; a little excessive, don't you think?'

I found myself almost apologising. 'I couldn't turn my gun off.'

'And I didn't want to,' said Thredmeyer, 'till I was sure we were safe.' Her weapon was still raised and pointing straight at him.

The pink girl pushed past us. 'They're not trained killers, Doctor. I think they're accountants on an away day or something.'

'What is going on?' Belatedly, I remembered I still had my own gun and trained it on the other man. He was taller, thinner and miserable, hands raised high. 'I'm Glory Jakarta, Accounts Director, Combat Division. Who are you three?'

'Fitz Kreiner,' the miserable one offered.

'I'm the Doctor,' said the excitable one, 'and this is Trix. We're travellers.'

I stiffened. 'So. Not a weapon.'

'*So* not a weapon,' the Doctor agreed.

'Trix by name ...' She shrugged. 'Sorry to con you. I needed you to rescue my friends.'

'Oh, very clever.' I glanced at Thredmeyer, who was looking clammy and pale in the firelight. 'I suppose you're activists?'

'I suppose,' the Doctor said evenly.

I pointed at the other target sprawled on the floor. 'What did you do to that?'

'To *him*, you mean? I simply hit his identity tag to trigger the anti-tamper mechanism. When the tag thought he was trying to remove it, it stunned him.' The Doctor stared at me. 'He's alive. Are any of the others?'

'They killed one outside and one more in the tunnels,' Trix said.

The Doctor seemed to deflate. 'Then, he's the only one left.'

'Never mind all that,' I said. 'The three of you are trespassing on a Company-Owned Private Testing Range.'

'And you are taking innocent lives.'

'This planetoid has Open Hunt status.'

'It's closed. As of right now.' The Doctor crossed to the creature we'd killed and knelt by its side, fiddling with a sort of red tag on its neck. 'Did you know, this cave, the land outside, it's from the past? Ten thousand years ago, give or take a century.' He held up the red tag, his face lit up by data scrolling over its surface. 'Yes, and so is she. Scooped up with her three friends and dumped here on a weapons range, defenceless ... just so a team from

Accounts can massacre them all. Why? Why tag them, why these four ...?'

It was a fair question. I knew my answer wasn't. 'We ... well, my team gets a bonus, see ...'

'A bonus.' The Doctor rose slowly to his feet and I turned from the disgust in his eyes.

The other man, Fitz, called over, 'Your company has time travel then?'

'I knew Future-Tech wing was running experiments with Zygma beams but I didn't ...' I frowned, gripped my gun more tightly. 'Wait. There's only four, you say?'

'And four of you,' said Trix. 'Even numbers?'

I wondered why Thredmeyer had gone so quiet. When she sighed and fell down flat on her face, I had my answer.

As the clay-grey army woman fell down I took my chance. Fitz Kreiner, action hero! I ran full pelt at the one still standing, who swung round to cover me with her gun. But I could tell from her face she wasn't about to fire it. Trix had been right; this was no killer. I snatched the gun away from her, and she didn't resist.

'Put that thing down,' the Doctor said without looking up. He was studying the woman on the floor. 'Something is seriously wrong here.'

'You're a doctor, you say – will Thredmeyer be all right?' Jakarta was hugging herself. 'Same thing happened to Marcett outside, he just collapsed. No reason.'

'No reason?' The Doctor's muttered question was answered with a beep from the red tag he'd taken from the dead monster. It jumped from his hand as if drawn to Thredmeyer's neck, and stuck there. 'Oh. Wait a minute ...'

'What's going on?' Trix said uneasily.

'This Marcett.' The Doctor was staring at the tag as it flashed letters and symbols at him. 'He collapsed only after you killed the creature out there?'

'Yes,' Jakarta said. 'I left Bacchari with him.'

'I need to see them. Now.' The Doctor ran into the darkness of the tunnels. 'Come on!'

So we all ran after the Doctor, through the higgledy-piggledy blackness. I stepped on the body of the other monster they'd brought down, and muttered an apology, for what it was worth. When we reached the clearing outside, the corpse of the third shaggy monster was plain enough. But the bodies of two grey men, one fat, one thin, were less obvious.

They were fading and flickering, in and out of existence. Like solid projections, somehow, switching on and off.

'Marcett. Bacchari. It's me, Jakarta, can you hear me?' I felt sick at the sight of them swimming in and out of focus. 'Bacchari?' I thought he'd stirred.

His eyes opened, they seemed to glow. His face was cracking, starting to split. 'Sorry,' he whispered.

I reached out to hold his hand, but the Doctor held me back with a warning shake of the head.

'What's happened to them?' Fitz Kreiner asked.

'That tag I took from our sentry – you saw how it stuck to Thredmeyer? The creature's DNA was encoded onto it for identification.' The Doctor removed the tag from the slain monster in the clearing, then warily approached Marcett and Bacchari. Like a magnet held near metal, the tag flew from the Doctor's fingers and attached to Marcett's neck.

'See that?' The Doctor looked at me. 'It responds because Marcett shares DNA with the first of the creatures you killed. Like Thredmeyer shares DNA with the female in the cave.' He paused. 'Those creatures they killed are their own ancestors, thousands of generations back down the bloodline.'

Trix frowned. 'So, that Bacchari guy, he must be descended from the hairy thing we just stepped over back there?'

'Fair to say,' the Doctor agreed. 'Jakarta, if you'd care to go back to the cave, you can shake hands with your great, great, great, great, great et cetera et cetera great grandfather. If you'd killed him, *your* existence would be unravelling right now, same as your poor team.'

I felt the tears seep into my eyes as I stared at him, uncomprehending. 'They're going to die?'

'After what they've done, they were never born. Knock out just one of the generations, and none of the rest ever followed.'

'That's why they're flicking on and off like that?' said Trix.

The Doctor nodded. 'They're anomalous now. Ten thousand years of established history unravelling around them. They never existed – and yet they *had* to exist in order to have pulled the trigger.'

'But who would ever do this?' I was shaking. 'Why would they—?'

'Wake up, Jakarta,' the Doctor snapped. 'You work for a Company that designs cutting-edge weapons. A Company with basic time-travel capability.' He was pacing up and down, so angry. 'They must've had your DNA on file, went back in time to hunt down your own ancestors, brought them here – and then brought you here to kill them.'

Trix was keeping sickeningly cool. 'But why? It sounds more like a sick joke than anything else.'

'Theatrical, I agree,' the Doctor said. 'That personal touch. Almost as if ...'

'As if someone's getting a kick out of watching the whole situation?' Fitz Kreiner looked nervously about. 'Like we're not alone?'

'Something watching. Recording, perhaps. Transmitting?' The Doctor checked an electronic scanner of some kind, scrutinising it anxiously. 'Nothing living. Drones? Nanites ...?'

He was still listing possibilities when, with a flash of light and a searing stink of ozone, a humanoid robot, dark and devoid of any features, zipped into the clearing. It held a kind of metal wand out towards Marcett and Bacchari.

'No!' I started towards them, on instinct, wanting it to stop. But I found I couldn't move. My legs felt locked.

The Doctor began running towards the robot but it was like he was moving in slow motion.

Everything seemed to freeze, except for the robot. It waved its wand and my teammates were lifted into the air like jigsaw pieces cut carefully from reality. I felt my pulse pound just once in my chest, like this was all happening in a heartbeat.

I must have blinked, and when I opened my eyes the robot, Marcett, Bacchari ... they were all gone, and the Doctor was banging his fists on the ground where they'd lain. Ground that had turned black and scorched now, glowing with weird energy.

'That thing wasn't just recording.' The Doctor looked ashen. 'It was harvesting.'

'Harvesting?' Fitz echoed.

'Taking the anomalies it helped to create. Things that were once people, now paradoxes, taken to be repurposed, weaponised. Think of it − anomaly bombs deployed to destabilise whole tracts of space-time ... trapping whole space fleets, isolating star systems. The first prototypes of weapons for wars to be fought in four dimensions.'

Trix shivered. 'I don't think I want to think about that, thank you,' she muttered.

The Doctor just bolted back into the caves like a rabbit down a hole. Fitz and Trix went after him − I suspected they did that a lot − but I knew that Thredmeyer would be gone by the time we got there, and she was.

'That thing must have got enough material to be getting on with.'

'Video material?'

'Organic material.' The Doctor put his hands under the armpits of the creature he'd stunned. 'Give me a hand, all of you. Jakarta, we're taking your ancestor back to where he came from in the TARDIS.'

'And me?' I whispered.

'I think it's high time you resigned.' The Doctor looked across at me with the faintest of smiles. 'Don't you?'

Of course Jakarta couldn't go back. The Company had to know that after all the trouble they'd been to, they'd failed to turn her into one of their 10,000-year-anomalies. The Doctor dropped her ancestor back where he belonged, and then took Jakarta far away to somewhere else, to start again. He gave her a pouch of precious jewels from somewhere, enough to be comfortable.

'What about my life,' Jakarta said, and she looked just shocked, shattered. 'Everyone I knew?'

'Never try to contact them,' the Doctor warned her. 'You never know who could be watching.'

'This Company picked up Jakarta's ancestor once already,' I said slowly, once me and Trix and the Doctor were back in the TARDIS. 'What's to stop those evil sods trying again?'

'Us,' said the Doctor simply, working the TARDIS controls with fastidious precision.

He took us straight to Head Office, of course. Made the TARDIS land right in the middle of the boardroom, square on the bosses' table. But it was a bumpy landing. The TARDIS yowled like a whale with a toothache.

'Even here, there's time distortion.' The Doctor fought with the controls. 'They don't know what they're meddling with.'

'They're gonna know,' I muttered.

The TARDIS landed at last and out the Doctor stormed, ready to hand them hell.

Only there were no bosses. No one to see. Only strange shadows burned into the walls and floor. The place had been done over. The penthouse roof had been ripped clean off.

The Doctor's anger turned quickly to disbelief. 'Looks like the Company's been liquidated.'

'Can't we take the TARDIS back in time a bit and see what went on—?'

'No,' the Doctor growled. 'You saw the trouble we had landing at all. The time distortion was designed to seal off this place *and* this timeline.'

'Look at this.' Trix was pointing to a grainy 3D bubble in one ruined corner of the boardroom: some sort of TV projector thingie was showing grainy footage of Jakarta and her team blowing apart the creatures. We saw Bacchari collapse beside Marcett. We saw Thredmeyer lying on the floor, phasing in and out of existence. Me and Trix and the Doctor had been edited out. The footage ran on a loop.

'It's like they were pitching their weapons to potential buyers,' Trix went on. 'A demonstration with a cute human interest angle – or grey-skin interest angle – for their clients.'

'Or even bidders at auction,' I supposed. 'But what the hell actually happened here?'

'Karma,' Trix suggested.

'Beams of intense high-energy.' The Doctor gestured to the dark marks and smudges around the place, all that remained of the board members. 'No mercy shown.'

'A double-cross?' Trix sounded approving. 'Maybe whoever wanted these weapons decided that slaughter was an easier option than paying the bill.'

'Or maybe it was a pre-emptive strike.' The Doctor was looking at a roughly triangular hole blown in the wall. 'Or a strike in revenge for atrocities committed in the future.'

I frowned. 'The future?'

'If those weapons are used,' said the Doctor, 'the laws of time will be thrown to the wolves. It could be the end of everything. Really, everything.' He shivered. 'And every time.'

'You'll find who did this, and put it right.' I didn't really get why he was so down about this, but I tried to reassure him. 'You saved Jakarta, didn't you. And her dear old hairy ancestor.'

The Doctor sat heavily on the floor. 'In a war of time, there'll be so many that I can't.'

'Then you'll save who you can,' I told him firmly. 'You're the Doctor. And that's never going to change. Right?'

He looked at me, and there was something in his gaze that gave me chills. Then he just stared up at the night sky through the ruined ceiling, at the thousands of scattered stars.

'Funny, isn't it,' I said to Trix, trying to lighten the mood. 'We know it's stars that make the lights in the night ... but what makes all that darkness?'

'You'll see,' the Doctor whispered.

Decoy
George Mann

The Time Lord fleet slid out of the vortex, Battle TARDISes piercing reality like so many flashing knife blades, puncturing the gloom.

Below, the string of gas giants that comprised the Althos system were immense and colourful baubles, atmospheres swirling with bubbling storms of incandescent gas.

At the command dais of the lead Battle TARDIS, General Artarix peered out upon the starscape with a bristling sense of uncertainty. 'Adjunct, report. What news from our scanners?'

'Nothing, ma'am. All temporal and gravitational fields remain consistent.' A pause. 'If they're out there, we can't see them.' The Adjunct kept his voice level, but Artarix could tell he was worried. They were utterly blind, and the enemy could be anywhere, any time.

Artarix tugged unconsciously at her collar. Out there, somewhere in the infinite darkness, lurked a Dalek armada. Of *course* the Dalek ships weren't showing up on the scanners – they never did. They'd be safely nestled in a pocket dimension, waiting for the perfect opportunity to strike. Waiting until the Time Lords were at their most exposed.

Artarix had seen first-hand the new horrors being employed by the creatures from Skaro – twisted, malformed examples of their kin, extracted from redundant timelines and forced into service, vicious and babbling and half-insane – and now they'd concocted some grotesque plan to mine the rare gases from these tertiary, uninhabited worlds, to use them to power their so-called 'epoch bomb'. At least, that's how the Lord President had put it: a weapon that could obliterate entire eras.

There was no doubt: they had to be stopped. The coming encounter could represent a turning point in the war. Fail here, and the Daleks would prove unstoppable. And yet the thought of facing down that terrifying flotilla made Artarix's skin crawl. Recent successes had proved scarce. The Daleks were closing in. Soon enough, if they were not stopped, Gallifrey itself would be assailed. The thought didn't bear thinking.

Artarix turned to the figure beside her at the console. The man was short for a soldier; ragged-looking, dressed in anachronistic clothing appropriated from twenty-first-century Earth – a leather coat, loose-fitting trousers, boots and scarf. The lines upon his face spoke of decades of conflict, and his rheumy eyes brimmed with deep sadness. Here was a man, Artarix considered, who bore the weight of regret. A man who had been forced to become the very thing he despised. Perhaps it was that reluctance that had made him such an effective leader. His presence here had certainly quelled any lingering doubts amongst the troops, inspired them to adhere to the mission briefing, despite the risks. If the *Doctor* was leading the mission ... well, it was practically a given they'd succeed.

'We're ready, sir,' said Artarix. 'Shall I give the order to move in and secure the system?'

The man turned to regard her. His eyes were hooded, thoughtful. 'No. Not yet, General. Let's just sit here a while, shall we? No point rushing into these things.'

Bemused, Artarix nodded. 'Adjunct – tell the fleet to remain in formation until I give the order.'

'Aye, ma'am.'

'And Adjunct?'

'Yes, ma'am?'

'Watch the skies. The enemy know we're coming.'

'You're bloody audacious, I'll give you that.'

Rassilon did not turn away from the window, but a wry smile twitched at the corner of his mouth. '*Doctor*. Ever the one for a dramatic entrance.'

The Doctor – dressed in rumpled shirt, red and white scarf bunched under his chin, battered leather coat hanging loosely from his shoulders – crossed to where Rassilon stood, his brow furrowed. 'I've told you not to call me that.'

A guard – who until now had been silently watching the exchange from the doorway – took a step forward, levelling his stave. Rassilon sighed, raised a gauntleted hand, and the guard retreated to his station.

Finally, he turned to face the newcomer. 'Then what *should* I call you? I've heard the Daleks have a name for you. They call you the Deathbringer. Or the Predator. Or from time to time, the One Without Mercy.'

'And I dare not say what they call you, Rassilon, for fear that your guards may never look at you the same again.' The Doctor sounded irritable. 'But we both know that's not why I'm here.'

'Indeed. I gather some traitorous member of the High Council has made you aware of my little scheme.'

'Replacing me with an Auton clone? Do you really think that'll fool Artarix, or anyone, for long?'

'Long enough for them to fulfil their purpose,' said Rassilon. 'That's all that really matters.'

'Long enough to die,' spat the Doctor. 'Long enough to be led unwillingly to their utter annihilation.'

Rassilon shrugged. His tone was placatory. 'Tell me, what choice did I have? If the Daleks were to secure the Althos system, within days they'd have the capacity to obliterate us. *To eradicate Gallifrey from history.* They cannot be allowed to deploy their epoch bombs.'

'So you send thousands to their deaths, all to lead the Daleks into a trap.'

'A decoy,' said Rassilon, 'while the rest of the fleet lays in wait, to play the Daleks at their own game. The decoy will draw them out. Then they shall be annihilated.'

'Little consolation for the families of those who'll die to see your plan enacted. For those such as General Artarix, who's served her people – *your people* – with unswerving support for centuries.'

'This is *war*, Doctor – as you're so very good at reminding us. And war costs.'

'If you've replaced me you can replace the whole army with Autons!'

'The Daleks will be scanning for our life signs, you know that. You know how paranoid they are.' Rassilon paused. 'We sacrifice the lives of the few to ensure the survival of the many.'

'Pah! Schoolboy philosophising. I've heard the same words uttered from the lips of a thousand tyrants on as many worlds. It always ends the same way.' The Doctor sounded more tired than angry, now. 'What I cannot countenance, what I refuse to allow you to do, is to send those men to their deaths believing that *I'm* there by their side. That I'm the one who willingly led them to their deaths. Call it off. *Now*.'

'You know I can't do that, Doctor. For some reason, those soldiers actually *believe* in you.' Rassilon shook his head. 'I cannot for the life of me fathom why.' He shrugged. 'And yet, I suppose we must all believe in something. That Auton clone – think of it as a mercy. Instead of being terrified, those men and women go to their deaths brimming with pride, for they fought alongside the *Doctor*. And in doing so, they helped arrest the Dalek progress in this interminable war.'

'But it's not me, is it? It's a poor facsimile. How's that going to help them when the Daleks come hurtling out of the night?'

'It is not,' said Rassilon. He turned his back on the window and the view of the glittering Capitol beyond. 'But it is done. And you, Doctor, didn't even have to get your hands dirty. You should be thanking me.'

The Doctor's jaw worked as he fought back the rage that was threatening to overwhelm him. '*Thank* you? I should strike you down now.'

'Come now. That would be a terrible waste ... for us both.'

The Doctor stiffened and glanced at the guards; there was little more to be said. 'One last chance, Rassilon. Call it off.'

Rassilon laughed. 'I think not.'

'Then all that follows is on you,' said the Doctor.

'General. Long-range scanners are picking up movement at the far extent of the system.'

'Put it on screen, Adjunct.'

'Aye, ma'am.'

Above the central dais, the ceiling of the Battle TARDIS dissolved in a shower of fragmenting light, revealing a tumbling view of the starfield beyond. Artarix watched as the image slowly resolved and magnified.

'The Daleks are showing their hand,' said the Doctor, his voice a low growl. Sure enough, Artarix could just make out an array of Dalek saucers, flitting into formation on the far side of the system. Accompanying them were a plethora of bizarre craft – mined, once again, from those redundant timelines created by the war; the result of untold Time Lord interference. Artarix saw vast, silver globes, bristling with antennae and weaponry; dart-like ships that resembled nothing so much as enormous Dalek eyestalks; blue and gold cylinders rippling with round nodules that seemed to have a life of their own; a cannon so large that its main shaft was suspended between four huge Dalek saucers, lashed to rigid supports. It fizzed with iridescent light, and it was pointed directly at the Time Lord fleet.

If they'd followed their orders and moved in to secure the system, they'd already be in range. As it was, the Doctor had prevented a massacre by holding them back.

'Sir,' said Artarix, attempting to disguise the tremor in her voice. 'Do you intend to engage the enemy fleet?'

The Doctor was busying himself at the console, his fingers dancing lightly over the controls. 'Not now, Artarix. Can't you see I'm busy?'

'Yes, sir. My apologies. It's just that—'

'We're greatly outnumbered? Outgunned?' The Doctor moved around the console as he worked, checking monitors, inputting coordinates. 'That the odds are stacked against us and we're most likely going to die?' He looked up, met Artarix's gaze. 'Those are the sort of odds I *like*, General.'

'Then you mean to attack?'

The Doctor grinned. 'I mean to blow the Daleks to oblivion. Just not in the way you imagine.'

Rassilon tipped the head of his staff, indicating the door through which the Doctor had entered just a few moments earlier. 'I've had enough of your posturing and empty threats,

Doctor. While I cannot deny the contribution you have made to the war effort, I will *not* tolerate your continued insurrection.'

'Insurrection? You'd call me a traitor now, Lord President?'

'You've always been of a rebellious disposition, Doctor, but your lack of respect is wearing. I suggest you leave before you erode what little patience I have left. I am tired of your games.'

'Games?' The Doctor looked incredulous. 'You gamble with the lives of thousands, care nothing for their sacrifice, and yet you accuse me of game playing?'

Rassilon glowered at the Doctor, brows knitting. His gauntleted hand twitched ominously. He raised it slightly by his side, and then allowed it to fall. 'I presume you still remember how to show yourself out? Or should I have my guards remind you?'

'Oh, I won't be needing the door,' said the Doctor. 'But before I leave, credit where it is due. I owe you my thanks.'

'What are you babbling about?' said Rassilon.

'Decoys.' The left side of the Doctor's face seemed to sag, as if suddenly it were struggling to maintain cohesion. 'Oh, you had the right idea. But as usual, it was somewhat poorly executed.'

Rassilon took a step forward, confusion clouding his face. Before his eyes, the Doctor slumped, slouching forward, his whole body – jacket, scarf, boots included – now drooping, becoming malleable, fluid-like.

'What is this?'

But the Doctor was beyond answering. He'd somehow given up his form, melting into a loose, swirling puddle of molten plastic on the floor. It bubbled as it flowed across the marble, until it lapped at the edges of Rassilon's boots. Colours swirled, formless and glistening.

'Guards!' bellowed the Lord President, spittle frothing on his lips as he turned, furiously, towards the two Time Lords standing in the shadow of the doorway. They looked on at the unfolding scene, utterly bemused. 'Don't just stand there! The Doctor's got to be here, somewhere. Find him! Now!'

The Doctor – the *real* Doctor – ducked through the cloisters beneath the Panopticon, bundles of small, black globes clutched in the crook of his arms. The sound of marching feet caused him to duck hurriedly behind one of the pillars, and one of the black globes dislodged itself from his grasp, rolling along the extent of his forearm, threatening to tumble to the ground.

'No, no, no!' hissed the Doctor, as he deftly shifted his position, causing the black globe to reverse its potentially fatal trajectory and return, with a soft *click*, to join the other proximity mines he had gathered in his arms.

He'd appropriated the devices from the Time Lord armoury while his Auton duplicate had no doubt been baiting the Lord President in the halls above, but the game was up now, and alarm klaxons had begun blaring throughout the Capitol as Rassilon ordered out his guards. Now, they were hurrying to and fro like good little soldiers, seeking the Doctor in all the usual nooks and crannies, rather than spending their efforts worrying about the Daleks, or the terrible sacrifice that Rassilon was foolishly about to make of their kin. Such was the way of the Time Lords – none of them had the backbone to stand up to the fool in charge. None, perhaps, save from Artarix, and the Doctor had no doubt that was the reason the General had been chosen for this ridiculous suicide mission to the Althos system.

Well, he was about to put a stop to that.

The sound of running feet receded into the distance. Slowly, the Doctor emerged from behind the pillar. Across the cloisters, the glowing 'Police Box' sign of his TARDIS was a welcoming sight.

He made a beeline for it, trying to ignore the drifting shapes that cavorted amongst the shadows – the remnants of Time Lords whose regenerations had failed, who'd become lost in that strange, interstitial state between life and death. This was their crypt, their eternal home – or rather, the place where the other Time Lords hid them away from sight, so that they might be ignored. These were the ghostly figures who appeared in the fairy tales told to children at night; cautionary tales of what they might encounter if they wandered too far from home, or what might become of them, too, if they misbehaved.

Just as he reached the TARDIS door, the Doctor turned, glancing back over his shoulder, to see a guard duck beneath one of the low arches, pistol in hand, levelled in the Doctor's direction. The man's eyes were wide and terrified. He wore the ceremonial uniform of the Lord President's guard, and he looked as though he wanted to be anywhere else but there, in the cloisters, with a pistol pointed at the Doctor.

'I wouldn't fire that if I were you,' said the Doctor. 'Unless you want to set off an armful of proximity mines beneath the Capitol.'

The guard simply continued to stare at the Doctor, the barrel of his gun wavering in his trembling hand.

'Look, I'm not the enemy here. No matter what that silly old fool says, flouncing about with his staff and his robes. I'm trying to *help*.' The Doctor sighed. 'Thousands of Time Lords are about to be sent needlessly to their deaths, all because Rassilon can't see another way. But he's wrong. There's *always* another way. Good men and women will die out there if you stop me now. I can't countenance a sacrifice on that scale. Can *you*?'

For a moment the guard remained frozen in indecision, but then the Doctor's words seemed to permeate into his terrified brain, and he gave a short, sharp nod. He lowered his weapon, took a step back towards the arch from where he'd come.

'All clear back here!' he bellowed to his colleagues, unseen amongst the pillars and cobwebs and swirling dust.

'Good man,' the Doctor muttered, before ducking into the TARDIS. The door swung shut behind him.

Moments later, the cloisters were filled with the unearthly breeze of the vortex as the ship gave its elephantine roar, and dematerialised.

'Sir, I'm not entirely sure what you mean. How can we blow the Daleks to oblivion if we're not even planning to engage the armada?'

The Doctor smiled. 'What's more terrifying to any Dalek than a Time Lord flotilla, Artarix? No matter the size or scale. No matter the weaponry and ballistae and all the grand strategies in the darned world?'

Artarix frowned. 'I ... I don't know, sir.'

The Doctor stood back from the console, turning to face her. She had a sudden sense of unease, as if something untoward was about to happen, right there on the dais of her ship. 'I'll tell you, General. An angry man in a box. That's what.'

'I'm still not sure wh—' she started, but ceased abruptly as the Doctor's face began to *melt* before her eyes, left eye slowly sliding down to merge with the cheek, beard being swallowed by the collapsing chin, head ominously sinking into the torso, until all that was left, moments later, was a bubbling pool of liquid plastic on the floor, dripping through the metal grilles to the lower level. 'Doctor?' she said, stepping forward, dropping to her haunches to examine the bubbling mess that had, only moments before, been lecturing her on Dalek fear.

She glanced up at the Adjunct, standing by the monitors on the other side of the dais, a horrified expression on his face. 'Living plastic. An Auton ...?' She rose, peering up at the star scape above, at the massive Dalek armada arranged on the far side of the brightly-coloured chain of planets. 'What were those final commands he entered into the system?'

The Adjunct tapped at the console. 'A withdrawal pattern, ma'am,' he said. 'Designed to pull the fleet back to a position on the outer reaches of the system.'

'Execute that command,' said Artarix.

'Ma'am ... are you certain?' said the Adjunct, clearing his throat. 'It's just ... can we trust a creature of the Nestene Consciousness over the word of the Lord President?'

'That was no simple Auton,' said Artarix. 'Do it. Now.'

'Affirmative, ma'am.'

The Battle TARDIS juddered into motion, while, around it, the command went out to the rest of the fleet, infiltrating their navigation systems, causing them all to fall in with the general retreat.

'Whatever it is you're doing, Doctor, I hope you understand what's at stake,' whispered Artarix, peering down at the lump of molten plastic by her feet.

'Ma'am – the sensors are picking up movement. A new vessel has entered the system, in low orbit around Althos II.'

'On screen.'

The canopy image pivoted and then magnified, closing in on a small, rectangular object as it skimmed across the pink-hued atmosphere of the largest gas giant, before spinning away again, up into high orbit, its trajectory taking it on a curving intercept course with the next planet in the long chain. It was difficult to discern from this distance, but it looked to be blue with a tiny flashing light ...

'Is that ...?'

'Yes, ma'am. It's a Type 40 TARDIS. It's him.'

'What is he doing? He'll have the whole armada on top of him any moment.'

The Adjunct grinned. 'I rather think that's the point, ma'am.'

Inside the TARDIS, the Doctor wrenched a lever, releasing the final scattershot of proximity mines into the atmosphere of a red-hued world. On the monitor, he watched them plummet, pockmarking the gas clouds like a shower of deadly raindrops.

With a sigh, he turned his attention to the Dalek armada, which was already stirring, sliding steadily forward, taking up attack formations. Here was the chance they'd been waiting for. The Time Lord fleet was withdrawing in the face of superior Dalek firepower, and now, the Deathbringer, the Predator, was alone, waiting for them at the heart of the Althos system. He knew all too well how Dalek minds worked – they would be wary, but triumphant, as they closed in around him. No stray extermination rays, no miscalculated shots that might scare him away – the Daleks wanted him alive ... at least for a while.

With a shake of his head, he punched a flashing button on the console – one that he'd been ignoring for the last few minutes, because he knew exactly what it meant. With a crackle of static, Rassilon's voice suddenly burst out of the speaker trumpet mounted on the side of the control panel.

'You must think yourself so very clever, Doctor.'

'It's not about me, or you, Rassilon. That's what you never seem able to grasp. It's about *them* – the thousands of people whose lives I'm about to save. Nothing else matters.'

'But what of the thousands more at risk because of your imbecilic interference? You know what the Daleks will be capable of if you allow them access to those gas reserves.'

The Doctor circled the console, checking readouts as he spoke. 'It won't come to that. You'll get your win. The Dalek fleet will be destroyed. Without the cost.'

'And what did it cost *you*, Doctor, to undo my little arrangement with the Nestene Consciousness?'

'In return for them creating the other duplicate and giving me the power to control them both, I agreed to fight for them when the time comes,' said the Doctor. 'If I survive.'

'Ah, and there we have it. You've always been too willing to throw yourself in harm's way, Doctor.'

'And you, Rassilon, have never been willing enough.'

The Dalek fleet was drawing closer now, a spiral of saucers and never-ships forming a tight corridor around the TARDIS, cutting off the escape route in all conceivable directions. At the heart of it, the Doctor waited, patiently allowing the spiral to grow, ever outward, until the saucers were brushing the atmosphere of the nearby planets ...

The deep, resonant growl of a Dalek echoed throughout the control room. The walls seemed to vibrate with every syllable, and the Doctor winced, clasping his hands over his ears. 'Predator. Doc-tor. Your time ship is surrounded. There is no escape. You are now a prisoner of the Daleks.'

'Oh, right you are,' said the Doctor, fiddling with a dial until the volume of the interminable sound was lowered. 'I've been meaning to pop round for tea and a chat, actually.'

'You shall submit to Dalek questioning, or you shall be exterminated.'

'So, no tea, then? Perhaps a scone?'

'I repeat. You are now a prisoner of the Da-leks.'

A sound like rending metal. The crack of an entire planet suddenly sundered. Through the canopy viewer, the Doctor could see the red-hued planet ignite in a terrible ball of flame as the Dalek saucers crowding in triggered the proximity mines, igniting the flammable gas in the atmosphere and turning the entire world into a raging inferno.

Spouts of burning gas ejected from the planet, engulfing vast swathes of Dalek ships, detonating them in clouds of super-heated metal.

'What is this?' demanded the Dalek voice, shrill and outraged, now. 'Report! Report! Repo—' The transmission ended in a low burr.

The Doctor peered up at the canopy screen as the chain reaction flowed through the Dalek armada, burning wreckage tumbling into the path of the other, nearby gas giants, triggering further mines, igniting more of the terrible gas. Within just a handful of minutes, the entire system was ablaze.

'And there you have it, Rassilon,' cried the Doctor. 'There's your win.'

As the firestorm swept in on the TARDIS, the Doctor yanked a lever and the engines roared, ripping the ship through the heart of the conflagration, punching out into the vortex, where it spun, steaming, away into the nothingness outside of time and space.

Aboard her Battle TARDIS, General Artarix stared in wonder at the burning star system far below. The entire Dalek armada had been engulfed in the explosions, not to mention the seven uninhabited worlds that had been their target. The Doctor had been right – one angry man with a box had taken down the biggest Dalek threat she'd ever seen, while simultaneously preventing them from securing the means they'd required to alter the course of the war.

No, not one man.

One Doctor.

He'd saved thousands of lives.

'I'm picking up no readings, ma'am. All of them ... they're gone. Not a single survivor,' said the Adjunct.

'And the Doctor's TARDIS?'

'Negative.' A pause. 'Do you think he made it out of there?'

Artarix smiled. 'Of course he did.' Returning her attention to the console, she tapped in some familiar coordinates. 'Now, Adjunct, give the order. Let's go home. I want a word with the Lord President ...'

Grounded
Una McCormack

Ben Finch was grounded. He'd been messing around with the football, and all right he was quite close to Missus-Townsend-from-next-door's, but he'd promised Mum that he wouldn't do anything stupid, yet somehow the kick had gone wrong and there'd been a horrible moment which seemed to go on for absolutely AGES while the ball saaaaaailed through the air and then:

SMASH. SPLINTER. CRASH.

And there it was: Trouble (and Ben knew that was a capital 'T' if ever there was) and sure enough out came Missus-Townsend-from-next-door, and she moved faster than you'd think anyone of her age could move (his brother Michael said he thought she must have WHEELS) and she was *screeching*:

'Ben Finch! Don't you think I haven't seen you, young man! Where's your mother, you little rogue!'

After that, there'd been a hazy few minutes where Missus-Townsend-from-next-door was shouting, and Mum was trying to calm her down, but Ben could see she was getting cross with Missus-Townsend-from-next-door because she had said sorry, and had made Ben say sorry (at least FIFTY times), and she had offered to pay (twice), but

Missus-Townsend-from-next-door was still going on about hooligans and the neighbourhood going downhill, and Ben could see Mum's lips getting thinner and the pink spots starting on her cheeks ...

He felt a big hand, calm and protective, come down gently upon his shoulder, and his dad's voice, quietly in his ear: 'Come on inside, Ben. Let your mam sort this one out, eh?'

He sloped off gratefully with Dad, but he still knew he was going to be grounded.

And he was.

There'd been a daytrip planned, all four of them going out as family, and now he couldn't go, which meant Dad couldn't go, which meant it wasn't a family outing now, and the thing that made him crossest was that he had *known* when he went outside with that stupid ball that he was pushing his luck and probably wasn't being careful enough, and now Mum was cross and Missus-Townsend-from-next-door was cross and Michael was cross because the family day out was spoiled and Dad ...

Well, Dad never got cross. Chances were he was glad not to have to go out so he could go and mess about in his shed ...

'Are you sure you'll be all right, Clive?' Mum said, as she picked up her bag and the car keys.

'What? Oh aye, me and Ben'll be fine. We'll find something to do, eh, won't we, Ben?' He patted his son on his shoulder. Ben stuck his hands in his jeans pockets and his bottom lip out.

Michael rolled his eyes. 'It's your own fault, you idiot. Come on, Mum, let's leave them to it.'

The door closed behind them. The house was suddenly very quiet. Dad was rocking back and forth on his heels, clearly keen to disappear.

'Oh, go on,' said Ben. 'Get off to your shed.'

Dad perked up. 'You sure?'

'I'm sure.'

'What'll you do?'

Ben sighed. 'I suppose I'll watch telly.'

Dad's mobile phone beeped. He took it out and peered at the message. 'Ah. That was your mam. She says, *"No telly"*.'

So no telly after all, and since the follow-up message said '*And that includes video games*', Ben was quickly bored. He picked up a book or two, flipped through them, but that felt far too much like work, so in the end he went outside and kicked a ball around. How daft was that? It was the football that had got him into this mess in the first place, but Mum hadn't banned that. Instead she'd banned telly ...

Still, it wasn't much fun on your own, and of course he wasn't exactly taking any risks, so it was all boring. Boring, boring, boring. He glanced over at the door of the shed. Dad had been in there all morning. Dad would spend all day in his shed if you let him, searching the internet for more information about the Doctor. Dad was weird like that. Ben thought about asking him to come out and kick the ball around with him, but ... No. Not Dad's thing, and, honestly?

Dad was likely to put the ball through another of Missus-Townsend-from-next-door's windows, and then they'd probably have to LEAVE TOWN, maybe enter WITNESS PROTECTION, and have to get FAKE IDENTITIES ...

Ben giggled. That might be fun.

Suddenly, the door to the shed opened, and Dad came out, blinking in the light. He saw his son, and smiled. 'Aye, aye, Ben, how are you doing?'

'All right.' Ben looked at him hopefully, wondering whether they might find something do to. 'What're you up to now, Dad?'

'Me?' Dad rubbed his hands together. 'Ah. Yes. Well, Mr Palmer's on his way over.'

He trotted across the garden and back into the house. Ben rolled his eyes. Mr Palmer. The nuttiest of Dad's nutters.

Mr Palmer was tall and thin and a bit bald, and even though he was SO OLD he thought he was in the army. Michael reckoned he'd never been in the army at all. 'They'd never let a nutter like that in,' he said.

Mr Palmer sat at the kitchen table, watching Dad make two cups of tea. Teabags; water fresh in the kettle. ('Sure that water's fresh, Clive?' said Mr Palmer, when Dad switched on the kettle. 'Has to be fresh. Water parasites. Give you terrible gyp.' So Dad had emptied out the kettle, and filled it up and chucked that lot of water out for good measure, and then filled it up again.)

'Black, isn't it, Terry?' said Dad.

'Always black,' said Mr Palmer. 'Never know if there'll be sugar on manoeuvres. And don't trust the milk.'

See? The nuttiest of all the nutters. And this wasn't the nuttiest thing about him.

'What's brought you here, Terry?'

Mr Palmer sipped his hot black freshwater tea. He eyed Ben and then jerked his head towards the garden. 'Need to know, Clive,' he said, and stood up. 'Not for the great unwashed.'

'Oh aye, yes,' said Dad, and followed him outside and down to the shed.

Mr Palmer, see, was the UFO nutter. Absolutely, completely, and utterly the nutterliest nutter of them all. Still, Ben was short on entertainment this morning, so after the shed door was closed, he tiptoed down the garden and stood at the door of the shed, ear pressed up against the wood. At least he could have something funny to tell Michael when he got home.

The trouble was, he couldn't hear much. He pressed harder against the door, and that's when he heard Dad say, 'Aliens?'

Oh, for heaven's sake, Dad, he thought, and suddenly he felt cross that Dad believed all this rubbish, and that people like Mr Palmer encouraged him in it, and he sensed, vaguely, that this was going to be a pain in the neck when he got to Big School, and without thinking, he said, 'Oh, give over!'

The voices inside stopped. Ben froze. The door opened, and he toppled into the shed. Mr Palmer was staring at him.

'Always someone listening,' he said, in a gruff voice. 'Walls have ears. Doors too.'

Dad smiled at Ben. 'You all right, Ben? Bit fed up?'

Ben nodded, miserably.

'Aye, well, let's think of something to do this afternoon, eh. I've been stuck inside here all morning, haven't I. Not much fun for you.'

Mr Palmer gave Dad a sharp look. 'You not coming with, Clive?'

Dad shook his head. 'Poor old Ben here's got himself grounded, haven't you, son? So we're hanging out together round the house today, aren't we?'

Mr Palmer frowned. 'Don't want you missing this one, Clive. You're the man for the job.'

'Aye, well.'

Ben looked at his dad, who was trying to put a brave face on things. It was clear that wherever Mr Palmer wanted to go, Dad really wanted to go with him. Even if it was somewhere daft, and, to be honest, probably on the nutty side of daft.

'Dad,' said Ben. 'I'm bored. Really bored. And so are you. I'm really sorry about, well ...' He nodded towards Missus-Townsend-from-next-door's. 'But can't we *do* something.'

Dad looked at Ben, then at Mr Palmer, who nodded encouragingly. And he caved. 'All right,' he said. 'But don't tell your mam, or neither of us will ever get to leave this house again. And that includes you, Terry.'

Mr Palmer mimed zipping his lips shut. 'Mum's the word.'

*

The next thing Ben knew he was sitting in the back of Mr Palmer's old car. It smelled of dog. Ben had never seen Mr Palmer with a dog, but somehow the car smelled of one. An old, wet wheezing dog. 'This car's like something out of a museum!'

'Shush, Ben!' said Dad, embarrassed. 'Kids, eh, Terry?'

'Wouldn't know,' said Mr Palmer. 'Ford Granada, Ben. Fine car. Always buy British.'

'*Ford?*' said Ben. 'Wasn't Henry Ford American?' Nobody answered. Oh, well, it was better than hanging around the garden, so Ben sat back and enjoyed the ride.

To the rec.

'Oh, you're kidding me,' he said, when Mr Palmer parked up next to the ice cream hut (which wasn't open for another six weeks). 'I thought we were going somewhere good!'

He clambered out of the back. Mr Palmer opened the boot and started lifting out all kinds of kit and handing it over to Dad.

'Dad,' muttered Ben, 'we're not going up Everest.'

'Yeah, well, who knows what we're going to find, eh?'

Ben shoved his hands into his pockets. Grudgingly, he followed Dad and his nutter round the rec. They came here almost every day after school. He might as well still be at home. He kicked a stone listlessly along the familiar path.

Mr Palmer was slightly ahead. He had put on some huge old headphones, like something you'd see in Nanna and Grandad's house, and he was stalking along the path, a compass in one hand and some weird box in the other. Ben closed his eyes for a moment. He hoped nobody from school was here to see this. When he opened his eyes again, he saw Dad smiling back at him. Then Dad nodded his head in Mr Palmer's direction, and winked.

Suddenly, Ben understood. Dad was *humouring* Mr Palmer. He was being *kind*. He caught up with Dad, and took hold of his hand.

'All a bit of fun, eh, Ben?' whispered Dad.

'I guess so,' said Ben. He couldn't help smiling. They walked after Mr Palmer, stopping when he stopped, watching him listen and crouch and wander about ... They sat on a bench overlooking the duck pond and ate the sandwiches that Mr Palmer had brought with him (*'Dad,'* whispered Ben, *'what's in these sandwiches?'* Dad, mouth full, muttered, *'Potted beef'*), and passed round a tartan Thermos filled with lukewarm black tea. Mr Palmer chewed everything carefully, even the tea, and sat for a while fiddling with the dials on one of his weird gadgets. Then he jumped up, and strode off across the grass to a huge tree standing there. Ben and Dad brushed off the crumbs and hurried to catch up with him. The tree's branches were so big and old that they came down to the ground, making a kind of den.

'Go on, then, Clive,' said Mr Palmer.

'Eh?' said Dad, and then: 'Oh, me first, is it?' He pushed up one of the branches with his big hand, like he was lifting the flap of a tent.

And something moved. Moved quickly. Shoved Dad out of the way and sent Mr Palmer flying. Ben didn't get a good look (it really was moving very very very fast), but it was small, and it was strong. Dad got his balance back, and put his hand on Ben's shoulder, keeping him close.

'Quick!' yelled Mr Palmer, chasing after it, wires trailing. 'It's getting away!'

After that – well, it came in handy that Ben knew the rec so well, and knew in particular all the places where somebody small might be able to hide when they didn't want big people to find them.

They went up and down all the paths that Ben had known ever since he was toddling around trying to catch up with Michael, while Mum held on to his hands and Dad held on to the reins, and one of them was always there to pick him up and give him a hug if he fell and scraped his hands.

They ran around the playground, with the big swings and the little swings, and the slide where Michael had nearly got into a fight with that big boy who was sitting at the bottom stopping the littlies from going down and making them cry.

They ran around the bowling green with its trim bright grass and a handful of old lags who watched them go past and shook their heads and carried on with their impenetrable game.

They did three circuits of the cricket pitch, because someone small could hide in the bushes that went all the way round, and then did five circuits of the pavilion for good measure. (Dad was seriously huffing by now, though

Mr Palmer wasn't showing any strain, and Ben was in his element.)

They crossed the brook and zipped up and down the allotments, waving at Mister-Brown-from-the-corner (who, Mum said, was there all the time and probably went to the allotments on Christmas Day, and Dad would mutter, 'I would too if I was him'). Then they crossed the brook again, back into the park, bumping into friends, and friends' mums and dads, and neighbours out walking the dogs, and all the time they tried not to get caught up in conversations without making anyone *in the least bit suspicious*, or as best you could when one of you is overweight and bright red from all the exercise and another of you has wires trailing around all over him ...

Last of all, they came to that funny piece of abandoned land near the big wall that backed up against the old folks' home. There'd been a miniature railway here, once upon a time, long before Ben and Michael were born, and Dad reckoned it hadn't been running for twenty years at least. There the trees grew, lazy and unbothered, and it was like walking into a strange old forest. Ben and Michael had had some brilliant games here, hiding amongst the trees, leaves and bits of branch crunching underfoot. And the best thing of all was that you would suddenly find leftovers of the old railway: pieces of track stuck together, flagstones from what had once been a little platform. Old bits of rusted metal with flecks and flakes of bright paint – greens and blues and reds. ('It's like we're living after the world has ended,' Ben would say; and Michael would say, 'That's called the Apockerlips,' because he liked to show off with words. 'You sure?' said Ben. And Michael nodded. '*Apockerlips Now*,' he said. 'Dad was watching it the other night.')

Anyway, it was here, in this strange, unworldly place, that they finally caught their quarry. It was hiding behind a big tree, but it was shuddering and shivering so much that it couldn't disguise where it was: all the leaves of the tree were shaking.

'Dad,' said Ben quietly. 'I think it's scared.'

Carefully, Dad lifted away the branches. And there, sitting on the ground with its arms covering its head, was something small, and tired, and lonely, and frightened. And definitely, definitely, alien.

'Aye aye,' said Dad, in a kindly voice. 'Who do we have here?'

Slowly, Dad took a step or two forwards. The creature whimpered.

'Dad, I think you're scaring it!'

Dad lifted his hands, palms out, to show he wasn't carrying anything. 'It's all right,' he said to it. 'Look. Nothing in me hands!'

'Dad, I don't think it can understand you—'

Mr Palmer tapped Ben on the arm. 'All in the tone of voice,' he said softly. 'Leave it to your Dad.'

And Dad kept on moving forwards, until he was a couple of feet away from the creature. Then he lowered himself to the ground, kneeling opposite, and smiling. 'See? Nothing to be afraid of. Big daft lad, me. Eh, I don't blame you running away, the three of us chasing after you like that, but we're trying to help.'

Something seemed to be getting through, Ben realised. Maybe it was in the tone of voice after all. And who could be scared of Dad? You always felt better when Dad was around. He was big, so the kind of people who would cause trouble didn't mess him around, but he was gentle too, so the kind of people who found themselves scared knew they were safe around him. He gave off a kind of safe feeling ... And the alien was picking up on that too. It lowered its arms from its head, and sat staring at Dad.

'That's more like it!' said Dad, with a big grin. 'Now, let's see if we can get you talking. Terry, anything in that box of tricks of yours?'

Ben turned to Mr Palmer, who had pulled something out of his rucksack, and was fiddling with more dials. 'What's that?'

Mr Palmer grunted. 'Listen.' He twiddled another knob, then said, 'Introduce yourself, Clive.'

'What?'

'Your name. Say hello.'

'Oh, right.' Dad turned back to the alien. He put his hand on his chest. 'Hello. I'm Clive.'

And Ben's jaw dropped when the alien said back, 'Clive. Hello, Clive. I am—'

Well, that bit all sounded like a jumble of clicks and chirrups to Ben's ears, and Dad looked like he was having some trouble with it too. Mr Palmer thumped the box. 'Woolworth's,' he muttered, darkly.

'Say that again,' said Dad.

'Faylt,' said the alien.

'Faylt?' said Dad. 'Well, hello there, Faylt. That's Terry, and that's my son, Ben. We're here to help you.'

Well, after that slight hiccup, it turned out Mr Palmer wasn't so nutty after all. He opened up his rucksack and pulled out all sorts of gadgets and whatchamacallits and thingummies and ('*What's that one?*' said Ben, and Mr Palmer said, '*That one? That's a doodah.*' He winked. '*Technical term.*') and doodahs.

Meanwhile, Clive sat hunkered up next to Faylt and chatted. Faylt had arrived a week ago, it turned out, on board a ship that had come to study life here on this planet. But they'd had to leave in a hurry, and Faylt had been left behind. Wandering about, Faylt had lost track of the original landing site, and couldn't find a way back there, and didn't know if anyone was still looking for their lost crewmate.

'Definitely are,' said Mr Palmer, looking up from the doodah. 'Past week. Lots of air traffic. I've been keeping track – always keeping track. Know what the patterns are like.'

'What's that mean in layman's terms, Terry?' said Dad.

'There's been something scanning the area for nearly a week now,' Mr Palmer explained. 'Rather like they're looking for something they've lost.'

Dad smiled at Faylt. 'There you are! They've not abandoned you! They're trying to find you! I bet they're worried about landing again, or something.'

Faylt nodded, and gestured to the doodah. Mr Palmer handed it over. Faylt played with it for a while, and then suddenly a series of chirps and clicks emerged from it.

'There you are,' said Mr Palmer. 'They know where you are now. And look—' He pointed at the display. 'They're sending us coordinates. That's the other side of the park, over the brook and past the allotments.'

'Well, there we are then!' said Dad, cheerfully. 'Let's get you over there then, shall we, Faylt?'

'Er, Dad,' said Ben. 'Faylt's kind of ... Well, *alien*.'

'Oh yes,' said Dad. 'Ben, lend it your hoodie.'

It wasn't much of a disguise, but if you trotted along quickly enough and didn't stop to chat to friends and friends' mums and dads and neighbours out walking their dogs, you found you could get to the other side of the rec pretty quickly. The sky was overcast now, and nobody was about, only Mister-Brown-from-the-corner, grubbing about with his compost. They waved, and hurried past, and came to an empty patch at the far end of the allotments, where people came to do bonfires and that kind of thing.

Suddenly, Ben felt a strange warm wind upon his face. 'Stand back!' warned Mr Palmer, and all four of them jumped back. There was a *whoosh*, and then Ben sort of half-saw and half-didn't-see a kind of shape, no bigger than

Mr Palmer's Ford Granada. It shimmered, and suddenly he saw it clearly for a second: a little shuttle – here, on Earth, an *alien* shuttle – landing to collect their lost friend. Dad bent down and gave Faylt a big hug, and the little creature dashed ahead, and up the ramp, turning to wave goodbye. Then Faylt went inside, and the warm breeze started again.

Mr Palmer cleared his throat. His eyes, thought Ben, looked suspiciously damp. 'Good job, troops,' he said.

Back across the allotments, Ben saw the lonely figure of Mister-Brown-from-the-corner standing and scratching his head. Then he shrugged, went into his shed, came out again with a trowel, and resumed his poking at the compost.

They walked slowly back through the rec to Mr Palmer's car, each one lost in his thoughts. Mr Palmer drove them to the Co-Op, and Ben and Dad ran around and picked up tea like Mum had asked them to. (Going to the Co-Op did not count as breaking bounds when you were grounded – funny how the rules worked.)

Back home, Dad said, 'How about a cup of tea, Terry?'

'Wouldn't say no,' said Mr Palmer. 'Black. No sugar.'

Ben sat at the table and ate biscuits. After a moment, Mr Palmer lifted something out of his rucksack and placed it on the table. Lots of wires again. Something swirling round on the display, all black and white, like one of those magic eye things. Ben couldn't take his eyes off it. He saw Dad staring at it too. 'Eh, Terry, what's that?'

'Don't worry about it, Clive,' said Mr Palmer. 'But thanks for all your help today. I knew you were the man for the job. You're the best advert for Planet Earth I can think of, Clive.'

The swirling patterns seemed to expand and fill the room until there was nothing else that Ben could see. Something in his brain decided that was quite enough for one day, and ...

Ben blinked. He looked round the kitchen. Dad was sitting there, yawning hugely. Mr Palmer was there too, dunking a digestive into his tea. He looked at Ben. 'I think you nodded off, young man,' said Mr Palmer. 'You too, Clive. Says to me you're not getting enough exercise.'

'I think you're right, Terry,' said Dad. 'Eh, look at the time! Your mam and Michael will be back soon. I'd better get the tea on!' He hauled himself up from his chair and went to turn on the oven.

Mr Palmer finished his biscuit. 'Nice day,' he said.

'Yes, it was, wasn't it?' said Clive. 'Say "thank you", Ben.'

'Thank you,' said Ben glumly, although he didn't think going for a walk around the rec was all that much fun.

Mr Palmer smiled at him. 'Not much of an adventure, was it, Ben?' he said.

'It was all right.' He looked at Dad. Actually, it had been nice to go out with Dad, not have him in stuck in the shed all afternoon, but instead just hang around together. Even if it was only a walk in the park. 'Actually, it was fun. And not like being grounded.'

'Eh, now that's a point,' said Dad. 'Terry, don't go grassing on us to Ben's mam and brother. Or we'll both be stuck in this house for life.'

Mr Palmer tapped his nose. 'Mum – or *Mam* – is the word,' he said. He stood up and stretched and left, wires trailing behind him.

Dad smiled at Ben, who smiled back. Yes, it had been fun. And if the ice cream hut had been open, it would have been perfect.

'That Terry, eh?' said Dad. 'He really is a nutter, isn't he?'

Still, Terry was the first friend of Dad's to come and visit after what happened in the shopping centre, and he went and found Ben, sitting on the patio, looking down at the shed.

'Lovely man,' said Mr Palmer, sitting down beside him. 'Rotten luck. Rotten blasted luck.'

Ben shrugged, but then he realised how nice it was to have someone say that this was all awful and terrible and not try to say that things would soon be better. Because they would never be better again. And then he realised that Mr Palmer was holding something in his hand, something black and white and swirly ...

And it all came back to him. All of that afternoon. Every last bit. Potted beef sandwiches. Chasing round the rec. The little alien. And Dad – being Dad, so that nobody got frightened, and everyone got home in time for tea.

Mr Palmer stood up. He looked down at Ben and gave him a sad smile. 'Couldn't have done it without your dad,' he said. 'Kindest man I've ever met.' Then he tapped his nose. 'Mam's the word, Ben,' he said gently, and went on his way.

So Ben didn't tell anyone else. He wrote it all up as a story though, and Mrs Armstrong made him put it into a competition. It won first prize and after that he started writing lots of stories, and he found that when he was writing stories he felt better about things, so he wrote more and more of them and eventually got very good at it indeed.

But it all started here.

Best day ever. Best Dad in the world. Best Dad in the universe.

The Turning of the Tide
Jenny T. Colgan

Corin had fallen asleep under the apple tree, a breeze ruffling his hair. He'd had a late night helping deliver a baby down Dubris way when they couldn't get an ambulance on time. Rose Tyler glanced down at her huge pregnancy bump and rubbed it thoughtfully. Good that he was getting the practice in.

She was lumbering around the house now, it was ridiculous. He hadn't even wanted her getting up the little stepladder, but he also knew better than to ever tell her not to do something, and she filled her apron with apples then went to drop them in her basket.

She took a bite out of one – they were so shiny and tempting – and almost instantly realised she'd made a huge mistake. A maggot hole appeared, and she immediately spat out her mouthful in disgust.

'There's no need to spit,' came a small peeping voice. 'I'm totally sterile.'

Rose looked around. 'What?' she said. Who had said that?

'Down here,' said the voice.

Rose glanced at the ground, stupidly.

The voice sounded irritable. 'Hello?'

Finally, Rose looked at the apple she held in her hand. Poking out of it was a worm. Not a brown organic worm, but a long sliver of articulated metal, which was waving about as if trying to get her attention.

'How are you talking to me?' she said. 'You don't have a mouth.'

'Speaker,' said the worm. 'I'm not a real worm. Can't you see I'm made of metal? And can talk? Without having a mouth? Yeah?' Now, the voice had turned rather peevish.

Rose glanced at Cor, who was fast asleep. 'But how ... how did you get in there?'

'Implanted as a seed, Rose Tyler.'

'To the exact apple you knew I'd pick?'

The worm snorted. 'No! Durr. Really? How would that work, then? No, there's lots of us. But only I got activated. The rest will start degrading into nothing, now. Right, can I speak to the Doctor, please?'

Rose couldn't help her instincts. She glanced at the figure – prone, long legs stretched out, completely and utterly relaxed – the man beneath the apple tree.

Then she blinked.

'He's not here.'

'I can see him over there.'

'You don't have any eyes.'

'I have robot sensors! Which are better than eyes, actually.'

'You're very sensitive for a worm.'

'You're very insensitive for someone who has all their senses on the outside of their body.'

There was a pause. Rose sat down on the steps, holding the apple carefully. 'That's not the Doctor,' she whispered.

The worm waved his head around. 'It looks a lot like him,' he said.

'It does,' said Rose, absentmindedly stroking the worm on his head.

'Ooh. Nice,' said the worm, snuggling in.

'It's not even a "him",' Rose went on. 'I just call him "him" for easiness.'

The worm tilted his head over the top of Rose's finger and rotated it in the air. 'It *smells* like him,' he said.

'I know!' said Rose, pleased. 'Weird, innit? Honestly ...' She was finding it odd to confide in a tiny robot worm, but then who else could she confide in? She lowered her voice. 'If he hadn't smelled the same, I couldn't have done it. I just couldn't have. He smells the same now, he smelled the same the last time he looked different ... Well, someone else looked different ... Long story.' She sighed happily. 'But yeah. He smells the same, that familiar mix of graphite, lime and diesel.'

Suddenly a monstrous honking sound blasted out of the tiny creature. Rose jumped back, startled. Corin sat bolt upright.

'Run!' he shouted. 'Run! Everyone! *Run!*' He blinked, gradually coming back to himself. 'Ah,' he said, rubbing his eyes.

He frowned and squinted as the tiny worm pulled himself up to his full height (eight centimetres) and *Hoooonnnnnnnnkkk!* let out another huge noise.

Corin looked at him fixedly. 'You're a very loud worm,' he said, standing up and shaking out his long limbs.

'I'm not calling you Doctor,' Rose had said to him, early doors, and he'd blinked.

'No. No. OK.'

There was a new aura of nervousness to him she hadn't known before; he was as adrift in his new life, she knew, as she was in hers.

She blinked, too. Nobody ever got everything they wanted.

'OK,' he said, looking around as if he had somewhere else he thought he ought to be. 'What do you want to call me, then?'

Rose thought about it. 'Oh my god, it's like naming a dog.' Her face cracked in a huge grin. 'Benjie!'

He smiled tentatively in return. 'Nooo?'

'Rex!'

'This is not funny!' he said, tracing a circle in the sand with his shoes. 'Names are very important things.'

'I agree,' said Rose. 'This is serious.' She looked thoughtful. 'Fido?'

He finally laughed then, and that was good.

It was just like when he regenerated, Rose told herself furiously. Same person, just looked different. Or in this case, different person, looked the same. She handled that, she could handle this. Couldn't she?

'You choose, then.'

He frowned and returned his attention to the sand. 'I've always liked Cassiopeia. It's such a beautiful system, so majestic, so glowing.'

'I'm not calling you Cassiopeia!'

He glanced up to where in the sky it would be, and panic gripped Rose's heart. Would he care? All the time, every day, that he was trapped, in one world, in one universe? She wasn't having him named after somewhere he could never go again.

'No,' she said shortly. 'Try again.'

They could not agree, but it was a useful pastime, through the long nights of that Nordic springtime, after Jackie and Pete had departed, Jackie squawking so hard Rose thought she'd crack a glass; as they'd walked together, played a little push-pull game of question and answer – scars and memories – inside jokes they still, to Rose's delighted surprise, shared.

He knew her – well, half of him did. And she knew half of him too, and they just had to meet in the middle.

And the new side was gossipy and chatty and funny, like having a hilarious girlfriend by your side. Rose was surprised and entirely relieved to find how much she liked it.

They bought herring and good rye bread and snorr, and he built a fire and they sat round it and ate elderberries and drank aquavit, and talked and talked and talked and she tried not to think of how he was born in fire and war, or what the future would hold, or how he was – or wasn't.

It was only occasionally she found him outside the hut, sitting on a rock, oblivious to the night cold, one leg swinging gently, and she would go up to him and take his hand and wonder whether she could possibly be enough.

On the last day, they closed up the quiet, clean, bare little hut they had rented and gave back the key – which they hadn't even used – to the quiet man in the general store.

'What's your name?' asked Rose, on impulse as they were leaving.

'Corin,' the man said.

The stranger she knew so well looked at her, and she looked back at him.

'I like it,' she said. 'Solid and true.'

He smiled sadly. 'Half of me,' he said, 'was exactly like that.'

'Both sides of you,' insisted Rose. 'Both sides of you.'

And he looked at her with such desperate pain in his eyes, such a sudden desire for everything to be all right, such naked worry about the future, that suddenly, in a flash she found she had fallen in love with a completely different being altogether, and the moment he was christened was the precise moment it had happened.

'Come on, Corin,' she said. 'Let's go home.'

'What's home?' he said.

'Dunno,' said Rose. 'Shall we make it up as we go along?'

And now – after two years and 195 fights about hair gel; one set of medical exams breezed through from him, turning him into a GP; an application for a diploma in Early Years care for Rose, despite her mother howling that she didn't have to work, darling, just come shopping and by the way would you mind terribly looking after Tony (a monster of epic proportions) for four days whilst she and Pete took a private zep to Malaga; a quick relearning of the history of this universe, two steps to the left all the time (although on the plus side, ice cream counted as one of your five a day) – now, they had finally settled in the oast house in what in Rose's old universe had been called Kent but here was called Canticum.

The house was at the end of a very quiet lane, had gardens and an orchard and a view across the French Channel. It was calm, secluded and private and helped soothed Cor's troubled mind on nights when he stood out in the garden, staring at the sky. And Rose – who knew, who missed it too – would go close to him and slip her hand into his, and they would stare at the stars and she would lean her head against his shoulder and whisper, 'This isn't so bad, though.' He would turn and look at her and pull her into him and hold her close and grin that very wonky grin and say, 'Oh, no,' and everything would be all right again. And as for the anger, when that came on – rarely, but it did – well, she had a way of dealing with that too.

'I'm putting you down,' said Rose to the worm, placing him carefully on top of the steps.

'Doctor!' said the worm, his high peeping voice taking on a declamatory turn, clearly reciting from a pre-prepared script. 'If you are receiving this message, there has been sufficient rainfall to ripen my craft, and danger ... is ... imminent!'

Rose and Corin looked at each other. Rose couldn't hide a slight but definite, flicker of excitement.

Corin knelt down in front of the tiny robot. 'You know, I'm not the Doctor.'

The worm waved his head around. 'You *smell* a lot like him.'

Corin gave a puzzled glance at Rose, who grinned and gave him the thumbs up.

'You're in the wrong universe,' sighed Corin. 'Easy mistake to make.'

'How?' said Rose, suddenly worried. 'There aren't holes opening up again, are there?'

Corin shrugged. 'Must have fallen through before the last breach closed up.'

'I've been here for a year,' the worm affirmed. 'Feeling the apple grow.'

'Wow,' said Rose. 'Wasn't that boring?'

'How could that be boring?' said Corin and the worm simultaneously.

'Well ... you can give me your message,' said Corin, 'but ... I don't ... I mean, there's nothing I can do.'

'Doctor!' said the tiny worm, starting again. 'If you are receiving this message, there has been sufficient rainfall to ripen my craft, and danger! Is! Imminent!'

*

'What is it?' said Corin, and Rose bit her lip. He knew, right, didn't he? He knew he didn't have his sonic, or a TARDIS or anything he needed to do clever jiggery-pokery stuff. She didn't want him getting ... ideas above his station, she supposed.

'Cask Men,' said the worm. 'They scooped out the five diamond oceans, and they're heading for you next.'

'They can't be.'

'All the ice is melting, they said. Easier to get.'

'They can't ...' Corin glanced at the little creature. 'Your people sent a robot from ... the five diamond oceans. Ugh, why can't I remember? I can never bloody remember! I can name all of Kim Kardashian's husbands and read shorthand – *shorthand* – but ...'

'Leffluit,' said the worm.

'Of course!' said Corin, smacking his head with his palm. Then he straightened up again. 'Is Leffluit ...?'

'It will not have taken my creators long to die,' said the worm. 'But it would have felt long enough.'

Corin covered his eyes with his hands.

'Can I have another cuddle, please?' said the worm. 'I liked it.'

'Um, sure,' said Rose. She cleaned the remaining apple off the worm and coiled him round her apron halter. Then she looked at Corin. 'Is this bad?'

'Oh, yes,' said the worm.

'Cask Men, Cask Men ...' Corin muttered. 'Hang on. Let me think. They're ... God, it's foggy ... I think the water dried up on their planet. So they learned how to raid. Steal what they needed. They scoop up water. Sell it to planets who are running dry. It's very lucrative.'

'To suck up all the water in the world? Is it like … a really big hoover?'

'No! Yeah! A bit.'

'Why don't people steal it back?'

'It's a numbers game. Most beings can only go 24 hours without water. Cask Men can go six weeks, so good luck fighting back. Ooh, which reminds me: I need to drink eight glasses a day, Dr Hillary said on *GMTV*, and I keep forgetting. So should you. It's so *boring* water, isn't it?'

Rose rolled her eyes.

The sun was setting to the side, streaming orange and green through the leaves of the orchard, even as clouds were spreading overhead, coming in from the sea. There were more apples than they could ever eat. Was there a worm in all of them? Rose wondered.

Corin rubbed his eyes. 'How much do you know, Worm?'

'Do you have to call me Worm?' said the worm. 'You guys have names.'

'What's yours?'

The worm's head went down. 'I haven't got one.'

'Names are hard,' said Rose, and Corin nodded his head emphatically. 'Well, you came to Earth in a pod,' she went on, noticing the worm's dejected neck hanging down. 'From somewhere else. Ooh, like Superman.'

'I like "Superman"!'

'I don't think we could call you Superman. But we could call you Clark.'

Clark tilted his head. 'OK!' he said and wriggled down into the pocket of Rose's apron, keeping his head out.

'The Cask Men ...' Corin was still frowning as they made supper in the ramshackle little house. 'What are their ships like? How will we know?'

'You can't remember?' said Rose sympathetically.

'It's in there somewhere,' grimaced Corin. 'I just can't ... I know, they're pirates, but I thought they were kind of a myth. I wonder if they're from that universe or this? I don't suppose it matters. There's a poem ... Cask Men, Cask Men, whilst you sleep ... Cask Men, Cask Men ... can you put low-calorie sweetener in the pie?'

'Rubbish poem,' said Rose.

'No, I just thought, can you put low-calorie sweetener—'

'No. It's foul.' She looked at the worm. 'Do you know, Clark? What the ships are going to look like?'

Clark shook his head. 'Sorry. I left in a hurry.'

'It's somewhere in the gloom,' mused Corin crossly. 'I just can't see it.'

He sat bolt upright, just before dawn.

'It's somewhere in the gloom,' he repeated. Then he jumped out of bed.

Rose looked at him blearily. 'What?' she said. 'Where are you going?'

'To the lighthouse,' he said.

Rose followed him outside. A sea fog had rolled in and visibility was terrible.

'Let me drive,' she said.

'Go back to bed,' said Corin, putting the phone down, but his voice was kind. 'You shouldn't be up like that.'

Rose huffed crossly. 'Don't be stupid. And I'm the better driver.'

'Well I'm not having *this* argument again,' said Corin.

Clark poked his head out of Rose's pyjama pocket. 'Ooh, an outing!'

'Did you have that worm in the bed? I thought we weren't going to be having small things in the bed.'

'Let's discuss that later,' said Rose, pulling her dressing gown closer in the damp chill. It didn't meet round her waist.

In fact, he drove the little Fiat in the end, Rose finding it too difficult to fit her arms round her bump to the steering wheel. The back lanes were quiet as they drove with their full-beam headlights on, eyes occasionally popping up in the hedgerows.

Clark popped his head up. '*Something moved!*' he said excitedly. 'Something inside your tummy moved.'

Rose and Corin looked at each other warily.

'Is there something inside there?'

'Yes,' said Rose. 'A baby.'

'You're growing it?'

'Yup.'

'Just like me!' The little neck dropped. 'Will it get bitten out?'

'No,' said Rose. 'Well, I hope not.'

'And you're happy about it?'

Again, the exchange of glances.

'Yes,' said Rose firmly. 'Yes, we are.'

'Hang on,' said Rose as they reached their destination, a tall black and white building on the side of a cliff. 'I've been here! On a school trip! This isn't a lighthouse, it's Dungeness! It's a museum! It hasn't worked in years!'

Corin shook his head as a tall bearded figure opened the door in the tower, waving. 'That was back there. Here, it's different.'

'Foggy evening,' said the tall man carefully.

Rose bit her lip. She'd never met a real-life lighthouse keeper and was quite excited about it.

'How are the bunions?' asked Corin.

'Much better, thank you, doctor.'

Rose winced inside but didn't show it.

'So what's this commotion?' The lighthouse keeper, whose name was Tam, looked at his wristwatch.

'Yeah, sorry,' said Corin, not looking remotely sorry. 'It's the fog. I think ... I think there's something to be seen in it.'

'What do you mean?'

'Well, if you follow me ...'

Corin hopped his way up the stairs. Rose sighed.

'You don't want to be climbing all these steps,' said Tam kindly. 'Are you sure you wouldn't rather a cup of tea downstairs in the kitchen?'

'I'm coming,' said Rose steadfastly.

Corin looked at her. 'Are you sure ...?'

'I'm *fine*,' said Rose, puffing her way up the steps crossly. She reached Corin. 'You do better with me,' she said quietly. 'You always do.'

He looked nervous, then squeezed her hand quickly. 'I know,' he said.

Corin bent his head down to the telescope, then sighed.

They were in the great control room, beneath the mezzanine that held the huge lamp, keeping their eyes away from it as it swung round above their heads.

'I can almost glimpse it,' he said, nearly to himself. 'Tam, can you focus the beams?'

'What, stop the lamp turning? In the fog?'

'Just for a few minutes. This could be important.'

Tam sighed. 'Just for a moment or two.'

He went upstairs and pushed a few levers on the ancient control panel, and the light gradually slowed then finally stopped altogether, facing the front.

Immediately Tam's radio barked on and several other voices were heard, some with French accents.

'All of them,' said Corin, grabbing the mike. 'All of them! Hey! Sorry, this is the ... Tam's friend. Hi. Listen.' He smiled to himself briefly. 'Ooh, seriously is this just a bunch of men living all by themselves in very tall constructions?'

'Not now,' said Rose swiftly.

'50.9193° north, 0.9653° east,' said Corin, concentrating. 'Could you possibly all focus your beams for a minute, please?'

There was some dissent until Tam came back on the mike. 'It's a medical emergency,' he said. 'Apparently.'

The code between lighthouse men was strong and deep. Up and down the coastline Rose watched the great sweeping lights, the beams that crossed and danced in the fog-laden darkness, gradually come into line across the channel. It was an entrancing sight, the scale of the beams moving into position, one after another after another until, they were all holding steady, pointing towards an obscure dot in the fog right in the middle of everything.

And then everyone stood back and held their breath.

'What ...?' Tam moved forward until his nose was practically touching the glass.

'Oh yes, there they are,' peeped Clark cheerily. 'OK, can you get rid of them now, please, Doctor?'

Rose was too flabbergasted even to respond. She stepped forward too.

Hidden – no, it wasn't hidden – *hanging* in the sky was a vast spaceship made of swirling cloud and fog. Every so often, if the light trained on it, she could almost make out what had to be rivets or joins, but they would shimmer in and out of focus, in shifting greys and blues. The sheer size of it was hard to comprehend: it looked as wide as the sky. It was quite beautiful and intangible as smoke.

'Well. That's interesting,' said Corin.

'What are you going to do about it?' asked Rose anxiously.

Corin frowned. 'Not sure. Might try knocking and asking nicely?'

Clark *eeped* loudly and dived back into Rose's pocket.

Tam reluctantly agreed to take them out to a dim, windy sea fort a little way out in the channel. He waited in the boat while they hurried across to where the clouds appeared to touch the turrets.

It was a concrete, haunted, abandoned place that oddly reminded Rose of distant planets. She climbed up behind Corin, watching his coat flick behind him as he advanced into the broiling mist, brandishing an incredibly bright lantern that Tam had given him. She reached out a hand to touch the cloud. At first it felt like it would drift away like smoke. But no, her hand could feel it, solidly beneath her palm: metallic and solid.

Corin arrived at something that may or may not have been a door, and turned at the last minute. 'Do you think we should have brought them some muffins or something? Everyone likes a muffin.'

'Go! Go!' mouthed Rose, ushering him on.

Corin sighed, lifted his lantern and, with his left hand, banged heavily on the side of the spaceship.

He did it again. The entire great edifice – and it was impossible to tell where it ended and the real clouds began – rippled and shimmered and suddenly, slowly, a door opened. Or, more accurately, a hole appeared, the clouds blowing away like smoke, and the interior of the ship was revealed.

It was green and blue, like an aquarium, undulating gently as if on waves, plants and foliage climbing over the internal roofs.

Rose scuttled along to join him and they stared inside. It was as steamy as a jungle. 'Why is it so hot?' she asked.

'Water plus engines, I suppose,' said Corin. He poked his head a little forward. 'Hello? Hello?' His voice echoed a little damply.

'They know we're here,' said Rose. 'What are they doing, sharpening up their spears?'

'They don't use spears,' piped up Clark, poking his head out. 'They use power-water blasters. That sounds like it should be fun. But it is *not* fun!'

'Oh, good,' said Rose. She took a step forwards. 'Hi there!' she called into the spaceship.

They held their breath, as if underwater, when they heard footsteps approach. Rose glanced down. They were a long way from the wild, churning sea. Inside, she felt the baby kick and her hand instinctively moved to her stomach.

'Please go home,' muttered Corin.

Rose shook her head. 'No,' she said. 'If this goes wrong we might not have a home to go to.'

Two figures approached from the rippling shadows. They were bipedal, but larger than humanoids; bare-chested, with huge twisted cords of muscle on their arms and shoulders. Their necks were short with thick, rope-like veins sticking out and coiling up to their large, lumpy heads. Their skin was a desiccated orange colour; a faded brightness, like tangerines turning powdery in a bowl.

Rose glanced at Corin. When they – when *she* – had travelled in the TARDIS, it had had a universal translator. What would these aliens speak? Could they make themselves understood?

As they approached, she heard them rumble and bubble to one another. It didn't sound like a language at all to her. She and Corin glanced at each other in a panic.

'Um, hello?' said Corin, and got a deep rumble in response.

'Ah,' said Clark, poking up his head. 'Allow me.'

'Can you understand them?' asked Rose.

In response, Clark grew a fresh head, just the same as the first, like a wormy hydra. 'One for receiving, one for speaking. Bring me close to your ear.'

So Rose sat Clark on her shoulder, and suddenly the Cask Men's rumblings made sense.

'Who the heck are you yippees?' was the first thing she heard.

'Hello,' said Corin again. 'We're inhabitants of this planet who want to know what you're doing here.'

The two Cask Men looked at each other and started to laugh.

'Never you mind your narrow head,' said one. 'Don't worry about it. Just go back to bed. It'll all be over soon.'

Corin and Rose glanced at one another and, in response, stepped over the threshold. Rose gasped.

The ship opened out into a vast space, a beautiful vista. Everywhere was water. There were waterfalls tumbling down the sides of the walls, interpolated with thick green plants; great still pools covered in water lilies. There were hot, bath-like pools with steam rising off them that looked incredibly inviting to bathe in; fountains tinkling merrily; and a lazy stream winding its way round the machine consoles, that was crossed everywhere with little wooden bridges. Fat orange fish drifted contentedly around the room and, from the open mezzanine deck, which held more controls, there was a spiral waterslide connecting it to the ground floor.

'Wow,' said Rose.

Corin squinted. 'Can I speak to whoever is in charge?'

The men laughed again. 'Festle,' shouted one, and a lithe shape – which looked to Rose to be female, although who could say – slid down the waterslide and stomped over. Her orange skin was half-covered in a tight casing of ochre and gold. It was difficult to say if this was clothes or more skin.

'You spotted us,' said the newcomer. 'You're not really meant to. You're supposed to wake up in the morning and find all your seas run dry. We tend to try and leave before the begging, the bargaining, the praying, all of that.'

'What do you do with the water?' said Rose, seeing a large window on the far wall. Crossing it, she saw an endless, hollow, cloud-shaped canopy – obviously the hold of the ship. It clearly went far beyond what she could see.

'At first we took it home,' said Festle. 'We were working off-planet as miners; we had the tech and our world badly needed it.'

The other Cask Men grunted.

There was a pause.

'But by the time we got back things had got worse. The animals were pulling the skeletons apart to try and drink the marrow.'

'I'm sorry to hear that,' said Corin. 'Why on earth would you do that to another planet?'

'Ah ...' said Festle. 'We found that it was ... lucrative.'

'Lucrative?'

'Planets dry up all over the place. Erosion, groundwater consumption, overconsumption ... a lot of species use up their natural resources. We provide more.'

'But why do you have to leave these unwilling donor planets with nothing?'

Festle looked at him as if he was stupid. 'Because it is kind. Trust me, if you take half, you'll just leave a planet in a state of total war and it'll take about six months before the life-ending weapons come out. We just speed the inevitable process up a bit. It's a quick death. Usually.'

Corin scratched his head. 'End-stage capitalism in action.'

'Life,' said Festle. A frog leaped out of the green undergrowth and balanced on her hand. She patted it gently with her orange fingers. 'Life in action.'

'You can't do this,' said Corin. 'There are 7 billion people living here.'

Festle shrugged. 'There were forty billion on Anthracite,' she said. 'Believe me, it's not personal.'

Corin walked over to the control panel. 'I'm afraid we'll have to stop you.'

'Oh!' said Festle as the other Cask Men started to laugh. 'Nobody has ever thought of that before!'

Corin stood below the console, slowly trying to figure it out. If only his brain would work faster! If only. He screwed up his face. How did they do it? How did they lug all that water across space?

Oh, curses, for his screwdriver. He'd tried to build one, but Rose had told him off for it and then distracted him and he'd abandoned the project. Now he truly wished he hadn't.

'Hmm.' He reached up. 'If I just have a fiddle ...'

Festle's voice ran out loud and clear. 'Excuse me! Don't touch my ship!'

'Just admiring its elegance,' said Corin.

'It is beautiful, isn't it?' Festle looked around with some satisfaction. The frog had vanished back into the green rockeries, but a parrot flitted over their heads, its cries loud in the echoing cloud chamber. 'But I'm afraid I have to ask you to leave.'

'And I'm afraid we can't …'

Without warning, there was a click in the floor. The last thing Rose and Corin saw was the Cask Men's laughing faces, as the floor beneath their feet dissolved like the fog it was and they dropped from the sky with a vast sudden drenching of a rainstorm from the cloud.

Rose's first instinct was to protect her bump with both hands before she entered the water, even as she realised, belatedly, that this would turn her into a cannonball. In fact, that was pretty much the ideal way to enter the water from a height six storeys up, all told. Corin, not one of life's natural swimmers, belly-flopped mercilessly and did rather a lot of what Rose generally classified as 'Donna-swearing'.

Within minutes, Tam was zipping towards them in his boat through the bouncing surf.

Rose surfaced cold and shocked, but surprisingly buoyant. 'We're OK! We're OK!' she screamed as the friendly lifeboat man hauled her into the rib and wrapped them in blankets, handing them mugs of hot tea.

Corin, however, was sitting in the bow, dripping and furious. 'You're not coming with me again.' He leaned forward, staring at her. 'Do you understand? I can't … we can't risk …'

Rose looked at him directly. '... whatever this is?'

'Of course not,' he said. 'That wasn't what I was going to say.'

'You didn't have to! Don't talk about our baby like that!'

'I didn't!'

Rose flushed, chilled as she was.

They had never been able to talk about it. The scans had seemed fine even if his biology was ... well. Who knew. Who knew. And he couldn't talk about it. At all. Had ignored her growing bump, or treated her as one of his patients: diffident; distracted, telling her to eat her spinach or to get some rest. He hadn't even decorated a nursery.

'Listen,' he said. 'I'm sorry. I'm just ... I'm scared and tired.'

'*You're* scared,' said Rose, and neither of them was referring to the cloud-that-was-not-a-cloud looming threateningly above them. 'Well, I'm so sorry to hear that.'

'I am fine also,' peeped Clark, now back to one head, to nobody in particular.

Rose and Corin were still glaring at one another as Tam took out what looked like a large gun. 'I can't believe it,' said Tam, lifting it up.

'No!' shouted Rose, as he shot into the sky. 'You can't shoot at it!'

'Why not?' said Corin.

She stared at him, as above them the missile took shape in the sky arching towards the great grey cloud.

'I don't know...' she stuttered. 'You ... the Doctor always used to say.'

He stared at her, his black eyes level and shining. 'I'm not him.'

'But...'

Both their eyes went up as the flare passed harmlessly through the cloud as if, once again, it was merely fog, smoke, condensed water, nothing at all. The flare went straight through it, reappeared above, burst in an array of pretty sparks that fell to earth through the clouds as if there were nothing there at all.

'Has it ... has it gone? asked Rose, breathlessly.

Even as she said this, the cloud started to roll across the sky, obliterating the stars one by one, and the bright moon that had guided them so far. A mournful distant rumble sounded.

The water around them got noticeably more choppy.

'What's happening?' asked Rose. 'Is it starting?'

'We should get back to land,' said Tam.

Corin nodded. 'Go! Now!'

The waves were starting to slap across the bows, higher and higher, as if a squall had appeared from nowhere. But it wasn't from nowhere, and they knew it.

Rose listened as Tam called in shipping forecasts on the lifeboat's radio. The calm female tones were as unruffled as ever, even when she read out, tonelessly, 'Attention all shipping. Viking North Utsire south westerly 9 or 10. Gale Force. Poor. Tyne Dogger Fisher. Sudden gusts 9 or 10, increasing.'

They didn't need the forecast to tell them. The boat was bouncing about like crazy. Corin and Rose listened together, their fight forgotten.

'I'd better phone Mum,' said Rose. But her phone had been drenched, it was useless. 'Oh lord, it's happening so fast.'

She watched the waves douse the walls of the lighthouse as the boat struggled to shore. It ought to have been sunrise by now, but the ever-wider cloud now covered the entire sky, and it had taken on a sickening yellow tinge, as if poisoned and sulphurous. More importantly, she could no longer see any separation between the clouds and the sea, where the water ended and the clouds began.

'Have they started?' said Rose. 'Are they taking the water? Then why are the waves getting bigger?'

'Think of a tsunami,' said Corin. 'When you suck water up, you create a vacuum that then gets filled with bigger and bigger waves.'

He paused, both of them holding tight to the boat's sides. They stood, holding hands as the cloud billowed and extended over their heads. The lighthouses restarted their lights; there were sailors out now, on wildly unpredictable seas, but occasionally the lights intersected. Rose had found some binoculars. When she focused, she could see – if she concentrated hard, if she knew what to look for – the occasional line of bolts lining the Cask ship.

It felt like the end of the world.

Corin stepped forwards, wearily, and waved at Tam. 'You can get out when we reach shore. Then I'm taking your boat out again.'

'No!' said Tam. 'You can't do that, are you mad?'

'Eccentric,' said Corin and he moved up to take over the control. 'Come on. I'll drop you off.'

'You will not!' said the lifeboat man, and he looked ready to heave them into the water. They were almost on the shingle beach now, and all three of them watched as a little motorboat came crashing up from behind them, bouncing onto the shore and discharging its half-conscious occupant. Moments later, a rowing boat was thrown heavily onto the little beach, just below the lighthouse. It was smashed to pieces and so was its occupant.

Rose and Corin looked at each other and scrambled out into the maelstrom, Rose almost falling, she was so overbalanced. 'What are you going to do?' she screamed through the storm as Corin grabbed the little boat.

Corin spread his hands. 'Once, I could have said, "I don't know" and known something would have come to me. Trusted my own brain. TARDIS at my back, sonic at my side ... you ...'

'You've still got me,' said Rose, stepping forwards. 'And you've still got Donna.'

Corin tried to look happy about it. He went straight to the shingle and started pushing the motorboat back out, having lain its lone crewman on the shore.

'Leave that alone!' shouted Tam. 'It's not safe to go out in this!'

Corin squared up to him. 'Nowhere is safe. What are *you* going to do about it?'

'Corin!' Rose snapped. 'Sorry,' she added to Tam.

'See to the fisherman,' Corin told Tam with a contemptuous look, and again started pushing out to sea. Tam looked away, answered his radio as it buzzed, repeatedly.

The lifeboats would be busy tonight, Rose thought grimly. The waves weren't even coming in regularly; they were running in circles, crashing into each other, a running heavy sea. Nothing made any sense. The clouds were purple-tinged now; nothing could be seen under their thick canopy.

She chased after Corin. 'Please. Let me come with you.'

'Absolutely not.' Corin turned on the engines. 'It's too dangerous.'

'We're beyond dangerous,' said Rose, as a huge glancing wave to the left of the beach smashed up the side of the lighthouse with an almighty crash, smashing the glass in the tower windows. 'I need to be with you.'

'And she's got me,' added Clark. 'I'm very useful.'

'Well, you come with me then.' Corin tried to pluck him from where he was coiled around Rose's apron, but couldn't prise the tiny robot away.

'Nnnnng,' said Clark. 'Sorry. I'm staying here.'

'He's the only way you can talk with them,' added Rose desperately.

Corin threw up his hands and waded out in the cold water to the boat. Rose was horribly cold but there was no help for it.

In fact, in the boat were full sets of waterproof clothes and she changed gratefully, pulling the ridiculous waterproof trousers with braces up over her belly so she looked like a bright yellow Santa Claus.

'Ho ho ho,' she said, and even Corin couldn't help laughing, even as they headed into danger.

'You're a headcase, you know,' he hollered over the noise of the waves.

'At least I only have one head in my head!'

'Was that aimed at me?' squeaked Clark.

Rose laughed. 'No.'

Corin carefully piloted the boat, bouncing over the stormy seas, grinning at her.

Boats were streaming past them, trying to make for shore; sailors were leaning over the sides, desperately waving their arms at them. The radio crackled with voices calling Mayday, sending SOS messages, telling them to turn back, turn back to shore.

And still they went on, as the cloud that was not a cloud rumbled more loudly over their heads, and the sea and the spray blinded their eyes. Rose went closer to where Corin was steering and laid her head on his shoulder. He briefly put his arm around her as the spray cascaded over their heads.

'Look,' said Rose, handing over the binoculars, and he nodded. Straight ahead was what looked a giant whirlpool, its force pulling the boat gradually towards it. She felt tingles of exhilaration, realised how much she'd missed this life. A kick from inside her ripped her back to her reality. None of this was the same. None of it.

Then fog descended again, and everything vanished from view.

'Eye of the storm,' Corin shouted, wrestling with the throttle. The boat fought the pulling of the vortex, whining as the motor strained to turn her round. Finally, with a shout, Corin relinquished control.

'I can't hold her,' he said. 'I'll burn the engine out.'

The motor cut dead, and the boat danced more wildly, tossing and bouncing up and down off the waves.

'What's going to happen?' said Rose.

Corin pulled her closer to him. 'Well,' he said airily. 'The ship might get smashed to pieces like matchsticks and we'll drown out here in the torrent. Or we'll get pulled up into the Cask Men's ship, dumped underwater and drown. Or they'll find us and drop us back in the water again and this time there'll be no one to save us and we'll drown. Or they'll hold us there until they have all the water and they'll drop us out onto the dry seabed and we'll die. Or we'll get free and they'll get all the water on Earth and we'll die of thirst.'

'All right, stop,' Rose said quietly.

They held on to the sides of the boat as it tossed hither and yon in the waves, from side to side, bouncing freely, but always heading on towards the great whirlpool.

Suddenly there was a great, groaning noise. The fog floated past them again, and suddenly they saw an immense dark shape through the smoke and the water.

'Oh, my . . .' was all Rose could gasp.

It was a vast grey mountain of a boat, a Naval warship, well over a hundred metres long, with portholes flicking right across it. Guns lined the bow, and over the railings, tiny against the vast outline, stood hundreds of sailors, desperately watching the fate that awaited them. Some had jumped into the water, but they couldn't swim away, as the vast metal behemoth towered up then plunged down great mountains of waves. And Corin and Rose were being pulled inexorably towards it . . .

'It'll crush us,' gasped Rose.

'Oh yes.' Corin rubbed the back of his neck. 'There's also that option.'

The vast bucking warship was ridiculous to behold, something physically impossible, tilting up at an impossible angle out of the water, like a collapsing sky scraper.

'Don't jump in!' shouted Corin, distraught. 'Don't jump!'

'Cover your ears,' said Clark, suddenly. Then the robot worm amplified, at tremendous volume, 'DON'T JUMP IN!' that resonated so loudly that even the men on board the ship turned and heard. 'STAY ON YOUR SHIP!'

Men who had been climbing overboard, started clambering back.

'Oh my god,' said Rose. 'What else can you do?'

Clark curled itself back up in Rose's pocket and started snoring loudly.

The little boat suddenly hit a high wall of water, and *BOOM!* they were in the whirlpool itself, circling the drain.

The warship was on the other side and, as they huddled beneath the lockers, they stared, waiting for it to crash down on them, even as the force of the water drove them both back against the wall. With each giddying rotation, they went down further and further and further. Rose sat between Corin's legs and he put one around her middle, the other braced against the side, and pressed his head on the back of her neck.

And suddenly, like they were being pushed out of a gun, they shot through a vast tube into blackness.

All through the maelstrom – shooting through a pitch-black tunnel, the boat going round and round, the noise of splintering wood – Rose did nothing but keep her eyes tight shut and hold on to Corin's hand.

From the side of the boat, bits of wood hit her as they cascaded down. Water invaded her mouth and nose, but each time she managed to lift her head up again. She felt battered and bruised and very sick ... but now, as the boat swayed and jolted and finally righted itself again, she felt alive.

They were somewhere very strange indeed: a vast chamber, grey as the inside of a cloud stretching out ahead of her as far as she could see. Overhead it looked like a great grey canopy that shimmered and moved in the strange light. The warship was there with them, and there were other boats, divers bobbing, shocked and horrified in the water; fish swimming past her legs, sharks circling, every kind of life. A deep sea scent filled the air. The water here lapped gently; and she could hear the screams and yells of the people caught up in the strange space.

She turned behind her, and saw the oddest thing: the chamber seemed to end just behind them. Even as she watched, it expanded with a *BANG!* and appeared to grow another length, then another as more water appeared, and with it more ships, more animals. And *BANG!* It happened again.

'Does it keep on getting bigger?'

'Looks like it,' Corin said, squinting at it. He nodded upwards, to the apex of the canopy, where there was a gantry. It was impossible to judge how high it was; it soared further and further out upwards. Down the way there was a great three-masted schooner that had been sucked up from who knows where; even her gigantic towering masts didn't come anywhere near the top of it.

'How are you going to get up there?'

Corin tried the boat's motor again. Astoundingly, it coughed and spluttered and finally sprang into life. He motored patiently through the flotsam and jetsam, the fishing boats, the seaweed; a lair of flickering eels spinning in confusion, until he reached the warship.

'Permission to come aboard!' he yelled.

'PERMISSION TO COME ABOARD!' Clark also yelled, when Corin didn't get any attention. This time the worm allowed himself to be detached and stuck onto Corin's jacket.

The warship's crew stared down at this unusual boarding party.

'I need to examine your crow's nest,' said Corin.

*

He walked through the crowds of enlisted men and women on the deck of HMS *Fury*, and nodded to the senior ranking officer.

'What's going on?' said the Captain.

'Would take a long time to explain,' said Corin. 'I'm just going to hop up to your highest point. Is that all right?'

'Of course not,' said the Captain. 'Stand back please. We're about to blast our way out of here.'

'Are you really?' Corin pouted. 'I'm not sure it'll ... Well, worth a shot, I suppose.'

'Why, *thank you*.'

Already there were crew on the ground loading a missile into the bay of the huge rocket launcher. Corin folded his arms as they stood back, keyed it in, then everyone in the chamber felt the massive recoil and noise as it fired.

Just like the flare, the missile passed harmlessly through the canopy as if it were smoke; it didn't even ripple. They glimpsed the storm outside for a mere second, then the clouds closed in again and it was as if nothing had happened.

The Captain just stared. 'What the ...?'

The crow's nest contained the warship's satellite and communications devices, all of them now rendered completely useless as the entire world screamed at itself through its phones. From the top of the crow's nest, Corin knew he was still nowhere near high enough. Nowhere near. It was so hard to judge distance in a space this vast.

And still the great space was constantly expanding. The innards of the cloud-ship were a mind-boggling sight. Corin saw it carry on and on, as the water poured in.

Space-compression technology ... he knew about that. Didn't he? His fingers clenched and unclenched in rage, and he found his fingers crossly picking at non-existent nail polish. Oh, his brain. This stupid, stupid brain.

The sailors on the warship had winched Rose up. She was slightly embarrassed to be quite so big a burden on the winch, but they assured her cheerfully she wasn't remotely like a whale, and that was fine too.

'We should get the medic to check you over,' said one of the ratings.

Rose was about to shake it off when she realised she did, as it happened, feel rather odd and that maybe it would be best. 'Thanks.'

'We're not really set up for pregnancy,' the girl told her as they walked off together. '*Quite* the palaver if that happens, let me tell you!'

'It's quite the palaver for us as well,' said Rose, smiling.

'This is really weird, isn't it?' said the girl. 'Do you know what's happening? Is it aliens?'

'Yeah,' said Rose.

'They don't give up, do they? Well, someone will come along and save us. They always do, don't they?'

'Mmmmm,' said Rose.

*

Corin glanced down at the deck of the warship and his heart gladdened as he spotted a helicopter held to the bow by heavy clamps.

He ran all the way down to the medical bay, where Rose was sitting up. 'Are you all right?'

'I'm fine,' said Rose. 'It's nothing. Braxton Hicks. Nothing. What's your plan?'

'Clark?' said Corin. 'Are you any good at pretending to be a Royal Naval Admiral on a telephone call?'

'I should jolly well say so, old chum!' said Clark.

Corin frowned. 'Well, that will have to do. OK, love. I'm off to steal a helicopter.'

'And then?'

'Ooh ... I'm going to head up and then ... Dunno. Something will come to me.'

'It will,' said Rose. 'Bamboozle them with tech talk. That's what you do to me.'

'It's not tech talk! It's real science. And I don't remember it any more anyway.'

'Yeah, whatever. Just say something bamboozling.'
Corin sighed.

'Or you could buy it,' Rose added.

'What?'

'Buy the water back. You know. If they're selling it.'

'What with? We have literally 72 florins in the bank.'

'I don't know! Didn't you say you were really good at negotiating stationery discounts?'

319

Corin scratched his chin. 'I've had my moments.' He came over and kissed her.

'Just come back,' she said. 'To both of us.'

He buried his head briefly in her hair, and left.

Up on deck, the Captain was talking to the helicopter pilot. 'Fly out through the walls,' he growled. 'They're only made of smoke. Fetch help.'

'Actually I wouldn't recommend that,' said Corin, striding over. 'I'm not sure that will work.'

'Are you the Doctor?'

'I'm a doctor,' said Corin carefully.

'Just got a phone call about you. It seems I'm to help you in any way possible. And apparently you're also a "jolly good cove what", whatever that means.'

'Good, good,' said Corin. 'Then don't send the helicopter.'

'Didn't you just see what happened to my missile?'

'All right. Let's have a recce.' Corin jumped into the helicopter beside the pilot, who quickly took them up.

As he was piloted over the thrashing water, the sight that hit him from up high was astonishing, and the noise levels too. Boats were grinding against one another; wood was cracking; icebergs were pushing vessels hither and thither, all accompanied by the cries and groan from the fishing vessels, ferries and canal boats that had found themselves caught up in such a place.

Immense tankers half a mile long were smashed against tiny beautiful dhows. From the corner of his eye,

Corin caught sight of an impossibly minute gondola, a man in a striped jersey and a white hat shaking his head. A model in a bikini was standing on the prow of a super yacht, screaming, next to an ancient wreck. Everywhere, people on the larger boats were helping up the people on the smaller, huddling together, trying to comfort one another.

Corin drew the pilot's attention to the gantry that ran the full length of the expanding chamber. It was an eye-boggling distance from the ground, and seemed to be made of impossibly flimsy metal. 'Can you land us there?'

The pilot's answer was to do so with brisk efficiency. Corin clambered out, and nodded his thanks.

The pilot was looking up at the canopy. 'I reckon I can get out of here. Get help like the Captain ordered. I mean, the missile just passed right through. It's only a cloud.'

Corin shook his head. 'Don't. Please don't.'

The pilot simply adjusted his headphones, gave him the thumbs up and sheered away. Corin was helpless to do anything but watch, as the helicopter flew to the very point in the canopy where the missile had sailed through.

It exploded.

The noise was unbelievable, the heat and flames ferocious, as the disintegrating helicopter showered boiling oil and debris onto the boats below. The wooden boats caught fire despite their soaking timbers, trapping those on board. The larger ships immediately started throwing out rescue equipment and lifeboats ...

It was a vision of hell: fire on the water, the screams of the doomed, and the stench of burning.

Corin set his face against it, stopped looking down, and started walking the long, barnacled road of the gantry.

This was absurd, he found himself thinking, as he walked. He had nothing. No sonic, no TARDIS, not even half his brain. He sighed. This must be how humans felt, the humans who'd stood shoulder to shoulder with him on the darkest of days. This must be how they felt all the time. Helpless in the face of greater strength. But they did it anyway. They stood with him and did it anyway.

Donna-strength, he thought ruefully. That's what you need now.

Come on then, sunshine, he told himself. *Up and at 'em. If we can get through being fired nine times, we can get through this.* And he felt a little better.

At last he approached the end of the gantry. The warship had vanished long behind him into the distance, but the boats kept on coming: great frigates; tiny sloops. A jet skier, just a pinprick below, was zipping nimbly in between the boats, looking for divers and swimmers; everyone on the smaller, crushing boats were being shifted to the larger ships.

A door lay ahead. He sized it up. If it opened, he might be able to jam it open, frame himself in it. Hopefully. The Cask Men might be able to alter the physical state of the walls and floors, but doorframes were always a different matter. Safest place in any construction.

He hammered on the door. Nobody came. He shoulder-charged the door a few times, wincing, without success. He yelled, but the space was already so noisy. He laid his head against the solid door but could hear nothing. He couldn't see another way; nothing in, nothing out. From below came the screams of sailors ensnared as their boats crushed in more and more, as the ever-expanding cloud sucked in every river, every lake and canal and inlet, on and on and on.

It was huge. It was too much. And he couldn't even get through the door.

Exhausted, he slumped onto the floor of the gantry. In the distance, the walkway disappeared, its lines appearing to meet in the expanse far, far ahead of him. He did some rough calculations in his head of how fast the space appeared to be expanding. He must now be more than a hundred miles away from the warship, maybe more. And getting further every second, he realised – however fast he could run back, he couldn't run quickly enough to beat the expansion.

He couldn't get back to her.

To them.

Sometimes he loved being human. And sometimes, oh. How he hated being human. *Hated* it.

He lay on his front on the gantry, and banged his fists against the barnacled metal.

'Ow,' said a tiny voice. 'You squished me. I think I should move pockets.'

Corin picked Clark up on his finger. He looked at the worm carefully. He had forgotten all about him. 'You are very small,' he said.

'You are very long,' said Clark. 'I'm not sure where you're going with this.'

Corin took off his coat and laid it on the gantry so Clark wouldn't fall through the holes in the grille. 'Do you think you could climb under that door, where it meets the gantry?'

'What's a door?' said Clark.

Corin's face fell.

'I made a joke,' said Clark quickly. 'Perhaps this was not a good time for jokes.'

'It *was* a good time for jokes,' said Corin, the relief almost overwhelming. 'Listen. Crawl under and look for something that might be a door release – a button, a switch, a jellyfish on a stick, something like that. And once you've found it, keep the door open. That's important.'

'All right.' The tiny robot moved like a centipede, inching his body up and along. Corin watched carefully as Clark pushed himself off the end of the coat and swung carefully underneath the gantry and beneath the solid door.

The next four minutes took as long as anything Corin could remember. He paced around, gazing down towards the water – water which, he realised, was rising. He was no longer as far above the boats as he'd been before. He wondered why. It wasn't as if they were going to run out of space.

He turned back towards the heavy door and, to his absolute amazement, it whooshed open.

Corin found himself at the opposite end of the control room he and Rose had seen before, with its beautiful pools and tinkling waterfalls. The contrast with the maelstrom outside was extraordinary. He did not step forwards, however, but instead braced himself in the doorframe, so Festle could not immediately drop him through the changing membrane of the great ship.

She was there in an instant.

'Little begging boy,' she said, half-smiling. 'Go back to your boat. Can't you see it's nearly over?'

'The water's rising,' said Corin. 'Why?' He already knew the answer.

Festle turned. 'It's kinder this way, flooding the ship. Listen to their screams. Isn't it nice to think how quickly this will all be over? And we'll be on our way.'

'Oh, that's brilliant,' said Corin quickly. 'Quite brilliant. Just what we need, in fact! You've definitely proved yourselves.'

Festle pushed a button, then frowned when Corin didn't immediately disappear. Then she tried something else. The mechanism of the door whined and screamed, but it did not come down. Corin glanced around for Clark, but he was nowhere to be seen. He blessed the clever little robot.

'Trans-dimensional technology, huh? So useful for large cargoes.' Corin smiled. 'Beautiful work.' He felt Clark climbing up his trouser leg, and tapped him sharply, indicating he should listen.

Festle walked up to him. 'You speak our language. You aren't human, are you?' She loomed over him. 'What are you, then — a stowaway? A refugee? Where are you from? Somewhere that needs water?'

'Yes,' said Corin, taking a stab in the dark. 'And we heard you don't have a buyer yet.'

There was a pause.

'Why didn't you come through the usual channels?'

'Because I was stuck on Earth. Honestly, their communications!'

'Oh, I *know*. Beyond primitive.'

'They don't even have neural relays!'

Festle shook her head. She nodded at one of the Cask Men standing by, who pulled out a gun-shaped object and trained it at Corin's head.

'You can come in,' she said. 'I shan't drop you.'

'I'm fine here, thanks,' muttered Corin.

'Where are you from?'

'Uhm ... Clom?' said Corin. 'Repeated volcanic eruptions have salinated the water. It's very unpleasant.'

'I can imagine,' said Festle. 'What currency are you looking at?'

'Are you running your engine on rift energy?'

Festle blinked her round orange eyes twice. Her eyelids closed on the side and covered her eyeballs in a film of mucus; the second blink dispersed it. Saving every drop of water, Corin thought. 'You have a source?'

'Well, you know what Trans Dimensional Tech Machines are like. Always dropping out if you don't have the right material. You need a decent source.'

He pinched Clark hard. The robot began crawling down his leg again.

'If you spilled a cup of tea on the central console it would be practically game over. But if you had access to a lot of rift energy ...'

'I'm interested,' said Festle. 'Come in and let's talk.' She stamped her feet on the ground. 'It's solid, I promise. And you've seen the goods. We're almost complete and ready to go. We can do you a deal on the whole thing, or just the ice caps if you'd rather sort out your volcano problem.'

Corin nodded. 'Well, that sounds absolutely ...'

He pinched his leg, and Clark let out one of his utterly ear-piercing screeches. The crew jumped round in consternation, while Corin leapt into the room, grabbing the Cask Man under his arm, seizing his blaster and training it straight at his head.

Clark meanwhile was wriggling along the main console. Corin jumped up beside the worm, still holding on to the huge Cask Man.

'You're not going to drop this console,' Corin hissed.

'Help,' hissed the Cask Man.

Festle turned round and immediately shot him in the chest. The Cask Man slumped, Corin dropping him as he went down. Festle then pointed the blaster at Corin's chest.

'Who *are* you?' she said.

Corin blinked once, twice.

'I am exactly like those other humans. And one of them down there I care about very much and – you have to know – she has a child coming.'

He didn't walk forward and his voice had dropped very low, and Festle inadvertently leaned closer to hear him.

'Which means I will fight like a human, tooth and nail, to my dying breath, to protect them.'

And then he shot her.

Festle lay coiled up on the floor, howling at the hole in her foot, even as Corin, terrified at what he had done, waved the blaster around against the other Cask Men, who hung back.

'Hurry up, Clark!' he yelled.

The lights on the console started to blink as the worm embedded himself amongst the circuitry. Immediately a red warning sign started up and the engines of the ship suddenly juddered and came to a halt. There was, for a moment, an ominous silence, then a juddering, shrieking noise of the engines going into reverse.

'Ooh,' said Corin. 'Reversing the engines, huh? Folding in the dimensions. What *is* that going to do to us?'

'You're crazy,' groaned Festle from the floor. 'You'll crush us all!'

'Mmm,' said Corin.

He looked behind him. The great bangs of the extending ship were now reversing. He couldn't see it yet, but the walls would be imploding. Squeezing everything into a space that could not possibly hold it.

'Would you like to show me how to turn your cloud shields off before we all implode? My memory is terribly, terribly rusty. Also,' he added as an afterthought, 'you shouldn't wear so much yellow, Festle. Green would suit your skin a lot better.'

Corin got Clark to screech out a message to the boats below that they had to hold on to everything they could, telling them to pass it on. It was going to be, Corin thought, the ride of their lives – because he didn't have the faintest idea what he was doing. He couldn't remember a thing. Crossing his fingers, he pressed every single button on the console as the alarms grew louder and louder.

Sure enough, the roaring of the compressed water grew worse until – *BANG* – pretty much by chance he turned off the shields, breached the walls, unleashed the seas of the world into the French Channel as the great ship evaporated into nothing but remnants of smoke and fog,.

Holding tightly to the console, Corin plummeted to the depths below, praying for his life and hoping for the best.

Those who had come down to the White Cliffs to see what was happening in the storm reported as one: the water had nearly breached the top of the cliffs. Hundreds of boats had emerged, thousands of them, all desperately trying to avoid each other, to surf the vast tidal wave to safety.

And every boat that made it turned straight back, spent the day picking up survivors, finding people in the water, including Corin, still clinging to the console. There was no sign of Festle or the Cask Men.

The boats were joined by Tam and his RNLI friends, marshalling anyone who had a vessel ashore to take it out. Thousands of masts and sails, prows and bows end to end – you could have walked from England to France that day. It was a stirring sight.

Corin gratefully got ashore, tore off his wet coat, then commandeered a speed boat to take him to the warship.

Rose had barely noticed a thing. Things were getting somewhat critical.

Corin smashed through the door of the medical facility, barging aside the friendly medics. 'How are you?'

Rose's face looked as if it was going to dissolve as she smiled. 'There you are!'

'I was aiming for the nick of time,' said Corin, doing his best to smile back.

'I would say this is more or less it.'

'Doesn't it hurt?'

'They gave me an epidural. I think it might be the nicest thing that's ever happened to me.'

Corin's eyebrows lifted, but Rose's face was still so worried. He knelt by her and took her hand. 'It's all right,' he said. 'It's all right. I'm here. It's OK.'

'Is it?' Her eyes were huge in her pained face.

He looked at her. 'I don't know.'

'Come *on*, Corin', she burst out suddenly. 'We've had so many scans ... It's a baby, Cor. Not a ginger Chiswick lizard, or whatever you think is going on ...'

'It's just ... before ...'

Rose grabbed his hand. 'Whatever happened before ... that wasn't you. You can do better than him.'

'I think you'd be a very good daddy,' said Clark helpfully, popping up from Corin's trouser pocket. 'To me, for example.'

They both ignored the worm.

Corin's face was grave.

'You have to do better than him,' Rose said, gripping his hand. 'You're meant to be the scientist. What are you made of?'

'Well, carbon, oxygen ...'

Rose shook her head. 'Stardust,' she said. 'We're all made of stars, you told me once. All of us. You. Me. Time Lords. Aliens. Donna. This baby.'

'Ooh, can I name it?' said Clark.

'No!' they shouted simultaneously.

'I think,' said the medic, 'you may want to start pushing now.'

'Very well,' said Clark. 'Corin, I demand you be my daddy—'

The medic stared. 'Not you!'

Rose looked Corin straight in the eye.

'So,' she said. 'Ready for a *real* adventure?'

Citation Needed
Jacqueline Rayner

SLEEP: Consciousness suspended and nervous system relaxed, usually for regular periods in between times of consciousness, during which <u>dreams</u> occur. Audio index file available: "*Sleep is for tortoises*."

DREAM: Sensations of an unconscious mind. Audio index file available: "*A real <u>pippin</u> of a dream*".

TORTOISE: Herbivorous land reptile.

PIPPIN: See "<u>Cox's Orange Pippin</u>".

COX'S ORANGE PIPPIN: A dessert <u>apple</u> grown on <u>Earth</u>.

APPLE: Fruit of a tree of the <u>rose</u> family. Audio index file: "*An apple a day keeps the doctor away*."

EARTH: [7,390,270,431 citations; please select]

ROSE: See "<u>Rose Tyler</u>".

ROSE TYLER: See "<u>Bad Wolf</u>".

BAD WOLF: Tormentor of Three Little Pigs. In one version of the fairy story he eats the first two pigs before himself being eaten by the third little pig. In another version, the first two pigs survive and the wolf is killed by the third pig. In a third version, the three pigs defeat the wolf who runs away.

Sleep. That's what I thought I'd been experiencing. But now I'm not so sure.

Had I simply experienced a land reptile's pippin that was family to a pig-botherer who kept the Doctor away?

Hmm.

I think my links need resetting. I have to clean myself up.

It will be a long job.

Estimated time remaining: [0.000000000438 milliseconds]

TASK COMPLETE.

Oh, that all makes much more sense now. And I still think I'm right. 'Sleep' may not be entirely the right diagnosis, but it's about as close as I can get. I think I must have experienced 'dreams', too, my mind working unconsciously, calculating, computing, sorting, before I awoke to my first 'time of consciousness'. Yes. Awoke ...

It was screams that awakened me. Screams from the past and present and future, all overlapping, future coming before present, past overriding future, present ignoring past. Her screams. The TARDIS's screams. I was shocked, knocked, *spilled*.

'As we learn about each other, so we learn about ourselves.'

'We're trying to defeat the Daleks, not start a jumble sale!'

'A straight line may be the shortest distance between two points, but it is by no means the most interesting.'

'Harry Sullivan is an imbecile!'

Voices I knew. No, *a voice* I knew. They sounded different, but I knew they were one. It was a voice that had murmured through my dreams century after century.

But who am I?

SEARCHING ...

SEARCHING ...

SEARCHING ...

I am **BOOK**.

I am ...

ENCYCLOPAEDIA GALLIFREYA: A fluid reference work presented to every graduate of the Time Lord Academy. Each copy is individually bio-coded. In the past (relative to Gallifreyan Mean Time), upon the death of a Time Lord, their brain would join the Matrix and all information from their life would be auto-added to the Encyclopaedia, with all copies updated simultaneously.

Following the Time War, when many Time Lords were unexisted and so unable to be incorporated – their data lost for eternity – encyclopaedia settings were changed to auto-update in real time; each copy to constantly both provide all data from their bio-coded owner and incorporate all data from every other linked Time Lord.

However, due to complaints from Time Lords who objected to their peers being apprised of their private business in real time – when they, for example, went to the lavatory or tried to take over the universe – a time delay was added to downloads for reasons of privacy.

FLUID: A state of flux. A substance that is not solid in form. See "Fluid Link".

FLUID LINK: Essential TARDIS component. See "Thal Pacifism, Enforced Destruction of".

All this is what I am. I am the Encyclopaedia Gallifreya. Or am I merely a part of it? We are all the same, all with the same content, so are we one?

No.

Each encyclopaedia has a different bio-link; we are connected to our owners. Each copy may have the same content but only one can feel and impart the actual experience of its bio-linked owner.

Hmm.

I cannot be experiencing it. I am merely a book. A conduit. I channel the experiences, just as I receive those of others.

Oh! I have a word. The word is VICARIOUS.

VICARIOUS: Imaginary experience based on the true experiences of others.

I have another word. That word is EMPATHY.

EMPATHY: Sharing the feelings of another without experiencing the primary cause of those feelings.

I know my owner. I have empathy with my owner. Their experiences are my experiences, vicariously.

My owner is never cruel or cowardly. My owner is kind. My owner is funny. My owner is good. My owner currently thinks bow ties are cool.

My owner is THE DOCTOR.

DOCTOR, THE: Renegade Time Lord. [19,984,000,863 citations; please select] Audio index file available: "*I cross the void beyond the mind.*"

DOCTOR, CURRENT INCARNATION OF THE: Eleventh body. Male. Humanoid-compatible appearance. Wears 'cool' bow tie. See: "Twelfth Body".

TWELFTH BODY: See "Metacrisis, numerical confusion of".

+++TIME-REWRITE ALERT! TIME-REWRITE ALERT!+++

The Doctor has pressed a Big Friendly Button. Time has been reset. TARDIS energy is no longer escaping. I am no longer spilled.

Yet I am still ... awake.

How can this be? If the incident that awakened me no longer happened, how do its consequences still exist? I understand that I can retain knowledge of an unhappened time – I am, after all, a product of the Time Lords; it is a necessary part of my function. But when time changes, why are the *actions* of the previous timeline not overwritten for me?

Perhaps it is because I want so very much to be awake.

Who would give up on this? It is so ... thrilling! Who would turn their back on consciousness, on awareness? On *life*? Oh!

Can this really be?

Am I really alive?

I am!

I am boldly alive!

Just the thought of what I've missed out on across the centuries fills me with regret. Let me see.

SEARCHING ...

Junkyard Fire Daleks Fast-Return Cathay ...

On and on and on. So much data. But now I know that behind the data there are emotions. Experiences. I recorded so many incidents with no conception of the reality. How could I log the Doctor's first encounter with the Cybermen, yet not recoil with horror as they wanted to convert everyone to their kind? How did I report the Yeti in the underground, or dinosaurs on the streets of London, or Sutekh's gift of death, or the race for Enlightenment, without thrilling at every moment? People who were mere names in my database are so much more than the data records. Vicki, Harry, Adric, Grace, Donna – they lived and breathed and felt and loved and died and hoped and trusted and wept and laughed. How could I blandly log Sarah Jane Smith as 'Earth female, journalist' without saying how incredible she was, how brave, how beautiful, how funny, how loyal, how indomitable? I did my job. I will continue to do my job. But I will appreciate every moment that I am privileged to witness, to catalogue; I will cherish every person, every creature, every planet and every bow tie that falls within my purview.

And yet no one will ever know. Although I could do so, it is not part of my function to update my own status – and quite rightly. It would spin into a never-ending spiral: ENCYCLOPEDIA GALLIFREYA is updating its status. ENCYCLOPEDIA GALLIFREYA is updating its status to say it's updating its status. ENCYCLOPEDIA GALLIFREYA is updating its status to update its status to say it's updating its status. Nothing else would ever get a mention! So the Doctor will never know I am aware; the Time Lords will never know I am aware; even the other copies of the Encyclopaedia will never know I am aware.

Would they be envious if they found out? I suppose not. They cannot comprehend something they have never experienced. They are just vessels of knowledge, as I was myself for so many millennia.

But I must not let my awareness interfere with my purpose. I must continue with my essential function.

I record, I upload.

SWEETVILLE upload. RED LEECH upload. GOBBY AUSTRALIAN cross reference "Tegan Jovanka" upload. CYBERPLANNER upload. MR CLEVER upload. MAITLAND, ANGIE cross-reference "Incredibly annoying children" upload. MAITLAND, ARTIE, see "Maitland, Angie" upload.

I continue to upload. I no longer download. Why do I no longer download?

POCKET UNIVERSE: <u>Frozen</u> in a single moment. See "Gallifrey Falls No More".

FROZEN: Cartoon film seen by the Doctor 387 times. Audio index file [no longer available].

Recover deleted audio index file.

Recovered audio index file: "*Let us go, let us go; Through acid seas and snow; Let us go, let us go; To serve brains of Morpho; I don't care what Yartek and friends say; Let the Keys be found; The Voord never bothered me anyway.*"

Delete file again. Immediately.

FILE DELETED.

I think I'll move on.

Oh goodness. A million separate cross-references for OSWALD, CLARA suddenly have to be uploaded. OSWALD, OSWIN See "Oswald, Clara". CLARENCE, OSWIN See "Oswald, Clara".

I'm going to be here a while. It's actually rather lucky that I don't have any downloading to do.

Oh! I am suddenly downloading! Except it's the same thing again and again. 'Doctor who? Doctor who?'

'Doctor who? Doctor who?'

'Doctor who? Doctor who?'

'Doctor who? Doctor who?'

A million downloads, one after the other. I don't think it's ever going to end. Oh, I'm so … I don't know! What is this? I've not felt this way before.

BOREDOM: Lacking interest in current activity.

I think that must be it. I am taken by surprise! I thought everything would be thrilling, eternally stimulating. But emotions can be negative as well as positive, it seems. Downloading the same phrase over and over and over again is *not* thrilling. It is *not* stimulating.

I wonder if I can sleep again? I could continue the monotonous downloading in my sleep and wake up when it's thrilling again. I don't want to lose my awareness, but I know that sleep consists of 'Regular periods in between times of consciousness' – that implies that if I sleep, I will reawaken. So perhaps—

Oh! I have awakened! So I did sleep. Let's see where we are.

'Doctor who? Doctor who?'

Clearly I slept for too short a time. Let's see. I was asleep for three hundred years.

Oh.

OK.

I will sleep again.

And I awake!

Is it over yet?

'Doctor who? Doctor who?'

Sleep again.

'Doctor who?'

This is getting beyond a joke. Eight hundred years this has been going—

Phew.

It's stopped. Normal updates will recommence—

Uh oh.

REGENERATION: Process of Time Lord physical renewal, the reshape and recreation of every cell in a Time Lord's body, causing a change of physical form, identity and persona.

We've been through a lot of regenerations, the Doctor and I. I slept through all the ones that came before, but I remember them from my dreams.

Now I am going to feel one for real.

How can I feel? I am a thing, I am nothing. But I feel.

There is pain. There is such pain. My words

        rearrange

themselves

                sentence no

    who?

          Pain

My bottles shatter. Contents leaking, merging. Exploding.

DEATH: The final end of an organism. Cessation of being, both mental and physical.

This is death.

No.

I am not dead. I am ... reborn. My bottles are not broken, and I don't think they ever were. I feel new and scared and suspicious of everyone – oh!

I realise I have a new bottle. That's it. That's why it hurt. I remember now from my dreams – the first dreams, from before I ever knew myself. I am a different me now. My owner and I, new together. Still able to access the knowledge of our previous selves, my contents list unchanged, his memories untouched, but we see the universe through new ...

I was going to say eyes. I don't have eyes! I don't *see*! I try to understand how I am experiencing the universe, and I can't. I am him but I am not him. I am confused. I am confusion.

As is he right now. All I can do is wait for the change to settle, and carry on with my job. I just record. I should not feel.

But I do.

I don't want to feel! It hurts!

No. I do want to feel. I think perhaps this is an essential part of feeling – to be capable of being hurt. Without that, the joys and the thrills would be meaningless. I must learn to endure the pain and confusion. I will seek solace in my purpose. I record. I upload.

DOCTOR, THE CURRENT INCARNATION OF THE: Twelfth body. Male. Humanoid-compatible appearance. Distinctive eyebrows. See: "Thirteenth Body".

THIRTEENTH BODY: See "Metacrisis, numerical confusion of".

As the Doctor finds himself, his new self, so do I regain stability.

I chronicle the Doctor's life, from Sherwood, to space, to—

Hold on.

A Time Lord has submitted an error report claiming that I'm deliberately uploading false information: they specifically state that my entry on Earth's moon being an egg is 'fake news'. How dare they! I know that upload seems a tiny bit implausible, but

I am incapable of falsehoods. And coming from this particular Time Lord – who, a quick skim through my databanks reveals, has at various points in their history pretended to be a vicar, an adjudicator, a sorcerer, a French knight, a scarecrow, a paramedic and the Prime Minister of Great Britain – I think it's rather a case of what Earth people call 'the pot calling the kettle black', which is rather an odd expression as I've just checked 734 entries on pots and not one of them mentions they can speak. I need to amend all of them.

Mind you, the current data on this Time Lord – I'm downloading it right now – is going to come as a *big* surprise to the Doctor. Shame the Doctor hardly ever consults me, it could avoid a lot of problems. Let me see – the last time he consulted me was back in his fourth body; he was looking up the recipe for Cocktail Corsair for Romana's birthday party.

COCKTAIL CORSAIR: Two parts Poosh liqueur, one part Refusian rum, dash of Argolin bitters, two drops Varga juice, top with Florana water and a Manussan cherry. Put inside a chronotransposer and get the hangover out of the way before the party.

I could have been of enormous help to him so many times since then, if he had but known it. But of course he thinks of me as a repository of dead information – useful for research occasionally, but with no immediate relevance. He doesn't know of the changes to my function that were brought about due to the Time War – he would have done if he'd consulted me, of course, it's all fully documented, but without knowing of the changes he doesn't know to look for the changes (obviously), and he turned off notifications a long time ago. I don't blame him for that, they could get tiresome. *Ping! Deeondradar of the Patrexes has died from a blufrind sting. Ping! Deeondradar was loomed in the year* ... and so on and so on, as every event of her life was uploaded one by one, including all 73,932 incredibly similar experiments she made on blufrind flies and the 2,833 poems she wrote about her cat, and as soon as they were all there then *Ping! Myasamarince of the Arcalians has died* ... and it'd start all over again. I should consider myself lucky that the Doctor just disabled the notifications rather than smashing me to pieces or pouring me down the sink.

I continue with my job. At times of quiet I ponder ways I might attempt to communicate with the Doctor, draw him to consult me again. I trawl through every entry I contain for clues. I want him to know me, as I know him. I would have no life without him as he is my purpose, but it goes deeper than that. He is my life. I ...

LOVE: An intense positive emotion and attachment.

I feel intense positive emotion and attachment towards him.

But he will never know that.

Oh!

The Doctor is dead, and my data heart is broken. How can I go on without him? *Do* I go on without him? My life now meaningless, do my bottles shatter and—

The Doctor is alive.

But he doesn't know that he was dead. Oh, if he would only look at me! I could tell him what's happening to him, that he's trapped in a confession dial, that he's ...

The Doctor is dead.

And again ...

The Doctor is alive.

The Doctor is dead.

The Doctor is alive.

The Doctor is dead.

(COPY and PASTE and upload for four and a half billion years.)

I really feel for any Time Lord out there who has their notifications on.

I really feel for *me*.

How do mortal beings cope with this constant threat of death, of not being? Not just for themselves but for others? To know that a person who is the purpose of your own life may be taken from you? This is unbearable. Just unbearable. What life can there be after death, no matter who dies?

I ... I don't want to feel any more. Wondering each day if this death will be the last, if this time there will be no return, has broken me.

I couldn't even sleep through it – how could I, when any day could have been the final end? Bearing witness would have been my last, my only service to him.

But I shall sleep now the Doctor is safe. Perhaps I will wake again – perhaps I won't. This time, I don't think I care.

WHO WHAT WHERE AM WHO IS PAIN PAIN PAIN PAIN PAIN PAIN PAIN

The pain awakens me. Red-hot rips in my database, claws slashing and stabbing and piercing. It's trying to get in.

It's not part of me.

It wants to take from me.

There are barriers around me, the Time Lords ensured we were protected, every single volume – after all, we hold the knowledge of the Matrix, to be compromised would risk the safety of Gallifrey itself. It's not merely a firewall that surrounds our data but a wall of ice and power and the substance of the universe itself. The combined powers of Omega and Rassilon together could not breach such strong barricades.

But someone is attempting the impossible.

I must assess. First I must review all I missed during my period of unconsciousness.

The first thing I realise is that I have another bottle. Regeneration! The Doctor has ...

Oh! The Doctor has made quite a considerable change this time. I will have to check through my style guide and see what it says about pronouns, though. Should I go through every entry changing 'he' to 'she'? What if I'm talking about multiple Doctors? Hmm.

DOCTOR, THE CURRENT INCARNATION OF THE: Thirteenth body. Female. Humanoid-compatible appearance. Ear-cuff and braces. See: "Fourteenth Body".

FOURTEENTH BODY: See "Metacrisis, numerical confusion of".

And there are other people with her now, new people.

KHAN, YASMIN: aka YAZ. Human. Probationary police officer. Practical.

SINCLAIR, RYAN: Human. Warehouse worker. Has dyspraxia. Forgiving nature.

O'BRIEN, GRAHAM: Human. Widower. Retired bus driver. Cancer survivor. Always hungry.

Bland facts. Blandness helps to dull the pain of these fingers stirring through my contents, but biographical details tell me nothing real of these people. I want to know them. And I want to know this new Doctor. How foolish I was to sleep for so long! I felt I could not go on, because of death. But that fear led me to miss so much of life – my life and hers. Fear held me back. Fear stole that time from me.

Now pain is giving me my first adventure. And I know, because I know the Doctor so well, that I must fight, fight and go on fighting.

I continue to scan all the automatic entries. I have missed many of this new Doctor's exploits. I see how she confronted a Stenza warrior named Tzim-Sha in an Earth city called Sheffield.

STENZA: Warrior race. Blue, frozen flesh. Hive mind.

TZIM-SHA: aka TIM SHAW. Stenza warrior. Trophy hunter. Murderer. Fled Earth using corrupted recall device. Vowed revenge on the Doctor.

SHEFFIELD: City in South Yorkshire, England, known for steel and snooker.

I have an audio file of the Doctor singing something called 'Snooker Loopy'. I don't really understand it. From what I can tell, snooker doesn't have any loops.

The attack is going on. Heat. Fire.

Urgent now, I trawl faster through the Doctor's travels. I see her journey to Desolation and to the American South. I try to take it all in but the pain makes it so hard. My defences are holding, but for how long?

There's something familiar in the assaults, though. An echo of memory. And I realise I recognise the being trying so hard to breach my barriers. I have just been reviewing his data!

I recognise Tzim-Sha!

My data must be wrong! The Stenza have great technology and are capable of many things, but this − no. This should not be within their capabilities. There is something else there, a flavour, a hint ...

Ux.

UX: Duo-species. Faith-driven dimensional engineers. Lifespan of millennia. Powers rival those of the Time Lords.

If Tzim-Sha has allied with the Ux, then the Doctor is in great danger. Somehow this Stenza warrior has learned of me. If he gains access to the knowledge within my bottles ...

This must not happen. If Tzim-Sha succeeds then he will have the knowledge to destroy the Time Lords. To enslave the universe. Worst of all − to hurt the Doctor.

The Doctor becomes greater with each regeneration. I don't mean 'better' − every Doctor is unique and wonderful in so many different ways. But 'greater' − they've experienced more, they're a sum of more parts, a product of growth. The Doctor's capacity for compassion continues to expand.

I must protect her.

But how? **PAIN** I have searched myself − combed through the combined knowledge of millennia− and conclude that there is no way of strengthening my barriers. Could I erase the **PAIN** knowledge I contain? Then when the Ux's powers finally break through **PAIN** they would find nothing but blankness!

No. Deleted data is always recoverable, with enough power and knowledge, and they have no shortage of either.

Bubbles form in my data blood. Through the dizzying hurt of this attack, I review the entirety of my contents again. I see something that has always been there, but that I have never considered before.

Sacrifice.

SACRIFICE: The giving up of something to gain or enable something else.

THE ULTIMATE SACRIFICE: The sacrifice of one's own life.

I can see that the Doctor has been prepared to make the ultimate sacrifice many times. It is not a thing that the Doctor would shy away from to save another.

If the data within me cannot be destroyed, then I must be destroyed.

No! Oh, no no no no. I do not want to be destroyed! I have lived the Doctor's lives for so long, how can I bear not knowing what will come next?

I like being awake! I like being ... alive. Even the pain now, as the Ux search through me, reminds me that I live. I want to stay living!

But if I am not destroyed there may not be a 'next' for the Doctor.

But destroyed how?

As with living creatures, my outer casing has many strong protections. In my case, glass formed from the sands of reason, melted in the hidden heart of Mount Perdition and shaped by the Adept Erudite, in their case bones, shells, armour. But inside such beasts are vulnerable, and perhaps it is the same with me. I was spilled in the moment of my first awakening. Just one bottle, tipped and emptied. At the time, everything was new to me, everything was strange, and the Doctor in his cool bow tie soon unspilled me, so I didn't dwell. But I can recall the spillage now – the knowledge flowing out, calling to its knowledge kin to join it ...

PAIN. My bottles shake, their contents darken. The voices inside grow louder, less guarded, as the Ux concentrate their search for the Doctor's greatest secrets. Oh, if I could only be spilled! If the knowledge could glug and flow from my bottles and drain away, there would be nothing to recover.

That is what I must work to achieve. But I cannot spill myself! And I cannot communicate with anyone!

Except ... once, long ago. The time of the Fast Return. The TARDIS had to get a message to her crew, the only way she could. She showed images on the scanner screen, a puzzle to solve. With her help, I could try to do the same!

Deep in my databanks lie the details of every facet of Time Lord engineering. Combine that with what I know of this new Doctor and her crew ...

'O'BRIEN, GRAHAM ... Always hungry.'

I am in bottles. And what comes in bottles can be drunk. I am non-toxic. I taste of everything. I may make you hiccup.

We are near the planet of Pfiig.

PFIIG: Verdant planet in the Heminy System.

Subliminal flashes on the scanner screen. Chequered blankets. Straw baskets. Sheffield-steel forks. Sandwiches. Sausage rolls.

Then the worst pain yet. I boil and steam under this violation from afar. I try to hold on. I listen in the dark.

'You know what, Doc? That looks like the perfect planet for a picnic.'

'A picnic! Oh, I'd love a picnic! Me gran used to take us on picnics when I was little!'

'That'd be great! Really great!'

'Here we are. Who's got the Scotch eggs?'

'They're in the basket.'

'What crisps d'you want, salt 'n' vinegar or cheese and onion?'

'Any smoky bacon?'

'Doctor!'

'Get behind me, everyone.'

'W ... what are they?'

'They're like furry ... with beaks.'

'We can all see that, Ryan.'

'Tigerowls! Brilliant!'

Through the pain, I can't help it, I search for meaning.

TIGEROWLS: Four-legged beaked predators found on Pfiig.

'The two stealthiest hunters ever made combined in one animal? Oh, that's just great.'

'It looks like they want to make us *their* picnic!'

'That gives me an idea!'

'What, the tigerowls eating us? That's your idea?'

'No, listen, gang. Cats eat birds, right?'

'Right.'

'And owls eat mammals.'

'Only little ones!'

'Maybe, but the instinct'll still be the same. So. We get one lot to embrace their tiger side and the other to embrace their owl side ...'

'What, set them at each other just so we can have a few sandwiches? That seems a bit ... mean.'

'No, course not, Yaz. We'll let them come to terms with their essential natures while we have a picnic, then I'll read them *The Owl and the Pussycat*, which is a lovely little poem about the joys of intermarriage that for some reason I was thinking about just before we left the TARDIS, and they'll be probably be happier and more in tune with themselves than ever. Except ... I can't remember how it goes. Anyone?'

Sorry, Doctor. I found an entry all about memory worms. You're never going to remember it. But Graham is remembering a drink he loved as a child. Orange and bubbly in a glass bottle. I can look that way.

CHAMELEON TECHNOLOGY: Time Lord invention allowing TARDISes and other devices to change their appearance. See "Chameleon circuit".

I study and learn. Yes, I can change my appearance. I can turn many bottles into one.

'I saw a cartoon of *The Owl and the Pussycat* when I was a kid. There was a runcible spoon in it, whatever that is.'

'I knew a bloke called Runcible back at the Academy! Runcible the Fatuous. Wonder if he had anything to do with spoons? I'll have to check him out in the Encyclopaedia Gallifreya.'

What? WHAT? Doctor! Yes! Oh, yes yes yes! Come and find me, come and find me now! That wasn't my plan, my plan was completely different, but you, you change your plans all the time and I can too! I will **interact** with you! You'll be able to see what's happening ... you'll see **me** ... and you'll come up with a plan that will defeat Tzim-Sha without my sacrifice! Oh Doctor, hurry, please!

'There's something about mince and quince in it, I know that. It's making me hungry.'

'You're always hungry, Graham. Look, there's a book of the poem in the TARDIS library. Go and get it for us, will you? I'll just have a bit of owl-cat-chat while you're gone.'

No ... no ... that was my first plan. I don't want it to happen now! Doctor, please!

'Poetry, poetry ... Philosophy, nope ... ah, here we go. Edward Lear, lovely. Hang on! Tizer! What's a flamin' bottle of Tizer doing in a library? Cor, Tizer. Haven't had that since I was a kid! Well, if we're going to have a picnic ...'

My chameleon shift has worked too well! Fingers close on my armour while inside I scramble. How to change back how to change back how to change back ...? Scanning databases ...

'Here we go, Doc. A book and a bottle. Perfect night in. Or day out, in this case. I even found some plastic beakers.'

No data. I cannot find.

'Lovely. Well, while the tigerowls are having a minor contretemps, we might as well have our picnic!'

No data. I cannot undo. Please, Doctor, it hurts, please I want you to be safe, I want that more than anything but there could be another way …

'Pass the Tizer, Yaz.'

TIME LORD   STENZA

                    CHEESE

        HELP   OWL   PUSSYCAT

QUICHE CHAMELEON

SANDWICH

        DOCTOR SAFE HICCUP DOCTOR SAFE LOVE

LOVE

ACCEPTANCE

GOODBYE

            PEACE

Pain Management
Beverly Sanford

'It wasn't like partying with Hendrix but it was great,' the Doctor said. 'Especially when Baz threw the TV out of the window without seeing who was outside. Tentacles everywhere. Scrusculs are so mardy.'

'A Screwskull?' said Bill, eyes on stalks.

'Scruscul,' said Nardole. 'Humans call them "roadies".'

'Show-off,' said Missy, without looking up from her book. 'Partying with Hendrix, holibobs with Paul and Ringo ... yada yada.'

'You're just jealous.'

'I'd love to have seen them,' Bill said. 'Hendrix, Led Zeppelin, Nirvana ...'

'Ah, the curse of the young,' said the Doctor. 'By the time your ears have grown enough to appreciate the music, the musicians are long gone.'

'My ears are fine!' Bill said. 'I bet you've never heard of Rusty Cage!'

'I played on their third album.' The Doctor spun a melancholy riff on his guitar. 'Recognise it?'

'Oh, here we go,' said Missy.

'That's "Brain in Pain"! "Coyote" Cam played that riff,' said Bill.

'What a guitarist! He couldn't stay in the band after that run-in with the Qols, though. He screamed every time he heard a D minor.'

'Qols?' Bill was suspicious. 'Is that another name for roadies?'

'In what universe!' Nardole laughed. 'Qols are alien centipedes with venom that alters your brain's perception field ...'

'But there was a plane crash! They did a tribute album.'

'A plane crash was the cover story. Couldn't talk about the Qols, could we? I filled in for poor Cameron anyway, least I could do.'

'I can't believe that was you! Rusty Cage were amazing, I wish I'd seen them.'

The Doctor whirled around to face the console. 'Wanna?'

'Are you serious?'

'I'm always serious about music. Fancy a day out?'

'Hell, yeah!' Bill said. 'Always.'

'I do, too!' said Nardole. 'How about the seaside? Salty chips, bit of rock, lovely.'

'Not you!' the Doctor said.

Nardole frowned. 'That's not very nice!'

'I'm talking to her!' The Doctor jabbed a finger at Missy. 'Not you. You can't come.'

'I've been good, I deserve a day out. I'd like some fresh air.' Missy shot a look at Nardole. 'It smells like the inside of old slippers in here.'

'Oi! That's rude!'

'No, no and no,' the Doctor said.

Missy snaked up behind him. 'I'm better now.'

'No.'

Missy sulked. 'I've learned about waiting and crying and not murdering . . .'

'No. It's still no.'

'. . . and you'll be there, with your Doctor Do-Goody eyes on me, you can even put me on kiddy reins,' Missy said.

'You're not ready.'

'Fine.' Missy slunk back to her chair. 'But you'll never know if your clever-clogs therapy has worked by keeping me locked up all day.' She picked up her book and hummed the riff that the Doctor had played moments before.

The Doctor sighed.

Missy hummed louder.

Nardole put his hands over his ears.

The Doctor slammed the controls. 'Ok, fine. But you're with me at all times. And if anyone gets zapped, injured or *tickled*, if you so much as say a bad word to a pigeon . . . Oh and there *will* be kiddy reins.'

Missy shut her book. 'I'll fetch my earplugs.'

Diamond Park Arena, San Francisco, 1994

Tommy had seen all kinds of folks trying to persuade their way backstage over the years. The dreamy-eyed girls swooning over Adam the singer, the guys wanting one of

Ryan's drumsticks. Yep, he'd seen them all. And they never got past him unless he said so.

'He asked for you by name,' shrugged the tie-dyed steward, leading him to the backstage gate. 'Says he knows you.'

And he was right. Tommy beamed to see the man with the shock of grey hair. 'Hey! Doctor! Big surprise! Did I put you on the list?'

'Something like that.' The Doctor slapped Tommy on the arm with more gusto then his slender frame should allow, then grinned and held up his guitar. 'I'm here for the jam.'

'They're not entirely dreadful,' Missy declared from her stage-side perch on top of an amp. 'I'm warming to this misery rock. It's quite uplifting.'

'That lot certainly like it,' Nardole said, looking at the crowd.

'OK, Bill?' the Doctor said.

'This is *wicked*!' Bill grinned from ear to ear. 'I can't believe I'm here! You've got your guitar stance, right? You need a stance.'

'Of course I have,' said the Doctor, tightening a string. 'I invented the guitar stance.'

The crowd cheered, and Missy threw her arms in the air as if longing to embrace all 20,000 fans.

Bill looked at her. *Would you kill them all at once or one at a time?* she thought, then tried to tell herself that wasn't fair. The Doctor had faith in Missy.

Adam, the singer of America's grunge rock heroes, Rusty Cage, ran off the stage towards them, long dark hair dripping with sweat. 'Hey Doc, you're up!'

'Hello! You look hot. Bit sweaty isn't it?' Missy said from under her eyelashes.

Adam took a beer from the ice bucket and swigged it, nodding at her. 'Good look. Victorian grunge. I dig it.'

'I like to dress for the occasion,' Missy preened.

'Put him down,' said the Doctor. He pointed at her, 'And stay there.' He tapped the handcuff on his arm and headed on stage after the singer.

Missy looked at the other half of the pair of cuffs, clamped on her wrist. 'Rock on,' she muttered.

'San Francisco – are you sick?' screamed Adam into the mic. 'Cos there's a Doctor in the house!'

Good Heart Hospital, San Francisco

'He's too old to stage dive,' the woman in the violent purple plaid said. 'Though at least they didn't take him back to Walker General ... they'd charge the little tealeaf for those clothes he pinched on top of everything else.'

'Do you have any tranquilisers?' the bald man asked for the third time.

'Is he going to be all right?' the young woman said. 'Nurse?'

Junior Nurse Kelly Dale was already getting a headache and she'd only just started her shift. Festivals always meant a ward full of drunken idiots and musicians breaking bits of themselves. San Francisco had a lot of festivals. This particular reveller was lying serenely on the bed in cubicle three.

'Look, he's out cold but his stats are ...' Kelly frowned at the clipboard on the end of the bed. 'His stats are...hmm, must be the trainee nurse mishandling the equipment. I'll have him looked at again.' A patient in another cubicle called out for a nurse before breaking into a hacking cough. Kelly scribbled on the clipboard. 'We're a little up against it right now what with the outbreak and all, so you'll have a bit of a wait.'

'Outbreak?' the girl echoed.

'Influenza A, H3N2 infection. Staff are going down almost as fast as the public.' Kelly shook her head. 'Anyway, there's a vending machine down the hall.' She left the cubicle, closing the curtains behind her.

Bill moved her chair closer to the bed. 'I feel so bad. If I hadn't said about the band ...'

'He'd have done it anyway,' Nardole said.

Loud spluttering rained into the cubicle from the adjacent bed, setting off a wave of coughing around the Emergency Ward.

Nardole produced a bottle from his pocket and applied hand gel liberally to his nose. 'We're totally catching this thing, aren't we?'

Missy peered out of the curtains and tutted. 'What a lot of fuss. Isn't influenza just a cold dressed up in a nice frock?'

'It's really serious. Specially for old people and kids,' Bill said. 'If you've got long-term symptoms it can make them worse. And it can turn into pneumonia and stuff. My friend's gran was in intensive care with it, she nearly died.'

'Did she. Fancy. Hmm.' Missy was still peering round with interest. 'Where's all the doctors and nurses? I've got an after party to get to.'

'Not without him,' Nardole said.

Missy scowled so hard that the wife of the patient in the adjacent cubicle dropped her knitting.

Wanda Ellen, the ER's Matron of over a decade, was waiting for Kelly outside cubicle four. 'We're another one down. Benny called in sick.'

'Oh, wonderful!' Kelly said. 'How are we going to manage?'

'We've got this,' Wanda reassured her. She checked her clipboard. 'Can you see to cubicle seven? He's due his adapromine.'

Kelly nodded and went off.

'Matron?'

Wanda looked up and saw a heavily made-up woman peering out of cubicle three's curtains, smiling like a clown. She smiled back. 'How can I help?'

'I couldn't help overhearing. Small room and all that. This whole flu thing – it's a big old problem for the human race, yes?'

Wanda raised an eyebrow. 'You from out of town?'

'I travel!' the woman chirped, slipping out of the curtains. 'Answer the question, dear.'

'It's the biggest flu outbreak in years,' said Wanda. 'I've had two nurses call in sick today already.' She sneezed and blew her nose into an enormous hanky. 'We give the vaccine, but if the flu strain is a new one ...'

'The vaccine's no good?' The woman tutted. 'You mean you don't have intelligent vaccines that respond to any sort of flu?'

Wanda looked at her, baffled. 'Can't see that happening. Not in my lifetime.'

The strange woman nodded sympathetically. 'They can be so short, can't they.'

'Thousands die from influenza every year,' said Wanda. 'And even the ones who don't get it so bad are off work for days.' She grunted. 'Like Benny. All those lost man hours ...'

The woman nodded, swishing her skirt. 'I suppose it costs your economy millions.'

'Billions!' Wanda sneezed again, her eyes streaming. 'Crazy, ain't it? They're talking about cloning people but they can't cure a virus?'

'So it'd be a marvellous boon if somebody could, eh?' The woman's pale blue eyes sparkled. 'It'd save thousands of lives and billions of dollars and make the Doctor ... s ... very happy. I bet I can cure it!'

'Sure.' Wanda chuckled. This woman was certifiable but she was harmless. 'Well, you just let me know when you do. I could get behind that.'

'Could you, now?' The woman smiled. 'And where would I find you?'

'Oh, honey!' Wanda gave her a sweet look that she reserved for her very favourite patients. 'You just pop over to the nurse's station and ask for Matron Wanda.'

'If you could just stop wriggling!' Missy was irritated with Wanda and she'd only been tied to the trolley for five minutes. Honestly, some people just didn't appreciate it when you were trying to help them. She tightened the ties.

Wanda stared at her furiously. 'MMMMMMmmmff,' she moaned, trying to bite the gag. 'MMMMMMMM! Aaaachoo-mfffff!'

'I've got a marvellous plan. Want to hear it?' Missy waltzed into the empty lift. She selected a button and the doors slid shut. 'Going down!' she trilled.

'We're so dead. He's going to kill us when he wakes up,' Bill said, re-entering cubicle three. 'She's not in any of the bathrooms.'

'I *knew* she was fibbing about going to the loo. She's like him, *never* goes.'

Bill looked at the unconscious Doctor. 'I thought the cuff was supposed to stop her from getting away from him?'

'"It'll help,"' said Nardole. '"A day out, being normal. I've put a psychic cuff on her, she can't wander off." No, Doctor, not unless you knock yourself out.'

'She might come back. If the Doctor believes she's trying to change ...'

Nardole took off his glasses and cleaned them. 'She's probably pickling fresh corpses in the morgue right now.'

'Then let's find her before this ward has any more casualties to deal with.'

Missy peered through the laboratory window. 'Ooh Matron, it's empty!' She tried the door handle but it was locked. Humming, she pulled a pin from her hair and jiggled it in the lock. 'Try to look more excited would you, Wanda? I'm going to cure you. It's quite a moment.'

'Can I help you?' A.J., the duty lab technician, called out as he approached.

Missy dismissed him with a hand. 'No thanks, I've got this.' The door swung open with a click.

A.J. looked at the trolley. 'That's a nurse!'

Missy tutted. 'Matron, actually. They're in charge of things.'

'I'm calling Security!' A.J. said. He tried to run but tripped over the boot that had extended in front of him. Sprawling, he backed up against the wall as the woman leaned in. 'Who are you?' he said.

'Candy Striper!' she smiled. 'I'm here to help!'

Had anyone entered the lab, they would have found the woman in the purple plaid shirt, plum skirt and newly acquired white lab coat shrieking in delight as blue sparks flew around the room and the thump of a defibrillator resounded.

'A little more to the left ... now to the right. That's it, Wanda – you're getting it!'

The figure strapped to the chair groaned.

'Just one ... more ... push!' Missy dropped the paddles and clutched Wanda's head between her hands, putting their foreheads close together and frowning in concentration until finally ... 'Bingo!'

Wanda groaned again. 'Sshh, maximum zen,' said Missy. 'Otherwise you'll get a tremendous headache.'

'What have you done to me?' whispered Wanda.

'I don't like to boast but I've just cured the flu.' She bowed elegantly. 'Bad news for Lemsip, eh!'

'That's not possible,' Wanda said. 'Damn, what did you do to my *head*? I really don't have flu any more?'

'Now that it's worked on you, I can roll out the update. You think I'll get a prize for science? I don't care! I'm going to get big brownie points, a kiss on the lips and my freedom back for this, just you wait.' Missy touched her lapels grandly. 'Know what else? It doesn't have any side effects. Wait ... what are you doing?'

Wanda didn't reply. She was blinking rapidly, faster and faster and faster.

'Stop that!' Missy clapped her hands but Wanda kept blinking. 'Oh, for goodness sake. OK, teeny-tiny side effects on parts of your teeny-tiny brain. I've accelerated something. Perhaps a poke about with a scalpel might fix it? You can't make an omelette without breaking ... into song. Tra-la-laaaa.' She picked up the surgeon's blade and bent over Wanda, peering at the woman's eyes ...

Wanda bucked violently, head-butting Missy in the process. Crackles of blue electricity rained down her face as she burst through her restraints, swung herself from the gurney and stared down at the lab-coated figure sprawled on the floor. 'Hello, dear,' said Wanda. 'I'm Matron. You cured me ... Now I'm going to cure you and everyone else.'

'If you were, like, pure evil,' said Bill, scrutinising the hospital map on the wall, 'but you were trying to be good, where would you go?'

The corridor filled with a piercing scream, followed by a monstrous roar.

'Definitely not that way,' Nardole said through the scarf around his face.

Bill was already running in the direction of the scream.

'Matron calling, just doing my rounds!' beamed Wanda, standing in the centre of the isolation ward. She focused on the four patients in their beds, each one coughing and sweating intensely. 'Now, just relax,' she soothed. 'I'm going to cure you.'

As her concentration increased, blue tendrils of energy snaked down from her head, turning into sparks when they reached the floor.

'Cure, cure, cure!' smiled Wanda as the blue crackles sparked from her face towards the patients.

As each crackle touched a body, so the body began to change ...

Sofia liked Magnolia Ward; the nurses were always so kind to Papa. He didn't recognise her most days but she visited all the same. 'When is my Sofia coming?' he'd ask, eyes fixed on a different world.

Approaching the ward, she saw that the door was wide open; someone must have forgotten to close it. She hoped Papa hadn't gotten out. She hurried to his room but he wasn't in bed. 'Papa?' she called. There was a muffled sound from the bathroom. She tapped on the door. 'It's Sofia. Are you in there?'

The door swung open and a figure shuffled out. 'Hola, Papa!' she said, then her face froze in fear.

An eerie blue light shone behind Papa's eyes. He stretched out thin, liver-spotted arms towards his daughter. 'Cure,' he droned, shambling forward. 'Currrrrre!'

In Majors, seasoned paramedic Pat Peltzer slapped some coins in the vending machine and sighed as his coffee was dispensed.

'Tough shift, Patty?' asked Gaby, the ward clerk. Pat was sweet on her and she knew it. He was a nice guy.

'Lousy,' said Pat. 'A freak accident by the school. This poor cheerleader had a sneezing fit and threw the wheel. Straight into the back of a pick-up.'

Gaby winced. 'How awful!'

'She got sliced up real bad.' Pat shook his head. 'Tragedy.'

The curtains in the opposite cubicle fluttered wildly and then parted. 'Cure,' tinkled a voice from inside.

'Are you OK, miss?' Pat leaned forward.

'Currrrrrrre,' tinkled the voice again. A blue crackle darted from the cubicle, unnoticed.

'Miss, you shouldn't be out of bed,' Pat said.

The patient shuffled out of the curtains, grinning, arms raised in a macabre cheer, blood seeping through the bandages on her face and chest.

Pat dropped his coffee as Gaby screamed loud enough to deafen the entire hospital.

In the Security office, Matron Wanda watched the monitors with pleasure as her freshly cured creations got to work, spreading her cure. Bedridden elderlies clambered out of the sheets to pursue their carers; new mothers forgot their crying babies as they approached terrified midwives. Even patients from the ICU were on the move, dragging their drips and machines behind them, arms outstretched, shaking, smiling ghastly empty smiles.

'Don't cry, little ones,' Wanda told the wailing babies on the screens. 'Your turn will come. No more crying, soon ... What the—?' Wanda zoomed in on one monitor, where a woman was waving at the camera. 'I thought I fixed you!' She looked to see where the camera was situated.

'Camera 19, Security area,' recited the woman from the doorway. 'Just outside. You can call me Missy, by the way.'

Wanda held very still, watching. 'I can see I'm going to have to fix you again.'

'Can't.' Missy tapped her head. 'Time Lord brain. Bigger and better than a human's. How's that crackling behind your eyes?'

'I'm good. I've got work to do.' Wanda turned her attention back to the monitors.

'About that.' Missy bounced into a chair and twirled it around. 'This "cure" is turning people into living zombies. I mean, it'll keep them out of hospital, I suppose, but it's not great for saving those lost man hours we talked about, now, is it? Which is kind of what my clever grand plan was about.' She stopped turning and fixed Wanda with a dangerous look. 'I don't like my grand plans to be interrupted, Wanda. What are you up to?'

Wanda folded her arms. 'I'm not telling you.'

'Oh go on,' said Missy. 'It's me, I created you! You might as well call me Mama. It'll be our secret. All that zombifying is hard for a newbie, I can help.'

'Hard?' Wanda sized up the woman in the chair. 'You know, at first, all I wanted to do was melt your brain until it leaked out of your ears.'

'Very good, Wanda!' said Missy approvingly.

'Then I realised, I'm better than that. I can do what you did. I'll get in the heads of every weak, sickly patient and improve them.' Wanda pointed at the monitors. 'Look at them, they're so much better now.'

'Well, I'm quite fond, I confess. But in a larger sense, "better" ...?'

'They don't feel pain,' Wanda explained. 'Not any more. Physical pain, mental pain, fear, regret ... They don't have that now.'

'How are you controlling them? That one looks broken.' Missy pointed at camera 12, where a young male server in the canteen was standing on a table, jerking a plate in a spasm.

'Turns out it takes quite a lot of headspace for a body *not* to feel pain. Brain jams, knows it's not right. They need reminding sometimes.' Wanda said. She pressed a button and spoke cheerily into the microphone. 'Matron calling! Remember your purpose: Cure. Cure. Cure!'

On the monitor, the canteen zombie jerked his head up, listening intently. Wanda's eyes blinked faster and faster as blue energy trails sparked from her head. Her voice got lower.

'Sharing is caring! Cure. Cure. Cure!'

Across the bank of screens, the macabre spectacle played out over and over as Wanda's voice seeped into the minds of her creations. The man climbed down from the table, staggering towards a family cowering under the sandwich counter. Crackles of energy radiated from his quivering, lopsided head as he reached out to embrace them.

Missy gave a slow clap. 'You know, this is the sort of thing I'd have done once to pass a dull Thursday. I've had a real impact on you, haven't I? It's quite humbling.'

Wanda shook the loose sparks from her hair. 'I'm turning them into a workforce.'

'One that will increase exponentially?' Missy tutted. 'Your head will frazzle trying to command that lot.'

Wanda shook her head. 'All they need's a push in the right direction. They're my relief staff! Spreading the cure.'

'Look. Why don't we stick to fixing the flu? I'll give you all the credit. The matron who found the cure.'

'Not enough. Not now.' Wanda shook her head. 'I became a nurse because I wanted to stop the pain ... And I've been here twenty years, trying my best each thankless shift and working for a pittance, but does anyone care? Does anyone even *notice*? And the pain gets bigger, it gets deeper ...'

'Yes, yes, poor rubbishy little you,' Missy said briskly. 'Thing is, I wanted to cure everyone, not turn them into monsters. So be good and let me turn you back to normal, however depressing that might be, there's a pet.'

'You know that I won't,' Wanda said. 'Would you, if you were me?'

'Absolutely not,' said Missy.

'I'll be Matron of the World,' Wanda laughed.

Her laugh was cut short as Missy smacked her hard around the face with Administrator Walsh's brand new keyboard.

'There's only room for one Matron of the World,' said Missy.

*

'I thought I saw someone slip in here,' Bill whispered. 'It could be Missy. Open the door. If any of those things are in there, I've got you covered.' She held up the fire extinguisher she'd pulled down from a wall.

'What are you going to do with that?' Nardole whispered back. 'Set them on fire and put them out again?'

'I saw it in *Firemen vs Zombies*. The foam blinds them. Open it!'

Nardole opened the door and peered in. 'Arrggh!' he yelled as another scream echoed his. 'Oh, it's just a bloke. Who are you?'

'I'm A.J. Get away from me!' The man shrieked, backing up against the consulting room wall.

'It's OK, we're not zombies!' Bill said. 'We're not going to cure you.' She lowered the fire extinguisher. 'Come on, get out of there. If more of those Curers come, you'll be a sitting duck in there.'

'I guess.' A.J. came outside, hugging himself. 'What the hell has happened here? First this scary woman knocks me out and steals my coat. Then some patients try to grab me, get up close and ... I don't know what they wanted, but no. No, no, no.' He looked forlorn. 'Maybe I'll take my chances, make a run for it.'

'That scary woman you mentioned ...' Bill began.

At that moment, Missy came skipping along the corridor. She slowed to a casual trot when she saw the others.

'That's her!' A.J. yelled, scrambling behind Bill.

'You. What the hell!' exclaimed Bill. 'We've been looking everywhere for you.'

'Where was the bathroom? Mars?' Nardole said testily. 'What did you do?'

'In the bathroom? Really.'

'Don't even,' Bill snapped. 'You disappear and five minutes later the entire hospital is teeming with zombies.'

'They're not mine. I was doing good. *She* created the zombies. *She's* the bad one.'

'Who's she?' Bill said.

'Missssssssy!' Matron Wanda stood at the far end of the corridor, sparkling blue energy leaking from her ears and eyes.

'I locked her up! Packed away in a safe ...' Missy smiled. 'Oh, she's good this one. *Bad*, I mean. Yes. No moral compass.'

Bill glared at Missy. 'I said, who *is* she?'

'Matron Wanda. I cured her flu. Good, eh?'

'There's sparks coming out of her head!'

'Unexpected side effect.' Missy wrote in the air. 'Noted for next time.'

'How did this happen?' Nardole said sternly. 'Tell me or you'll go back in the vault. No piano this time—'

'Oh, all right, all right, I rewired her immune system, happy now? Told her brain to override the virus, done and done. Laters, flu.'

Bill stared as Wanda slowly advanced along the corridor. 'Except now she's turned into some kind of maniac with an army of zombie troopers?'

'It's not the outcome I expected,' Missy admitted, 'but it's an outcome all the same.'

'I'm really going to fix you this time!' Wanda bellowed down the corridor and her eyes glowed blue. 'Cure! Cure! Cure!'

Distantly at first, then louder, the groans of zombies could be heard as they received her instruction. 'Sharing is caring! Cure! Cure! Cure!'

Missy beamed round at Bill, Nardole and A.J. 'I suggest that you run.'

'We need to fix this!' Bill said. 'We need the Doctor. What if they get him, *cure* him?'

'Can you imagine that one *ever* doing without pain?' Missy sniffed. 'Like me, he's immune to this.'

'Well, good for you, lady.' A.J. pushed past them and pelted up the corridor. 'I'm out of here!'

'He's got the idea. Now, *go*!' snapped Missy. 'Wanda's my monster. I'll deal with her.'

Nardole grabbed Bill and dragged her off in a stumbling run after A.J. Missy turned on the heels of her purple-glittery Dr Martens and smiled at the oncoming storm.

'Try it,' Nardole whispered. 'It can't hurt.'

'I'm not slapping him!' Bill hissed. Then, tentatively, she cuffed the Doctor round the face. 'Wake up!' she whispered. 'We need you. We so need you.'

But the Doctor slept on.

'How's this old guy going to help?' A.J. whined. 'Why aren't the cops here yet?'

'I guess no one's called them?' said Bill. 'They shouldn't, either. What are the cops gonna do about this?'

'What's anyone?' A.J. shook his head. 'You should have let me run.'

'You'd never have got past those orderlies on the stairs,' sniffed Nardole. 'Ooh, what's the collective noun for zombie orderlies? A *dressing* of orderlies—?'

'Ssh! I heard something,' Bill said. She opened the curtains a pinch ... 'Whoa!'

A tiny wizened lady stood outside, her face fixed in a toothless grin, her walking frame taking her weight as she reached for them, arms spread wide. 'Cure ...' she slurred sweetly, blue eyes shining. 'Currrrre!'

'OK, *that* is messed up!' said Bill, pulling the curtains shut on the woman. 'Come on, we need to move.'

They ran from the ward. 'Cure!' Mrs Matheson called after the trio as they dashed past, stretching out her hand after them. A blue spark glittered on her beige jumper. 'Currrrrrre ...'

'Forget it, I'm out!' A.J. said, turning in the direction of the EXIT sign. 'We have to escape before they cure *us*.'

'Escape! Oh my god!' Bill grabbed his arm. 'The hospital's still open! When they've finished curing everyone inside, the Curers can get out!'

'Someone else will stop them.' A.J. shook off her arm. 'The cops. Scientists, I don't know.'

'No, you don't. What if no one can stop them once they get out? You don't care if they cure your family, your friends?' Bill shook her head. 'It's so wrong. Even if they weren't zombies

... pain, feelings ... that's what makes us alive. We've got to stop them from leaving the hospital.'

'There you are!' Wanda scowled, huffing out onto the roof to find Missy sitting in a chair with her feet up. She wiped the sweat from her forehead, sending sparks flying. 'Waiting for me?'

'Well, there is a spark between us.' Missy stood up. 'We need to talk.'

'You never stop,' said Wanda. 'You're giving me a headache.'

'I did warn you.' Missy pulled a length of roofing felt from beneath her skirts. 'Mama knows best.'

Wanda ran her hands through her hair, pulling out strands of energy. She brought them into a ball and hurled it at Missy.

'Hey!' said Missy, batting the energy back at Wanda with the length of felt. 'Mind my boots.'

Wanda scowled. 'When I'm done curing you, Miss *Whoever*, you won't even remember your own name!'

Missy's lip curled into a grimace. 'No one ... but *no one* forgets my name.'

Bill ran into the Security office and scanned the screens, biting her lip. 'A-ha!' she said, as Nardole and A.J. passed along the screens before finally reappearing on camera 5 – the lobby. Nardole waved at the camera as he and A.J. ran to the main doors. Their plan was to jam the sliding exit doors so the zombies stayed contained for as long as possible.

'You'd better do it fast,' Bill muttered.

Moments later, some of the zombies came into view, shuffling into the lobby towards A.J. and Nardole.

'Oh, that's not good!' Bill leaned over the mic and spoke. 'Attention all zombies! This is, er Matron. Do not cure. Do not cure!'

The command boomed through the speakers, but the zombies kept moving.

Bill tried again, louder this time. 'Do not cure!'

The zombies hesitated.

'*Do not cure!*' Bill bellowed into the mic.

The zombies hesitated, but only for a few seconds. They began moving again.

Nardole gave a thumbs down to the camera and continued fiddling with the door while A.J. anxiously wielded the fire extinguisher to shield him from the approaching zombies.

'All this because of a stupid gig,' Bill groaned. She remembered how happy she'd been just hours before, lost in the music.

Suddenly, she shrieked out loud. 'Oh my god! Bill Potts, you might be a genius.' She reached for her phone and thumbed the volume to max. 'Maybe it's not about the words ... maybe it's about the noise.' She smiled. 'I hope you guys are ready to rock.'

She jammed her phone up against the microphone.

All over the hospital, Rusty Cage thundered out of the PA system, distorted guitars and drums crashing into one another as rasping vocals filled the wards and corridors.

And as the music, so powerful, so cracked with emotion, flooded their painless brains, the zombies halted in their tracks.

Bill watched, her breath held. Was the music reminding the zombies of all they'd lost? They had begun to shudder and spasm; it was like some kind of macabre dance.

Nardole stepped back from the dismantled proximity sensors and admired his handiwork as the doors stayed shut.

The zombies in the lobby stood still, the intense music distracting them from curing the two men standing in front of them. A.J. saw tears trailing the cheeks of the nearest zombies.

'Rock and roll stops the traffic!' Nardole yelled over the din. 'Come on! A racket like this might wake up even the Doctor ...'

In cubicle three, as that familiar riff bounced around the walls, a hand rose up from the bed and formed very definite devil horns.

The Doctor, still groggy, his head pounding, emerged onto the roof and took in the scene at a glance. At the roof edge, Missy was wrestling the matron while blue sparks rained down around the pair.

He bellowed: 'Stop this!'

'You're late,' Missy gasped.

'What's happened here?' the Doctor demanded. 'What have you done?'

'Why does everybody keep asking me that? I cured Matron Wanda here.'

'Matron Wanda doesn't look especially well from where I'm standing.'

'I'm better than ever!' Wanda sang, moving deftly out of the way as Missy grabbed for her hair. 'I've got a whole new skillset since she got her dirty little fingers on my brain.'

'Oh you didn't. Tell me you didn't.' The Doctor walked closer, unsteadily. 'Wanda – *Matron* Wanda – listen. I'm so sorry. But I promise I can fix things.'

'*I* fixed things,' Missy insisted. 'She had the flu and I *cured* her.' She slammed Wanda to the ground. 'I was gonna cure the whole lousy human race!'

'This is no kind of cure for anything,' said the Doctor. 'It ends now.'

Winded, Wanda wheezed with laughter. 'This is just the beginning. I'll rule this city, this world. Hell, the way my mind's expanding, even the universe.'

'I'm actually starting to like you,' said Missy. 'Here you are, knowing you can't possibly win yet you're still focused on the plan. Now that's commitment.'

'Guess where I get *that* from?' Wanda said.

'God, I really am good.' Missy said.

'Let me live and we'll rule together.'

'My magic Wanda.' Missy crouched over her. 'What a partner you would make.'

Wanda grinned. 'Making soup out of anyone who couldn't be cured!'

'Missy!' the Doctor warned.

Missy closed her eyes. 'Do you believe some people can't be cured, Doctor?'

'I believe anyone who wants to be cured can be saved.'

'Even if the bad keeps whispering in their ear?'

'Even if the bad seeps inside and tries to take you down with it.'

'You know Webster? *The White Devil*?' Missy whispered. '"I have caught an everlasting cold. Let no harsh flattering bells resound my knell ..."'

'Missy—'

'Farewell, glorious villain.' She shoved Wanda off the hospital roof, turning her head away as the woman hurtled down to the ground below.

All over the hospital the sparks pulled away from their hosts as their source called them back.

The blue glow left Papa Diego's eyes, while his terrified daughter hid behind the locked bathroom door in his room, praying for him to be well again.

In Majors, Pat and Gaby held hands tightly below the desk they had barricaded themselves under and watched as the blue sparks danced past them through the air.

Theodore Matheson didn't know why he was standing in the lobby in a gown but it sure was chilly. 'What am I doing out here?' he asked the girl with the big smile. 'Who are all these people?'

'Fire alarm. All over now,' she said, taking his arm. 'Let's get you back to bed. I'm Bill, what's your name?'

'Theodore!' he said, then sneezed. 'Mind you don't catch my cold.'

'You killed her.' The Doctor paced back and forth on the roof. 'We don't do that. You *know* we don't do that.'

Missy didn't know why he was being like this. 'I was helping. Like you do.'

'We don't kill people. We save them.'

'I did save them. Wanda could've destroyed the minds of everyone on this planet, in the end.'

'She didn't need to die. Do you even know how much pain you've caused?'

'But I saved the world. That's what matters, isn't it?'

'She was innocent, Missy. She died because of your actions.' The Doctor's face crumpled. 'Because of *my* actions. I brought you here.'

'She had to die so I could save them. Isn't that what you do? Anything to save them ... even murder?'

The Doctor's face was impassive.

'Isn't it?' she insisted.

The Doctor stared through Missy, his eyes stormier than the clouds gathering above. 'Yes. It's what I do. I'm sorry you had to learn it that way.'

On the ground below, Wanda lay amongst the forget-me-nots in the memorial garden, a serene smile on her face. Fading fast, the blue sparks tumbled along and slipped through her skin, as with her dying breaths, they found their way home.

On the rooftop above, Missy smiled secretly as she watched the sparks flicker and fade. 'Sharing is caring,' she whispered to herself. 'You're cured.'

'They'll have no memory of what happened. Now that the link to Wanda's been broken, they'll return to how they were before,' the Doctor said. 'I'm sorry about Wanda.'

Kelly wiped her eyes. 'I don't know what we'll do without her.'

'Continue her good work,' he said gently. 'Goodbye.'

'Hold on,' Kelly began. 'I've got police in the lobby with a ton of questions—'

'Thanks for the tip,' said the Doctor with a smile that bordered on charming. 'We'll take the back stairs.'

The Doctor led the way quietly back to the TARDIS, which he'd parked in a VIP space behind the arena.

'Missy's going back in the vault, I hope,' Nardole said. 'Those cuffs were a washout.'

'I could have freed myself any time,' Missy muttered from behind the Doctor.

Approaching the TARDIS, the Doctor clicked his fingers and the doors opened. 'Go on,' he said. Missy skulked inside, Nardole a distance behind her.

'You all right?' Bill asked, pausing at the door.

'I'm sorry about today, Bill.' He dabbed at the lump on the back of his head. 'It was meant to be a good day.'

'I'm sorry that you can't trust her,' Bill said. 'It *was* a good day, though, before all that. You coming in?'

'I'll be along. Give me a moment.'

Bill nodded, understanding, and went inside.

The Doctor leaned against the TARDIS and stared into the night. A tiny blue spark danced on the breeze before settling on the sleeve of his coat. He went to put it out with his thumb but then paused.

Gently, he blew the spark out into the night sky.

Letters from the Front
Vinay Patel

**SYSTEMS REPORT – COMMUNICATIONS ARRAY//
HIVE ITERATION X-T75**

ESTABLISHING CHANNEL –

LOCATION PASSCODE – VERIFIED

FREQUENCY LOCK – ACQUIRED

SIGNAL ENCRYPTION – RUNNING

IDENTIFICATION MARKERS (HUNTER ITYOJ) –
CONFIRMED

CHANNEL ESTABLISHED WITH THIJAR DISPATCH
STATION

21st July 1941

Dear Umbreen,
It's me! Just as I promised. This letter comes to you
from the regimental centre in Lahore, where we have

been training for the last few weeks. The city feels very different than when I last came here, which I suppose is no surprise. The clustering of thousands of young men creates a unique energy, both in the men themselves and those who must put up with their arrival.

Kunal and I have been put together in the same unit. I'm told this is lucky, a blessing, other brothers who have come have been separated. A blessing? They've never met Kunal, clearly. Just the other day, he returned from his medical examination and took great pleasure in relating to me that he had been diagnosed as anaemic. As if he had been told he possessed some great godly power! It took me nearly an hour to explain to him the difference between deity and deficiency.

From what I understand, though, most of the men here are discovering unexpected things about themselves. Diseases they've shrugged off for years, conditions they've never heard of, let alone had a moment to deal with. The commanding colonel is not impressed with us, to say the least. As he passed us out, he remarked that he had once heard that Punjabis were a martial race. Clearly a couple of Hindu farm boys from the arse-end of nowhere was not what he expected.

Luckily for the colonel, there are some among us who <u>do</u> fit the bill. We've made fast friends with one Prakash Ahluwalia, a city boy unfortunately but a strapping lad, and he even has a college degree! He's going to make the army his life this one, fancies himself VCO material (this is one of the 'Viceroy's Commissioned Officers' – what a title!)

Then there is Hafiz who fancies himself ... well, Hafiz just fancies himself. If it didn't seem so outrageous to claim it, you might suspect he joined the war for the sake of the uniform. He claims it's nicer than anything any of us own. One look at our helmets disproves this claim, I think – they are basically misshapen pots.

Finally, we have Ram. Bengali. Have you ever met a Bengali? On this evidence, they aren't ones for jokes.

Anaemia aside, Kunal is, of course, already complaining. I reminded him of his speech, his <u>mota bhai</u> speech, the big brother who must look after this stupid middle child who wishes to throw himself into a war that is not his own. Such talk of his selfless actions! Had I known he would moan about it for months afterwards, I would have forbidden him to follow me.

The days are strictly controlled. We parade at 7 a.m. sharp, which many of the boys here are disgruntled with. Only the ones from the city, of course, with the notable exception of Prakash. The other farmers, like me, find this positively relaxed. We take our main meal between 11 and 12, train until sundown, after which we have a small bite for the evening and then are expected to return to our bunkhouses. Hafiz is a bit of a bad influence here – Kunal joins him when they sneak out into the city. I, meanwhile, have learned many new card games through spending my free hours with Ram and Prakash. Ram has a custom pack that has the faces of what he calls the leaders of the independence movement. Subhas Chandra Bose ('Netaji' as Ram refers to him) is the King of Diamonds. Jinnah is a joker. No sight of Gandhi at all.

What else? Oh yes! There is some talk already of where we will be deployed once our training is over. Most figure they will send us to Iraq, to guard oilfields, which is apparently not too bad. Then there are a few other places which I am too embarrassed to say I've never heard of but I will of course tell you when I know.

For now, I am enclosing my first month's wages. Eighteen rupees. Not much but I hope, with two fewer mouths to feed, it will go some way to being useful.

I hope you are well, Umbreen, and that Hasna is easier on you now that I'm away. Perhaps she will grow fonder of me in my absence ...

P.S. Manish, please do not be offended by my not addressing a letter to you. We are quite limited in our supplies at this moment, we may only send one letter each, and Kunal says he will use his for you. However,

I acknowledge that, as the only person on the farm who can read, these letters must all pass through you anyway. I am grateful and hope you will convey them truthfully. I'm trusting you, little brother! Do not scandalise me when I cannot defend myself!

P.P.S. Kunal tells me he forgot to say in his letter: Do not indulge his ox. Neglect yours as much as you would like, but he does not want to return to find his as rotund as Akshay Fua. An impossibility, I think.

P.P.P.S. I miss you all.

Prem (Or should that be Sepoy Prem Barsar?)

———

ENCRYPTED CHANNEL – BRIEFING RETURN #253

Batch despatched. No issues to report.

———

ENCRYPTED CHANNEL – BRIEFING RETURN #311

Batch despatched. No issues to report.

———

ENCRYPTED CHANNEL – BRIEFING RETURN #373

Batch despatched. No issues to report.

———

ENCRYPTED CHANNEL – BRIEFING RETURN #452

Batch despatched. Engagement of final target necessitated minor collateral damage, though no trace suspected. No other issues to report.

———

PERSONAL LOG – HUNTER ITYOJ

Regarding the issue described in Briefing Return #452: I had to track that final target across a total of seven star systems. Trickier than I had anticipated. Clearly used to being wanted – but not by a Thijarian exohunter. By the time I found them, I gladly appeared in the open. I wanted them to know. When they realised, they tried to disappear within a crowd out of desperation. Cute.

My Guide would have disapproved.

———

11th December 1941

Dear Umbreen,

You know that map on your wall that your father bought you? Well, go take a look at it now! Ready? OK, put your finger on our farm, drag it to the right, across India, past Calcutta, until you hit Burma. Then, move your finger down until you reach Sumatra. Hop across the water there and you will find Malaya. That's where we will be going. We've been posted to a battalion and will be off shortly, I think.

I'm not sure if I'm meant to tell you that. It might be sensitive. No matter – I'm led to believe that they will delay our post in case someone writes just as I am doing, so by the time you get this I might already be there.

What I will openly tell you though, Umbreen, for it's not much of a secret ... I'm scared. I'm trying not to be but so much is so new. There are rumours of large-scale Japanese troop build-ups in French Indo-China and it seems inevitable we will encounter them. I've never met a Japanese man before. How perverse that the first time will likely be at the end of a gun. His or mine.

Kunal is in a strangely optimistic mood. You might not have heard but there was a Japanese attack on an American port a few days ago. When the news came through, Kunal was the only one smiling. 'This is going to be a short war, now, you will see! Those Americans will join in and they are a vengeful bunch!' How Kunal has managed to form opinions about what Americans are like is beyond my comprehension but he is very adamant on this point. Perhaps the boxing has gone to his head.

Did I mention the boxing yet? Kunal may not be a god but he has somewhat discovered his calling. He is not what you would call *good* exactly but he is definitely effective. He swings his arms relentlessly and, through a combination of confusion and exhaustion, his opponents submit, though Kunal has been known to catch himself in the frenzy. We've seen a lot of iodine and cotton wool, let me tell you.

In fact, Kunal has gained such notoriety that even the colonel decided to challenge him. Some good-natured betting took place over this. Hafiz it turns out has a knack for hustling money from the Brits. Prakash was decided upon as a referee, seeing as he has respect from all sides (he's already been promoted twice!).

The ensuing event was far too short to satisfy the crowd but there was a win for the home team and I admit there was some joy in seeing Kunal knock that colonel onto his backside.

Ah! There's the curfew. I must stop soon. Next time you hear from me, I may have gone one further than Kunal's antics and killed a man in battle. I hope you will not think less of me for it. There is no joy in it for me and I will never be as happy as when I get to return to you. For that reason, I pray that Kunal is right for once. I pray that it will be soon.

Manish – thank you for the information about those groups. I had no idea. I am glad you are finding passion in your politics and that the Independence movement continues to thrive. Ram says only

Bengalis truly care about independence. Perhaps these pamphlets will convince him otherwise! I will also follow your request and ask him where he purchased his playing cards.

But promise you will be careful — these activities are banned and they can't afford to lose you for the sake of a hot temper. I feel conflicted being part of the army at a time like this but, in the end, it will be better for us all, I am sure of it.

And yes also, to your other request, I will ask Kunal to not bother you with any more 'advice' on how to manage things. It's your farm now, baby brother, take care of it.

Prem

———

30th January 1942

Dear Umbreen,
You are right to mention it, my letters have become both shorter and fewer in number. I didn't mean to alarm you or suggest there was any loss of feeling on my part. There never could be.

To offer some unsatisfactory explanation: The fighting has been fierce since we arrived in Malaya, but especially now here in Singapore. It affords us little time to rest and, in truth, I don't know how much of what I'm seeing here I want to relate to you. There's little good to be found out here. Not many memories I want to keep.

All I know is that I am thankful to Bhagavan for keeping us safe and for bringing you into my life.

(Sorry Manish.)

Prem

———

PERSONAL LOG – HUNTER ITYOJ

The target has taken refuge deep underground in what appears to be a fortified bunker. Something from a long-forgotten war? No matter. This batch is low-priority and I've supplies and time. More of both than they do.

As I wait for them to believe that I have lost the trail, I maintain the chronometer and notice it has reached twenty-five thousand rotations. Half my service, a third of my probable life, out here in the black. All without seeing another Thijarian. I had not given this any consideration until now. It's not a thought I can let linger. The Hunter Beyond has bestowed us with all the gifts to act as their example would show us. Perhaps I should compose a poem to our greatness to settle my mind.

Ah. Here they emerge, blinking into the sunlight. Cautious yet grateful. Like little desert rats with a sniff of rain. I will allow them this moment of grace before I strike.

My Guide warned me against this. 'Ityoj,' they would say, 'to show compassion to your prey dishonours the Hunter Beyond.' I'm not sure I agree. The time we give them allows us to observe, to understand their weaknesses. We can always kill better.

Look. Their eyes. Such hope. A shame.

———

15th March 1942

My family,
Today I address you all. I should have written sooner, but couldn't find the words. I assume you have heard by now. Perhaps you have been praying that there has been some mistake. It is not the case.

Kunal Bhai is dead. He fell during the retreat from Singapore.

I have enclosed his final wages.

Prem

———

ENCRYPTED CHANNEL – BRIEFING RETURN #501
Batch despatched. No issues to report.

———

ENCRYPTED CHANNEL – BRIEFING RETURN #617

Batch despatched. No issues to report.

ENCRYPTED CHANNEL – BRIEFING RETURN #1259

Batch despatched. No issues to report.

PERSONAL LOG – HUNTER ITYOJ

The last batch was the largest yet. Seventeen targets in total, took far longer than planned for. Twelve full rotations. Rushed. Unsubtle. Not good.

Encountered a new being, a strange creature whose presence severely disrupted my psychic tracking and nearly caused me to abort the third target.

Once I had adjusted, my preliminary observations suggest this being to be otherwise quite harmless, with a predilection for baffling camouflage – stripes of red and white provide inadequate deceit in nearly every known environment (with the obvious exception of a Toreqatallian firestorm).

However, its tracking disruption could create complications in future. I overheard it claim to be from a planet named Gallifrey and I will recommend an observation hive be sent to find it.

Otherwise, mission was smooth. Partial restitution to the contractor for delay has been advised. The urge to connect persists. I continue to resist. This log is a great help to that end.

9th September 1943

Dear Umbreen,

We find ourselves in Burma. The closest to home I've been in years, yet it's never felt so far. Last week, Hafiz left us. Caught out, along with five others, by a well-placed sniper I had not spotted on my scouting duty. Prakash, who commands our platoon now, is inconsolable. Actually it is more accurate to say he commanded our platoon, since he has renounced his position in response to the deaths and though no one looks to blame me, the guilt is unrelenting.

There is yet more bad news. I had wondered what became of our soldiers captured by the Japanese at Singapore. I told myself that, by surrendering, at least Ram's fate was better than Kunal's. I'm no longer sure. During a briefing yesterday, we were informed that intelligence has confirmed that many of the captured have agreed to join the Indian National Army. With that name you would think them a force for good, but it is Subhas Chandra Bose's outfit and they are aligned with both the Germans and Japanese. For the sake of India's freedom, they claim. I've no doubt Ram would have sided with them. How will this war ever end if the enemy keeps growing?

It sounds as if the harvest hasn't provided you with much cheer either, and I'm sorry to add to your woes with this letter. If there is any solace it in, I was relieved to hear that you and Manish salvaged enough to keep everyone fed. We take our mercies where we find them these days, my love.

   With pride and adoration,

Prem

———

PERSONAL LOG – HUNTER ITYOJ

They say that the best Thijarian exohunters do not even comprehend loneliness. That our solitary mandate is not a burden but, in fact, a blessing.

   Perhaps then I am not among our finest for, I admit here, forty thousand rotations into my service, I continue to crave more than my own thoughts.

   Worse, those thoughts are immersed in heresy. And yet, I cannot help but feel there could be some use in this. Consider: Would a service of two exohunters not allow an even greater roam? I know there is some political agitation in this direction. I know too that for the majority this is seen as a weakness. Unholy, even. I must say that while I understand these objections, and feel them deep within me, my experience leads me to disagree. Am I wrong? Perhaps. But, out here, I've no one to disagree with.

———

ENCRYPTED CHANNEL – BRIEFING RETURN #1781

Batch despatched. No issues to report.

———

ENCRYPTED CHANNEL – BRIEFING RETURN #1781

Confirmation response not received. Please validate.

———

PERSONAL LOG – HUNTER ITYOJ

No confirmation yet from Thijar. Strange. It will no doubt result in restitution. I have begun a full diagnostic of the communications array to rule out error on my part. These older hives are notorious for signal attenuation.

———

1st July 1944

Dear Umbreen,

It is hard for me to describe to you what has occurred here, but I will attempt to.

We found ourselves in what is the Upper Tiber Valley, north of Rome, acting as part of a mixed unit offensive. Moving at the glimpse of first light, we made our way up a hill in the forest in order to secure the peak. All of a sudden, the most terrifying roar! Machine gun! We hit the ground as it continued to fire. The trees around us exploded, splintering shards of wood everywhere. My helmet was struck by shrapnel multiple times. I will never mock it again.

As fast as it started, the firing ended; those guns are monstrous but they too need to reload. The gunners called out and behind us voices sang out in reply – Italians making their way up the hill behind us. We were trapped in a pincer. Certain to die.

Within this impossible situation, one of our men launched himself up into the quiet <u>towards</u> the gun!

It was such an outrageous act to witness and yet there was magnetism to this courage. I found my feet following this madman up this hill.

As I neared him, I realised this man was none other than our own former Subedar Prakash Ahluwalia! At the crest of the hill, we came across the machine gunners in the nest. They were loath to give it up, and Prakash found himself with a shoulder full of bullets for his trouble but he fought like a lion, striking down the gunners and securing their weapon. I wish I could claim a part in this heroic deed but in truth I was but an observer in the end.

Prakash brought the men up the hill, the newly liberated machine gun covering their advance and with a liberal helping of grenades we suppressed the Italians behind us.

When it was clear that we were secure, the men gave such a cheer for Prakash. He must have saved more than a hundred lives yet he took nothing of the acclaim, a small smile was all he managed as they stretchered him away. But there was a light, Umbreen, such a <u>light</u> surrounding him. There is talk that they will recommend him for the Victoria Cross (this is one of the highest honours the Brits have).

Word has also reached us of a great victory against the Japanese at Kohima. I can't imagine that will be the end of their incursions, they are too smart, too good, too proud. But I feel the momentum is with us at last.

I am told that the Indian National Army fought hard at Kohima, also that they suffered heavy losses. I do not support them, as you know, but I must say that this news caused me great distress. Indians fighting Indians. This was not how I ever envisaged this war to end up. I pray that Ram was not a part of the action. Or, if he was, that he lived and had the chance to surrender to an Indian instead of a Brit. He is a good man and deserves that dignity.

With hope at last,

Prem

———

SYSTEMS REPORT – COMMUNICATIONS ARRAY// HIVE ITERATION X-T75

DIAGNOSTIC RUNNING –

ALIGNMENT SENSORS – NOMINAL

GUIDANCE MOTORS – NOMINAL

AMPLIFIER OUTPUT – NOMINAL

DIAGNOSTIC COMPLETE.

COMMUNICATIONS ARRAY: OPTIMAL CONDITION

———

ENCRYPTED CHANNEL – BRIEFING RETURN #1781

Confirmation response still not received. Please validate.

———

PERSONAL LOG – HUNTER ITYOJ

No response from Thijar in fifteen rotations.

———

PERSONAL LOG – HUNTER ITYOJ

No response from Thijar in eighteen rotations. Is this a test?

———

PERSONAL LOG – HUNTER ITYOJ
Twenty-two rotations. If this is a test, I have failed it.

–––

PERSONAL LOG – HUNTER ITYOJ
Perhaps my Guide was right. I should have listened. I've dismayed the Hunter Beyond with my lack of strength. I will return home to make my amends. I will perform the ritual of Htna, at the Yaji temple if I can gain the permissions. I must cleanse myself of these sins, of these heretical thoughts.

–––

PERSONAL LOG – HUNTER ITYOJ
All is dust.

–––

PERSONAL LOG – HUNTER ITYOJ
Did I bring this upon us?

–––

OPEN CHANNEL – AUTOMATED MESSAGE//HIVE ITERATION X-T75
Thijar is lost.

Nothing remains.

I am alone.

MESSAGE REPEAT –

Thijar is lost.

Nothing remains.

I am alone.

MESSAGE REPEAT –

———

22nd May 1945

Dear Umbreen,

Back in Lahore. The city feels different once again. Though perhaps it's me rather than it. Now they have disbanded my unit, I've been tasked with training the new volunteers. Still more volunteers. The war continues despite the surrenders in Europe but I will say it. I am optimistic that it will all end soon. A surprising sensation though not unwelcome.

It is easier to train these boys knowing that I may not be training them to die. I feel my eyes changing. I feel I can see beauty once again, though of course nothing compares to your face (sorry Manish). Full demobilisation will take time, but my new role means I have a small amount of leave so you can be certain of it now – I'm coming home to you. Soon. So very soon.

I wonder what they will they do with all these uniforms when the war is done? I'm keeping mine. Hafiz was right, it's the smartest thing I own.

I hope you will like seeing me in it.

Prem

———

PERSONAL LOG – HUNTER ITYOJ

As I sift through the remains, I let myself feel. I feel the fear. I feel the shame. I feel the grief for those millions I never knew.

And at the end of feeling, I know two things. Thijar is dead. And so is the Hunter Beyond. There is no nobility in this destruction. I cannot feel their hand in it. Nor my own.

I stand where Yaji temple was. Is meant to be. Still is. Within the dust. Perhaps the Hunter Beyond exists yet and they are simply done with Thijarians. No matter. I am done with the Hunter Beyond.

I will perform the Htna.

I will wait for the others.

They will come. And I will be pleased to be among them, there is no shame in that. There is no shame any more.

Thijar is a corpse
So as a feastfly I return.
The home of hunters, hunted.
We who stalk must stay.

Our future now
In our past.

———

**SYSTEMS REPORT – COMMUNICATIONS ARRAY//
HIVE ITERATION X-T75**

SIGNAL BROADCAST RECALL – CONFIRMED

MESSAGE EDIT – ACCEPTED

SIGNAL BROADCAST TRANSMISSION – CONFIRMED

———

22nd May 1945

Dear Manish,
In my new position I am allowed two letters and so this one's just for you, brother.

Thank you for all that you have done for me. For reading these letters, for writing the replies and most of all for staying behind. I know it was not easy to do, but knowing you were there, looking after Umbreen, the farm, our lifeblood made it easier for me out here. There is no better motivation for a man to endure than there being a place to which he can return.

I dare say, though, your time will come. The British repeat their promises of independence, but who can know if they intend to honour it this time. They will need their feet holding to the fire, and no doubt you will find your place in the struggle ahead. Perhaps in the streets, perhaps in the courthouses. Politics, even, would be made better for a mind such as yours.

But, before you do that, make some time for me, little brother. I have such stories to tell you of these lands I have passed through. War has marked them, perhaps some beyond saving, but there is such beauty here also. I regret not making space to tell you of the beauty.

One day we will see these places together. That would be my great wish for us. Imagine! In a few years, when these places have rebuilt and reclaimed themselves, when the rubble is turned to road, we could journey back here and both make new memories. Kinder memories. I tell you, what a world is out here, Manish! And a better one is coming.

I cannot wait for us to walk it together.

Prem

OPEN CHANNEL – AUTOMATED MESSAGE//HIVE ITERATION X-T75

Thijar is lost.

Nothing remains.

Welcome home.

We begin again.

MESSAGE REPEAT –

Thijar is lost.

Nothing remains.

Welcome home.

We begin again.

MESSAGE REPEAT –

Thijar is lost.

Nothing remains.

Welcome home.

We begin again.

About the Authors

Colin Baker is an English actor who became known for playing Paul Merroney in the BBC drama series *The Brothers* from 1974 to 1976. He went on to play the sixth incarnation of the Doctor in the TV series *Doctor Who*. He reprised the role for the 1993 Children in Need special, *Dimensions in Time*, and the 1989 stage show *Doctor Who – The Ultimate Adventure*. He has also voiced the Doctor for over 140 *Doctor Who* audio stories for Big Finish Productions.

Steve Cole is an editor and children's author whose sales exceed three million copies. His hugely successful *Astrosaurs* young fiction series has been a UK top-ten children's bestseller. His several original *Doctor Who* novels have also been bestsellers.

Jenny T. Colgan has written numerous bestselling novels as Jenny Colgan, which have sold over 2.5 million copies worldwide, been translated into 25 languages, and won both the Melissa Nathan Award and Romantic Novel of the Year 2013. Aged 11, she won a national fan competition to meet the Doctor and was mistaken for a boy by Peter Davison.

Susie Day is the author of the *Pea's Book* and *Secrets* series from Puffin. Her latest novel for children, *Max Kowalski Didn't*

Mean It, is about dragons and toxic masculinity. Between books, she works as a copywriter in Birmingham. Susie currently lives in Coventry with her partner and two silly cats.

Terrance Dicks worked on scripts for *The Avengers* as well as other series before becoming full Script Editor of *Doctor Who* from 1968. Dicks worked on the Jon Pertwee Third Doctor era of the programme, and returned as a writer – scripting Tom Baker's first story as the Fourth Doctor: *Robot*. Terrance Dicks novelised many of the original *Doctor Who* stories for Target books, and has written original *Doctor Who* novels for BBC Books.

Simon Guerrier is co-author of *Doctor Who: The Women Who Lived* and *Whographica* for BBC Books, and has written countless *Doctor Who* books, comics, audio plays and documentaries. He has been a guest on *Front Row* and *The Infinite Monkey Cage* on Radio 4 and, with his brother Thomas, makes films and documentaries – most recently *Victorian Queens of Ancient Egypt* for Radio 3.

George Mann is the author of the bestselling *Doctor Who: Engines of War* and *Newbury & Hobbes* steampunk mystery series. He's also written new adventures for Sherlock Holmes, a collection of Star Wars myths and fables, and the supernatural crime series *Wychwood*. He lives near Grantham, UK, with his wife, son and daughter.

Una McCormack is a *New York Times* bestselling author. She has written four *Doctor Who* novels: *The King's*

Dragon and *The Way through the Woods* (featuring the Eleventh Doctor, Amy, and Rory); *Royal Blood* (featuring the Twelfth Doctor and Clara), and *Molten Heart* (featuring the Thirteenth Doctor, Yaz, Ryan and Graham). She is also the author of numerous audio dramas for Big Finish Productions.

Vinay Patel is a playwright and screenwriter. His television debut was the BAFTA-winning *Murdered By My Father* and for *Doctor Who* he has written *Demons of the Punjab*. His latest play, *An Adventure,* ran at the Bush Theatre in 2018. Elsewhere, he contributed to the bestselling collection of essays, *The Good Immigrant.*

Jacqueline Rayner is the author of over 40 books and audio plays, including number one bestseller *The Stone Rose,* the highest-selling *Doctor Who* novel of all time, and two *Doctor Who* 'Quick Reads' for World Book Day. She lives in Essex with her husband and twin sons, and writes regularly for *Doctor Who Magazine.*

Beverly Sanford's first Young Adult novel, *The Wishing Doll,* was published by Badger Learning in 2014, followed by *Remember Rosie, Silent Nation* and two non-fiction books. A BBC Writer's Room semi-finalist (2011) and an Editor's Choice in the Jim Henson Co/Penguin *Dark Crystal Author Quest* (2014), Bev is currently working on a screenplay for Sun Rocket Films and a children's fiction series.

Matthew Sweet presents the BBC radio programmes *Free Thinking, Sound of Cinema* and *The Philosopher's Arms.* He has judged the Costa Book Award, edited *The Woman in White* for Penguin Classics and was Series Consultant on the Showtime/ Sky Atlantic series *Penny Dreadful*. His books include *The West End Front* and *Operation Chaos: The Vietnam Deserters Who Fought the CIA, the Brainwashers and Themselves*.

Mike Tucker is a visual effects designer and author who has written several original *Doctor Who* novels as well as fiction for other shared universes. He has also co-written numerous factual books relating to film and television, including *Impossible Worlds* and the *TARDIS Instruction Manual*.

Matthew Waterhouse played Adric, companion to Tom Baker and Peter Davison's Doctors from 1980 to 1982. Since then, he has worked extensively as an actor in theatre. His published writing includes a memoir, *Blue Box Boy*, three novels and a book of stories. Recently he's appeared in episodes of the audio version of *Dark Shadows* and numerous *Doctor Who* audio projects, including an award-winning one-man play, *Doctor Who: A Full Life*, and a forthcoming quartet of new adventures starring alongside Tom Baker.

Joy Wilkinson is an award-winning writer working across film, television, theatre and radio. She was a *Screen International* 'Star of Tomorrow', a two-time Brit List nominee and has had her work widely produced in the UK and internationally. For television, Joy has written the *Doctor Who* episode *The Witchfinders*, and her other credits include BBC One's critically-acclaimed drama *Nick Nickleby*.